THE GUARDIAN

Of Might & Manners

Highland Heroes
Book One

by Maeve Greyson

Dragonblade Publishing, Inc. is an imprint of Kathryn Le Veque Novels, Inc.
P.O. Box 7968
La Verne CA 91750
ceo@dragonbladepublishing.com

Produced in the United States of America

First Edition November 2019
Print Edition

ARE YOU SIGNED UP FOR DRAGONBLADE'S BLOG?

You'll get the latest news and information on exclusive giveaways, exclusive excerpts, coming releases, sales, free books, cover reveals and more.

Check out our complete list of authors, too!

No spam, no junk. That's a promise!

Sign Up Here

www.dragonbladepublishing.com

Dearest Reader;

Thank you for your support of a small press. At Dragonblade Publishing, we strive to bring you the highest quality Historical Romance from the some of the best authors in the business. Without your support, there is no 'us', so we sincerely hope you adore these stories and find some new favorite authors along the way.

Happy Reading!

CEO, Dragonblade Publishing

Additional Dragonblade books by Author Maeve Greyson

Highland Heroes Series
The Guardian
The Warrior

*** Please visit Dragonblade's website for a full list of books and authors. Sign up for Dragonblade's blog for sneak peeks, interviews, and more: ***
www.dragonbladepublishing.com

CHAPTER ONE

Kensington Palace
Early spring 1693

G RAHAM MACCOINNICH EYED his surroundings, rubbing his hands
together with slow, purposeful movements. Several grim
outcomes had come to mind since receiving the strange summons
from the crown. This situation had not been among them.

Graham shifted in place and pulled in a deep breath, hissing it out
between clenched teeth as he stole another veiled glance around the
small but opulent chamber—unoccupied except for himself. An ill-
feeling permeated the air of what appeared to be a private library of
the palace. Bookshelves lined each wall, laden not only with books but
also all manner of useless baubles and trinkets, the likes of which
Graham had never seen. Luxurious chairs and couches sat in clusters
of twos and threes, crowding every available space. Tables littered
with gilded boxes and cut-glass decanters filled to their stoppers
highlighted the cozy arrangements of gaudy furniture.

Graham wet his lips. He wouldn't turn away a drink about now. A
bead of sweat trickled down his spine and settled in the crack of his
arse. He didn't care for this place a damn bit. A chamber made for
secrets. Dark. Ominous. The room reeked of deception.

He shifted positions again, turning with as nonchalant an air as he could muster. Places such as these always held spy holes, riddled with them, in fact. Someone watched him. He'd bet a barrel of fine MacCoinnich whisky on it. The king's personal guard had escorted him here with a rudeness that had come close to forcing him to teach the man better manners. Graham had managed to refrain. Barely. He still itched to put the insolent bastard in his place. But he wouldn't dare. It was too great a risk. After all, he was a Scot in the heart of hostile soil. For his own sake and the sake of his brother Alexander's new clan and young family, he'd behave. At least for now.

A quiet click to his right made him turn—a paneled door swung open.

"Come this instant, daughter. His Highness will join us presently. Your maid can fetch your journal later. We've greater matters at hand than the whereabouts of your silly sketches, and I will not be humiliated by running after my progeny like an incompetent nursemaid." A tall man, once broad across the shoulders but now stooped with age, held tight to the hand of a fetching young woman. He yanked her forward with a rude, impatient jerk.

"Papa! I beg you—"

"This instant, Mercy! Heed me now. Not another word, do you understand me?"

The scarlet-cheeked beauty careened to a bouncing halt as her alarmed gaze fell on Graham. Her chin jerked to a prideful angle but her full lips quivered, and her slender throat flexed as she struggled to recover a calm, gracious appearance.

Graham's heart went out to the lass for suffering such an embarrassment at the hands of her brute-of-a-father. He stepped forward with a warning glare at the man and lifted his fists to a more noticeable level. The old bastard better change his behavior or rue the day he stepped into the presence of a MacCoinnich. Women were precious and meant to be treated with respect.

The lady's father made a weak attempt of jutting out his chin but took a half step back and cleared his throat.

Good. The old fool understood the warning.

Graham shifted his attention back to the sweet lass peering out from behind her father.

A rare vision. She had glossy black hair and skin fairer than any ivory Graham had ever seen. And those eyes... Fathomless. Curved as though smiling and colored the rich hue of a well-aged whisky reflecting torchlight. A man could get trapped in those eyes, completely ensnared with the promise of discovering the rest of the lady's charms.

Graham wrenched himself free of her spell. Such a dalliance could prove dangerous. Not only was she a Sassenach but more than likely a noble, judging from the looks of her father and her regal, genteel demeanor. The situation begged careful handling. He made a polite nod toward the beguiling lass and stepped between her and her intolerable father. "M'lady. Graham MacCoinnich at your service."

The lass curtsied and dropped her gaze with a coy turning of her head, but Graham didn't miss the glances she stole at him through those long, dark lashes. Aye. A fine, rare beauty, this one was.

Her father edged his way back in front of her. "Duke of Edsbury, sir." The man growled out the words in a low, huffing tone that said the name should impress Graham.

It didn't.

"Sir." Graham gave the duke that much politeness but no more 'til the man proved he deserved it. He'd march straight through hell's gates before he called the man *m'lord*.

Lord Edsbury's eyes narrowed the slightest bit and the crease between his twin thatches of bushy, gray brows deepened. He stood taller, his spine stiffening into as challenging a stance as the man could muster. He might have been a worthy adversary at one time, a courageous lion, strong, and noble. But now the man moved with the hitched gait of one battling the ill health of overindulgence and advancing years.

"Papa." The word floated through the air as soft as a whisper, slipped between the two men, and hovered like a spirit.

The duke recovered his composure. The required shroud of polite court manners fell across him like a veil of mist tumbling down a mountain. He turned and took his daughter's hand, pulling her out from behind him to stand at his side. "Allow me to introduce you to my daughter, Lady Mercy Rowena Claxton."

"Honored to meet ye, m'lady." Graham graced her with a smile intended as a gesture of truce. After all, it wasn't the woman's fault her father was an arrogant arse—and an English one at that. "Might I call ye Lady Mercy?"

"You may." Lady Mercy curtsied again and held out her hand, lowering her gaze as she waited for him to take it.

Take it, he did. Graham relished the opportunity to graze his mouth across the softness of her long, delicate fingers. He knew well enough it was considered ungentlemanly to press his lips to the lady's skin rather than hover above her fine hand, but he'd never been accused of being a gentleman nor possessed the desire of gaining the title.

He took pride in his brazenness, breathing in her enticing fragrance as he drew a step closer. The earthy florals of a heather-filled glen paired with the intoxicating sweetness of a nervous young woman floated around her. What a treasure she was—sadly, a Sassenach, aye, but a treasure to be won and enjoyed, nonetheless.

She rewarded him with a deeper blush across her high cheekbones and an endearing gasp as she slipped her hand out of his grasp and tucked it to her middle.

"Damned, ill-bred Scot. I would expect no less."

Graham turned and laughed in Edsbury's face. "Aye, man. A Scot doesna leave a woman guessing after his intentions. They ken verra well when they're wanted." He returned his attention to the lady. As much as he enjoyed tormenting her pompous father, he wished the dear lass no unease. "Forgive me if I've offended ye, m'lady. I assure ye 'twas no' my intent at all."

Lady Mercy fluttered his words away with a gracious wave. "No offense taken, sir." With a modest lowering of her gaze, she retreated to a corner.

Were circumstances different, he'd take great pleasure in getting to know this lass better—despite her being a danger. The strange summons from the crown returned to the forefront of his thoughts and all levity left him. He turned back to the duke. "I assume your presence here means ye have a meeting with the king as well?"

Edsbury gave him an unsettling scowl, one that made Graham wish he could read the man's mind. "His Highness will be with us anon. Bentinck, Lord Portland, assured me of such."

"Bentinck?" Graham wasn't familiar with the name.

"The Earl of Portland. His Highness's Groom of the Stole." Edsbury gave a haughty sniff and looked at Graham as though he should be envious of the man chosen to wipe the king's arse after His Majesty took a shite.

King William's entrance cut off the less than complimentary retort burning on Graham's tongue.

"Your Highness." Edsbury bowed long and low, and Lady Mercy rushed to give the perfect, gracious curtsy.

Graham made the required respectful bow, then straightened and met King William's gaze.

The royal, known for his heartless scheming and tenacity, looked worn, far older than his forty-some-odd years of age. His Majesty appeared travel weary and ready for a drink and it was no wonder. The king wintered but a few short months in Whitehall or Kensington, traveling the remainder of the year and entrusting the everyday duties of ruling the kingdom to his wife, Queen Mary. He had proven himself more interested in the expansion of his empire and the battlefield rather than in the running of the kingdom. It was a rare occurrence for him to darken the doors of his own palace for more than a few days during the spring or summer months.

King William didn't speak for a long moment. Just stood there. Motionless, except for the occasional shifting of his impeccably arranged long brown curls whenever he took in a breath. He peered at Graham, studying him as though weighing his merits to decide if he was lacking. After what most would consider an overlong stare bordering on rudeness, His Highness pursed his thin lips and gave a slow, imperious nod. He moved to sit in a luxurious chair situated on a raised platform near the entrance. With a lazy turn of his head, he shifted his focus to the almost invisible young lord standing beside his chair like a well-trained dog waiting for his master's command. "Pray tell, is there a reason our glass is bereft of port?"

The thin lordling's eyes flared wide with alarm, then he sprang into action, snapping his fingers at the pair of servants flanking the king's private entrance to the room.

The older of the servants bowed and bobbed as he hurried to snatch a decanter from the cabinet beside His Majesty's chair. "Sincerest apologies, m'lord, but Her Highness—"

Before the young, attending lord could administer a more severe reprimand, King William held up a bejeweled hand.

"We are well aware of Her Majesty's position on sobriety, but as you should know, if you wish to continue in our service, when we are present at the palace, it is our command and our rule. Not the Queen's inclinations."

"Yes, Your Majesty." Still bobbing and bowing as he scurried to fill more glasses, the addled servant waved his counterpart forward and gave a jerking nod toward Graham, the duke, and Lady Mercy.

King William took a slow sip from his glass, all the while continuing to study Graham.

Graham clenched his teeth harder and lifted his chin. Royal or not, he would not give the man the satisfaction of a Scot cowering at his feet. The ominous echo of a ticking clock filled the room. Graham felt the minutes of his life slipping away, and the feeling shattered his ability to curb his impatience. Time to end this waste of time. "Your summons appeared urgent." He gave a stiff nod. "How might I be of service to His Majesty?"

The king's gaze slid from Graham to Edsbury. "The Duke of Edsbury is in need of your service, and it is our most adamant wish you see fit to accept the task." A sincere smile wiped the weariness from the king's long, drawn face as his attention settled on Lady Mercy. "Edsbury and his daughter, the lovely Lady Mercy, are our particular favorites here at court." With an affectionate tilting of his head in her direction, King William extended his hand and wiggled his fingers. "Come to us, child."

With the barest rustling of her full skirts, Lady Mercy hurried to the king and knelt at his feet, placing her fingertips up beneath his. She bowed her head, pressing a kiss over the jewel-encrusted rings sparkling across his knuckles. "My king," she murmured as she lifted her face to his and gifted the king with a reverent, adoring smile.

Graham studied the king as His Majesty gazed down at the lass, fully expecting to witness the signs of a lascivious royal sizing up his next mistress. But such lust was not there. Surprising. A genuine fondness filled the king's face. He gave Lady Mercy the adoring look one would expect from a benevolent guardian toward a most beloved charge.

"Explain to him, Edsbury," King William said as he kept his pleased countenance fixed on Lady Mercy. He took tight hold of her hand, steadying her as she seated herself on the small, upholstered stool beside his chair. "Your loveliness is a welcome balm to our weary soul, my dear. A welcome balm, indeed."

With a graceful nod, Lady Mercy lowered her gaze. "You are most kind, Your Majesty."

His patience thinning even more with this royal parlor game, Graham turned to the duke. "The task?"

Edsbury's jaw flexed. He took a fortifying sip of the dark liquid in his glass, then scowled down at the port as he swirled it in a slow, methodical circle. "Lady Mercy has a great interest in the flora and fauna of Scotland. The Highlands, in particular." He leveled an even sterner scowl on Graham. "My late wife's influence, I fear. I blame her for the indulgence of my daughter regarding such. And with both my wife and my son's untimely deaths, Lady Mercy appears to need a distraction from her grief or there will be no peace in my household." He snorted, then coughed as though his words left a detestable taste in his mouth.

"Ye have my condolences, sir." Graham considered the man a rude cur, but he'd not be heartless toward him. 'Twas a raw thing to outlive a wife and a child. He'd witnessed such when cousin Ian had lost his wife and unborn child in the attack at Glencoe. "My *genuine* condolences, sir," he stressed.

Edsbury responded with a stiff nod.

"May they ever rest in peace." Graham raised his glass to Lady Mercy, holding it high as he gave her a respectful bow before downing the contents.

The duke responded to Graham's kind words with another jerking nod, then turned away, settling a long, studious glare upon his daughter still seated beside the king. He drained his glass, accepted another from a servant, then turned back to Graham. "It is Lady Mercy's wish to compile a book, an enhanced journal of sorts, cataloging the plants and animals of the Highlands. She wishes to dedicate it to her mother and brother since they were both avid lovers of nature."

"And she has our blessing," King William interjected with a look that dared Graham to argue. "We have vowed to see this journal

properly published and added to all our libraries across the kingdom."
The king gave Graham a menacing smile. "Hear this and mark our
words when we say Lady Mercy has our royal sanction for this
venture. We are certain you understand our meaning, do you not?"

"Oh aye, Your Majesty," Graham hedged. *"Your* meaning is quite
clear."

Clear as a murky fog floating above the bogs. Whatever they were
about to ask was an order, not a request. *That* part, he understood. But
what were they asking? Had he been summoned here merely to
describe the Highlands to a fetching Sassenach noble who more than
likely had never set foot past Hadrian's Wall? What a waste of his
time. Beguiling lass or not, he was no storyteller or some foppish bard.
Why the hell had they chosen him? Time to sort this foolishness out.
"What exactly is the task? I'm no' so much for telling stories of my
beloved Highlands. My time is better spent patrolling them, ye ken?"

"I require a guide, Master MacCoinnich."

So, Lady Mercy could speak something other than the demure
murmurings of a highborn lass seeking favor at court. Graham heard
an underlying strength in her sultry tone and something more,
something he couldn't quite put his finger on, but it drew him in just
the same. Determined, she was. Aye, that was it. She might play the
part of a shy lass, but he'd lay odds the woman was sly and unpredict-
able as the wind. A thrilling, ominous shiver, a shudder of expectation
shot through him. He relished a challenge.

"A guide, m'lady?" Graham took a step closer, noting the king's
sharp-eyed perusal as he did so. "Surely, ye dinna mean to travel
through the Highlands to make your wee book."

"That is exactly what she means to do," Edsbury said as he positioned himself closer to the king and his daughter, behaving as though
he'd be an impenetrable barrier should Graham decide to attack. "And
to do so safely, she needs someone who will not only guide her
through the Highlands but also protect her." He widened his tensed,

defensive stance and glared at Graham with red-veined nostrils flaring as though he smelled a stench. "Your reputation as a mercenary precedes you, sir. Are you not for hire?"

A warning tingle rippled through the hairs on the back of Graham's neck. The same instinctive alarm he always felt when danger neared. He'd best choose his words with care. He felt it clear to the marrow of his bones. With the king involved, if he failed at this, Alexander's clan could be in danger. King William had sworn to cleanse the Highlands of treasonous rumblings, and his edict played well into the hands of those seeking political gain and also wishing to settle old scores. The murdered MacDonalds of Glencoe lay restless in their graves as a testament to that.

Graham forced himself to appear a damned sight more relaxed than he felt. He even managed a congenial demeanor to go along with his polite half-bow. "Aye. I am a soldier for hire." He gave King William a look he prayed the royal would understand. "For the right price and the right reasons."

King William rewarded him with a smug but thoughtful smile as one, gold-ringed finger twitched with a slow rhythmic tap atop the lion's head carved into the arm of his chair. "Your loyalty is so noted by us, sir."

Lady Mercy rose from her seat beside the king, so graceful and lithe in the sumptuous yardage of her silk gown, she seemed to float across the floor, suspended in the folds of rich purple framing her coloring to perfection. She eased closer to Graham, hands clasped in front of her in an almost pious pose. With a shy incline of her head, she flashed him a smile that Graham felt sure was meant to beguile him. "I would be most grateful if you would agree to this duty. My father assures me you shall be well paid for your services."

"Gold coin," Edsbury said, spitting out the words as though it was a struggle to say them. "As much as you can lift. Bags, of course. Both hands."

"Quite a sum." The generous offer made Graham even more wary. Was it truly that important to Edsbury and the king that the charming Lady Mercy be indulged and allowed to make her wee book rather than just disposing of the lass by marrying her off for political gain? There was more here, more than what had been said; damned if he could figure out what it was.

"Then you will agree?" Lady Mercy blessed him with a genuine smile and a look that stirred him in places better left unstirred by an English lass who was clearly a favorite to the king—especially if they were to be traveling through the Highlands. Alone.

Alone? Nay. Surely not. Graham cleared his throat and huffed away Lady Mercy's enamoring spell, shifting his attention back to Edsbury. "I need more details. How many will be in our party? I assume the lady has her own retinue accompanying her?" Royals traveled with herds of servants to see to their every need. If he was both guide and guard to all concerned, he needed to know the number.

"Myself and my maid," Lady Mercy said after a quick glance back at her father. "And a few servants to handle the horses and wagons, of course."

"And one of our own personal guards," King William added with a warning, narrow-eyed glare. "After all, parts of the Highlands are quite uncivilized. A lone man, even one with your rumored skills, could do little against a band of highwaymen."

Graham knew damn good and well why the king was sending one of his own. The man would be a bloody spy. If the king was so worried about highwaymen outnumbering him, he had a better solution. "My brothers, Duncan and Sutherland, might be available to join us." He turned to Edsbury and grinned. "Of course, they'll be wanting their own payment of gold."

The duke opened his mouth to speak, but King William cut him off. "We find your terms acceptable." He paused, gave Edsbury a hard look, then continued. "However, one of our personal guards shall still accompany you. We will not negotiate that point."

Three Scots against one red-coated Sassenach? Aye, that would do. Fair laughable odds it was and a great deal more acceptable. Graham settled his focus back on the lovely Lady Mercy, searching her expression for signs of guile or deceit. More was at stake here than the spoiled daughter of a duke getting her way. But what was it? Could the lass really just wish for a grand tour through the Highlands to honor her mother and brother? And why was the king so intent on accommodating the girl and her father? Graham understood the concept of favorites at court, but this…this was more than a little odd.

"Will you agree, sir?" Lady Mercy asked, looking like a child begging for sweets.

"Aye, m'lady. I agree to the terms set forth today." Graham accepted with a curt bow, then turned to Edsbury and the king. "My brothers can be here within a few days. All I need do is send for them. When shall I tell them we plan to leave?"

Edsbury sniffed and turned aside, glancing at the king before giving Graham a dismissive nod. "All shall be set in motion as soon as your brothers arrive."

"Do have them make haste," King William intoned. "We have little patience for waiting."

A warning. Graham acknowledged it with a bow, clenching his teeth to keep from saying more than he should as he turned and left the room.

CHAPTER TWO

"D ID HE SEEM like a wild barbarian, m'lady? I've heard about those Scots, I have. And did you know..." Janie paused and leaned in close, charged excitement arching her sparse, reddish blonde brows up to the ruffles of her white cap. "I heard some of them kidnap their wives! Have you ever heard such? Did your Scot look all that fearsome? You know I can protect you if need be, m'lady. I'm not afraid of any man."

"Master MacCoinnich is not *my* Scot," Mercy corrected as gently as possible, trying not to smile at the thought of fearless Janie boxing Master MacCoinnich's ears and taking him to his knees with a coarse tongue-lashing.

Janie—or Hughson as everyone else called her, had been an odd sort of choice for this position. A faint sigh of futility escaped Mercy. Sadly, Janie Hughson had been the *only* woman interested in the job of her lady's maid.

The girl was nice enough. Sort of—in a scrabbling, fighting-to-survive sort of way. A bit coarse for a maid and quite the solid build. Mercy had always secretly thought Janie could pass for a man should she ever wish to do so. At the time of her interview, Janie had begged Mercy to give her a chance, and something about the plea had touched Mercy's heart. She understood what it was to battle for acceptance.

Her conscience bade her help Janie and give the girl a try. So, Janie had joined their household and become more than a little protective over Mercy. She couldn't imagine life without her maid.

"And the Scotsman looked to be quite the gentleman, I assure you," Mercy hurried to add. A *handsome* gentleman that made the very act of breathing a chore. She stiffened, sitting straighter as Janie pulled on another heavy hank of her long, dark hair, hacking the brush through its thickness as though waging war on it.

"*Such is the curse of our ancestry,*" Mama had always said with a proud smile as she brushed out Mercy's hair every morning. She had never left the task to the maids. Mercy swallowed hard and released another frustrated sigh. Thick, heavy hair was but one of the curses. She lifted her chin, determined to mimic her mother's tranquil optimism. Mama had never flinched or acted as though she noticed the shunning. She had ignored the ostracism, the rude, haughty glances. Her mother rose above it all. A cool, poised beauty, Mama had held herself above their slurs. If only she had inherited Mama's ability to find a state of serenity no matter the circumstances.

Mercy assumed the epitome of calm control as Janie worked through another troublesome strand of tangled hair. The snarls were easily endured. The slurs and slights of a heartless, narrow-minded society—not so much, especially when those insults followed her home. Her reflection in the looking glass scowled back at her. She would never be as forgiving and graceful as Mama. She'd rather spit in their faces than ignore their hatred.

"I just love your hair, m'lady. All straight and gorgeous like a fine, full river of black silk. Not all curls and orange fluff like me own." When Janie got wistful, her Irish background grew more pronounced in her speech.

"Thank you, Janie." Mercy's black mood eased a bit. Janie was the best sort of tonic. The protective girl kept her grounded. She smiled at their reflections in the large oval mirror hanging above the dressing table. "But you know you mustn't feel such. Human nature always wishes for what you don't have and usually, if you ever get it, it's not nearly as wonderful as you thought it might be. My hair is quite the chore, as you well know since I'm lost without your help in taming it."

Janie shrugged away the words and kept brushing. "Tell me about this gentleman Scot so I'll know what to expect on this trip past the borders of civilization."

"Past the borders of civilization? You've been talking to Mrs. Frances again, haven't you?" Mercy preferred Janie stay away from Mrs. Frances. The astute housekeeper could be the undoing of Mercy's grand plan should Janie slip and divulge any of Mercy's meticulously laid out details.

The guilt reflected in Janie's freckled face told all.

"I cannot fail in this, Janie." Mercy clenched her hands atop the polished surface of the dressing table. "I beg you, keep to yourself and speak to no one about my trip. Please."

"I didn't tell her nothing, m'lady. I swear it." Janie chewed at the corner of her bottom lip, her brows knotted over her troubled eyes. "I overheard her speaking with his lordship, I did. That's where I heard that saying about the Highlands not being civilized."

Mrs. Frances spoke to his lordship about the trip? That was worse still. "What did she say to him?" Mercy reached up and slid her hair from Janie's grasp, stilling the brushing.

Janie shook her head, then leaned over Mercy's shoulder, and lowered her voice. "She feels you shouldn't go. She's afraid those Scots will sully your good name and prevent you from obtaining a good match in the future."

"There will be no match for me, Janie, and the only name I have in English society is *a low born of questionable breeding*, among others I shan't repeat." The sentiment tumbled from her lips before she thought. She shouldn't say such in front of Janie. She'd never wish to offend her, and the girl had been known to slip and say things she shouldn't whilst amongst her peers.

"So sorry, m'lady," Janie whispered, her crestfallen face flushing under the ruffles of her cap. "Truly sorry I am that they've been so mean to you. Such fools, they are. They don't have a clue to your sweet nature and kind heart." She nodded so hard, her cap fluttered atop her curls. "You can trust me, m'lady. I'm proud to be the maid of such a courageous woman. I'm not afraid to help you do what you're about to do."

Determination and hope surged through Mercy, filling her with renewed calm. She reached up and patted Janie's plump hand resting on her shoulder. "We will make this happen. Together." She squeezed the girl's hand and gave her a meaningful look in the mirror. "But please, Janie, you must guard your words more carefully than you have ever guarded them before. Promise me?"

Janie dipped her dimpled chin and smiled. "I promise, m'lady. I swear it on me mam's grave."

A hard rap on the door cut the conversation short. Mercy pulled her nightgown closed as she rose from the stool. She stared at the door, struggling to calm the rapid pounding of her heart. She flattened a hand atop her dressing table, drawing a strange sense of calm from its cool, solid surface laden with hair combs, perfumes, and lotions. Janie hurried to the latch, then looked back to her mistress before pulling the door open. Mercy took a deep breath and nodded.

"Yes?" Janie cracked open the door, blocking the space with her stocky frame.

"I would speak with my daughter." His lordship's voice floated through the door with a soft harshness but loud enough to shoot a chill straight to Mercy's heart.

"The lady is already retired for the evening, m'lord," Janie said in a borderline, insolent tone.

He couldn't have discovered the plan. Couldn't have. Papa never came to her suite of rooms. Since Mama's death, whenever he wished for Mercy's company, he sent a servant to fetch her, and those requests for her presence had been few and far between. Mercy understood why. How often had Papa remarked she was the image of her mother? Her only trait attesting to her English ancestry were her light, golden eyes inherited from her paternal grandmama, or so Mama had once said. But Mercy knew that information to be untrue. She had seen portraits of Papa's mother. The grandmama she had never met had light blue eyes in every painting. An ominous shiver rippled across her. The tawny amber of her eyes might have come by way of the rumor she'd overheard at Mama's memorial.

"I must speak with Lady Mercy. Have her meet me in her private sitting room at once." The door pulled out of Janie's hand and clicked shut with a firm thud that brooked no refusal of the order.

Red-faced and frowning, Janie turned from the closed door and faced Mercy. "M'lady?"

"Best do as he says." Mercy clasped her hands tight in front of her to stop their shaking. She nodded toward a garment hanging on the side of the mahogany wardrobe filling one wall of the room. She had to remain calm. She had to appear pure and truthful. Above suspicion.

She swallowed hard and did her best to settle her pounding heart as she slid her dressing gown off her arms and tossed it to the foot of the bed. Thankfully, both corset and shift were still in place.

Without a word, Janie removed a simple gown from its hanger, gave it a snapping fluff, then hurried to slip the day dress over Mercy's head. This was the garment Mercy wore on days she kept to her private rooms whenever they stayed in their house here in London. She smoothed her hands down the vibrant yellow panels of linen and cotton, bereft of lace, ribbons, and all manner of fussiness found on the dresses she wore when going out. Janie yanked the laces tight and secured the bodice, brushing out the skirts as she stepped away. Mercy pulled in another deep breath and forced herself to assume the calm grace she'd always seen in her mother. She could do this. She would see this through.

"Shall I wait for you here, m'lady?" Janie looked ready to fight, hands fisted at her sides.

Mercy laid a gentle hand to the girl's arm and steered her to a chair next to a bay window looking out across the private gardens. Beside the seat stood a small, claw-footed, round table with a pitcher of water and several glasses. She poured a bit of the water into one of the glasses and handed it to Janie. "Wait here and have a sip of water to cool your temper. I'll need your help to prepare for bed once I've finished speaking with Father. It'll be all right, Janie. I promise."

"Yes, m'lady." Janie accepted the glass, then bowed her head and set to rocking back and forth. "I'm such a disgrace to you as a lady's maid, m'lady. I beg your forgiveness and thank you for your patience. You shouldn't have to bother with the likes of me."

Mercy took hold of Janie's shoulders. "You are a treasure to me, Janie. Someone I can talk to. Someone to trust. Now no more talk of being a disgrace."

Janie didn't answer, just gave Mercy a noncommittal shrug and returned to rocking in place as soon as Mercy stepped away.

Best get this done. With a slide of her palms against her skirts to rid them of their nervous dampness, she hurried to the door, then paused to breathe in a steadying breath as she held the latch. *Help me, Mama. Please give me your strength and wisdom.* She lifted her chin, set her shoulders to the poised position expected of a lady, and pushed through the door.

Her father sat in one of the wingback chairs flanking the small mahogany table nearly buried beneath the books Mercy had left piled atop it. At the sound of her entrance, he looked up and smiled, or at least attempted a pleasant expression. Mercy recognized the familiar scowl of discontentment that had always hollowed out her father's features and grown even darker since her mother's death. It pained her no small amount to know that the mere sight of her fueled his irritation like wood thrown to red-hot coals. Yet another reason to hasten her departure and disappear. She did her best to set the feeling aside, forcing a vague, demure smile. Papa had to believe her an empty-headed female that thought of nothing other than dresses and invitations to parties. It was imperative to her plan. "Yes, Papa? You wished to see me?"

"Yes, daughter." He waved a hand toward the other wingback chair flanking the table of books. His gaze settled on the thick, leather-bound tomes. "I must stay, quite an unusual choice of reading material for a young lady. Maps of Scotland, clans of the Highlands, and the history of abbeys and priories." He paused for a deep sip of the golden liquid in the glass he always clutched in one hand until it was time for him to retire for the evening. He selected one of the larger books bound in black leather and squinted closer at the faded lettering on its spine. "Ah yes, and the Holy Bible, of course."

"Preparations for my trip, Papa." Mercy lowered herself to the chair, perching on the edge of the seat. A proper lady never lounged back in a chair. She wished she'd returned the book about abbeys and priories back to the shelves. That book might draw too much scrutiny to her itinerary.

Her father returned the Bible to the stack of books, frowning at the pile as though the mere sight of the collected readings disgusted him. "About your trip..." He leaned forward, cupping his glass of whiskey between both hands and scowling down at the shimmering liquid as though he hated it.

Mercy's thumping heart threatened to steal her breath. With a hard swallow, she tucked her fists against her middle and willed herself to remain calm. "Yes, Papa? It's my understanding that all stands at the ready. We merely await the arrival of Master MacCoinnich's brothers."

He looked up at her then, locking a piercing scrutiny upon her. His bloodshot eyes narrowed. "It is very important to me that Master

MacCoinnich…" His words faded away and the down-turned corners of his mouth tightened and twitched as though he fought to speak in spite of some inner demon attempting to keep him silent. He trembled, his frustrated scowl growing even fiercer. "Master MacCoinnich must…"

"Must what?"

"He must grow measurably fond of you." He downed the contents of his glass, rose stiffly from his seat, and shuffled across the room to the table of bottles and decanters beside another wall of books.

A sense of doom tightened in the pit of Mercy's stomach. It was all she could do to keep her voice controlled and even. "Fond of me?" she repeated, nearly choking on the words. "What exactly do you mean, Papa?"

The Duke of Edsbury refilled his glass, emptied it in one long drink, then filled it again. He meandered along the wall of bookcases, perusing the shelves as though looking for a nightly read. "It is important to me, daughter. Important that you are…accepted." He turned toward her with a jerk. "I cannot begin to tell you how I have regretted the ill treatment you, your brother, and your mother—and myself, I might add—have received over the years." He lifted his quivering chin and bared his yellowed teeth, biting out his words. "No amount of wealth or status protected the three of you from society's cruelty. It failed to protect any of us—myself most importantly." Pulling in a deep breath, he appeared to grow calmer. "But I mean to change all that." He gave her a perfunctory nod. "So, you need to ensure MacCoinnich becomes enamored of you. You must understand my intent and obey me as your mother always did."

"Enamored of me?" The request pushed her to her feet and made her take a step closer to the door. "You wish a Scotsman to fall in love with me? Why?" What political game did her father play at, and how could the love of a Scotsman help him win it?

The thought set her stomach to churning. This did not fit well with her plans at all. And now that Mama was gone, was Mercy expected to assume the role of primary pawn for Papa's political scheming? How much had Mama endured because of Papa's machinations? "How can you ask such a thing of me, Papa? How?" Did he possess no kind feelings toward her at all?

Her father plunked his glass down among the decanters. Hands trembling as he knotted them into fists, he knuckled them down on the long heavy table. He leaned over it, swaying from side to side as though the strength of the furniture was the only thing holding him upright. Head bowed, he stared down at his fists as he spoke. "If you can make a Scotsman love you and then spurn him, society will see that you are above the low morals they saw fit to brand you and your mother with because of your ancestry. They will see you as a proper daughter of an English gentleman. They will see me in a better light."

Her father lied. Mercy felt it more surely than the over-tight corset biting into her ribs. The slow, simmering fury she'd carried with her ever since she'd been old enough to recognize the ill treatment of herself and her mother bubbled to the surface. "I fail to see how spurning the love of a Scotsman will make people stop calling me a low class aberration of muddied breeding, whelped from a prostitute you rescued from pirates off the coast of Siam."

Her father spun about and faced her, mouth agape. "Mercy Rowena Etain Claxton! Where did you learn such language?"

"From those with whom you seek acceptance." Mercy stood taller and drew in a settling breath, holding in the tears burning her eyes. "Now tell me the truth. Why do you come to my rooms and tell me to seduce a stranger, then cast him aside? I shall never be accepted, and you know very well why."

The duke sagged into a nearby chair tucked up against the small hearth on the opposite side of the room. He massaged his temples, then leaned his head into hands. "I tried to cherish you, Mercy—just as I tried to love and cherish your brother and your beautiful mother after I made the mistake of falling under her spell and throwing my life into ruin." Without lifting his face from his hands, he drew in a heavy breath. "I am a weak man, and now I must pay the price for it." He dropped his hands from his face and glared at her as though he'd love nothing more than to beat her. He pointed at her. "You are the key to my redemption, daughter."

Mercy studied her father, attempting to fathom what he meant. He made even less sense this evening than he usually did after a few glasses of his favorite drink. "I fear I still don't understand."

"You are to secure my place at court, dear child. Permanently." The duke settled himself back in the chair and folded his hands in his lap with a coldness that filled the room. "And Jameson Campbell owns my soul due to several of my recent debts, but you shall remedy that problem as well."

"But the king—" Surely King William would help him—especially against a Scot. After all, her father had been a court favorite for as long as she could remember.

"I have fallen from his majesty's favor since your mother's untimely death. Disregard all you have seen over the past year and what he told MacCoinnich during our meeting." Mercy's father propped his elbow on the arm of the chair and set his chin in his hand as he stared into nothingness. He gave a disheartened shrug. "All that kept the king from banishing me from court after your mother's fatal accident was a promising opportunity I offered him."

A sick sensation washed across Mercy. Whatever her father was about to say couldn't possibly be good. "What opportunity?"

"The MacCoinnichs fought alongside the MacDonalds at the massacre of Glencoe." The duke studied her, his expression unreadable. "They are considered a possible problem to the crown. The king does not trust them or the Neals, with whom they forged an alliance through marriage to rebuild their clan."

"What has that to do with Jameson Campbell, your debts, and an opportunity for the king?" Her father still wasn't making sense.

"Jameson Campbell was once betrothed to the current wife of Alexander MacCoinnich." Her father frowned at her as though this information should mean something. It didn't. He rolled his eyes and continued, "Alexander MacCoinnich is Graham MacCoinnich's eldest brother. Clan MacCoinnich's chief. When Campbell attempted to claim his betrothed, along with her generous dowry, MacCoinnich not only dishonored Campbell but also convinced Lord Crestshire to toss him into the Tolbooth at Edinburgh."

Mercy hugged herself, scrubbing her arms against the oppressive sense of evil settling across the room. Mama had warned her of Papa's political scheming before. He enjoyed the games of politics far better than any challenge of backgammon or chess. "Spurning a Scot seems weak revenge for Campbell's time in prison and however much money you owe him."

"Not if that Scot reacts as predicted."

"Which is?"

"When a Scot wants something, especially a MacCoinnich, he takes it, and if it escapes him, he fights to make it his own, even steals it if need be. MacCoinnich's brother proved that." He sipped at his drink, never blinking in his plotting scrutiny of her. He lifted his glass in a toast. "King William wishes the MacCoinnichs tested and neutralized the same way the Campbells quelled the MacDonalds, but His Majesty would like the task to look more plausible this time, cleaner—especially after the debacle at Glencoe." He gave a dissatis-fied shake of his head as he rose from the depths of the chair. "Glencoe turned gruesome and risked the image King William wishes to maintain." Pointing a finger at Mercy, a cold, mean laugh rumbled from him as he returned to the decanter and filled his glass. "But the kidnapping of a Duke's daughter, the one and only favored godchild of the king, would give His Majesty good reason to silence a dangerous rumbling in the Highlands before it becomes a deafening roar."

Mercy turned away as her father continued sharing his grand plan, wishing she could cover her ears to shut out his words.

"And what better form of repayment to Jameson Campbell than the opportunity to destroy the family who shamed him without fear of reprisal from the king?" The wood flooring beneath her father's large frame groaned and creaked as he made his way to the door. "You will do this for me, daughter, and for our king. With Lord Crestshire's military reports of no treasonous issues with the MacCoinnichs, this is the only way to destroy them honorably."

"Honorably?" What honor existed in setting such a snare? "And if I refuse?" She had to say the words even though she heard her mother's soft warning in her mind. *You must never challenge Papa.*

"I shall disavow you as my daughter and name you as a bastard of one of your mother's numerous affairs. Trust me. It won't take anything to prove my claim." Her father's words echoed low and deadly through the room. "And I shall have you sent to the wharf where I met your mother, and you can survive as best you can among the pirates." He paused and gave her a slow up and down look. "I'm sure you'll fetch an even higher price than what I paid for your mother all those many years ago."

The door creaked as he opened it "I am not completely heartless. Accomplish this task to my liking and you shall be sent to the abbey on the Isle of Iona. The abbess there was well acquainted with your mother and felt a kindness toward her." He gave a casual flip of one hand. "At least, from what I gathered from your mother's journals, the abbess had no issue with a reformed whore and adulteress." He stared at Mercy, his watery, bloodshot eyes squinting. "I can barely stand to look at you, daughter. You remind me so much of her. My misbegotten lust for her. The way she drove me mad beyond reason. The damned foolish mistake I made in marrying her for which I've paid a thousand times over. I could have achieved greatness without the lot of you attached to my name."

As much as she wanted to look away, Mercy couldn't tear her gaze from him as he stood in the doorway, this monster of a man who had once been her trusted papa. Yes, he'd always been detached but never this cruel.

"I refuse to lose any more opportunities because of an error in judgement I made years ago. One way or another, you shall make this right for me or rue the day you were born."

"Too late, Father," Mercy whispered. "I already do."

CHAPTER THREE

'TWAS A GRAY, bone-chilling day–typical for early spring in England. A drizzling rain soaked through everything. Graham swiped the back of his hand across his forehead, then yanked his long, dripping hair away from his neck. He hated the feel of clammy hair shoved down his collar and stuck to his skin.

The rhythmic *clop-clop-clop* echoing ever closer pulled Graham's attention away from tightening the leather straps of the bags to the rear of his saddle. He turned and scanned the bustling area in front of the public stable. His dark mood lightened somewhat at the sight of his younger brother, Duncan, riding a dapple gray down the narrow alleyway cutting between the tall buildings lining one of the city's busiest thoroughfares. Good. It was about time. With his brothers here, they could be shed of this crowded, stinking hell and be on their way back to the Highlands. He sidled to one side, craning his neck to see behind Duncan and catch sight of his youngest brother, Sutherland. But the alley behind Duncan was empty.

"Where's Sutherland?"

"Greetings to ye as well, dear brother." Duncan fixed him with a go-to-Hades look as he dismounted. His brother rolled his shoulders and glanced around the paddock. "Sutherland's in France. Left the day before the messenger arrived with your strange request." He slapped a hand to Graham's shoulder. "So, tell me, brother, what manner of shite have ye stepped in this time?" He leaned in close and winked. "I'm proud to see ye're at least not in prison, so it canna be too serious."

"Ye willna believe me when I tell ye." Graham turned back to his mount, running his hand over his sheathed sword, to his holstered musket, and across the rolled bundles in one last check of all he'd need for this venture. He'd been ready since the day of the meeting but still couldn't believe all that had transpired. With his hand on the braided lip of his saddle, a frustrated snort escaped him. "King William and the Duke of Edsbury have hired our expertise for a safe, informative tour of the Highlands. Gold to be our payment."

"A tour of the Highlands, ye say?" A dark brow hiked and disbelief sparking in his eyes, Duncan laughed. "Since when does the king and one of his pawns hire a mercenary, a Scot no less, to take them through the Highlands?" He propped his shoulder against one of the stone columns of the stable. All humor left him as he gazed at Graham. "I smell a trap, brother."

"Aye, I got a whiff of that stench as well." Graham stole a glance around the area and edged a step closer to Duncan. "And we're nae taking *them* through the Highlands, mind ye. 'Tis Edsbury's daughter. Lady Mercy Claxton and her retinue, and we'll be nursemaids to them through the wilds of Scotland."

"The *Lady* Mercy Claxton? A genteel woman of noble birth? Camping her way across the Highlands?" He pushed off the wall and looked about, confirming their privacy. Still scowling, he strode back to within a hairsbreadth of Graham's nose. "This reeks of a dangerous snare, ye ken that, aye? What the hell do they play at?"

Graham felt the same. It was as though he and Duncan were a pair of clueless rabbits about to be caught. "I have yet to discover their game, but the king made it quite clear this was not a request. There was little choice to be had."

"Ye mentioned gold," Duncan reminded, his avarice always at the forefront.

"Aye. Bags of it, they said. As much as ye can carry."

"Christ Almighty, 'tis one hell of a trap for sure then." Duncan scrubbed a hand over the dark stubble of his beard, then raked his fingers back through his hair. He studied Graham, the muscles in his square jaw flexing. "Ye told them half now and the rest when the job was done, aye?"

Shite. Why the hell had he not thought of that? Graham knew exactly why. Because he'd been done in with the strangeness of the entire situation. He ducked his head, ashamed to admit a failing to his younger brother. "Nay. Payment in full once we return her here to London."

"Ye're daft, ye are." Duncan gave him a damning glare. "Ye always get the money first—or at least a good bit of it. She must be quite the fetching lass."

"If ye'd been there, ye would understand," Graham defended. A private audience with a king who'd as soon hang your arse as to look at ye, paired with a beauty begging to be swept away to the Highlands, well... Hell's fire. At least he'd ensured they'd be paid at all.

The sound of an approaching rider silenced them both. A soldier in full redcoat uniform headed his horse toward them at a fast clip. The man sat tall in the saddle, his scowl locked on Graham. He yanked his horse to a halt, squared his rain-soaked shoulders, and squinted down his nose at Graham. "Master Graham MacCoinnich?"

"Aye." Graham rested one hand on the hilt of his sword sheathed in front of his saddle and the other on the butt of his second pistol tucked into his belt.

"Lieutenant George St. Johns, sir. I shall accompany you and your brother on Lady Claxton's journey." He gave a nod at Duncan as though this small, polite gesture should be taken as quite the blessing.

"Well... that's verra reassuring, I grant ye, but I fear we've yet to be notified when her ladyship wishes to leave. So ye might as well be gone for a bit." Graham clapped a hand to his brother's shoulder. "My brother here just arrived. He'll need a bit of time to refresh himself before our departure."

Mouth ajar, the lieutenant darted a quick glance behind him as though the devil himself nipped at his coattails. He motioned back down the alley. "Lady Claxton and her company await us at Gray's Inn Fields. They are ready to leave." A jerk of his head in that direction expressed the urgency. "Now."

This was not the way any trip should start. Graham shook his head. Time to take control. The king could order him to do this task but, by damn, the man wouldn't control how he did it. "Tell her ladyship we set out at dawn, aye? 'Twould be better than leaving midday today."

"That is not acceptable, sir. Her ladyship is ready to leave now." The lieutenant sniffed. "If you wish to incur her ladyship's wrath, you may do so in person. I shall not be the errand boy for a *Scot's* messages."

"I'm not a gutless worm afraid to inform her ladyship, I grant ye that." Graham mounted his horse and nodded to his brother. "Are ye coming or no'? Could be a fine time for ye to meet our lovely charge."

Duncan grinned and saddled up. "I wouldna miss this for the world, brother."

The lieutenant took the lead. The main thoroughfares of London crisscrossed their paths, slowing their progress as they allowed buggies and carriages to pass. Graham urged his horse ahead when he spotted a group clustered in one corner of a rolling green field bereft of buildings or any of the city's worrisome clutter.

He easily picked out the esteemed Lady Mercy Claxton as she emerged from a colorful wagon. The woman had to have inherited her beauty from her mother. Thankfully, the Lord had blessed her with an absence of her father's features. The lady's attire today appeared more sensible—less lace and ribbons and more lightweight wool, linen, and cotton. It suited her, fitting her lithe figure in all the right places and giving the impression of a rare, willowy orchid.

Rather than wearing the awkward fontange headwear Graham had seen women struggling to manage at court, Lady Mercy wore a simple straw hat with a wide brim bereft of useless plumage and held in place with a ribbon dyed the same deep purple as her skirt and coat. She carried another garment clenched in one gloved hand, a drab-colored thing that looked like it was made from the same material as a tent. With a scowl up at the overcast day, she shook out the strange looking, long-tailed coat and slipped it on over her clothing. The misting rain beaded up and rolled off her odd apparel.

"Well, isn't she the canny lass." Duncan observed. "Shielding herself with that coat."

"Aye," Graham agreed. But how odd for a lady of noble birth to be so sensible-minded. Most he'd met were more concerned with how they looked rather than the usefulness of their attire.

Lady Mercy stepped forward, greeting them both with a shy curtsy. "Good day, Master MacCoinnich." She motioned toward her servants, horses, and wagons. "As you can see, we are quite ready to begin our trip through the Highlands."

Graham propped his hands atop the saddle horn and leaned forward, studying all that Lady Mercy intended to bring along on the trip. A pair of flatbed wagons with low sides were parked side by side, filled and covered, their cargo secured with ropes across the tarps. On one of the wagon's benches, perched an old man holding the reins of the two draft horses hitched to it. The flatbed wagon next to it had a driver that looked like a younger version of the other wagon's driver. The horses shook their heads, rattling their harnesses and stomping in eagerness to pull. Each driver of the two, low-sided wagons was accompanied by a young man, servants more than likely. The lads looked to be at that gangly awkward age of not quite men but grown enough to provide some muscle for the more laborious chores the trip would entail.

A scowling, white-capped, chunk-of-a-girl dressed in the drab attire provided for the personal maids of high-born ladies waited a few paces behind her ladyship. Beside the handmaid, an older woman stood with her thick arms folded across her middle. Behind the matron was the box wagon in which Lady Mercy had taken shelter from the rain. Smoke filtered up from the tiny, crooked chimney jutting out of its side. The house-like carriage was daubed with bright colors, blues and reds and had all manner of pots and buckets swinging from hooks screwed into the narrow eaves of its roof. The cluttered contraption resembled a shed fitted with wagon wheels. From the gear attached to it and the older woman's stained apron, Graham assumed the scowling matron to be Lady Mercy's private cook.

A sleek, purebred horse stood tethered to the side of the cook's wagon. It appeared Lady Mercy not only intended to ride rather than view Scotland from the bench of a wagon, but also intended to ride astride rather than sit sidesaddle.

Lord Almighty. This wasn't a tour of the Highlands. This was a blasted invasion.

Her ladyship stood with gloved hands clasped in front of her waist and a demure smile aimed right at him. "I do hope you'll appreciate how we've winnowed down our accoutrements so we might travel lighter and with more efficiency."

"Aye, I see ye've been a' winnowing all right." Graham shifted in the saddle, an impending sense of doom settling heavy in the pit of his stomach. He forced himself not to falter beneath the lovely woman's golden-eyed gaze. "We should leave at dawn tomorrow rather than midday today. Makes for better traveling, ye ken? Gets more miles behind us afore we have to stop and make camp for the evening." He shrugged toward Duncan. "Besides, my brother arrived this verra day. A night's rest is needed for both himself and his mount."

Duncan snorted out a laugh as he made a dashing bow from his saddle. "Your ladyship. Duncan MacCoinnich, at your service."

Lady Mercy gave him a quick curtsy. "Master MacCoinnich," she said, her tone polite but strained.

"Your most welcome to call me Duncan, m'lady." He grinned. "Might help keep the Master MacCoinnichs on the trip straight, aye? 'Course, I am the better looking one." He gave Lady Mercy a knowing wink.

Duncan's familiarity with the lass, irritated Graham to no end. Before Lady Mercy could respond, Graham interrupted. "She'll do no such thing." He edged his horse a step forward. "Ye may call me, Graham, m'lady. Dinna fret about using Duncan's Christian name, if ye dinna wish to do so. Ye can call him plain ole MacCoinnich if ye like—or *boy's* a more apt title. 'Tis what the rest of us MacCoinnich brothers call him."

"Ye're an arse," Duncan observed with a belittling cut of his eyes in Graham's direction.

Lady Mercy's nervous gaze flitted back and forth between the two men, her dark brows arched in an attractive display of confusion and subdued amusement. "Perhaps, while we are traveling, I should use both your given names to avoid confusion." She cleared her throat with a light *ahem* and pressed her hands together in supplication. "But Graham," she paused and rewarded him with a kind, placating look. "Did I understand you to say we shan't be leaving today?"

"That's exactly what he said, your ladyship," Lieutenant St. Johns interrupted. "This Scot appears to think of no one's wishes but his own. I informed him such an attitude was not acceptable."

Graham almost laughed out loud at the cold haughtiness of Lady Mercy's glare as she turned it on the lieutenant. He held his tongue and winked at Duncan to do the same.

"Your name, sir?" Lady Mercy asked.

The lieutenant's Adam's apple skittered up and down his throat in a hard swallow. "Lieutenant George St. Johns, ma'am. His Majesty's guard—at your service."

"I shall thank you to refrain from commenting on questions not directed to you, sir, and everyone here will be treated with respect. Neither rudeness nor a troublesome nature will be tolerated on this trip. Is that understood?" Lady Mercy's eyes narrowed, reminding Graham of a wild feline about to pounce on its prey.

"Understood, ma'am." The lieutenant straightened his shoulders, then stared straight ahead.

Aye, now there's the strength he'd heard in her earlier. What a lass. Graham grinned, secretly hoping for a continuation of the redcoat's scolding.

Lady Mercy's attention returned to Graham, thankfully, with less ferocity than what she'd focused on the lieutenant. "I understand the soundness of your logic, sir, but I beg you reconsider." A wariness shadowed her features, and Graham swore the enticing lass almost cringed as though she feared something—surely, she didn't fear him? The thought gave him pause.

"Master MacCoinnich... I mean, Graham—others of the king's guard alerted us to your brother's arrival today." She clenched her gloved hands together in a sign of supplication. "I am quite certain you're not surprised to learn that His Majesty takes measures to watch everything."

"Spies, ye mean." Graham gritted his teeth. He'd thought as much, but he'd not expected the king to watch them so closely before they'd even left London. "Aye. I expected no less."

"I am sorry." Lady Mercy turned aside, looking back toward her wagons. "At the king's order, when your brother was sighted close to the city, we gathered here with all our equipment in tow. Might we not make our way into the countryside for a short distance today, then set up camp early so your brother and his mount could find their needed rest?" She faced him once more, her aura of grace, strength, and composure fully restored. After a quick glance at his horse and the packs strapped to his saddle, she nodded toward them. "You appear packed and ready to travel, are you not?"

"I am packed and ready, but that isna the point, m'lady." Graham distinctly heard Duncan chuckling under his breath and promised himself that he'd knock the wee fool on his arse at first opportunity.

"I can live with the lady's suggestion," Duncan said with a benevolent look that made Graham want to shove him off his horse even more. "Ole Jock and I didna run all that hard getting here. I believe we're good for a few more miles today."

"Ye couldha said that afore," Graham said.

"Ye didna ask," Duncan replied with a wide grin.

Duncan was supposed to be an ally not a thorn in his arse. He pulled in a deep breath and released it with a slow controlled hiss. He glanced up at the sky, then turned and studied the buildings lining the far side of the field. The position of the sun on the murky day escaped him, but mayhap he could estimate the time by the length of the shadows. Not only was it well into the afternoon, but an early fog was joining the dense misting rain blanketing everything with a cloying wetness.

Lady Mercy stood there, patiently awaiting his decision, not even blinking as moisture beaded up on her hat's brim and dripped off in front of her face. She shifted with a quiet sigh and gave him a tremulous smile.

Saints' bones, how could he refuse her? "Aye." Graham made a jerking wave toward the caravan of servants, wagons, and horses. "Mount up, the lot of ye. We'll be on our way."

"Oh, thank you, Master MacCoinnich!" Her smile no longer tremulous, Lady Mercy fair beamed up at him as she clapped her gloved hands.

"Graham, aye?" he corrected. He'd not let Duncan have the honor of being the only one her ladyship called by their Christian name.

"Yes. I shall strive to remember." Lady Mercy gave him a genuine smile that stirred him more than it should. "Thank you, Graham. I do appreciate your understanding."

Time to show the lady he was just as gallant as Duncan. Graham dismounted and held out his hand. "Help you to your horse, m'lady?"

"You are most kind, sir." She slid her hand into his and permitted him to walk her to her horse.

Rather than allow the muddiness to foil her attempt at the stirrup, Graham took the liberty of setting his hands on either side of her waist and lifted her up into the saddle.

"My goodness!" Her cheeks reddened as she touched his chest.

Graham chuckled to himself. What a delightful sound she made when startled. "Forgive me for taking such liberties, m'lady, but I didna wish ye to slip—not with your wee boot heels so glutted with turf and mud."

"Uhm… quite all right, Graham. Thank you," she said in a breathless tone as she maneuvered her skirts and long coat to sit astride without baring her legs above her ankles.

Graham hadn't a clue how she managed it, but he did know he was disappointed at missing a peek that might reveal more of her legs. He studied her outfit closer. The woman's skirt and petticoats were paneled, split down the center, and fashioned after a man's breeches. "I'll be damned. Your skirts and petticoats are made into trews."

Lady Mercy's cheeks glowed even brighter. She briefly bowed her head, taking refuge in the wide brim of her hat.

Remorse filled Graham. What was wrong with him? He shouldn't have blurted out such a personal observation. He took hold of her horse's reins and prevented her from moving away. "Forgive me," he said in a low tone meant for her alone. "I'm no' a gentleman, m'lady, and have never claimed such. I say whatever comes to mind, but please know I'd never shame ye on purpose." He waited, gritting his teeth, hoping she'd accept his apology. Damn his thoughtless hide.

She turned in the saddle, glancing back at him, her graceful demeanor seeming somehow saddened. "No offense taken, Graham. You cannot imagine how refreshing I find your honesty." She settled her damp skirts over her ankles. "And you are quite correct, I had my seamstress alter my clothes for the journey. I thought them more sensible for the trip. Like my cover coat. Don't you agree?"

A sensible Sassenach and a high born one at that. Admiration for the woman filled him. Mayhap this trip wouldn't be so wretched after all. "Aye, lass. I agree wholeheartedly." He turned away, having sense enough to give the lady some privacy after embarrassing her.

He slogged back across the muddy ground to his horse, mounted, then gave Duncan a warning look. "Dinna ye dare say a word about the lass's clothes or I'll string ye up by the short hairs of your ballocks. Understand?"

"Aye, brother." Duncan grinned, a smug, damning grin that threatened to get his arse kicked. "I understand more than ye know."

CHAPTER FOUR

GRAHAM APPEARED TO be a decent man, and his brother seemed the same. Mama would have liked them both—maybe even liked them enough to trust them. Mercy pressed the flat of her hand to her middle. A warm fluttering—a strange excited sensation she'd never experienced before—made her swallow hard and pull in a quick breath. Such feelings would not do at all. She was bound for the abbey. A life of peace and solitude removed from the torture of a prejudiced society and a heartless father's machinations. Yes. Such a life would be most welcome.

God willing, by way of her own carefully laid out plan and not that of her father's evil ploy, she would achieve the peace she craved. She snorted out a disgusted huff. She refused to deal with such wickedness. How her father lived with such loathsome tactics was beyond her. Although she knew little of the Highlander, from what she'd observed so far, Graham MacCoinnich possessed more honor in his little finger than her father had ever possessed. A satisfying sense of finality filled her. She would save Graham and his clan from her father's despicable plot, as well as free herself.

From her horse's position several yards behind Graham, she studied him with an interest that bordered on rudeness. But she couldn't help it. The man intrigued her. She'd never met anyone like him. He said what he thought, and his opinions were quite clear. He made no attempt to hide anything. Rare traits in this world, indeed.

Remembered moments from earlier in the day triggered a smile. Graham detested the lieutenant and made his opinion quite obvious by forcing the king's guard to travel separate from everyone else, bringing up the rear at his appointed station behind the wagons. St. Johns would be lucky if his mount didn't founder in the muddy ruts and mucked out holes the horses and wagons left in their wake. Incessant rain and the spring thaw made for treacherous traveling through England's countryside.

Mercy warmed toward Graham even more when she thought back about his treatment of every individual in her circle. He interacted with them as though it was unnecessary to deal with them unless it risked the journey. He didn't ignore them, he merely allowed them to go about their duties unless their actions somehow endangered them, and then advised *her* as to how to correct them.

The thought suddenly occurred to her that the only individual to whom he'd given a direct command was the lieutenant. All other orders, he routed through her. She smiled. Did that mean he respected her intellect? Such respect was something she'd not experienced before. A satisfied sigh escaped her as she took in the dreary landscape and soggy surroundings. But she must remember to give him liberty to issue orders directly. After all, he knew the Highlands whereas she did not.

She adjusted her hat to a better angle for deflecting the rain and swiped her damp glove across her even wetter cheek. Respect or not, at present, Graham MacCoinnich was ignoring her. He rode several yards in front of the group with his brother at his side. This observation pricked at her nerves. She made an impatient flicking away of the droplets gathered along her hat's brim. What an irrational emotion. Why on earth should she expect his attention? Graham would never fawn over a woman. He was a far cry from the shallow courtiers. He was her guide, for heaven's sake, and under no circumstances should she encourage him to behave otherwise. Both their lives depended on it.

Concentrate on the abbey. That's what she should do. Mercy sat taller in the saddle, lifting her chin to the proud tilt Mama had taught her to hold no matter her circumstances. She fixed her gaze on the broad backs of the two Scots riding in front of her, and a pang of worry hit her. Personal considerations aside, how could she protect these two men and their families from her father's hellish plot to execute them?

Graham held up a hand and reined in his horse, bringing the caravan to a stop. He turned and faced Mercy, waiting for her mount to catch up to his.

As her horse plodded closer, Mercy blinked and struggled to control her breathing. How could a man look so…proper words escaped her. Wild? Rugged? Yes. Graham sat his mount like a god-king sitting a prized war horse as he watched over his kingdom. Rain drenched the man to the skin, and yet he looked none the worse for it. His long black hair looked all the blacker, pulled back in a braid that snaked down his back. The rest of them looked like drowned rats, but he looked…undefeatable. Yes. That was it.

He looked strong, courageous, fearless even. She had never seen such a man. An appreciative sigh escaped her. Graham MacCoinnich personified what a real man should be. The excited fluttering in her middle strengthened, threatening to overcome the whole of her body.

"M'lady?"

Dear heavens. What had the man just asked? Mercy edged her horse closer. "Beg pardon, Graham. What did you say?"

Graham gave her a wicked grin. and the glint in his eyes said he was well aware of her scrutiny. "I said we'll make camp here for the night. With any luck, this weather will pass by morning. Have your men set the tents up beside those pines, aye? Or I can tell them. I wasna certain how ye felt about me ordering about your servants."

"By all means, issue whatever orders you wish to whomever you wish. I assure you, they will be followed to the letter." There. She'd remembered to tell him. Now he would know she trusted him without question.

Graham flashed her a wide smile.

Her cheeks warmed, and she pulled in a sharp breath. Perhaps, she could have chosen better wording. That hadn't sounded at all proper. Her statement almost seemed like an invitation for him to give her orders. She retreated and turned her mount toward the pines. "Do what you will," she said with a lighthearted wave. Perhaps, it would be best to retreat before she said something else she shouldn't.

She dismounted beneath the pines, very much aware of Graham's gaze upon her. She waved over Percy March, the senior driver of the wagons, pulling him away from the job of helping his son, Doughal, and the other two lads, Robbie and Wills, from erecting the tent slated to be her personal shelter.

"Yes, m'lady?" Percy squinted one eye shut against the rain. The gentle misting of earlier in the day had ended. Water fell from the sky in a heavy shower that threatened to become a drowning deluge.

Mercy handed him her reins. "The horses' tent first, please, Percy, and make haste. If we lose any of the horses to this damp, chill weather, it would end our journey before it's even started. As soon as we have them in the dry, I'll see to my own horse." She turned to the beast and whispered, "Please continue to behave, my friend. There's a treat for you if you're sweet. I'm proud of how you've behaved with everyone so far."

The great, black horse nickered in response, then nuzzled his wet nose up under the brim of her hat and gave her an affectionate nudge.

"Horse tent?"

The proximity of Graham's deep voice startled her. "Why...yes. We've brought shelter for the horses. Our journey is set to last weeks, and these horses are accustomed to being stabled." She rubbed a hand along the black, shining nose of her horse. "Ryū is strong and fearless, but I will not have him subjected to such conditions."

"If that's no' the damnedest thing I've ever heard." Graham tossed a hand toward the sky. "'Tis but a bit a rain. They dinna need a tent." He put two fingers to his mouth and emitted a sharp whistle that split the air. All in the camp froze in place and riveted their attention to him. "Shelter for the women first, then tents for yourselves," he instructed Percy and Doughal along with Robbie and Wills. He pointed to a line of pines closest to the wagons. "String a rope between those trees and tie the horses there." He turned back to Mercy. "That'll be shelter enough for the beasts, I reckon."

"But the horses—"

"The horses will be fine, and if they canna survive a mild wet night such as this, we've no business taking them into the Highlands." He took a step closer, close enough so she could feel the heat steaming off him. "And ye might consider the same advice for yourself, m'lady. This trip isna for the faint of heart. A traipse about the Highlands is no' an enjoyable stroll through the sweet shops of London. The Highlands are filled with glorious beauty, but ye'll find they're rugged and unrelenting."

Mercy clenched her gloved hands, fighting against the urge to shake her fist in his face. "Do not judge me as weak or pampered, Master MacCoinnich. You know not of what you speak." How dare he think her a foolish noble incapable of besting a challenge. Her entire life had been a battle against all who judged her as inferior and waited to see her stumble and fail. "I assure you, I am quite ready for this journey." The man had no idea how ready. "And my horses will at least be granted blankets from this weather if I have to cover them myself. I shall negotiate no further on the matter."

Ryū stomped a pace forward toward the Scot, ears flattened and teeth bared as he moved to stand beside Mercy.

"No, Ryū," Mercy crooned as she took hold of his bridle and

hugged the beast to her. "Leave Master MacCoinnich alone. He doesn't know us yet."

"So that's the way of it, then. Master MacCoinnich again, is it?"

He studied her with a jaw-clenched stare that made her want to shout at him that he couldn't possibly understand all she'd endured, but she held her tongue. Mama had taught her better. One did not give in to emotional outbursts. One proved others wrong with controlled actions. She lifted her chin and gave him a damning look she hoped he would understand.

"Verra well then. So be it, I reckon." He pointed a finger at her. "The order stands. No tent for the horses but blankets I'll allow. Get ye in the dry, m'lady, and seek your rest. We break camp at dawn." He turned and stomped away, his kilt snapping behind him like the whipping of a dragon's tail.

Mercy felt the intense desire to pelt him with anything she could find to throw.

"M'lady?" Janie's sharp voice broke through her haze of frustration.

"What now?" She turned so fast, Janie backed up a step and raised her fists as though ready to fight. Janie's reaction made her feel even worse. She'd never struck Janie, but the poor girl had no doubt received such mistreatment from previous employers. Mercy pulled in a deep breath, exhaled, then swallowed hard, struggling to compose herself. "Forgive my tone, Janie." She swiped a hand against the heavy drizzle, wondering how she'd ever dry out in such weather. "I had hoped our trip would begin in a more pleasant way."

Janie gave her a forgiving smile, then pointed toward one of the flatbed wagons that looked as though someone had shoved a spike up underneath the tarp and created a makeshift tent. "Doughal and Wills fixed us a place in the wagon after they pulled the tents out. Said we could sit there in the dry 'til they get the shelters up and ready. Cook's kept the fire going in her wagon and said she'll have you a nice cup of broth and toasted bread ready in no time at all."

A fire and hot broth sounded heavenly. "I think I'd rather sit in Cook's wagon. It's much nicer than the flatbed."

Janie made a face and shrugged. "No place to sit anymore in Cook's wagon. It got crammed full of last-minute supplies right before we left. Even her bunk's full of tins and sacks of food. The woman fair plans to sleep on the floor, she does. You ever heard such?"

Right about now, a pallet on a warm, dry floor didn't sound all that bad, but Mercy refrained from saying so aloud. She might be chilled and soaking wet, but she would not whine about it. This had been her decision. As Mama always said, *"Sacrifice makes success all the sweeter."*

"To the wagon it is, then." She forged ahead through the mud, struggling against the treacherous, sticky mire as Janie headed off in the direction of Cook's wagon. The ground, boggy and wet, grabbed at Mercy's boots, pulling at them and threatening to suck them off her feet. Every step was a chore. Halfway to the line of wagons, as she came up even with Graham and Duncan, the lacing on her right boot gave way. Her foot pulled free, leaving it behind in the mud. Unbalanced, Mercy careened first to one side then the other, arms flailing to keep from falling as she held her stockinged foot high above the mire. "Oh dear!"

Graham charged forward with the speed and agility of one accustomed to navigating across such ground. Before she hit the muck, he scooped her up into his arms. "M'lady," he said with a deep, heart-stopping rumble that sounded entirely too amused for Mercy's liking. He cradled her against his chest as though she were a treasured child. "Seems ye've lost your slipper."

How in the world could one attempt to remain dignified in this sort of situation? Especially when held in the arms of such a *man*. Mercy clutched her fisted hands to her chest and glared at him from under the sagging brim of her wet hat. With an irritated jerk, she shoved it away from her forehead. "My bootlace came undone."

The ribbon of her hat chose that auspicious moment to pull free of the bow beneath her chin and plopped backward to the ground, exposing her fully to nature's downpour. Mercy closed her eyes and prayed for divine guidance, especially for deliverance from the traitorous feelings triggered by finding herself in Graham MacCoinnich's strong arms. *This is the first day of many. Give me strength, I beg you!*

Graham snorted out a laugh, then clamped his mouth shut. Sheer joy sparkled in the dark blue of his eyes.

"This is not amusing." Mercy swiped the rain out of her face and clutched at the heavy wet coil of her hair escaping its pins. Her attempts failed. The soaked tresses unwound down over Graham's arm, reaching almost to the ground in a shimmering river of soggy, black stubbornness. "Not amusing at all," she repeated through gritted teeth.

"Aye, lass, but it is." Graham chuckled as he repositioned her higher in his arms, hugging her close as he slogged across the camp. "Verra much so, in fact."

She thumped his chest. "Put me down this instant, Master MacCoinnich. A true gentleman does not hold a lady in such a fashion. I appreciate the gesture, but it is high time you released me." Her words sounded harsh and ungrateful even to her.

"Verra well then." Graham stomped forward a few more steps, then dropped her into the rear of the wagon. He jerked his arms out from around her, then retreated a step, scowling at her. "I already told ye I was no' a gentleman, m'lady, and I shall tell ye something more. As I see it, whether ye like it or no', ye need a man like me who'll snatch your arse up out of the mud instead of a man like that *gentleman* over there." He turned and jerked a thumb toward Lieutenant St. Johns tiptoeing and simpering his way around camp, as though the mud and muck were hot coals.

Her bottom still smarting from her hard landing, Mercy scooted deeper beneath the shelter of the tarp. A shiver rippled across her, making her miss the warmth of Graham's embrace. How could she have spoken to him in such a haughty manner? She swallowed hard and drew her wet coat closer around her, tucking her feet up under her skirts. She dropped her gaze and stared down at Graham's boots currently ankle deep in mud and puddled water. Her mother's teachings nudged her. She knew better than to behave like a spoiled, ungrateful child no matter the actions of her champion. After all, he'd done nothing unseemly, merely held her close to keep her high above the mud.

"Forgive me," she said without looking up. "Please believe me when I say I am grateful to you and all you do. I would never wish you to think I felt otherwise." She stole a glance up at him, praying he'd accept her apology.

Graham's dark, irritated scowl melted away, turning almost sheepish. He glanced aside, squinting against the rain as he looked out across the camp. "No harm done, m'lady," he said without looking back at her.

"Please, Graham. Sit here in the dry with me." She patted the rough boards of the wagon. "Bateson has promised hot broth and bread." Perhaps she could bribe him to forgive her tantrum. "Janie's gone to fetch it, and I'm more than happy to share."

Graham stared at the spot beside her, then shifted his gaze up to hers. "I should be helping set camp not sitting in the dry drinking broth."

"I'm sure Percy and his men would be happy to set your tent and your brother's. Duncan is more than welcome to take refuge in here, too." Mercy stole a nervous glance around the back of the wagon. There *was* enough room for both the men, herself, and Janie, but it threatened to be a mite cozier than she would certainly find comfortable. She bit her lip and turned back to Graham. The look on his face said he knew her thoughts as though she'd spoken them aloud.

Frustration pricked her. The man's opinion of her would never improve if she kept behaving in such a manner.

He shook his head and slicked his dripping wet hair away from his face. "Duncan and I dinna have tents. All we need is our kilts to shield us from the weather. We've endured much worse than this many a time."

Mercy couldn't imagine such. The men needed shelter from what looked to be a long night of heavy rains. "I can't abide it. You and Duncan must sleep in the men's tent. I am certain there shall be room for two more pallets."

Graham didn't comment, acting as though she hadn't spoken. She watched the rain stream down the planes of his chiseled profile and drip off the tip of his nose as he surveyed the progress of setting up camp. How did one reason with such a man? Did he truly hate her that much for acting like such a pampered noble? Her heart sank, and she swallowed hard. How could she blame him? He considered her a part of the very same society she hated for the way they treated people. She closed her eyes for a brief moment. She had to prove to him she was different. Better.

"Please, Graham," she said in a coaxing whisper, patting the boards beside her again. "Please forgive my horrid behavior and allow me to show you I am better than this."

A gentle smile pulled at the corners of his mouth and the dimple in his left cheek deepened. With an endearing growl and a shake of his head, he hoisted himself up into the wagon and scooted to the spot beside her. After a stern glance at the tarp above their heads, he gave an approving nod. "'Tis a sight dryer in here for certain." He folded his long legs into a loose, cross-legged position and leaned his elbows on his knees. Clasping his large hands in front of him, he stared down at them as he spoke. "Your behavior wasna horrid." He shrugged. "Ye're a lady, and me mam taught me how to treat a lady, but I thought to save ye from the mud. Truly, that was my intent."

"And I am very thankful you did." Mercy rested a hand atop his arm for the span of a heartbeat, then drew it back. She shouldn't touch him. It wasn't proper and he might resent it—especially if he belonged to another. She glanced away and busied herself with twisting the water out of her hair. "You will relent and share the tent with Percy and the other men, won't you? I can't bear the thought of you suffering a night out in the rain."

He blew out what he played to be a long-suffering groan, then gifted her with a grin. "Duncan and I shall make our pallets with the men if that will please ye."

"It will." She returned his smile and before she thought about it, reached over and swept his dark, wet hair back from his face.

Graham stared at her, all amusement gone, replaced by something akin to longing in his gaze. "I wish to please ye, m'lady."

Mercy held her breath, staring at his mouth, mere inches from hers. What would a kiss from such a man be like? She swallowed hard, then raced the tip of her tongue across her lip, already tasting...feeling.

With a slow careful leaning, Graham drew closer, so close she felt the warmth of his breath brush across her mouth. She sensed the raw heat of him reaching out to encompass her.

"Your broth, m'lady," Janie called out, her announcement shattering the spell.

Graham jerked back and scooted out of the wagon, motioning Janie forward. "Come, lass. Serve your mistress. She's fair chilled to the bone, ye ken?"

"Yes, sir." Janie slid the tray up into the wagon, then lumbered up the lowered, rear panel to join Mercy beneath the tarp.

Shaking herself free of the aching disappointment washing across her, Mercy raised a hand to beg Graham to return and share her warm repast, but the man was already gone.

"Hot broth and bread cures all that ails a body," Janie said as she filled a cup, then handed it to her mistress.

Mercy very much doubted a warmed drink could help with what ailed her.

CHAPTER FIVE

A SENSE OF peace fed the fragile tendrils of hope within her. Strengthened her. Lifted her up.

Breathtaking yellows and vivid pinks of the rising sun spilled across the horizon, chasing the last shadows of the night away from the sleepy valley below. A cool morning breeze brushed her loosened hair from her shoulders, ruffling it down her back. The air smelled crisp and clean. The land stretched green and vibrant before her, washed by the rains and encouraged to blossom by the welcomed warmth of spring.

Her horse nudged her, grumbling for another bit of carrot he knew she had in the pocket of the coat she'd had her seamstress make for the trip. Madame Zhou had thought her mad to design such a garment. Called it ugly and masculine but Mercy didn't care. It was practical. The ankle-length, lightweight coat not only protected her clothing from the rain and grime of travel but was also perfect to slip on over her dressing gown for early morning walks. Her spoiled beast snorted and snuffled at her pocket again, butting his head against her side with a gentle, affectionate shove.

"Such a pampered boy, my sweet dragon." Mercy gave him the chunk of carrot, then laughed as he pressed his cheek to hers while he crunched it.

"Dragon suits him far better than Ryū."

The deep voice startled them both. The skittish mount jerked away, snorting and stomping.

"Ryū, no." Mercy caught hold of the stallion's halter, standing between Graham and the angry horse as she shushed and soothed him. "Graham is our friend, Ryū. You must not hurt him." Poor Ryū. He trusted people less than she did. "Graham is good. Look within him and see." Mercy believed animals sensed a person's true heart and spirit. She trusted her stallion's judgement implicitly.

"Aye, lad," Graham added in a calm, quiet tone as he held out his hand to the horse, knuckles extended. "I mean ye no harm. To neither yourself nor your lady. I promise, I'm here to protect her."

The horse calmed but grumbled, ears still flattened to his head.

Graham shook with a silent laugh. "He's protecting his lady and merely wishes to be appreciated." He turned and squinted at the dazzling blaze of morning colors painted across the horizon. "And I'm surprised his lady rises this early to feed him treats."

"I find the gloaming, especially the twilight of early morn, fills me with the inner peace I seek." She cast a glance over at Graham's state of dress. "Not a wrinkle in your kilt. Did sleep escape you, sir?"

Graham clasped his hands to the small of his back and walked closer to the edge of the short cliff upon which they'd camped. "I dinna lay down and sleep whilst in England. 'Tis no' healthy."

Graham's leeriness gave her pause. Mercy joined him at the edge, very much aware of his silent strength as she stood beside him. Perhaps Graham was wise to be so cautious. King William trusted very few. Both her father and the rumors said His Majesty hated Scotland. Some said he even feared it. She glanced at Graham again. 'Twas little wonder the king felt such concern if the Highlands were filled with men like Graham. A calm knowing overcame her, coupled with a mildly disturbing growing affection for the man beside her. Graham could be trusted. He was a good man. She would never fear him.

"I would hope your health is quite safe among my camp. You must have sleep. Not all of us are *bloody Sassenachs*," she said in her best imitation of a Highland brogue. "We're a great deal alike—you'd discover that if you'd but take the time to get to know us."

Graham studied her a long while, long enough to make the simple act of drawing breath a chore. When she feared she could bear his scrutiny no longer, he shifted his gaze back to the vista below. "If England were filled with such as yourself, m'lady, I would consider an opportunity to visit the land and get to know her people a blessing. And I would sleep." He took a deep breath and shuffled his feet. "But such is no' the case. Tell me..." He turned and nodded toward her precious mount. "Why do ye call him your dragon?"

"It fits his spirit," Mercy said, allowing Graham to shift to a safer subject. Perhaps, 'twas best. She stretched out her hand to the horse, but he snubbed her with a toss of his head. "And it's also the meaning of his name. Ryū is Japanese for dragon."

"Japan," Graham repeated with a thoughtful nod. "Isolated country. Closed to foreigners." He gifted her with a gentle smile that encouraged her to keep talking. "Your ancestry, I presume?"

"Yes." Mercy struggled not to grow defensive, but a lifetime of rejection was difficult to overcome. "My mother...of course."

"Of course," Graham said in a quiet, respectful tone, seeming to sense her discomfort.

"And what of your ancestry?" She'd rather not speak to him about Mama. Not just yet.

Graham grew thoughtful, frowning at the land, eyes narrowing as he studied the skyline. "Before Alexander married into Clan Neal and they took our name and made him chieftain, there werena many of us MacCoinnichs left." He gave a shrug as though his words didn't matter. "The clan died out, fell to illness. Only four of us brothers, two cousins, and half a dozen more I havena seen in years survived. We lost the ones we loved." He shook his head. "It took so many from us.

Morbid sore throat, it was. Didna leave enough of us to even give the dead proper burials."

"I am sorry," Mercy whispered, wishing she could offer him some sort of comfort. She understood the agony of losing everyone you had ever loved. "So, you became a mercenary?" Her heart ached for all Graham had suffered.

"Aye." Graham nodded. "My brothers and two cousins. We lost our lands, so we banded together and left. Included one of our friends as well. Magnus de Gray. We consider him blood, and the seven of us traveled the world together."

"Lost your lands? How?" Had Graham and his brothers gambled away everything like her father had? Mercy retrieved Ryū from foraging too close to the cliff's edge and led him to a safer distance from the precipice. Surely, that wasn't the case. Not a man like Graham.

"Political games, m'lady," Graham said. "Campbells claimed our lands with the king's blessing. He didna feel enough MacCoinnichs were left to give a damn."

The hatred and revulsion in Graham's voice were unmistakable, and Mercy didn't blame him. It was bad enough to lose one's entire family, but to be stripped of ancestral lands at the same time? Unforgivable. Without thinking, she reached out, took his hand, and squeezed. "Again, I am very sorry."

Graham looked down at her hand and covered it with his own. "Ye're a kind woman, m'lady. I thank ye." He looked up at her then, tilting his head and studying her before unleashing the smile that always touched her heart and deepened the one dimple in his cheek. "Ye should always wear your hair loose. I like it. If possible, it makes ye even lovelier."

The compliment rendered her speechless and sent a flush of heat to her cheeks. Mercy ducked her head and whispered, "Thank you." She turned away and busied herself with offering her horse another carrot. "Here, sweet boy. This is the last for today."

The gentlest sensation against her hair caused her to freeze. *Just the wind.* But she knew better. Without turning, she knew Graham had lightly riffled his fingers across her hair. The touch was innocent enough but more intimate than any she'd ever experienced. Mercy swallowed hard as she tucked a loose strand behind one ear.

Graham stood so close behind her, she brushed against him as she turned and peered up into his eyes. So dark blue. Vivid and full of...something, some fiery hunger she dared not imagine. The longer she gazed into his eyes, the more she felt as though she tumbled into an endless night, spinning through the stars.

Without realizing what she did, she pressed a hand to his chest. His strong, steady heartbeat pounded against the center of her palm, filling her with a yearning, an urgency she feared to address. She was at a loss. Mama had told her to avoid these situations. *"A true lady must never lose control."*

"Master MacCoinnich," Mercy whispered.

"Graham," he corrected in a rumbling tone that stroked her senses as expertly as if he'd reached out and caressed her. He didn't move closer or make an effort to touch her in any way, but he didn't retreat and put a proper space between them either.

"Yes. Graham," she struggled to find words, beguiled by those eyes of his and the way the loose strands of his dark hair fluttered along the side of his strong jawline. His hair was as black as hers. They made a perfect pair. She hitched in a gasp at such a shocking thought. She had to regain control, had to maintain a calm demeanor. "I-I am sorry. I appear to have lost our train of conversation. Please, forgive me."

"There's nothing to forgive, m'lady." His mouth crooked again into that one-sided smile that deepened the dimple in his cheek, but his eyes—something in them said so much more. He leaned closer. The heat of him, the aura of his soul swirled around her like an intoxicating perfume, daring her to succumb.

He wished to kiss her. She felt it as surely as she felt the nervous churning in her middle. What should she do? They'd nearly kissed once before, and she'd been so disappointed when they'd been interrupted. But she shouldn't have been. She was headed for the abbey, headed to safety, and if she dared allow herself the pleasure of drowning in his gaze and losing all control—what then?

A mild sense of panic battled with the aching emptiness within her, the loneliness she'd borne for so very long. The need to be needed. She'd become so lonely in this unfair world. To be cared for. To be cherished. What a wondrous gift. She stared into his eyes, then reached up and cupped his jaw. The stubble of his beard bristled against her fingers. The sensation startled her back to reality. She couldn't endanger this man. If she kissed him, if he happened to grow fond of her, what then? She'd sworn she would never play into her father's hands and do as he'd asked.

She allowed her hand to drop away from his face, easing back a step with an apologetic smile, praying he'd understand. "I should be getting back to my tent. Janie will rise soon to tie up all this unruly hair and help me into my riding clothes."

Graham pulled in a deep breath and slowly blew it out. "Aye, lass. Perhaps it would be best." His gaze shifted to a spot behind her, just over her left shoulder. "Besides, the camp is astir. I believe our opportunity has passed."

Bitter disappointment and loss filled her. A sense of allowing the world to once again dictate her actions threatened to smother her. Mercy tensed against the familiar unpleasantness of having little to no control over what she could or couldn't do because of society's opinion. It wasn't fair. Graham MacCoinnich wasn't trying to take advantage of her. He seemed a genuine admirer. She'd never had such before. Not really. Not one so kind and...real.

"I like you, Graham." The words spilled out before she thought. She caught her lip between her teeth, fearing she'd rudely overstepped her bounds.

Graham gave her a wide smile and rumbled out a low, pleased laugh. "I like ye, too, m'lady." He lowered his voice and glanced around as he continued, "A damn sight more than I should. But dinna fear, I would never endanger ye or put ye at risk of public scorn. I understand the constraints of your status." Then his tone changed, and the look in his eyes tampered with her ability to draw breath. "But by all the saints in heaven, I'd love to show ye things a great more enjoyable than status—if ye'd so allow it," he added in a husky whisper.

"You are scandalous."

"Aye," Graham chuckled. "That I am." He offered his arm with the gallantry of a perfect gentleman. "Shall I escort ye to your tent, m'lady? Your fine beast seems well enough where he is, and I'll watch him for ye whilst ye dress."

Mercy took his arm, sighing with an aching wistfulness. If only their private morning visit could last a bit longer. But, alas, such was not the case. Pots and pans banged and clanked from the direction of Cook's wagon, and the smell of wood smoke from a refreshed fire filled the air. The peaceful glade no longer belonged to only Mercy, Graham, and Ryū. The camp stirred with the others of the group.

"There you are, m'lady." Janie rounded the tent, coming up short when she saw that Mercy wasn't alone. "Beg pardon," she said with a quick curtsy and a hurried lowering of her gaze. "I was worried about you. Especially when I saw your coat gone."

Janie had never understood why Mercy wished to rise before dawn to ponder life alone. Mercy patted Graham's arm with a reluctance that made her sigh, then pulled her arm out of his. "I'm fine, Janie." She turned to Graham. "Thank you, Graham. I very much enjoyed our visit this morning."

"And I as well, m'lady." Graham gave a polite bow, looked as though he might say something, then clamped his mouth shut as though he thought better of it. He motioned toward the rest of the camp. "I'd like us to be traveling within two hours. Please bear that in mind." With a curt nod, he turned and hurried away.

"I'm not so sure I trust that man, m'lady," Janie said in a gruff whisper as she hurried Mercy into her tent. "Mrs. Frances says Scots are nothing more than brutes and savages. You best take care around that one."

"What did I tell you about talking...?"

Shouts shattered the peace of the glen. The enraged squealing of a horse and a loud crash followed.

"Ryū!" Mercy recognized her stallion's scream as though he were her child. She rushed from the tent.

Wills and Robbie surrounded the horse, waving sticks and shouting at the enraged animal.

"Stop! The both of ye!" Graham strode forward, shoving Wills back and giving Robbie a look that should have turned him to a pile of ash.

The angry stallion reared up and shook the woods with another angry shriek, pawed at the air, then came down hard with a pounding stomp.

"Easy now, lad," Graham crooned as he edged forward, hands held low with palms up. "They're young fools, Ryū, and deserve a good stomping, but 'twould upset your mistress. Come now, lad. Calm down and let me take ye to her."

Mercy came to a halt. What would her dear friend do? Her beloved horse's reaction would greatly influence her already high opinion of Graham. If Ryū fully trusted the man, then she would, too.

The horse snorted and tossed his head but stopped pawing the air. He danced from side to side, grumbling and snorting, then charged Graham, only to skid to a halt right before he hit him.

Graham didn't flinch. Just stood with hands extended, talking to the beast in calm, soothing tones.

Ryū pranced back a few paces, cut the ground with a stomping gallop, and charged Graham again, once more stopping as soon as he reached him.

Graham smiled and stood still, his attention fully focused on the animal.

The stallion paused, glaring at Graham for the span of two huffing snorts, then lowered his head and butted into Graham hard, square in the chest, bouncing him back several steps.

Mercy held her breath. Ryū was testing Graham to see what he would do. The horse had done the same to Akio upon their first meeting.

"Ye're a stout lad, I'll gi' ye that." Graham laughed and held out a hand. "Come now, lad, enough foolishness. Ye ken ye can trust me. I see it in your eyes."

The horse nickered and flipped his tail, sounding pleased with himself. He pranced forward and buried his nose in Graham's right hand, nuzzling and grumbling as Graham rubbed and patted his neck.

Ryū trusted Graham. Hurrying forward, she reached for his reins. "Thank you, Graham."

Graham nodded and handed her the reins, then turned to scowl at Wills and Robbie. "Take your friend here and tie him outside your tent whilst your maid helps ye dress. Ye dinna need to hear what I'm about to say to these two fools."

Mercy wound the reins around one hand. "I wish to speak to them first, if you don't mind." She didn't wait for Graham's response.

Leading her much calmer mount, she marched over to the two young men. "If I ever witness you raising a stick or any other weapon to threaten my horse again, I will use whatever weapon you threatened him with and whip you myself. Do you understand me?"

The two lads dropped their gazes to the ground and gave disrespectful shrugs. "Yes, m'lady," they said in unison, both in sullen tones that lacked sincerity. "We were only trying to corral the wicked beast."

They didn't believe her. They thought her a helpless woman. She glared at them both. Her father had insisted these two come along on the trip. At the time, she'd been unable to fathom why, but their insolence couldn't possibly be any clearer. These two came to cause trouble. How much trouble, only time would tell.

Ryū whickered in her ear and stomped. He was ready to attack, only waiting for permission to do so.

She turned him aside and drew closer to Graham. "I don't trust those two. Do with them what you will. You'll get no argument from me."

Graham gave her an understanding nod. "I agree, they need watching." He motioned toward her tent. "Get ye dressed, m'lady." He paused and glanced back at the two lads. "And take your time. There's a lesson in respect to be taught and it willna be quick, nor will it be pleasant."

CHAPTER SIX

'TWOULD TAKE THEM a month to reach the high peak, Ben Nevis. Longer at this rate, depending on how many times Lady Mercy insisted on stopping to draw in her wee book. Saint's beards, they weren't even in Scotland yet. Graham shifted in the saddle, doing his best to hold his tongue and not rush the determined woman. After all, the point of this trip was about stops such as these.

He studied her, wishing she'd abandon that damn hat and wear her hair loose like she did during her early morning walks. It was a shame to hide such beauty with a hat that would serve a far better purpose as a basket for gathering herbs. He clenched his teeth against a strained groan and did his best to think of other things. Lady Mercy was a lady. Of course she'd wear her hair pinned up and protect the creaminess of her skin with a hat. He shifted in the saddle, thinking of how she looked with her hair down and her face upturned to the wind. Aye. He liked her better that way. Very much so.

Blinking away the memory, he forced himself back to the matter at hand. They needed to be on their way—and soon. He cleared his throat for the umpteenth time and glared at her, willing her to rise and return to her horse. Lady Mercy ignored him. Instead, she remained perched on an outcropping of stones overlooking a verdant valley, writing and sketching in the large, leather-bound book she kept in a bag lashed to her saddle.

Graham released another impatient whistling under his breath and glanced up at the wisps of white clouds fluttering across the bright blue sky. At least the rains had ceased for a bit. Seven days of the accursed wetness was enough. Hopefully, today's sunshine would dry them all out and make their route easier. Graham relented to his impatience and dismounted. It was obvious they'd be here for a while. Her ladyship had paused in her writing to sharpen her wood-encased stick of graphite with the wee knife she kept tucked in the inside pocket of the journal. The current view must have inspired the woman to use an inexplicable amount of her precious writing tool. A wee nudge was most definitely in order. They'd never make it to Scotland at this rate—sunny days or not.

"Ye ken this is still England, aye?" He scanned the area as he joined her on the stone ledge. It was a fine enough view, he reckoned. Peaceful hills covered in a tapestry of spring's palette: greens, yellows, blues. Open countryside bereft of stinking, overcrowded masses of buildings, but still England just the same.

The lady didn't look away from her book nor slow in her shading of the hillside she'd outlined on the paper, just humored him with a distracted smile and a nod. "I am well aware this is not Scotland, Graham."

At least she seemed to have finally grown accustomed to calling him by his given name rather than Master MacCoinnich. She rarely reverted back to the formal address anymore, and that pleased him more than he cared to admit.

She glanced up from the book, pushing the brim of her hat up and out of the way as she looked out across the grassy valley. "I thought it a good way to begin the book. Mama so loved the greening of spring and the yellow blooms of the cowslip." She pointed her pencil at the rest of the caravan, keeping her attention focused on the view in front of her. "Besides, it seemed an opportune time to sketch a few pages while we wait for Lieutenant St. Johns and Duncan to return from the village."

And that was another thing. How ill-planned was this journey if they already had to stop in a village? Cook's wagon and one of the flatbeds bulged with supplies, the other was filled with tents and tools. What could they possibly lack?

England made him feel cross and ill-at-ease—even more so since the incident with Robbie and Wills. Their behavior nettled him. Openly disrespectful, an underlying current of hostility and treachery surrounded them. Hostility not only directed toward himself and Duncan but also at Lady Mercy. Those two were trouble incarnate.

They needed to hasten to the Highlands. He'd decided at the onset of the trip to head to *Tor Ruadh*. Alexander would provide reinforcements; men Graham could trust to continue the lady's safe passage through the remainder of the Highlands.

"What exactly did ye send for from the village?" He'd sent Duncan along with St. Johns because he didn't trust the man as far as he could toss him. "We've barely begun the trip. Did ye forget something?" Agitation crept into his voice, but he couldn't help it. They should be marking time in this fair weather, not sitting on the side of the road. He eyed their surroundings, half expecting an attack at any moment. Ill-tidings rode the wind. He felt it.

Graham waited. Lady Mercy didn't answer right away, just kept sketching. Guilt filled him. He shouldn't have spoken to her so. He'd sounded cross. "Forgive me for sounding worrisome, m'lady. It's just…" he struggled to find the words to make her understand. "We need to get to Scotland so ye can enjoy the rare beauty of the Highlands rather than see just another English field of weeds abloom." There. That sounded some better.

Lady Mercy shrugged. "I understand your reasoning, but it is my hope a very important correspondence I'm expecting will have reached the village." She glanced up at him then, those warm eyes of hers filled with a subtle plea for patience. "I sent St. Johns to check if it has caught up with us there. It's crucial to me, Graham."

"An important correspondence?" A warning uneasiness prickled through the hairs on the back of Graham's neck. He scrubbed a hand across his nape to erase the ominous tickle. "How would they know where to send it to reach ye?"

"I sent the information on ahead. A map of sorts. Remember? Janie had Wills post it for me when we passed close to Wembley."

The lass had been quite stubborn about his showing her the route he'd planned to take through the Highlands. Even double-checked the notes she'd taken by showing him the simple map she'd drawn from what he'd told her. To whom had she sent the map? Her father? The king? Why would they care? They'd ordered him to take her through the Highlands. They hadn't expressed an interest in how he accomplished it. "Who needed the map, m'lady?"

"Beg pardon?" Mercy peered hard at the vista before her, scowling as she made careful strokes with her pencil, then measured the marks on the page for accuracy.

Graham reached down and stilled her sketching with a touch to her shoulder. "Who needed the map of our planned journey?"

She was hiding something. He knew it as sure as he knew his own name. Enticing as she was, she was still a noble with strong ties to the king. Such an alliance could be lethal—especially to a Scot. He'd done his best to temper his behavior around her—as difficult as that had been—and warned Duncan to do the same. But the more time he spent with the lass, the less he gave a damn about any possible risks. He found the woman intriguing and wished to know her better—befriend her even. *Friend.* He huffed out a snort. Well…perhaps *friend* was not the best word to describe his inclinations when it came to Lady Mercy, but he did wish to get closer to her all the same. It troubled him to admit he liked her. She was braw, fearless, and tempting. He felt an innate need to protect her, even if it meant protecting her from herself.

"Who did ye send it to, lass?"

Lady Mercy placed her pencil in the inner pocket of her journal, closed the book, then hugged it to her chest. She stared ahead, a mournful look pulling at her delicate features. "Mother Julienne."

Graham lowered himself to sit beside Lady Mercy. "I assume Mother Julienne is at a priory somewhere along our route?"

"An abbess, actually." Lady Mercy's voice took on a hollow, pained sound. "She oversees the nunnery connected to the abbey on the Isle of Iona." She stole a glance back at the servants milling about the wagons, then leaned closer to Graham and lowered her voice. "I know our acquaintance is quite new, but you appear to be a man of honor—and Ryū likes you." She paused, her gaze darting about. She pulled in a deep breath before turning her smile full upon him. "If my horse trusts you—that's quite an accomplishment." Graham started to speak, but the Lady Mercy lifted a hand and silenced him. "You have won my trust, but I beg you confirm that trust is not ill-placed."

The warning tingle at the back his neck turned into a much warmer stirring quite a bit lower on his body. He'd thought often of the missed kisses and how he might finally claim them, especially when they'd sat together beside the fire in the evenings. But he'd forced himself to take the side of caution. It was risky business indeed for one such as him to dally with Lady Mercy. But caution was becoming quite the chore. He slid his hand under hers and brought it to his mouth for a warm brushing kiss across her knuckles. "I assure ye, m'lady. Ye may trust me with your life."

Lower lip quivering, Lady Mercy dropped her gaze and whispered, "You have no idea how much that means to me. My life as well as yours and the wellbeing of your family is at great risk."

Graham held tight to her fingers, cradling her hand his. "I have known ever since I was summoned to court by King William that wickedness was about, but I have yet to figure out the trap." He gave her hand a reassuring squeeze, "Tell me what they plan, and we shall see who is at risk and who shall be played the fool."

Lady Mercy studied him, her dark brows drawn together in a perplexed frown. She looked away with an abrupt shuddering and pulled her hand free of his grasp.

What troubled the lass? And what did it have to do with him? "Ye can tell me anything, m'lady. I swear it."

Lady Mercy lifted her chin to a defiant angle. "I seek sanctuary at the abbey. I shall never return to London if all goes according to plan. Mother Julienne extended an invitation earlier. I await further instructions and assurance I am expected."

Graham frowned. A protectiveness swept across him like a raging fire. Who dared threaten this kind, gentle lass? "Sanctuary from what?"

"My father and his political games." Lady Mercy's voice quivered. She focused her gaze straight ahead and set her jaw, her delicate features hardening. "Society." She turned away. "Life," she said in a strained whisper.

Graham stood and held out his hand. "Come, lass. Walk with me."

She looked up at him, startled. "What?"

"Walk with me. We need to speak without interruption or the fear of eavesdropping." He shifted his attention to the others in their group currently milling about the wagons and taking the opportunity of the stop to work the stiffness from their legs.

"Janie," he called out in a voice that brooked no disobedience.

Janie cut off her conversation with Percy and turned, giving Graham her full attention.

"I am taking Lady Mercy to a better viewpoint off the path. We are no' to be disturbed, ye ken? We shall return to the wagons anon." Graham gave the entire group a look that dared them to argue or think less of their lady for walking unaccompanied with a man. To save Lady Mercy's reputation further, he motioned toward a narrow sheep trail winding down the side of the grassy hill. "We shall be in plain view at all times, so dinna worry about chaperoning your lady. Ye can do so from atop this hill if ye so wish, understand?"

"Yes, Master MacCoinnich." Janie made an awkward bob of her head, then gave Lady Mercy a nervous dip of her chin. "As long her ladyship agrees?"

Graham supported the young girl's loyalty to her mistress. He turned back to Lady Mercy. "Ye agree, aye?"

She responded with a soft 'yes' and an almost imperceptible nod.

His arm proffered, he waited.

Mercy took her place beside him, tucking her hand in the crook of his elbow and matching her steps to his. "Thank you."

"For?" He had to admit, he rather liked walking this way with the lovely lass so close beside him and holding tight to his forearm.

"For attempting to save my honor." She held tighter as the downward spiraling of the sheep's trail grew steeper. "That was kind."

"I would do nothing to dishonor ye or start tongues a wagging about your taking liberties with a Scot." Although, deep down, he had to admit that he wished she would take liberties with him. She was a very fine woman, indeed—fine and tempting.

"Tongues already wag, Master MacCoinnich. They've wagged since before I was born."

"There ye go with the 'Master MacCoinnich' nonsense again. I've come to realize ye always do it when ye're upset. Have I offended ye?" He felt the tension in the woman's grasp and the stiff way she walked beside him. The poor lass was fraught with troubles. What had her so rattled today? "Did Robbie and Wills act out again? Do I need to *temper* their behavior for them? Tell me what they did."

"I assure you, my agitation is not because of you. Nor because of the boys." She paused, almost flinched, then shook her head. A deep sigh escaped her. "It is *so* complicated, Graham."

"Why do ye no' explain it to me then?" Graham gave her a wink and a consoling pat to her hand. "I'm quick to catch on to things."

Her resulting smile warmed his heart. "I shall do my best but first, if we are to be true friends, I insist you call me Mercy."

Graham's heart swelled with pride. He'd done well to think of this private walk. Usually, he struggled with saying the right thing to lassies but somehow, with Mercy, it was different. "Aye, lass." The name suited her well—her beauty could very easily drive a man to his knees and make him beg for mercy. "Now tell me what troubles ye so much that ye seek sanctuary at an abbey."

"I have never belonged anywhere." Mercy's mouth tightened into a hard line. "While my mother and brother still lived, I knew enough love and acceptance to endure society's prejudice and my father's ill will, but now that they're gone..." Her words trailed off and she stared at the landscape as though she hated it. "I am scorned because of my ancestry and how my mother survived before she met my father." She shook her head, trembling with emotion. "It was recently made quite clear to me that she endured a great deal *after* marrying my father as well."

Graham scowled down at his boots as they walked, unsure how to respond. He wished to comfort her, but he didn't know the best way to go about it. "Those who scorn ye because of your blood and your mother's deeds are fools." He came to a halt and turned her to face him. "And that includes your father." He dared a touch to her face, cupping her cheek. "Ye're a beauty, Mercy, and I have never seen a person so ready to care for others. Ye're a braw, fearless woman. Ye treat your servants as family, and ye love those horses as though they be your kin. To hell with those who dinna appreciate ye for the fine woman ye are."

She gazed back at him for the span of several heartbeats, wistfulness filling her face. "If only it were that simple," she whispered.

"It can be." Graham glanced up at the top of the hill. Janie, along with Percy, Doughal, and Cook, stood lined up like sentries along the crest of the hillside, watching them. Regret filled him as he eased his hand away from the satin of her cheek and tucked her arm back into his. For her sake, he mustn't give the gossips any fodder. "Ignore the fools. 'Tis their loss if they rebuff your presence."

"The fools cannot be ignored. Not when they have become so dangerous." She squeezed his arm. "My father means to hand you and your kin over to Jameson Campbell and his ilk with King William's blessing."

Jameson Campbell. The mere mention of the name sent renewed rage surging through Graham. The bastard had attempted an assault on his eldest brother, Alexander's keep, *Tor Ruadh,* and more than likely had a hand in the bloody massacre at Glencoe. Graham grit his teeth, forcing himself to maintain control. "And how does he think to do such?"

Mercy lowered her gaze and watched her slow, methodical steps, her face hidden by the wide brim of her hat. "I cannot bear the shame of the words I need to say."

Graham stopped their progress down the trail, once more turned her to face him, and took both her hands in his. Mercy's head remained bowed. "Look at our hands, lass, if ye canna find the strength to face me. Clasped together, our hands, we ourselves, are stronger for the bond. Keep your eyes on our hands and tell me. I swear I willna judge ye or shame ye."

"He told me to seduce you," she whispered. The brim of her hat trembled as she spoke. "Seduce you and ensure you wanted me, then spurn you and send you away."

With a hard swallow, Graham took his own advice, staring down at their clasped hands as he traced his thumbs back and forth across the smoothness of Mercy's skin. "And how would that hand me to Campbell? That doesna make sense." What foolish machinations did Mercy's father have fogging that addled head of his?

Mercy squeezed his hands as she shifted with a quick shrug. "He says when a Scot wants something and claims it as his own, he takes it.

Even by force, if necessary."

The man had a point about a Scot's passion—especially a MacCoinnich's—but Graham would never take a woman unless she wished to be taken. "I beg your forgiveness, but I fear I dinna follow the plot." A laughing groan escaped him. "Mayhap I'm no' as bright as I thought m'self to be."

"My father believes if you wanted me enough, you'd kidnap me. He's heard of such marital practices among Scots." She lifted her gaze to his. "And if you kidnapped me, Jameson Campbell could be unleashed to retrieve me and permitted to decimate the new MacCoinnich clan formed by joining with Clan Neal. Their growing strength is feared by the crown, and my father knows this. Campbell would be permitted to attack. Much as what happened to the MacDonalds of Glencoe—without fear of reprisal from the king or parliament."

"Poorly planned treachery, that—if ye ask me." Although Graham had no doubt that King William would celebrate the Scots killed in such a skirmish, whether they be MacCoinnich or Campbell. More questions surfaced. The intricate connections of the plan escaped him. "Why did your father choose Jameson Campbell—or was the man the king's choice?"

"Some sort of debts." Mercy looked away. "Father said Jameson Campbell owns his soul." She hissed out a bitter laugh. "If he had a soul." Her face pinched into a scowl. "He said his weakness with money pushed him from King William's favor." Her nostrils flared. "But I know the truth. The fact he can no longer offer my mother as mistress to His Majesty rendered him of no further use to the king." She averted her gaze and pressed a trembling hand to her chest. "I am so ashamed," she whispered, closing her eyes. "For everything." She bowed her head and hid beneath her hat.

The Duke of Edsbury's desperate and weak plan became clearer. King William wanted complete obedience from the Scots through whatever means necessary. The massacre of Clan MacDonald had been brutal and triggered the opposite effect. Many didn't fear the king. They hated him, hated the Campbells, and vowed revenge.

But if a Scot were to kidnap a Sassenach noble, the king's god-daughter no less, in essence—fire the first shot, it would only be natural for her to be retrieved by any means necessary, and if many Scots died in the process, so be it. Even a fellow Scot, thinking of their own daughters, might grudgingly agree. Clan wars had been started for less.

And then there was this poor, dear lass trapped in the middle. Graham didn't fear the foolish plot. He was a Scot and a mercenary. He'd bested worse than this. This lost lass—aye, that was something else indeed. He took Mercy's hands back and held them tight. "Ye've nothing to be ashamed of, lass. Ye've done nothing wrong. We canna control anyone's actions but our own." He let out a pained sigh. "I'm just thankful ye're bastard-of-a-father didn't sacrifice ye to the king as he did your mother." Graham turned her so he could peer up under the brim of that damn hat and see her face. "I'd surely have to kill him if he attempted that, ye ken?"

Mercy responded with a quivering smile, then squeezed his hands before slipping free of his grasp and turning away to continue meandering down the path. She fluttered her fingers as though shooing away the cares of the world. "I was recently informed that I am King William's only godchild because of his extreme fondness for my mother and the talents she exhibited as his mistress. In a drunken rage, my father confessed to me that's how she extracted my protection as godchild from His Majesty." Bitterness emanated from her every move as she stopped walking and looked back at Graham. "Do not dare to judge her though. It was not her fault. She did what she had to do to survive and protect her children."

"I would never judge her. I have no right to do so." Graham sensed Mercy's pain and ached to take her in his arms. "Speak whatever weighs on your heart, m'lady."

She lifted her chin, swallowed hard, and fisted her hands in front of her. "My mother was no longer a prostitute when she serviced the king. She had been wife to my father for several years, but my father saw great promise in aligning himself with the young Prince of Orange by offering him my mother for his pleasure." Pain and suffering muted the defiance in Mercy's stance. "My mother was a Japanese high born once. Almost like an English noble—long ago before a rival lord stole her away for refusing his offer of marriage. Intent on destroying her honor, the lord sold her to pirates and a life of prostitution. King William found the prospect of such a mistress intriguing and impossible to resist." She bowed her head. "And although King William has committed many an atrocious sin, an illicit affair with the godchild he promised to protect does not appear to be a sin of which he is capable."

Graham's soul raged for the lass. He hated all she'd been through and had yet to endure. He had to find a way to help her escape this cruel web of deceit and also protect his kin in the process. "Tell me what your father said for ye to do—exactly how he said it, mind ye. I need to know so I might help ye and save my clan as well."

"He said to seduce you. Then spurn you. Trick you into reacting." Sadness shadowed her features as she stared off into the distance. "If I do not succeed, he swears to send me to the wharf where he bought my mother from her captors and sell me to them." She shook her head and shrugged. "He said I'd be sold to the highest bidder." She swallowed hard, then jerked her gaze downward. "But if I succeed and please him, he said he would send me to the abbey. It's almost as though he knew of my planned escape." A bitter smile trembled across her lips. "And I feel quite certain His Majesty would rest easier with my removal from court no matter how much affection he has always professed for his *godchild*."

Graham mulled over all she'd said, turned back, and studied those standing at the top of the hill watching them. How many spies traveled with them? One? Two? All? How many watched to report back the details of Mercy's progress in her assigned quest? He felt for certain St. Johns was a spy, but for a man as ruthless as Mercy's father—and the king, he doubted very much if either man left anything to chance. Edsbury was desperate, and King William enjoyed the game. Neither would leave the gathering of information to just one informant.

Another thought occurred to him. The abbey. Her father had offered it as reward, but Mercy had said reaching the abbey was her goal as well. Did Mercy mean to seek sanctuary no matter the outcome? "Do ye mean to take vows, lass?" Such a waste. He caught the tip of his tongue betwixt his teeth to keep from speaking the sinful thought aloud. Mam would cuff him hard for such. "Do ye seek to join the order?"

Mercy lifted her hands as though at a loss. "I seek peace, Graham, and acceptance." She shook her head. "God has not called me, but it is my hope the sisters will allow me an indefinite stay." Her focus shifted to the group at the top of the hill. "Will you help me? If you deliver me safely to the abbey and Mother Julienne sends word to the king, that should ensure the safety of myself as well as you and your clan."

Graham shook his head as he noticed St. Johns and Duncan had returned. "I doubt your father will allow us to reach the abbey. He'd be robbed of the chance to unleash Campbell to repay the man. He'd ken well enough that once ye're within those walls, 'twould be difficult enough to touch ye without risking his name. Holy ground is holy ground, and not many would look kindly on him disregarding that no matter their beliefs about your ancestry." He nodded toward their watchers. "We've a spy among us, lass. More than just St. Johns, I'd wager. If your father or the king gets wind that ye've warned me..."

"He'll make good on his threat to sell me into whoredom." Mercy swept her hat from her head, then rubbed her knuckles across her forehead. "What can we do to stop this?"

"Seduce me," Graham said, a subtle plan falling into place at the back of his mind. "That's what ye must do, m'lady. Seduce me and make them all believe ye're determined to honor your sire's wishes."

CHAPTER SEVEN

ANGER AND THE slow burn of endless betrayal filled her. It was more than obvious the seal of the missive had been ever-so-carefully peeled away from the folded parchment and then reattached. Mercy turned and locked a cold, hard glare on Lieutenant St. Johns, willing the coward to crumble. The man looked guilty, glancing from side to side in an obvious attempt to avoid meeting her gaze. Without a word, she looked to Duncan. "Did he open this in front of you?"

"Aye." Duncan gave the lieutenant an up and down sneer that clearly said he despised the man. "He thought I didna ken what he was about, but I saw him."

"They bade me protect you!" St. Johns defended. "It is my sworn duty."

"Protect me from Mother Julienne? The abbess of Iona?" Mercy pointed at the stamped seal bearing Iona Abbey's insignia. What a fool the man was. It was a wonder England prospered with such men in its armies. She snapped the missive in his direction. "And just how did she threaten me, sir? With hellfire and damnation of my eternal soul?"

Lieutenant St. Johns jutted his chin upward. "You are under the king's protection. I do not apologize for my actions."

Mercy turned away before she said more than she should, lifting her face to the cool spring breeze and taking in great calming gulps of the sweet air. She must not overplay this game. The stakes were far too high. She stomped a few feet away from the circle of wagons surrounding the camp, the weight of the task set before her feeling even heavier than before. She chanced a glance back at Graham.

The ceaseless wind pulled at his dark, long hair and whipped at the tail of his kilt as he waited beside his horse. Graham watched her, he stood as a man who cared not what others thought. Such a great, bear-of-a-man, tall and proud. Wide shoulders, defensive stance, commanding—he was breathtaking. The oppressive despair she'd felt since the loss of both mother and brother, the burden she carried that snuffed out all possible hope and joy, lessened. At least she had one ally. One true friend. Thank Almighty God for Graham. She swallowed hard and clutched the parchment between her hands tighter. *"Help me save us both from Father and the king,"* she said in silent prayer.

Unfolding the letter and studying the contents, an uneasy pounding gained strength and thrummed at her temples. She blinked hard and read the words again, disbelief and dismay fighting for possession of her soul. One sentence, written in a delicate flowery scrawl, crept across the center of the page.

"God bless you and keep you in perfect peace, my child. My prayers are with you."

Mercy stared at the words inked across the creaminess of the parchment. They stood out in blue-black starkness like a damning brand. This wasn't a welcome or the assurance and direction she'd hoped to receive. Had Mother Julienne rescinded the offer she'd originally made in the letter she'd sent offering condolences and prayers after the loss of Mercy's family? The sentence sounded like a blessing meant for one headed to the gallows.

She cast an alarmed glance across the way to Graham.

Her trusted partner in this treacherous game hastened to her side. "What is it, lass?"

The fact he read her so easily brought some small comfort. She held out the letter. "I don't understand what she's telling me."

Graham took the page, scowled down at the script, then lifted his gaze to hers. "I thought ye said she expected ye, had invited ye even?" He turned the paper and studied the seal, then flipped it back and studied it again. "She's as much as dismissed ye."

"She felt a kindness for my mother. Expressed sincere regret when Mama and Akio died. Told me to come to her with anything I might need." Mercy wrung her hands. An uncontrollable shivering took hold of her. The early evening air suddenly felt much colder. "Did she just mean to come to her in prayer?"

"Akio?" Graham interrupted, repeating the name carefully.

Mercy turned away. How could she have so easily uttered her brother's Japanese name that only she and Mama had known and used? Because that was who he was to her, who he would always be. She once again faced Graham, forced herself to regain control, then continued, "Akio, known to everyone else as Lord Andrew Phillip Charles was my brother. Akio was his..." she paused. The name stirred such fond memories. Akio, older by five years, had been her devoted friend and champion. "Akio was his pet name." She couldn't bear to say more or dwell on the memories long. She'd be reduced to tears if she did so.

Graham studied her as he refolded the letter. "I need to know how your mother and brother died."

A nauseating chill shot through Mercy, making her take hold of the lapels of her riding coat and draw it closer about her. "A carriage accident." She looked out across the horizon, noting the clouds skittering across the delicate pinking of the sky as it blushed with the vibrant colors from the retreating sun. The wind rippled across the grasses of the hillside. In the distance, a small flock of sheep meandered through the undulating sea of green. "I was spared any further details."

"I see."

"What do you see? Tell me." She knew in her heart the accident had not been an accident at all, but she'd never found proof or anyone brave enough to discuss the matter in detail.

"I see that ye're in more danger than I first thought, m'lady." He gave her a sad smile as he returned the letter to her, then held out his hand. "Come. Let us see what Cook has prepared for our supper. There is little we can do from here."

She took his hand and allowed him to tuck it into the crook of his arm as they made their way to the fire on the other side of the wagons. Wood smoke and the mouthwatering-scent of meat roasting, its fat sizzling and dripping into the coals, filled the air. Percy, Doughal, Robbie, and Wills had already erected the tents. Her private shelter off to itself, feet away from the tent for the men. Janie slept in a small, partitioned-off space inside Mercy's tent and, as declared at the onset of their journey, Cook slept in the floor of her wagon. Although, Janie had recently informed her that Cook had managed to rearrange enough of her supplies to fit herself back into her bunk.

Before they neared the others, Graham stopped and drew her closer. With a cautious glance about, he pressed a hand atop hers where it rested on his arm. He gave her fingers a reassuring squeeze. "Ye must convince the spies that ye mean to seduce me. Ye must be believed, ye ken?" The look he gave her fueled a more frantic fluttering in her middle. "We can wait no longer in taking control of this game. I fear your survival depends on it, lass."

Mercy swallowed hard, struggling to speak in spite of the erratic pounding of her heart. "I'm...I fear I..." The intense blue of Graham's eyes mesmerized her, making the simple act of forming words almost impossible. "I don't know how," she whispered.

She'd never seduced a man before. Mama would have been shocked and ashamed at such behavior. Mercy remembered the severe scolding she'd received over a simple flirtation when she'd been little more than sixteen years old. Mama had come close to boxing her ears, swearing that Mercy would never suffer the same fate she'd endured.

You are a lady and will always behave as such.

Graham smiled, and the blue of his eyes darkened, once again reminding Mercy of a midnight sky filled with lightning. "Act as though ye like me, lass, and wish to know me better. Simple as that."

He made it sound easy enough—and if she was honest, it was the truth. She did like Graham and would like to know him better. "I can do that." She peered over at those gathered around the fire.

Cook was busy resetting the iron pans deeper into the coals, lifting lids, and scowling down at the steaming contents. Janie stood with a tray held between her hands, waiting for Mercy's share of the choicest parts of supper to finish cooking.

Taking a deep breath, Mercy forged ahead. She would do as Graham advised and do it well. "Janie—rather than eating off my tray beside the fire, please set the table in my tent. For two, please." She cast a smile back at Graham, then turned to the surprised faces around the fire. "Could you help her move the chairs, Robbie?"

"Yes, m'lady." Robbie tossed the armload of firewood down beside the fire, then dipped his chin as he brushed off his hands on his dark, worn trews. "Right away."

Janie stared at her, her shock apparent. "Uhm, yes, m'lady," she uttered as she tucked the tray under one arm and hurried toward Mercy's private tent.

"You will join me, won't you? I know you don't like formalities, but surely a quiet little visit while we eat isn't too proper?" Mercy took Graham's arm, sliding her hand up through the crook of his elbow and hugging it close. The feel of him pressed to her in such an intimate manner stole her breath. She thought for certain she'd choke on the pressure of her heartbeat pounding in her throat. She forced a smile, struggling to maintain control.

"Easy now, lass," Graham said under his breath as he gazed down at her. He stroked her arm with the touch of a man laying claim to what he desired and intent on making it known. "I'd be most honored to join ye." He glanced up at the sky ablaze with the setting sun. "'Tis a lovely night for a dinner for two," he said loud enough so all could hear. "But no' as lovely as yourself, m'lady."

Judging by their heat, her cheeks had to be flaming. How in the world could she make everyone believe she was a seductress when she couldn't even handle a simple compliment from the man intended as her prey? She lowered her gaze and fluttered her lashes as she'd seen her mother do a thousand times when attempting to placate her father and turn his anger aside. "You are too kind, sir, too kind, indeed."

"Wills!" Cook clanged her spoon against the lid of one of the iron pots hanging over the fire. "Fetch me that other rabbit. Sounds like there'll be two meat pies needed this evening." She bobbed a quick curtsy in Mercy's direction without looking up from the makeshift table at her side where she added another handful of flour to the ball of dough in front of her. "No problem at all, m'lady, no problem at all." Her gruff tone hinted otherwise.

"Thank you, Cook." Mercy took a deep breath to settle her nerves, then stepped forward, pulling Graham with her. "I sense you're flustered. I do apologize that I gave you so little notice on this evening's arrangements."

Cook shook her head with a defensive jerk, looking aside as she busied herself with the rolling out of the dough. "You must do as you see fit."

Mercy smiled up at Graham, leaning against his shoulder as she did so. "You wouldn't mind sharing my table every evening, would you?" She fluttered a hand along the edge of his coat lapel, then brazenly pressed it to the center of his broad, hard chest. "You tell the most delightful stories, and I so enjoy your company. Please say yes. It would assist Cook's planning in the future."

Graham looked down at her with a lazy, seductive smile that threatened to buckle her knees. "I'd cherish such company, m'lady. Every night. For as long as ye'll have me in your tent."

A light cough escaped her as she almost choked. She managed an even brighter smile and tightened her grip on Graham's muscular arm to keep from melting down to the ground. Such suggestive words. Graham played this game far better than she. With a graceful wave toward her tent, she gave him a coy look. "Shall we wait in my tent while Cook finishes our supper?" She needed to sit. Badly. Before she fell to her knees in the first swoon of her life. A drink would not be amiss either.

"As ye wish, m'lady," Graham said in the same evocative tone that rumbled through her every fiber in quite the delicious fashion.

Forcing herself to appear a great deal calmer than she felt, Mercy allowed Graham to lead her to the tent. Janie stood waiting beside the pinned back flaps creating the door.

"All is ready, m'lady." The color high on her cheeks and her white bonnet askew, Janie stood with her hands fisted in front of her apron. "Robbie and I took the liberty of blocking off your sleeping area so it wouldn't disturb your meal," she said with a pointed look. She made a flipping motion toward both sides of the tent opening. "And we fastened back both flaps so you can enjoy some fresh air whilst you dine."

"Thank you, Janie." Mercy struggled not to laugh or act as if she gave a whit that Janie did not approve of her private dinner with Master MacCoinnich.

"Be sure and bring us an extra bottle of wine, ye ken?" Graham said in a dismissive tone as he helped Mercy into her chair.

"Yes, Master MacCoinnich." Janie made a perfunctory curtsy and hurried away.

Seating himself on the other side of the small, round table, Graham chuckled at the trio of flickering candles illuminating the canvas walls and flooring of the tent with a bright golden glow. "Me thinks your maid disapproves."

"Janie's very protective." Mercy smoothed her hand back and forth across the fine weave of the tablecloth. "And sometimes oversteps her bounds because she's so close to me."

"Can she be trusted?"

The question caught Mercy off guard. "Of...of course," she stammered without a thought. "Janie's been with me for almost two years."

"Aye, but can she be trusted?" Graham repeated in a hushed tone as he glanced out the opened flaps of the tent.

"Most certainly." His insistence put her on edge, making her second guess everything. She picked up the handbell waiting beside the base of the candelabra and rang it. "We need wine. I can't believe she hasn't already returned with it."

Janie appeared almost immediately. She gave Graham a borderline sneer. "Your extra wine, sir."

"Thank you, Janie. Tha'll do." Graham opened one of the bottles and filled both glasses on the table. He paused and turned to Janie waiting at the door. "Was there something else?"

"M'lady?" Janie ignored Graham with a rude shifting of her gaze to Mercy.

"Yes?"

"I'll bring your supper soon as 'tis ready, but I shall be close until then, so you just ring that bell if you have need of anything at all, yes?" Janie lowered her chin, pinning Mercy with a fierce glare. "Anything at all," she repeated.

"Thank you, Janie." Mercy did her best to calm the girl with a reassuring smile. "I shall keep the bell close."

Janie turned and walked away after one last scowling look at Graham.

"There. You see? She's doing her best to protect me." Mercy took a fortifying sip of the sweet wine that had always been her favorite.

"Just be careful," Graham said as he peered down at his own glass of wine shimmering in the candlelight. "Mind your words with everyone." He reached across the table, scooped up her hand, and pressed a slow kiss across her knuckles.

She could feel the heat of his breath stroking her skin, his lips tickled the backs of her fingers as he spoke. "When someone entrusts themselves to my care, I dinna take their trust lightly." He kissed her hand again, then gifted her with a seductive smile. "And I always protect what I claim as mine."

Mercy's breath caught as she found herself ensnared in his gaze. Dark. Brooding. Fierce. Danger flashed in his eyes like lightning reflecting across a stormy sea. She allowed her thumb to stroke against the roughness of his hand. Calloused. Experienced. Strong. What wonders could such a man teach her? Did he truly mean to claim her, or was this just a part of their agreed upon guise?

A rustling outside the tent caught her attention. A faint shadow danced along the wall of the shelter, the silhouette of a person outlined on the canvas by the campfire in the distance. Mercy's heart fell. What a fool she was. Graham was but playing to the crowd as he'd advised her to do. How stupid she was to think his attentions were genuine. It was all an act to protect them both. Fine. She could do the same and accomplish the task as well as him.

She leaned across the table, clasped his hand between both of hers, and turned it so she might examine his palm. Keeping her voice loud enough to be heard by any who might be near but low enough to be considered private, she locked her gaze with Graham's as she tickled a fingertip down the center of his palm. "Our hands hold our life's story. Did you know that?"

"T-truly?" Graham's control slipped a bit. "And what might my hand tell ye?" he asked, then cleared his throat.

She rested her four fingertips atop the callouses at the base of Graham's fingers, taking some small satisfaction in the fact that Graham's palm had grown damp and he appeared unsettled. "Yours are the hands of a warrior," she said, then stroked the lines mapping his skin, noting with satisfaction that he jerked every time she moved her fingers. "A ticklish warrior." She bubbled out a flirtatious laugh, then pressed a kiss to the center of his open hand, tasting his skin with her tongue.

"God Almighty." A pained groan escaped him as he shifted in his seat. He yanked his hand away and scrubbed it back and forth atop his kilt-covered thigh.

"A problem, dear sir?" Mercy assumed as innocent a look as she could muster.

"I thought ye said ye'd never done this before?" Graham said from between clenched teeth.

"I haven't." Mercy glanced out the entryway and leaned across the table. "Am I doing it right?"

"Aye, lass." Graham emptied his glass, refilled it, then emptied it again. "If ye do any better, I'll be in dire need of one of two things."

"And what might those things be?" Mercy lifted her glass in a proud toast to herself. She'd managed it. Gotten under his skin.

Graham thumped down his glass, then stood. He studied her. His massive chest shifted with a deep intake of breath, then he strode around the table, and pulled her up into his arms. One hand at the small of her back and the other to the back of her head. He held her close, gazing down into her eyes. "I'll either need a swim in an icy loch or your embrace, m'lady. And since we've no loch nearby…"

Before she could respond, Graham silenced her with a kiss.

Mercy shuddered in his arms, reveling in the array of sensations he sent coursing through her. Such strength. Such fierce hunger. The hard length of his body pressed against hers triggered an almost unbearable urgency of her own. He tasted of wine and endless possibilities. She grew bolder, clutching him tighter as she opened to the kiss and flicked her tongue in a wanton swipe against his. He pulled her harder against him, and she was thankful. If not for the strength of his hold, she surely would have collapsed by now.

A throat cleared at the entrance to the tent, shattering the spell. "Your supper is ready, m'lady."

Mercy couldn't contain the sigh of regret that escaped her when she sank away from Graham's embrace. Holding to the back of her chair for support, she turned and faced the intrusion to what had definitely been the most wondrous thing she'd experienced up to this point in her life. She blinked and struggled to regain the ability to speak. Lowering herself into her chair, she politely motioned for Graham to do the same. "Thank you, Janie. We're quite famished. Are we not, Graham?"

"Ye have no idea how famished, lass," Graham said, his unwavering gaze searing into the depths of her soul. "No idea at all."

CHAPTER EIGHT

THE WATER OF the River Teviot couldn't be cold enough to suit him. Stripped of his clothes, Graham dove forward, submerged completely, and swam upstream. The fight against the current felt good as it strained his muscles and pushed him. He prayed the battle against the water would wear him down and get that tempting woman off his mind if only for a wee spell.

He came up for air. Whipping his hair back from his face, he sank into the water until his nose and eyes were just above the waterline, treading to stay afloat. He scanned the bank. Good. No one around but Duncan floating on his back in the part of the river catching the last of the afternoon sun.

Camp was farther downstream. Doughal and Percy were armed and standing guard. Graham doubted anything would happen. He and Duncan had canvassed the area well and deemed it peaceful enough for the pair of wagon drivers to protect it with no problem. As Graham swam around the bend, a flash of color halted him.

It was Mercy. The very temptation from which he'd sought relief.

He eased back into the shadows of the tall grasses growing at the river's edge. A gentleman would leave the lady to her ablutions. Graham smiled. He'd warned the lass on several occasions that he was not a gentleman.

Janie stood on the opposite bank in front of her mistress, helping Mercy step out of her trew-like skirt. Mercy's jacket and corset were already draped over the crook of Janie's arm, leaving Mercy blessedly bare from the waist up and soon from the waist down. Mercy straightened and freed her long dark tresses.

Graham swallowed hard. What a vision. Tall. Lithe. Curves as delicate and fine as a perfect blossom, and skin as fair as the ivory of a lily. Her black hair tumbled down her back, falling well below the sweet curve of her bottom and almost touched the backs of her knees. She turned and faced him, wading out into the water.

Graham clenched his teeth to keep from groaning aloud. Pert breasts, smallish but perfect with dark nipples tightened by the chill of the river. She disappeared under the water, the creamy whiteness of her skin shimmering just beneath the surface.

Sweet Mother of God. She was headed straight for him.

Graham backed deeper under the riverbank grasses, his toes squishing into the sticky mud and his arse hitting the knobby, protruding roots of a tree growing along the bank. What would the lass think if she discovered him? Graham knew damned well what she'd think. A grin overtook him as he followed her movement beneath the water. He was wicked—although not the dangerous sort of wicked.

She broke through the surface, eyes closed, back arched, and head thrown back. With a kick of one long leg, she pushed herself to her back and floated with those tempting breasts sitting above the surface of the water. The woman moved with the grace of a selkie. Mayhap she was one. Graham wouldn't be shocked if Mercy transformed into a seal right before his eyes. The woman was beauty personified, ideal for any myth or legend.

As she came closer, Graham couldn't retreat any further, so he did his best to shift sideways. A root caught on his shoulder and bounced back into place with a loud splash.

Mercy righted herself and faced him. Her eyes flared wide and her mouth tightened in shock.

"It's no' what ye think, lass," Graham whispered, taking care to stay among the long grasses. Janie still stood on the opposite shore waiting for her mistress. "Just stay calm."

"Stay calm?" she repeated with a hiss. "I find you spying on me while I bathe, and you expect me to stay calm? And Janie's right over there. What if she sees you?" She attempted to cross her arms over her breasts but sank deeper in the water. Bouncing back up, she did her best to keep her chin even with the surface and everything else covered.

Graham could still see the delightful flickering of her lovely breasts in the clear water.

"Is this part of your *plan* to make everyone believe we're involved? Don't you feel this might be a bit drastic?" Mercy's frantic whisper had shifted to a chiding tone that made him want her even more.

Graham couldn't resist. He risked floating a bit closer. "I think it a fine plan, m'lady."

Stealing a glance back at Janie, Mercy shooed him back. "It is *not*. I insist you behave yourself. Rumored to be *involved* is one thing. Acting as forbidden lovers is quite another."

"Is there something in the grass, m'lady?" Janie called from the shore.

"Uhm…yes. I think it's just a water vole, Janie," Mercy shouted back. "A common rat!" she added with a stern arch of a brow at Graham. But the high color in her cheeks and the glint in her eyes told him maybe the lady didn't mind his presence so much after all.

Graham held his breath to keep from laughing out loud. "Come closer," he whispered. "I dare ye."

"I will not!"

"Aye, but your voice betrays ye, lass." Graham wiggled his fingers, motioning her toward him. "'Tis excitement and the need for adventure I hear. Come, give me one kiss, then I swear I'll let ye bathe in peace."

"Shall I fetch one of the lads with a pistol, m'lady?" Janie shielded her eyes as she peered across the water.

"No, Janie." Mercy's unease disappeared and a plotting smile curved up the corners of her mouth. "It fears me more than I fear it." Her eyes narrowed into a competitive, daring look that shot a dangerous hot surge of hope through Graham. "But if you could fetch my sketchbook, please. I should love to get its likeness down on paper before I forget what it looks like in the wild."

"Yes, m'lady." Janie draped the remainder of Mercy's undergarments over a nearby bush, then scrambled up the low embankment and disappeared into the trees.

Mercy floated around to face Graham. "One kiss and you will leave me be—that's what you promised, yes?"

"Aye," Graham said low and slow. What dangerous game did the minx plot?

Holding up a finger to keep him at bay, Mercy shook her head. "Oh no. You have always been a man of your word, and I expect you to continue." Her teasing smile grew. "You may not touch me with anything but your mouth. A kiss is your fee. A kiss and nothing more you shall have. Agreed?"

The wily lass intrigued him. How could he refuse? "Aye, lass. Agreed." He held out his arms and kept himself in place by curling his toes into the mud. "I am ready, m'lady." The woman had no idea how ready.

With a last glance at the opposite bank where Janie had disappeared, Mercy swam closer, coming to a stop in front of Graham. Resting her fingertips atop his shoulders, she grew brazen and smoothed her palms down along his muscles, her gaze following her hands as she stroked from his upper arms to his throat.

Graham didn't say a word, just watched her rapid intake of breath and the way she wet her mouth as she touched him. The lass wanted him as much as he wanted her, and she longed to satisfy her curiosity. It heated his heart as well as a few other parts—cold water be damned—to know that she'd never been like this with any other man.

Graham held true to his word. Although it nearly killed him, he kept his arms outstretched and waited. She inched closer. If this didn't end him, nothing would. He leaned into her the slightest bit, connecting his mouth with hers.

Her fingers laced up into the back of his hair, her nails tickling into his scalp as she deepened the kiss. Graham fueled all his need into the sweet taste of her, entwining his tongue with hers, and fully possessing her luscious mouth. One of her legs brushed against his flank and a groan escaped him, vibrating against her lips.

Fists clenched, Graham kept his arms extended though he ached to embrace her, love her proper. When Mercy pulled away, he wanted to yank her back and never let her go. "Damn fine kiss, m'lady," he forced out in a rasping whisper.

Mercy didn't answer, just searched his face with an unreadable gaze while she shuddered in a deep intake of breath. Her pulse pounded, twitching at the base of her throat, and Graham ached to graze his fingertips across it. "I...must go now. Janie will return any moment."

She pushed away, paddling back to the other side of the river.

Launching himself off the riverbed, Graham dove back downstream. Stroke after long-armed stroke, he swam hard and fast until he'd returned to where he'd started and walked up the embankment to his clothes. The chill water did its job of easing his man parts. A good thing since Duncan waited for him, sitting on the rocky beach, sunning like a selkie.

"Enjoy your swim, brother?" he asked as he rose from his place on the beach and stretched like a cat awakening from a nap.

Mere words could not describe that swim. Graham grunted and

walked to the shrub where he'd draped his clothes. He'd never been good at games. He needed help for certain with this one, lest it become more than just pretense.

MERCY SAT ON the river bank and twisted the water from her hair, thankful for the slight breeze cooling the moisture off her skin. What on earth had she been thinking to do such a thing? She pulled in another deep breath and blew it out, struggling to calm her mess of emotions. If Mama had been here, she would have dragged her straight back to camp with a severe scolding the entire way.

A sad smile pulled at her mouth. If Mama and Akio had been here, Mercy and Graham would have already found themselves in front of a priest after their first heated look. A nude swim would never have happened until they were a proper man and wife. A fearful shudder chased away the scandalous idea. No. Father would never permit such. He would use the incident to incite a massacre of the MacCoinnichs. A sickening dread washed across her. How could she be so reckless? How could she even think of placing Graham and his kin in such danger?

Because the longer she was with him, the more she... Her thoughts muddied worse than the water's edge where her toes wiggled in the silt of the river. The more she what? Mercy yanked on her corset and managed her own ties, then rinsed her feet. She didn't dare even think the word. She'd known the man but a few weeks, and why on earth would he wish to trouble himself with someone such as her?

Her hands shook as she pulled her split skirt with sewn-in petti-coats from the bushes. Maybe she had only known Graham for a mere few weeks, but she'd witnessed more trust and more honor in him than she'd witnessed in anyone other than her brother in her entire life. And if she escaped Father and London society, would she be such a burden? After all, Graham had said the past was the past, and he hated political maneuvering as much as she.

She fastened her clothes and stared across the river at the place where Graham had hidden. Warmth spread down to her core. How could she have behaved in such a brazen manner? "Because when I am with him, I want to feel everything," she whispered. "He makes me fearless—and hopeful."

Twigs snapped and leaves rustled, pulling Mercy from her yearnings and forcing her attention on the copse of trees behind her. Janie tromped out from between a pair of leafy saplings, Mercy's sketchbook tucked under one arm and her hands clasping multiple bundles and baskets. "Since you didn't eat this morning, I thought you might enjoy a bit of food here whilst you sketched your animal you found."

The gesture touched Mercy's heart. "How thoughtful, Janie, thank you." Mercy helped with the bundles, then settled herself on the blanket Janie spread across the grass. She tucked her feet up beneath her, Graham's kiss still foremost in her thoughts. "Did you happen to see, Graham? He might like to join me to share this lovely repast."

Janie gave her a sharp look and returned to unwrapping parcels of cheese and small slices of brown bread smeared with creamy butter. "I didn't see Master MacCoinnich, m'lady."

Mercy accepted a cup of honeyed wine, studying Janie over the rim as she sipped. Had Janie known it was Graham in the grasses and not a water vole? "Have you ever seen a water vole, Janie?" Pointing to the other side of the river, Mercy motioned toward the now infamous clump of grass curtained over the water. "If you watch that area right there, you might spot it."

"I don't much care for rats, m'lady." Janie busied herself with positioning the bits of bread and cheese within Mercy's reach, then perched upon a nearby stump of driftwood and clasped her hands around her knees. With a prim sniff and a lifting of her chin, she squinted as she looked out across the river. "That's why I thought it ill-advised for you to be swimming in such a place. Who knows what's in that water?"

"Indeed." Mercy nibbled at her food and took another sip of wine. Spotting the rim of another cup protruding from one of the bundles, she nodded toward it. "Do pour yourself some, Janie. There's more than enough for both of us." And why was that? Had Janie seen Graham and assumed he'd be here with Mercy when she returned?

Janie brightened and hurried to help herself. "Thank you, m'lady. I was hoping you'd ask me to join you. I know it wouldn't be proper back in the city, but surely, it's all right out here. It is all right, m'lady, for certain?"

"For certain," Mercy repeated, her wariness relaxing a bit. She could trust Janie. The girl had always been an ally. She patted the blanket. "Do sit here. It's so much more comfortable."

"Yes, m'lady." Janie settled on the blanket and took up a piece of brown bread, biting into it with gusto.

Mercy studied the girl with covert glances between sips of wine and doodling in her sketchbook. The more she watched Janie scowl at the clump of grass across the river, the harder the knot in her middle tightened. Janie knew. Janie must have seen them. The girl must not have headed back to camp immediately. She'd tarried long enough to see what her mistress would do with the nude Scot hiding in the shadows.

"What is it, Janie?"

"M'lady?" Janie paused with another slice of bread part way to her mouth.

"You seem...distracted." Mercy had to know for certain, but she had to play this situation with care. "Are you unwell?"

Janie's eyes rounded and her reddish brows arched to her hairline. "I'm quite well, m'lady. I am sorry. Did I miss something you said?" Her cheeks grew rosy. "Mam always said I was the worst child she ever had when it came to wool gathering." She gave an apologetic shrug and lowered her voice. "Please forgive me, m'lady. I don't mean to complain, but this trip is a mite boring compared to staying in the city." She cringed and caught the corner of her bottom lip between her teeth. "But please don't dismiss me. You're true and for certain the kindest mistress I've ever had."

Perhaps Janie didn't know. *A guilty conscience punishes with many a useless thought.* Mama's words echoed strong and true. Thank goodness she hadn't asked Janie outright. She would've revealed her scandalous secret. "How could I dismiss you, Janie, after you've taken such good care of me?"

"Thank you, m'lady." Janie brightened and bobbed her head. "Thank you for your kindness." Then she settled back on the blanket, lifted her cup to her lips, and returned to staring at the dreaded clump of grass.

She knows. No matter how innocent the girl played it, she knew. Mercy felt it in her heart. Regret and resignation settled like rocks in the pit of her stomach. She bowed her head and flattened her hand atop her sketchbook. Not only had she just lost an ally, she'd lost a friend. She prayed Janie's devotion to her was as real as it had always seemed. Only that would keep the girl from profiting from the afternoon's secret.

"There it is again!" Janie pointed at the grass. "There it is, m'lady! See it?"

Mercy shielded her eyes, relief flooding through her as she spotted what Janie had spied. Never in her life would she ever dream the sight of a sleek dark rodent swimming in a river would bring her so much joy. "Thank you," she whispered to whatever benevolent power had seen fit to encourage the water rat to appear.

CHAPTER NINE

"A NOTHER TWO WEEKS or so of this 'til we reach *Tor Ruadh?*"
Duncan shook his head and gave him a look Graham
recognized all too well. Little brother thought him a fool. "Ye dinna
handle the playing of games well, brother. Pretending one thing whilst
ye feel another has never been your strong suit. There's no guile about
ye, ye ken? Never has been. Ye're a hard-headed, bull of a man. Ye
charge forward damned and determined with your whole heart or
nothing. And to attempt such a farce with a Sassenach whose ties to
the king appear strong? Ye're daft for certain." Duncan watched him,
concern showing in the set of his shoulders and the scowl on his face.
"I fear for ye, brother—fear both for your heart and your stubborn
arse."

Graham snorted away Duncan's concern, concentrating instead on
the rugged beauty of the surrounding land. Thank God they were back
in Scotland. He glanced back at the group following them at a
distance. Mercy had taken to riding at his side since their witnessed
kiss. But today, he'd quietly asked her to stay with the group. He
needed to learn the gossip of the camp. Duncan's job was to ferret it
out. His brother had a talent for blending in and becoming a best
friend to a total stranger. As their mam always said, Duncan could
charm a dog off a meat wagon. He made the perfect spy.

Graham ignored the critical points of Duncan's warning. His brother could also be a nettling pain in the arse. "So, tell me then. Lady Mercy and I, our affection, 'tis believable?"

Duncan rolled his eyes.

Graham shifted in the saddle, trying his best to ignore the fact that his brother might be right, and the amorous pretense ventured too damn close to becoming a reality. The more time he and Lady Mercy invested in their charades, the more impossible it was to ignore his feelings for the woman. Not just a beauty, the woman was sharp-witted, tenacious, and fierce. What a waste. Such a woman bound for an abbey. And no matter how many times he suggested they come up with another solution, Mercy insisted she was determined to go to the abbey—even though Mother Julienne's letter was less than welcoming. "I bid ye answer me, brother. Is our liaison believable?"

"Aye." Duncan scowled at him. "Believable because 'tis real. I dare say ye'll struggle something fierce when it comes time to carry out your plan. Just what will ye do, Graham? When the time comes to secret her *away*, when it's time to *get* her to the nunnery, will ye?"

"I will leave her there as she wishes," Graham said, staring straight ahead. "I'm no' like Alexander. I am a mercenary—no' a husband."

"Alexander swore the same yet now he's happy with Catriona and father to two bairns. Ye're a fool, Graham. A fool through and through, ye ken?"

"Who is our enemy besides St. Johns?" It was time to change the subject and devise a battle plan before they reached *Tor Ruadh,* then deserted the group and spirited Mercy away before any of the others suspected. At least—that was the plan for now. He tried to ignore the bleak feeling of hopeless emptiness the thought triggered. "What about Percy and his son?"

"Near as I can tell, neither of the Marches give a rat's arse about anything but horses and whisky." Duncan gave an appreciative shrug as the horses meandered their way around a particularly rocky patch of ground. "Damned wise if ye ask me."

That left Robbie, Wills, Bateson the cook, and Janie. Cook Bateson cared for no one but herself and her wagon, she'd made that apparent from the onset of the trip. The crotchety old woman kept to herself and none dared disturb her. Robbie and Wills still had a sullenness about them but so far, no other incidents of insolence had transpired. Mayhap they were just a pair of lads fed up with the life of servitude. And then there was Janie. Closer to Mercy than any of them. He prayed Mercy had taken his advice and not taken her into complete confidence. The outcome of such a mislaid trust could be deadly.

The sighting of three riders approaching fast ended Graham's mulling. He and Duncan reined in their horses. The angle of the sun to the back of the riders rendered them as silhouettes, dark, foreboding figures, their features impossible to discern.

"They dinna wear kilts. I can tell that much." Duncan drew his pistol. "Shall I ride ahead and greet them proper?"

"Nay." Graham motioned back toward the wagons. "Warn the others, and have the men draw arms 'til we see if they be friend or foe."

Highwaymen plagued the area but so did King William's regiments. If he had his choice, Graham hoped for highwaymen. There was a certain honor among thieves, and he'd seen very little of that among the British. A flash of red filled him with renewed trepidation. Soldiers. From the direction they'd come, more than likely they came from Fort William. Could be some of Lord Crestshire's troops which wouldn't be a bad thing. Most of Crestshire's men got along well with the MacCoinnichs. Graham readied his pistol and rested it across his lap. A man could but prepare for the worst and pray for the best.

Galloping from behind tore his attention from the soldiers in front of him. A gut-churning mix of protectiveness and irritation heated through him. He didn't bother looking back. He knew very well who approached. "Get back to the wagons, lass."

Mercy brought her horse up even with his. "Who do you think they are?" she asked, completely ignoring his order.

"I dinna ken." He jabbed a thumb back toward the cluster of wagons. "Which is why I bid ye do as ye're told and take shelter in the center of the wagons." He squinted at the progress of the oncoming riders drawing ever closer. They'd reach them soon. "Now. Mercy, please listen and dinna challenge me on this. I canna protect ye as well if ye're out in the open and vulnerable to attack."

"I need you safe, too."

Something in her voice made him turn and look at her. Chin lifted, she sat taller in the saddle and glared back at him, unflinching, defiant, and more beautiful a sight than any he'd ever seen.

Folly. Sheer folly, this was. His head knew it all too well. The only chore left now was convincing his heart this wasn't wise. "I shall be safe, lass. I swear it. Please."

With a glance at the approaching soldiers, she gave him an acquiescing nod and turned her horse. "I shall hold you to your word, sir. Do not anger me by getting hurt."

Her threat warmed through him like a shot of good whisky. He lifted a hand, drew Duncan's attention, then motioned toward the lady returning to the group as he'd requested. He felt some better then. His brother would guard her well.

"You, there!" The soldier at the center of the trio drew ahead of the other two. "Identify yourself, sir."

"Condescending bastard," Graham muttered under his breath. He puffed out his chest and bared his teeth. "Graham MacCoinnich of Clan MacCoinnich. Who might ye be?"

"MacCoinnich, you say?" The soldier halted his mount a few feet away. "The MacCoinnich leading Lady Mercy Claxton through the Highlands?"

This man knew too much for his own damn good. Graham made the pistol in his hand more apparent. "Your name?"

The man squinted at the weapon, scowled, then shrugged it off. He gave Graham a polite bob of his head. "Captain Herschel Marsden. Dispatched from Fort William to relieve Lieutenant St. Johns of his duties."

"I assure ye, it doesna take three of ye to replace that man." Graham rested his pistol back in his lap but kept it at the ready.

Captain Marsden tucked his chin to his chest, face growing red and shoulders bouncing as though trying not to laugh out loud. He cleared his throat. "Be that as it may, you may or may not be aware of an incident involving St. Johns back in the village of Benswick."

Duncan had reported a scuffle between the lieutenant and a local man, but Graham was not about to reveal his knowledge of the matter. "What incident?"

"As I thought." With an indulgent smile, Captain Marsden tilted his head in Graham's direction and urged his horse closer. "Officer James and Officer Carmichael will be escorting Lieutenant St. Johns back to Fort William to stand trial for the murder of one Franklin Samuels." The Captain's smile broadened. "I shall take St. Johns's place in your entourage as His Majesty's promised guard for the lady."

Graham studied Captain Marsden. This change in the game was proof that word of his and Mercy's feigned involvement had reached Edsbury and the crown. St. Johns hadn't murdered anyone in Benswick. The man had returned from his trip to the village with a bloodied nose, a swollen eye, and his tail tucked. Duncan had said he'd nearly pissed himself laughing at the drunken brawl the fool had lost.

So, Edsbury's scheme grew more entangled. A captain had been sent to replace the fool, and the man spoke as if he had a bit a sense. The remainder of the game would have to be played with greater care. Graham motioned the soldiers forward as he turned his horse. "Follow me. I wouldna wish to stand in the way of justice."

The one thing that troubled Graham was the speed with which the news had traveled. He and Mercy had introduced the appearance of their mutual infatuation but a little while ago and had gone through only a few villages since.

An aggravated growl escaped him as Mercy met them halfway. "I asked ye to wait with the wagons, m'lady."

"I waited as long as I could," she said. She dodged Graham, urged her mount in front of Captain Marsden, and blocked his way. "I am Lady Mercy Claxton. What is your business here, sir?"

Captain Marsden tucked his hat beneath his arm and offered a gracious nod. "Your servant, m'lady, Captain Herschel Marsden."

Mercy stole a look at Graham. He shot back a narrow-eyed glare, hoping she'd read his displeasure at her behavior. They would speak of this later.

"It appears the lieutenant is to be replaced by Captain Marsden here." Graham nodded toward the wide-eyed St. Johns being escorted away after having his wrists cuffed to his saddle. "Murdered a man in Benswick, they say."

"Murder? Lieutenant St. Johns?" Amusement and disbelief reflected in Mercy's expression and tone. She found the possibility as laughable as Graham did.

"Never fear, m'lady. The officers shall carry the rogue away, and I shall be here to ensure your safety." If Captain Marsden's wide smile shone any brighter in his plump face, it would surely pale the sun.

Graham rolled his eyes and snorted.

Mercy didn't grace the man with an answer, just turned her horse and returned to her place among the wagons in the cavalcade.

"Where are we bound, sir?" Captain Marsden asked as he brought his horse abreast of Graham's mount. The man's charming demeanor and almost puppy-like friendliness made Graham want to knock his Sassenach arse out of that saddle.

"*Tor Ruadh*," Graham replied.

"Your brother's keep," Marsden noted. "A fine keep, I must say. I enjoyed a visit there earlier this spring once the passes cleared of snow.

Your brother appears to be an exemplary chieftain." He glanced back at the entourage plodding along behind them. "About a two-week ride at this pace, wouldn't you say?"

Graham turned to answer, but Mercy's galloping approach stopped him. "A problem, m'lady?" he said with a growl, not attempting to hide his frustration.

"Sir!" Captain Marsden shot him a stern look. "I bid you curb your tone when addressing the lady."

"Do ye now?" Graham pulled his horse to a halt. "And what do ye mean to do about it if I dinna?"

"Now, Graham." Mercy steered her horse between the two men. "Captain Marsden," she said in a voice dripping with sweetness. "You mustn't read anything into Master MacCoinnich's tone. I fear I have been quite the trying charge, and he is not to blame for being curt. I assure you, he's been a most admirable gentleman even though I fear I have behaved like quite the spoiled child at times."

"Oh, my dear lady, I am certain that cannot be true." Captain Marsden beamed at her, the curls of his receding blonde hair stuck to the perspiration on his broad forehead as he clutched his hat in front of him.

Graham forced back a gag. He scrubbed a hand across his mouth and glared at Mercy, willing the woman to behave. "The lady is quite the challenge. I grant ye that."

Captain Marsden gave him a wink and a knowing nod. "I am more than certain she is, sir. Why else would His Majesty take it upon himself to see she is secured with such an advantageous match?" He shrugged, oblivious to the fact that both Mercy and Graham sat staring at him with their mouths open. "Of course, she is his only godchild. Both I and all the court find it more than natural he takes such a keen interest in her well-being." He turned aside toward Graham, lowered his voice, and shielded his mouth with one hand as though attempting to hide his words from the lady. "After all, there is the problem of her father's debts and the slipping of his status at court."

"What match?" Mercy asked, biting out the words as though they choked her. "After my journey through the Highlands, I am bound for Iona Abbey. My father has agreed to it."

Graham edged his horse closer to Mercy's mount. The poor lass had paled and looked ready to faint.

Captain Marsden's eyes grew wide, and he pressed a hand to his chest. "Forgive me, m'lady, but I was under the assumption you knew of your betrothal."

"Betrothal?" The word unleashed a possessive rage through Graham. He'd struggled to resign himself to Mercy dedicating her life to a nunnery, but he'd be damned if he handed her over to another man.

"You must be mistaken." Mercy shook her head. "I am not betrothed."

"Oh yes, m'lady." Marsden gave an adamant nod. "Louis Van Der Berg. A very influential Dutch cousin of His Highness's with close alignments to the House of Orange-Nassau. According to a reliable source, Van Der Berg is to receive the title of Duke upon the day of your wedding." Captain Marsden gave Mercy a glowing smile. "You shall not only be a bride but a duchess in your own right, m'lady. Quite fortunate, yes?"

Mercy stretched out a hand to Graham, fear and panic flashing in her eyes. "I knew nothing of this. I swear."

Graham took her hand and held tight, her pain and dread cutting through him. He laced his fingers through hers, then pressed a kiss to the back of her hand. Leaning closer, he whispered, "We will make this right. I swear it."

"Oh, dear," Captain Marsden interrupted, looking first at Mercy, then at Graham, then at their clasped hands. "So, it is true. I had been informed you two…but surely, m'lady, with a Scotsman, you didn't—"

"Ye dare sully this fine lady's name and I'll scatter your bones from one end of this glen to the other." Graham leveled his pistol at

Marsden. "Lady Mercy has done nothing improper, I assure ye. Christ, man, she is determined to spend the rest of her life in a nunnery, ye ken?" Graham hated to deny the kisses and the feelings they'd shared even though they'd gone unspoken, but he had to—for her sake and the sake of his clan—at least until he figured out a better plan and a way to make Mercy his own.

"I am not one to propagate disparaging rumors, I assure you." Captain Marsden glanced toward the retreating figures taking St. Johns toward Fort William. He turned back and frowned at Graham, then gave a slow shake of his head. "But I am also not one to lie. There have been reports of an *attachment* between yourself and Lady Mercy, and those reports have reached His Highness."

"And that is why I now discover myself betrothed? I am bound for the abbey. Does that count for nothing?" Mercy looked close to tears. "When?" she asked bitterly. "When am I to be handed over?"

The captain's shoulders slumped. "Upon your return from *Tor Ruadh,* m'lady. His Majesty—in his generosity—has allowed that you may finish your tour of the Highlands and are also granted a fortnight's stay with Clan MacCoinnich at their keep to better record the traditions of Scotland in your journal honoring your late mother and brother." He gave Graham and her an apologetic shrug. "Then you are to return forthwith to Kensington. Your wedding day is set for early September."

Graham studied the man. "Why are ye acting as though ye're sorry, man? What's this to ye other than an assigned duty to see that a bride is delivered proper and untouched to her betrothed?" Graham couldn't stand a placating fool that changed their colors according to the situation. "What is this to ye?"

Captain Marsden studied him. He adjusted the tilt of his hat and peered out across the valley. "Let us just say I know what it is to suffer a loss of the heart and leave it at that, shall we?"

The man was either a potential ally or a damned good spy. A spy with the ability to draw so close he'd slip under your skin and listen to your thoughts. Graham struggled to stay calm and figure out a way to overcome this new twist. Mercy had to be saved from the betrothal. And the nunnery. And he couldn't endanger his kin in the doing of either one. He clenched his teeth. Damned if he could see a way of accomplishing any of it.

His gut knotted, and the mercenary in him roared to run his enemies through and ride away with Mercy as his prize. But he couldn't do that. That was exactly what both the king and the duke wanted him to do.

"What are you thinking, sir?" Captain Marsden asked.

Graham gave a gracious nod to Mercy, then turned his attention to Marsden. "I'm thinking we'd best be on our way and show this fine lady the beauty of the Highlands."

"Graham?" A plea for help and hopefully something more, something he prayed she felt with all her heart, shone in Mercy's eyes as she kept her mount in step with his.

He urged his horse into a trot and waved a hand toward the land in front of them. "The land awaits us, lass. Come. Let's be about it." He gave her a more reassuring look than he felt. "The Highlands will give us our answers."

He stared out across the land and sent up a silent prayer, *"Show me how to win this woman and make her my own—safe and without bloodshed. Show me the way to make this right."*

❯❯❯❈❮❮❮

"TAKE CARE," GRAHAM said as he dismounted. He squinted up into the downpour, glaring at the gray blanket of sky. "Two days of rain makes the land treacherous. Dinna get too close to the edge of anything. Ye risk being washed away by water, mud, or rocks." He could hear the roaring waters of a swollen burn from here.

The Marchs and Cook heeded his advice and kept the wagons to the right side of the road snug against the rocky rise of the land. Mercy and Duncan followed suit and secured their mounts close to the wagons before walking a bit to stretch their legs and seek out some privacy to relieve their personal needs.

Only Marsden ignored Graham's advice. The man dismounted, left his horse standing in the middle of the road, and hurried off into a stand of trees sprouting up from the steep slope on the left.

"Fool." Graham shook his head. The man was headed straight toward the sound of the rushing water. "Marsden! Get back up here. Ye can piss behind the wagons."

"I have already started my task, sir, and I assure you, *pissing* is not what I'm doing."

The rain poured down, strengthening to a deluge. Graham slaked the water out of his eyes and glared at the woods. Past experience told him this was a grave mistake. It would be a damned shame for the man to die whilst taking a shite. Even an English.

Duncan appeared at his side. "Everyone's ready to move on. Too risky through here to make camp early."

Graham pointed at the woods. "Marsden isna back yet."

"Oh dear! Help! Help!"

"God's bones!" Graham charged into the woods. "Bring a rope!" he shouted back at Duncan as he sidled and slid down the slope, the soggy ground loose and shifting beneath his boots.

"Help!" Marsden screeched from farther down the hillside that turned out to be a jagged ravine with a river at its base.

"Graham!" Duncan shouted over the combined chaos of the rainstorm and the water rushing below.

A heavy coil of rope landed on the ground close to Graham. Duncan had tied one end of it around a tree at the road's edge. Graham scooped it up, feeding it through his hands as he worked his way lower. "Marsden!" he roared out. "Where are ye, man?" Visibility was terrible.

"Here!"

Graham turned. Marsden's shout had come from lower and behind him. At least the man hadn't already washed away down the
river. He might be British, but so far, had seemed decent enough and
beaten to death in flood waters would be a terrible way to die. Graham
hoped the rope was long enough.

The ground seemed alive, writhing beneath him like some great
serpent waking from the center of the earth. Hand wrapped in rope,
Graham held fast and scanned the area. "Marsden!"

"Here, I am! Here!"

The palest white flashed just beneath the trunk of an uprooted
tree. Graham leaned forward and peered closer, then smiled. It was
Marsden's white arse, shining through the storm.

"Hold fast, man! I'm nearly to ye." Graham let out the rope and
lowered himself to the tangle of branches Marsden clutched.

"My breeches," Marsden wheezed and coughed as he glanced
downward. His trews were tangled around his ankles. "Thank heavens
my boots kept them from washing away."

"Take hold of the rope, man. Quick now, or losing your trews will
be the least of your worries." Still holding tight to the rope himself,
Graham tossed Marsden a length of it.

Marsden wrapped the rope around one hand, released his hold on
the tree, and crawled his way up the embankment. Graham held tight
to the collar of his jacket as the man worked his soaked breeks back up
in place.

Face splotched and red, his body coated with mud and leaves,
Marsden held fast to the rope, gasping and sputtering as Graham
hefted them both back up to safety. As soon as they reached level
ground, he rolled to his back with a hand clutched to his chest. "Praise
God Almighty for strong, able Scotsmen."

Graham shook his head as he wound up the rope and untied it

from the tree. "Next time, ye'll listen to me, aye?"

"Absolutely," Marsden gasped as he struggled to stand. He wiped his muddy hand clean and held it out. "Allow me to shake your hand, sir, and give you my heartfelt thanks." He swallowed hard as he gripped Graham's forearm. "I owe my life to you, and I assure you, I will never forget what you did here today."

CHAPTER TEN

"**D**OES THE QUIET beauty of Loch Lomond no' inspire ye?" Graham's voice always triggered deep feelings within her. Even more so of late. His burr sent giddy anticipation thrilling through her. But not today. Today, the sound of his voice brought only regret, hopelessness, and despair.

Mercy smoothed her hands across the clean, unmarked page of her journal. She kept her gaze locked on the peaceful, blue green waters of the loch and watched the trails of sunlight sparkle and dance across its surface. "I was just thinking how peaceful it would be if I sank into those waters and never returned."

Graham took hold of her and pulled her close, knocking her sketchbook to the ground. "Never say such!" he said with such startling urgency it rattled her. He clasped her tight, showing fear she'd consider ending her life. "Ye've made me care for ye, woman. I'll be damned if I allow ye to give up and leave me now. We will figure this out together."

His words made her heart pound. He cared. She hitched in a sob before it escaped, forcing the warm, comforting security of being cared for away. No. He mustn't. For him to care risked too much.

"I would never give up," she reassured with a sad whisper. "But caring for you plays right into my father's hands. I will not endanger your family." Unshed tears stung her eyes, and the need to weep made her throat ache. She pressed both hands to the rock-hardness of his muscled chest, willing him to hold her, not caring if anyone saw. "I fear all is lost for us, Graham. The world is closing in and determined to see us separated before we are ever joined."

"All is not lost." He glanced over at the encampment, then released his hold on her and took a step back. "I never thought I would say this. Thought myself a soldier forever." His charged gaze held her captive, refused to let her look away. "But I swear I shall find a way for us to be together." He lifted his chin as he took a step closer and swept her hands up into his and held them to his chest. "That is—if ye can see fit to have me."

If her heart wasn't aching for all she would never have, Mercy would have laughed out loud. Her Highlander. Her guardian. Her courageous, caring heartmate. He stood before her offering himself as though he were the lowliest of the low. To her, a woman who had never belonged anywhere. "'See fit to have you, you say." She held his hands tight as though she'd never let them go. "If only I could have you, my fine, honorable man. No matter what comes to pass—you must know this, you will always be the only choice of my heart."

Graham pressed a kiss to the back of each of her hands, then gave her a reassuring smile. "When we reach *Tor Ruadh,* we shall have more heads to put to this quandary. We'll search out a way to make a future. We *will* find a solution, lass. I promise ye." He released her hands and retrieved her journal, brushing dirt from its cover. "No more talk of drowning yourself, my fine, wee selkie. I'll no' relinquish ye to the waters, ye ken?" He leaned closer and lowered his voice. "Unless ye fancy an evening swim and the gift of another kiss."

The burden of her black mood managed to lighten. Mercy tapped a finger to the end of his nose. "I see no grasses in which we can hide, my tempting water rat."

Graham chuckled as he caught her hand and brought it to his lips.

"I say there. Might I join you?" Pebbles and clumps of dirt tumbled down around them, dislodged by Captain Marsden's progress down the incline toward the water's edge.

"There's a body I wouldna mind surrendering to the loch," Graham grumbled in a low tone meant just for her.

"Now, Graham," she scolded gently. "He's not that bad, and if you'd admit it, I believe you rather like the man. You did see fit to save his life."

Since Marsden had joined their party, the garrulous man had befriended every person in the camp—even Cook.

He stumbled the last few feet to the shoreline, arms extended and flapping like an awkward bird attempting to take flight. "I never knew grasses could tangle a man's boots so. Do be careful, m'lady, when you make your way back to camp."

Mercy bit the inside of her cheek to keep from laughing at the poor captain. "Thank you, Captain Marsden. I appreciate the warning."

The red-cheeked man smiled, yanking his uniform back in place down around his rather full form as he settled in beside them. "Although my arrival brought the two of you ill news, I consider myself quite fortunate to have made your acquaintance. I feel as though we've become good friends."

Graham didn't respond, just glared at the man with that stoic expression that infuriated Mercy so. She nudged her elbow into his side as she spoke. "And we feel the same, Captain Marsden."

"Ye seem a good man, Marsden." Graham gave Mercy a sullen dip of his chin that told her she should be grateful for him saying that much.

The captain clasped his hands together, lacing his fingers so tightly his knuckles whitened. "Thank you, Master MacCoinnich." He nodded with a knowing wink. "I understand how much it pains a Scot to admit friendship with an Englishman."

"Was that all ye wished to say to us, Marsden?"

"Graham!" Mercy couldn't believe Graham's rude behavior. Well, she could, but his forwardness never ceased to amaze her. "Please forgive him, Captain Marsden. At least you know he always speaks his mind."

"Too true, m'lady. Which brings me quicker to the point Master MacCoinnich seeks." His jovial demeanor faded, replaced with a concerned look. "I am compelled to tell you I was sent here to replace Lieutenant St. Johns because the man failed to report any useful information regarding the two of you."

"Aye?" Graham held up his hands. "We all knew St. Johns to be a poor informant. What's your point, man?"

"If St. Johns was replaced for his failings as a spy, then how did His Majesty and the Duke of Edsbury come to possess such pertinent information involving the two of you and your, shall we say...*attachment*? The report I was given was more than explicit and extremely detailed." Marsden looked away and cleared his throat, shuffling back and forth in place as he continued, "Private dinners. Heated kisses and...dare I say...swimming without benefit of either clothing or chaperone."

"Janie." The name escaped her before she could stop it. Mercy felt the greatest sort of fool. Graham had warned her, but she'd been unable to believe her maid a spy. Not after the friendship she'd thought they'd formed. How could she have been so naïve?

"How many confidences have ye shared with her?" Graham asked in a patient, protective tone that made Mercy feel even worse.

"Of late—not many." Mercy shook her head, wringing her hands. "I had an ill feeling about her after the day at the river." A wave of nausea washed across her, making her grab hold of Graham's arm. How could she have been so blind? She'd risked so many lives by trusting that conniving girl.

"Take care, lass." Graham caught her up and held her. "If she doesna ken we are privy to her sly ways, mayhap we can use this." He looked to Marsden. "What say ye, man? Will ye help us?"

"Absolutely," Captain Marsden replied without hesitation. "My loyalty to king and country goes without saying. But I am also loyal to the protection of those who should be together. No greater pain exists than that of true love denied." He gave Graham a solemn nod. "And after all, you did save my life, sir."

Mercy's heart went out to the man. "You lost a great love, Captain Marsden?"

"Yes, m'lady. True love denied." Captain Marsden's voice faltered, and he pressed a clenched fist to his mouth. Eyes closed, he paused for what looked like a painful moment, then took a deep breath and turned back to face her with a forced smile. "But I shan't trouble you with the delicate details of the matter." He stood taller and cast a disparaging glance up the hillside where Janie and the others milled about the wagons, tending to their duties. "But I will help you both however I can—although I would be most appreciative if we could avoid anything treasonous."

"Ye can start by telling us the duke and king's reactions to the reports. Anything they might have told ye regarding Lady Mercy and m'self," Graham said. "Battles are won with information."

Captain Marsden frowned at the suggestion. He clasped both hands behind his back and walked near the water. "The Duke of Edsbury seemed elated at the news. Actually said that all was going according to his plan. A plan with which he'd never thought Lady Mercy would comply." Marsden turned and studied her as he continued. "But the king seemed quite..." He stopped, brow furrowed as he stared at her as though he'd never seen her before.

"Quite?" Mercy wished the man would spit it out but no matter how hard she glared at him, he remained silent. "Quite what, Marsden?"

"More than a little disturbed," Marsden replied. "What puzzles me is His Majesty's agitation appeared more directed at the Duke of

Edsbury rather than toward either of you."

"What makes you say that?" Marsden's observation made no sense. Surely the man had it wrong. Mercy wished she'd been at court observing her father and the king when they received the news.

"Because your father was immediately dismissed from His Majesty's presence and advised not to return unless summoned." Marsden gave Mercy a knowing nod. "Such a dismissal from His Highness is never good. Your father required assistance leaving the room."

Graham scowled, picked up a smooth round rock from the ground, and skipped it across the water. Staring at the point where the rock sank, his eyes narrowed. "King William didna go into detail as to how Edsbury displeased him?"

Marsden shook his head as he stood alongside Graham and joined him in staring out across the loch. "His Majesty merely cut off the duke's ill-timed bragging about how once again, he'd proven himself the pride of the court." Marsden shrugged. "The king then ordered the duke escorted out and not granted admittance again unless he so commanded it."

"When were you told of the betrothal?" Mercy couldn't even bear to say the unknown man's name she'd been slated to marry.

"That same day. Right after they led your father from the room." Marsden bent with a huffing grunt, selected a rock, and attempted to skip it across the water. It failed, sinking a few feet from shore with a disheartening *plunk*. Marsden frowned and bent to find another stone. "Although, come to think of it..." Marsden stood. "Your intended's name was not mentioned at that time." He frowned and gave Mercy a confused look. "In fact, I'm not certain the king even knew who your intended might be at that particular moment. The way he acted was quite peculiar for His Majesty. I wasn't made privy to your betrothed's name or status until the day I left London to return to Fort Smith and gather my men to intercept you. I was instructed to ride hard and fast and make the trip in record time. In fact, it was stated that the success of my future in His Majesty's guard depended on it."

Graham turned from the water and faced her, a grim knowing making his dark features. "Sounds as though the king is doing his best to protect your honor and recover you from this situation unscathed. After all, who in society would dare sully the name of a woman given in marriage by the king himself."

"But that would foil his plot to destroy your clan. How could he sanction Campbell's onslaught by having me safely married to some Dutchman allied with his family?" Mercy hugged herself against the cool wind coming off the loch. "None of this makes sense. My father explicitly stated the king was quite interested in a more subtle massacre of yet another Highland clan." The thought sickened her and made her swallow hard against the bitter bile rising at the back of her throat. "Father will be enraged by the king's dismissal." She clamped her mouth shut. "He will blame me," she whispered. Mercy had no doubt her father would attempt to do her harm.

Graham strode forward and took her in his arms, embracing her safe and tight to his chest. "The bastard willna hurt ye. I swear it."

His protective words rumbled against her, filling her with a comforting warmth, a fleeting sense of possibilities. Could they survive this unscathed? She closed her eyes, pressing her cheek against the rough weave of Graham's jacket. She breathed in the consoling scent of the man dearer to her than life. How could she fear anything with his strong arms around her? "I can't have you or your family hurt," she whispered. "Father will not fight fair."

Graham's laugh shook through her as he kissed the top of her head. "I dinna fight fair either when it comes to those I cherish."

CHAPTER ELEVEN

"I WILLNA REST easy until we reach *Tor Ruadh*." Graham rested his hand atop the butt of his pistol as he scanned the surrounding land.

Every tree, every rock, every towering crag could hide an intruder intent on hurting Mercy. Every sound from the group's movement seemed magnified in the tunnel-like pass through the silent mountainous sentries of Scotland. Horses clomped and thudded across the packed dirt. Harnesses rattled with their twisting and shifting. Wagon wheels creaked and groaned with the rhythm of every bump and turn. Christ Almighty. They couldn't announce their presence any louder if they shouted it from the mountain tops. The place made them easy targets, slow-moving and open to ambush.

Graham had no doubt the Duke of Edsbury had dispatched someone, and this was the perfect place for them to strike. He wished Marsden had seen fit to share the report of the duke's expulsion from court earlier. More time to plan a suitable defense and a different route.

"I'm torn betwixt riding ahead to warn Alexander and staying here." Duncan rode beside him on the road that was little more than a tramped down path. He twisted in the saddle and hurried the men forward. "Keep the wagons closer behind us, aye? No straggling through here."

Doughal and Percy March complied, urging the draft horses to pull at a faster clip. Cook's wagon swayed from side to side behind them, driven by the sour-faced cook herself with Janie sitting beside her clutching hold of the guardrail around the seat.

"I need ye here, brother," Graham said with a backward glance at Mercy. "I wish yourself and Marsden to flank Mercy through this pass. I've an ill feeling about this place."

Steep, rugged cliffs cradled the long stretch of overgrown woodland, walling in the towering trees and moss-covered boulders lining the narrow roadway. Instinct and experience bade him hasten them to the open glen on the other side. At least once they reached open land, he'd be able to better see around them.

"Someone watches us. I can feel it." Graham nudged his horse into a canter. "Stay together and keep up," he called back to others.

Suddenly, something whizzed past him, followed by another. Arrows from higher ground.

"Halt and take cover!" With the heavily laden wagons there was no outrunning the attack but by damn, they would hide and bide their time, and strike back when the marauders got within range. "Women, inside Cook's wagon. Now!" He thanked God when Mercy complied without argument. She dismounted and hurried back to climb inside the wagon.

"Bolt the doors and windows! Open them for no one!" he shouted after her.

She paused long enough to send him a fearful, longing look, then disappeared inside.

Graham, Duncan, Marsden, and the rest of the men took cover between the two flatbed wagons the men had steered off the sides of the road so Cook could draw her wagon up between them.

Pulling a pair of rifles out from under one of the wagon's benches, Graham motioned Wills and Robbie forward. "Crawl under and guard the back of Cook's wagon and see that none breaches it, aye?" he said as he handed each of them a rifle.

"Yes sir," Wills said, eyes wide as he stared down at the rifle Graham thrust into his hands.

"I wish we'd brought our bows," Duncan remarked as the rest of them crouched between the sturdy bodies of the draft horses and waited for the attackers' next move.

Dread grew inside him like a raging fever. Instinct warned him the arrows were a diversion. He cocked his pistols and turned toward the wagons. "They mean to charge the back of us. Come!"

Gunfire split the air from behind the wagons, followed by shouts and the sound of wood splintering. The horses reared and attempted to run, but Doughal and Percy held them fast.

"Go!" Marsden shouted. "These men and I shall hold the front." He aimed his rifle at the scattering of men headed down the hillside toward them and fired.

Graham and Duncan took cover under Cook's wagon, joining a pale, panic-stricken Robbie where he lay on his belly clutching his hands over his ears.

"Wills," Robbie said, taking one of his hands away from his head long enough to point at the lad's body lying in the leaves just behind the wagon. "Shot him dead, they did."

Graham propped the barrel of his pistol on the rung of the wagon wheel and fired, dropping one attacker to his knees. Duncan fired and finished off the man, who fell to the ground.

Elbow-crawling over to Wills, Graham grabbed hold of the boy's belt and dragged him back beneath the wagon. "He's no' dead," he told Robbie. He pointed to a dark red stain on the boy's leg. "Shot in the leg and fainted."

"Thank God above," Robbie whispered, then put his hands back over his ears, squinting his eyes shut against the racket of the gunfire.

Graham took hold of the boy's shoulder and shook him until he opened his eyes and looked at him. "Ye've got two choices, boy. Fight or die!"

A shot fired above them, sounding as though it had come from inside the wagon instead of from the woods. One of the men running toward them stumbled to his knees and dragged himself away, seeking cover behind a tree.

"Someone in the wagon has good aim," Duncan said as he reloaded, then fired on another man creeping down the hillside. The man growled and grabbed his arm as he retreated back up the rise.

Then the woods grew quiet.

The wagon boards above their heads creaked with scurrying footsteps. Graham rapped the butt of his pistol up against the boards. "Stay inside while the men and I ensure 'tis truly safe!"

The steps inside the wagon stilled.

"Are you well?" Mercy's voice, muffled and fearful, came to him.

"Aye, love. I'm fine," Graham called back. He crawled out from under the wagon and stood with a pistol in each hand. "Just a mite angry," he added under his breath. Except for the occasional moan and rustling of leaves coming from the hillside to their left, the skirmish appeared to be over.

Duncan rose from the ground, brushing dirt from his knees. He looked toward the sound of the moans. "I'll see what I can find out."

"Try not to kill them, aye? We need information." Graham knew Duncan's temperament. His younger brother had little patience with those who fired the first shot.

Graham bent and looked back under the wagon where Robbie crouched beside the still unconscious Wills, staring down at the red stain spreading along the thigh of the boy's trews. "Robbie!" he purposely barked the name to snap the boy out of his fear-induced stupor.

"Yes sir?"

"Drag him out so we can see to his leg. It looks to be nothing more than a grazing, but we need to be sure." Graham gave a disgusted shake of his head. Useless. Both of them.

A shot echoed through the woods. It came from the direction Duncan had taken.

"Duncan!" Graham skittered backward, pressing his back to the wagon with both pistols at the ready.

"The fool shot himself," Duncan shouted down from the mountainside. "Saw me headed toward him."

Coward. Graham had hoped for information. "Best come back down here among the wagons," he shouted. He was still none too certain the area was safe.

The door to Cook's wagon eased open. Mercy peeped through a crack in the door.

"Did I no' ask ye to say inside for a bit longer?" Graham asked.

"I needed to see you safe." Her eyes shimmered with tears.

Graham forced himself to speak in a kinder tone. "I told ye I was fine, lass. Ye must heed me during times such as these, ye ken?"

Mercy looked tempted to argue but responded with a jerking nod. "May we come out now? All seems quiet."

Graham took one last scan of the woods. All seemed quiet. "Aye, lass. Come out."

Mercy pushed open the door, jumped to the ground, and rushed to him, clutching hold of him in the best possible way as she threw herself into his embrace. She wrapped her arms around his shoulders and held on tight, tucking her face into his neck. "I was so afraid for you," she whispered against his skin.

Graham hugged her tight, grinning at the stares focused on them, not giving a damn what they thought. He held her close, reveling in the feel of her against him. What a perfect match they were. Their bairns would surely have hair dark as ravens and temperaments fierce and stubborn as mules. He looked forward to filling a keep with their brood. As much as he hated letting her go, he peeled her away from his chest. "We must go. I willna rest 'til we're out of this pass."

Mercy stepped back, sliding her hands down his arms with a reluctance that set him on fire. She gave a quick nod. "Agreed."

A pitiful moan came from Wills, lying at the side of the road where Robbie had dragged him.

"Oh no! Wills!" Mercy rushed to his side, bending to check the wound on his leg.

Wills sprang to life, snaking an arm around Mercy's waist and locking a dagger tight to her throat. Robbie hurried to stand beside him, holding a pair of pistols at the ready, one trained on Graham, and the other sweeping the rest of the group as though trying to decide upon a target.

Two men stepped out from around a cluster of large trees. A third man rose from behind a pile of boulders. He sauntered forward with an arrogant smile that fueled Graham's rage even hotter. "Gobs!" he shouted. "Bring the other one down so we can all have a wee chat before we're on our way."

A man taller and uglier than any man Graham had ever seen, half-shoved, half-dragged Duncan down the hillside. One hand held the barrel of a pistol stuck into Duncan's ribcage, and his other meaty hand clutched Duncan by the hair on the back of his head. A grimy knotted rag was jammed between Duncan's teeth and tied tight around his face. His hands were lashed behind his back.

"See, you stinking Scot? I ain't the coward you thought me." Robbie leveled a pistol higher, aiming it at Graham's head. "I'm a good shot, too." He clicked back the hammer.

"No!" Mercy screeched, lunged to the side, and landed a kick into the back of Robbie's knee, bringing him to the ground just as Wills sliced a cut across her throat.

"Stay still, Mercy, I beg ye." The sight of Mercy's blood staining the front of her bodice filled Graham with an icy panic, blinding him with unrelenting rage. The only thing that held him at bay was the gut-wrenching fear for her life.

The man from behind the rocks walked up to Wills and cuffed him hard on the ear. "Look what you done! She's worth more unmarked, fool!"

Wills jerked away, rubbing his ear against his shoulder as he resettled his grip on Mercy. "Caught me off guard, she did, Flynn. Lucky, I didn't cut her throat proper."

"I'll twist your head clean off your neck, ye wee bastard." Graham took a step forward, coming to a halt when Wills pressed the dagger harder against Mercy's already bleeding neck.

"Settle down, you. We'll be taking your lady with us," said the leader. "Got quite the prospects for her, we do." The man gave Graham a gap-toothed grin. "Her Da done promised us her weight in gold and told us whatever we sells her for is ours, too."

He took a step closer to Mercy, slid the tip of his rifle under the edge of her skirts, and lifted, bending to inspect her. "Well, will you look at that now, lads? She's wearing some kind of fancy breeches." Flynn shook his head. "We'll have to remedy that afore we get her to the docks, we will." He winked at Graham. "Gotta be able to show off them wares, eh? Get a better price that way."

Graham dove toward Flynn but came up short when Wills tightened his hold enough on Mercy to make her cry out. "If ye dare hurt her anymore, I'll kill ye slower than I'm already planning."

Flynn laughed out loud, then motioned to the others in his band. "Tie the Scots and the redcoat to the wagon wheels and be sure to gag them. Since they're such an ungrateful lot, I'll be lettin'm die slow. No blessing of a fast, clean bullet for the likes of them. Lock the rest in that there fancy wagon." He nodded toward the harnessed horses and those tethered to the wagons. "Shame we haven't got time to sell a bit of horseflesh, but no sense in leavin' the poor beasts trapped to suffer starvin' to death. Set'm loose, boys." He chuckled. "Any of these fools worms their way loose, they can walk."

"Stay alive," Graham roared to Mercy as they dragged her away. "I will find ye. Just stay alive, I beg ye!"

"Now that's right touching, that is," said the one called Gobs as he yanked hold of Graham to tie him to the same wagon wheel as Duncan. "Hold her up a minute!" he shouted to Wills. "Turn her this way."

"What for?" Wills halted, swinging Mercy around to face Graham.

"He won't be finding ye in this life, m'lady." Gobs gave a snorting laugh, then stabbed his dagger deep in Graham's side.

Graham held his breath against giving the bastard the satisfaction of any kind of reaction to the searing pain.

"No!" Tears streamed down her face as she bent over Wills's arm, flailing from side to side and sobbing uncontrollably.

"Thanks, Gobs. Now I gotta carry the wailin' bitch." Wills hefted her along, dragging her to one of the horses brought down from higher on the hillside. He threw her over the saddle, belly down, like a sack of grain, then mounted up behind her.

With a hard, chewing bite into the leather gag, Graham struggled to breathe through the ripping burn in his side as he watched the men ride away. The wound didn't hurt nearly as bad as the knowledge they had tricked him. Led astray by a pair of little bastards who had probably planned this day all along with Edsbury. Graham closed his eyes and leaned his head back against the wagon wheel. He'd missed the signs. How could he have been such a damned fool?

WITH HER BODY slung over the horse, the rush of blood drummed inside her head, and her skull felt ripe to split from the pressure. The ridges of the saddle dug into her ribcage. Her neck wound was still bleeding.

The weight of Wills's hand on her rump, groping and squeezing as they thundered through the forest repulsed and infuriated her. Fighting his touch proved futile, enraging her even more. She prayed for the opportunity to rip that knife from his belt and split him from gut to gullet.

The horse leapt over a crack in the forest floor. The rough landing made her wretch and cough, then gasp for air.

"Hold up, Wills!"

A deep, wheezing voice she hadn't heard before sounded somewhere close to her head. At this point, Mercy couldn't be certain of anything. A low buzzing filled her ears and she felt dizzy. When she dared open her eyes, lights flashed and distorted her vision. But one particular pain, one brutal image focused crisp and clear in her mind: Graham stabbed in the side and left to die. The cruelty of it twisted her heart. She let loose a piercing sob. *I am so sorry, my love. So very sorry.*

"God Almighty, Wills, pull her up so she'll stop that infernal noise," the wheezing voice said.

The horse stopped, and Mercy went limp, determined not to help the disgusting Wills in any way. She felt no fear, only a cold determination. Graham had begged her to live. Begged her not to give up. She wouldn't. But what she would do was escape and make her way back to him. She had to get back to him.

Wills grappled and yanked at her but lost his hold. She slid out of his grip and fell to the forest floor, hitting her right hip first, then slammed hard to the flat of her back. She gasped, curling to her side, struggling to regain the wind knocked from her.

"Dammit, Wills!"

Gunfire boomed and reverberated through the trees. Wills sagged to one side, then hit the ground with a sickening thud beside her. His sightless eyes stared into hers as he gasped his last breath.

"You killed him, Tracker!" Robbie said with a high-pitched squeak. Mercy recognized that little traitor's voice.

"You want to be next, boy?" The voice belonged to their leader.

"Naw." Robbie answered quickly, no doubt in his voice.

Mercy struggled to rise, head swimming and eyes so swollen from weeping and hanging upside down, her sight faded in and out.

"Get her up and on the horse, and tie her hands to the saddle," Tracker said. "We need to make some distance afore nightfall. We're too damn close to Ben Nevis for my likin'. MacCoinnich's brother has enough warriors to be a problem."

"What about Wills?" Robbie asked.

"Leave him," Tracker said. "Crows need ta eat."

The greasy, bloated man, the one called Gobs, and for good reason judging by the look of him, yanked her up and plopped her on the horse as easily as if she were a rag doll. Mercy forced back a gag at the rancid stench of the man. She flinched as he lashed her hands to the saddle horn, pulling the cord so tight it bit into her flesh.

"Damn, she be a tender one," Gobs said as he smacked a meaty paw across her bleeding hands and laughed. He gave her a slow wink as he took hold of her horse's reins. "You'll bring us a good price, hen. We'll do well 'cause a you."

Mercy clenched her teeth and stared straight ahead, determined to remain silent. *Give me your strength, Mama. Please give me your strength.* Head bowed and sagging forward, Mercy feigned the show of a cowering, hopeless female whilst stealing glances all around and assessing her captors. Mama had raised her to be a proper lady, but she'd also taught Mercy to be a fighter. Both Akio and Mama had seen to that. Poor Mama had seen too much in her lifetime and had known better than to trust Papa's title to protect them.

Five men. Now with Wills gone, Robbie knew her best, so she'd have to watch him closer. He'd worked at Claxton House for the past couple of years.

Gobs—the stinking mountain of flesh. Bald-headed Flynn, second-in-command. Tracker, the leader, dressed in black from his battered hat to the tips of his boots. A grizzled beard and stringy, gray hair roping down his back, the man looked as though he belonged at sea rather than on the back of a horse.

A weasel-like man rode behind Tracker, his beady-eyed gaze darting all around them. Mercy had yet to learn that man's name but decided, although he was the smallest of the group, he might well be the one that needed closer watching as well. He appeared to miss nothing. He cleared his throat and flicked a bony finger in her direction. "Ye keep bloodying her up like that and ye'll no' get as good a price for damaged goods. With her cat-eyed looks and that black hair, they'll already think her a whore rather than a real lady no matter what ye say. Ye better keep her all pampered lookin' and such."

Tracker gave Gobs a silent, narrow-eyed warning and nodded toward Mercy's bound hands.

Gobs rolled his eyes, dismounted with a labored grunt, and shoved a fist into one of the bags hanging from his saddle. He pulled free a length of dingy white linen that might once have been a man's fine neckcloth. He waddled over to Mercy and replaced the cords of leather he'd used to bind her hands with the cloth, anchoring it to her saddle. "There," he huffed as he barreled his way back to his horse. "Good enough for ye, Norton?"

"Good enough," Norton replied with a shrug. "We'll see when we get there."

They took off again at a brisk pace. Mercy used the opportunity to make a mental note of any landmarks that might help her get back to Graham. Unfortunately, she'd traveled the first part of the journey thrown over the side of a horse. She felt sure they hadn't made it that far from the wagons, for they were still in the pass leading to the glen that lay at the base of Ben Nevis.

She gritted her teeth against the pain left by the previous ties, working at the knotted cloth binding her hands. If she freed her hands, she might gain control of the horse.

Tracker, Flynn, and Gobs rode in front of her with her horse's reins tied to Gobs's saddle. Her heart fell. She'd never get those reins freed without a knife. Robbie and Norton rode behind her. Escape wouldn't be easy, but surely they wouldn't shoot her. She was worth too much to them.

Mercy explored the idea of throwing herself from the saddle. Akio had taught her how to dive and roll. A fond memory of him praising her after she'd nearly given her riding teacher a death scare by just such a stunt. *Give me your strength, Akio. Give me your agility.*

A glance forward warned her that the narrow pass would soon be behind them. She needed the woods to escape. She'd never get away in the open glen. With a final yank on her bonds, she pulled the ties free of the saddle and with care, untied her hands. Then she sent up a silent prayer and dove off her horse and to the to the left just as they passed a snarl of vines and saplings in the overgrown ravine running alongside the road.

Shouts followed her fall as she crashed through branches. Tucked into a ball as Akio had taught her, she rolled down the side of the ravine, jabbed and beaten by undergrowth and rocks. Upon her stop, she crouched low for the span of a heartbeat, glancing around to gather her thoughts, then launched into a limping run. She had to keep to the undergrowth to go undetected. The men would search for her but would never catch her. The small, nimble Norman would be her greatest threat.

Cursing behind her spurred her onward. She could not get caught. Branches ripped her clothes, clawed her arms, cut across her face, and yanked her hair. She didn't care. Nothing mattered but getting back to Graham. Horses thundered above her on the road. They thought to cut her off. The men behind her sounded farther away. *She could return to the road and go higher. They'd think her still in the ravine.*

She reached for the limbs of an obliging tree and pulled herself upward and toward the roadway. Just before she pushed through a dense tangle of leafy vines, she held her breath and listened. There was still definite movement in the ravine behind her. The voices had stopped, but the sound of knives slashing through vegetation was quite clear. She pulled herself up higher and crawled to the edge of the road, crouching behind a large boulder surrounded by several smaller rocks.

Glancing first one way and then the other, she held her breath, scrabbled across the road and shimmied into a ditch overgrown with grass and heather. Staying low, she wormed her way into a thick hedge and paused to catch her breath. She stole a glance higher. The risk of attack from above was now gone. Two to three of her captors were still in the ravine; from her current perch, she could just make out the swaying foliage below as they moved through it. She peered up the road and spotted Tracker and Gobs riding slowly, peering down over the edge of the road.

Another glance up filled her with concern. The higher she went, the less cover there was in which to hide. But if she remained here, they might discover her. She crouched lower, loosening her hair to drape around herself to hide the pink of her clothing as well as her fair skin. Thankfully, clusters of thrift colored the hillside above with vibrant shades of pinks and purples. She prayed the plant would help her blend in with the surroundings.

Voices grew louder, drew nearer.

"Any sight of her?" Gobs shouted.

"Not yet," Robbie replied. "But this vegetation be so thick, we might ha' stepped over the wily bitch if she holed up and hid herself."

"Don't be foolish enough t'come out without her, boy." Tracker meandered back up the roadway toward Mercy's hiding spot.

Panic building, she studied the lay of the land directly above her. With one last glance toward Tracker and Gobs, Mercy clawed upward toward her only hope.

CHAPTER TWELVE

DAWN BROUGHT NOTHING but more pain and a deeper, all-consuming rage.

Forcing his waning strength to feed on sheer stubbornness, Graham resumed yesterday's efforts to free himself. Today, he would succeed. There was no other option.

The wound in his side burned at every intake of breath. It didn't matter. He'd carried on through worse, and all that mattered was saving Mercy. Graham blinked and squinted against the sweat running into his eyes. Jaws working side to side, he battled the leather between his teeth, willing it to weaken and break with the steady grinding. A glance over at Duncan told him his brother was awake and did the same.

Hands lashed over his head, tied to the iron framework of the wagon, Graham snorted in a deep breath, then dug his heels into the ground and pushed, determined to stand even though he'd failed so many times before. He roared into the gag, powering through the pain.

Finally, Graham inched his way upward. Violent trembles nearly caused him to lose his footing. He thumped the back of his head against the side of the wagon. *Praise God.* He'd reached the point of standing, his bound hands caught between the small of his back and the iron bar. Inching his right thumb along the belted waist of his kilt covered by his waistcoat, he strained to hook the fingers of his tied hands around the bone-handled haft of the small dagger he kept tucked out of sight. He'd learned long ago that a secret blade could mean the difference between life and death.

Edsbury's hired men had relieved them of their daggers, swords, and guns. What weapons the thieves hadn't claimed for themselves and carried off, they'd tossed into the woods on the other side of the road. Thankfully, they'd failed to find his precious blade he kept tucked against his back. After a strained bit of sawing and twisting, he freed his hands. Ripping the gag away from his mouth, he gasped in great mouthfuls of air, then pushed away from the wagon and cut Duncan free.

"Pleased I am that ye still carry your wee blade, brother. But ye've gone soft. Since when does it take ye a full night and well into a new day to break your bonds?" Duncan gave him a smirk that darkened to a concerned scowl. "Turn so I can check where the bastard stabbed ye. Your kilt is dripping blood."

Graham waved him away. "No time. I've survived worse. Ye ken that as well as I." He handed over his knife and motioned toward Marsden. "Free him and set the others loose from Cook's wagon. Have the Marches search for the horses whilst the rest of us gather up what weapons we can find. With any luck, the beasts willna have wandered too far since they know us a good source for those treats Mercy always fed them."

Duncan took the knife and set about the task. Graham limped his way over to the side of the road, pushing through leaves and under-brush in search of his pistols. Special made and requiring a size of shot known only to him, the bastard called Flynn had shaken his head while examining the firearms, then tossed them aside.

A glance back at the wagons stirred his already raw emotions. Janie stood beside Cook's wagon, wringing her hands and sobbing. Graham had half a mind to leave that traitorous wench behind. He pressed a hand to his wounded side, applying pressure to ease the pain and slow oozing blood as he moved deeper into the thicket. He found both his pistols but not his *sgian dhu*. Losing that knife pained him. He snorted out a laugh and immediately regretted it because of his wound. He'd stolen that knife from Alexander's collection when they'd lost most of their clan to the morbid sore throat outbreak and banded together to seek their fortunes as mercenaries.

He tucked the pistols into his belt, slung the strap of a short-barreled musket over his shoulder, then headed back to the group. Marsden met him and helped him climb up and sit in the back of one of the flatbed wagons.

"What is your plan, sir?" Marsden frowned at the ever-growing dark stain seeping down the left side of Graham's kilt. "And does it include cauterizing that wound before you bleed to death?"

Graham squinted at a spot in the distance, far ahead on the roadway. "I ride as soon as I have a horse, even if it be one of the draft horses from the wagons. The rest of ye can follow as soon as circumstances permit."

Captain Marsden turned and scowled at the same spot down the road. "One wounded man bleeding to death against six. Poor odds, I daresay."

"If I dinna make haste, they will have her sold, and I risk never finding her." Graham ached to be on his way, the pain in his heart far outweighed the pain in his side. Every moment he sat doing nothing, Mercy slipped farther away. He'd heard a shot in the distance yesterday. He prayed to God his dear love was still alive.

"And if you die trying to reach her, how will that help the lady?" Captain Marsden glared at him. "The woman's own father sent a pack of miscreants after her to sell her into slavery. She needs you, Master MacCoinnich, and she needs you alive and well."

A steady thudding and clomping of hooves pounding against

packed dirt grew louder, ending Captain Marsden's unwelcome advice. Spry old Percy March rode at the front, astraddle Graham's horse, while his son, Doughal, brought up the rear on Duncan's horse and lead Marsden's horse beside him.

The four draft horses from the wagons plodded along between them. The only one missing was Mercy's pampered steed. The great black beast could be the devil himself when anyone dared get near him without his mistress's permission.

Duncan joined Captain Marsden and Graham at the wagon. "I say we ride hard to *Tor Ruadh*. Ye ken Alexander will provide men and fresh horses to fetch the lady and ensure they leave no trace of those who would do her harm."

"We could be there in less than a day, MacCoinnich," Marsden agreed. "We've but to cross the glen."

"We could leave the Marches to bring the wagons and the women." Duncan turned and gave Janie a hard look. "I assume we'll be bringing that one with us. Think it safe to trust the Marches and Cook as well?"

"The Marches love their horses, and Cook hates everyone. I dinna ken if any of that equates to trust or no', but I do feel that leaves Janie as the most guilty now that Robbie and Wills have shown their colors." Graham flinched as he slid off the wagon and stood. He studied the group, instinct, experience, and pure unwillingness to give up making up his mind.

He nodded to Marsden and Duncan. "We three ride ahead. Leave the rest here to either join us at *Tor Ruadh* or return to London. Makes no difference to me. I dinna trust the lot of them." He was done with this misbegotten game. He staggered to his horse and set to the task of ensuring his mount was ready to ride.

"Agreed," Duncan said, and Marsden nodded as both men went to their horses.

"When do we leave to fetch my mistress?" Janie demanded from behind them.

Graham clenched his teeth, not trusting himself to speak for a long, hard minute. He turned and glared at the girl, willing her to confess her sins so he might be justified in abandoning her. As it was, he couldn't do so, not in all good conscience—not yet. "Your journey depends on the Marches." He turned and faced old Percy and Doughal. "Go through the glen and find your way to *Tor Ruadh* or return to London. I leave ye to it." He motioned toward Janie and Cook. "These two go with ye, if ye wish. If ye choose to leave them here, it makes no difference to me."

Percy reacted with a puckering scowl, and Doughal looked bewildered. "Ye dinna trust us," Doughal said, taking a defensive stance. "Why? What have we done to show disloyalty? We've served Claxton house for years."

"Someone betrayed her ladyship. They provided detailed reports to the Duke of Edsbury and also to His Majesty," Captain Marsden said. "I very much doubt the two young men who assisted in the lady's kidnapping worked alone. Neither of them appeared intelligent enough to manage such a thing."

"That leaves you four," Graham said, then focused a damning scowl on Janie. "And some information given in the report was known only to yourself."

Janie's face flamed even redder. She shook her head violently. "Never," she rasped out. "Not ever—would I hurt her ladyship."

"I've no' time to play. Ye stay with the Marches. Your fate is in their hands—for now." Graham winced as he turned away. His bloodsoaked kilt slapped against his thigh. "Duncan, bind this damn wound so I can ride."

"In the wagon." Janie lumbered around him, glaring back at him with a defensive scowl. "In the wagon, her ladyship had me pack a box of bandages, herbs, and poultices in case of injuries on the trip." She hitched her way back and forth in front him as he strode toward a place to sit so Duncan could see to his bleeding. "Let me help you." She shook a fist at him. "If I help you, then I help her."

Graham reached for a tree and leaned against the sturdy trunk for support. "Get this nattering midge away from me!"

"Get the box, girl!" Captain Marsden ordered in a barking tone that Graham couldn't believe came from the ever-jovial man. He rested a hand on Graham's shoulder and squeezed. "Come. Sit. Duncan can bind your wound, then we'll be on our way."

Graham perched on a nearby rock flat enough to provide good support. He pulled away his waistcoat and stripped his tunic off over his head. Glancing down, he assessed the puncture wound low in his side. Good. Looked to be mostly damage to muscle. He'd had worse. At least the accursed man had only stabbed him once rather than slash his gut wide open.

Janie retrieved the wooden box, ornate and beautiful with black lacquered sides painted with colorful dragons in flight and framed with delicate pink blossoms. The box looked more like a treasure chest than a box filled with articles for healing. Janie deposited it on the rock beside Graham, then backed away as Duncan stepped forward. She motioned toward the handle of the domed lid. "I can tell you about the poultices her ladyship packed, if you like. Her ladyship's mother taught her all about herbs and such. She was quite the healer according to m'lady."

Graham gave Duncan the slightest shake of his head. No way would he trust the girl not to poison him by whatever was in that box.

Duncan waved her away. "No need. We've bandaged each other for years."

"Go back to the wagons, girl," Marsden instructed. "The Marches look to be ready with the horses harnessed."

Janie nodded, bowed her head, then shuffled her way back to the wagons.

"'Twill be interesting to see which direction they choose," Graham commented, a grunt escaping him as Duncan cinched the bandage tighter around his waist. "I need to breathe, man."

"Ye need to stop bleeding," Duncan shot back. "Stop your yammering."

Graham squinted up at the sky. They were losing daylight fast, and a storm looked to be coming. "Hurry it up. We need to be on our way." A storm might slow the thieving kidnappers but it would slow them as well.

Duncan helped him don his shirt, but the day had grown too warm and muggy for the waistcoat. Besides, the close-fitting garment rubbing against his wound would irritate it. He'd ride as a Highlander was meant to ride—kilt, *léine*, boots, and weapons. Nothing else was needed. Graham rolled up the waistcoat and stuffed it in one of the bags on the back of his saddle. Taking a long, hard swig from the leather flask he kept tucked into a hidden pocket of the saddle, Graham closed his eyes and savored the healing burn of the fine MacCoinnich whisky. Fortified by the alcohol, he mounted his horse and nodded to the others. "Let's be about this then. 'Tis a fine day for vengeance."

Graham set off down the road at a fast pace, scanning the landscape as he rode. He felt certain the highwaymen would stick to the roadway through the pass. The gullies, fissures, and overgrowth covering the landscape both above and below the path made any other plan impossible. Every jamming hit of his mount's hooves on the hardpacked ground shook him, sending jolts of pain through his side.

Duncan thundered up beside him. "They've chosen *Tor Ruadh*," he shouted with a jerk of his thumb back toward the wagons.

Graham didn't care. All that concerned him was Mercy.

Marsden rode on his other side, his pale face fixed on their surroundings. "Look there," he shouted just as Graham's gaze alit on the same sight before them.

Ryū. Mercy's horse. The beast stood to the right of the road, facing them, and pawing at the ground as though about to charge them.

Graham pulled to a stop as did Marsden, Duncan, and the wagons, still some distance behind them. "Could be a trap," Graham said more to himself than the others.

"Why would they set a trap this close to where they left us?" Duncan asked. "We've not traveled but a few miles."

"More to the point," Captain Marsden chimed in. "How on earth could they set a trap with that uncooperative beast? That animal borders on demonic if the Lady Mercy isn't present to control it."

"Maybe she is present," Graham said as he dismounted with slow movements to keep from startling the horse. A gnawing dread filled him. What if the kidnapping had gone horribly wrong? There had been that lone shot he'd heard yesterday. What if the fools had foiled their own plans and killed her? Graham held up a hand and looked back at Marsden and Duncan. "Stay here and dinna let those damn wagons any closer. I dinna want them privy to anything I might find."

"I'll ride back and advise them," Marsden volunteered, turning his horse and urging it onward in a fast cantor without waiting for Graham's agreement.

"I'll wait here for ye, brother," Duncan said in a quiet, somber tone. Duncan knew what troubled him, understood what he feared he'd find hidden by the thick sedge.

Hands held out to calm the horse, Graham eased closer. "Steady now, Ryū. Ye ken I care about your mistress just as much as ye do."

The magnificent horse snorted and took a warning stomp toward Graham. He tossed his head and stomped again.

Graham stood still, stretching to peer closer at the overgrown tangle of saplings, sedge, and heather that the horse guarded. He needed to get closer and search through the foliage if the horse would allow it.

Ryū split the air with a growling whinny, snorted again, reared, then danced forward a short distance before returning to his post beside the bushes.

The bushes were too still. Good news couldn't possibly await him. His sense of doom growing heavier, Graham swallowed hard and sidled closer. "I'm here now, Ryū. Ye've done your duty, lad. Step aside so I can find her."

Ryū grumbled out a low, deep warning but eased back a half step.

Keeping the horse in his periphery, Graham stole quick glances at the thicket beside the road. He saw nothing but the rugged wilderness the Highlands and God had seen fit to put there. There was no helping it. Danger of a stomping beast or not, he had to search through the overgrowth with greater care. Something there was the source of Ryū's distress. What could it be other than Mercy's body?

He waded into the thicket, dreading what instinct told him he would find. He pulled aside the vegetation, then dropped to his knees, and closed his eyes, an onslaught of raw, ragged emotion threatening to overcome him.

Mercy lay on her side, curled into a tight ball as though she'd returned to her mother's womb.

Crossing himself as he opened his eyes, Graham crouched down beside her. Heart breaking and rage flaring, a groaning sob escaped him. She lay so still. So serene. She appeared to have gone peacefully.

"I canna bear this," he choked out in a hoarse whisper. "Forgive me, m'love, for failing ye."

Her long, dark lashes rested on her pale cheeks. The pink of her sweet lips had already faded.

With a shaking hand, Graham reached out and brushed her hair back from her face.

"No!" Mercy screeched as she sprang to life, kicking and punching, rolling Graham back on his haunches, then off balance to his arse.

Graham crashed backward, floundering in the thicket, elated but gasping from the pain splitting through his middle. "Mercy, lass! 'Tis me!"

"Graham?"

That sweet voice he'd feared he'd never hear again. Graham managed to upright himself, half-wondering if he'd died and gone to Heaven in search of his sweet Mercy.

He caught her up as she jumped toward him, balling up in his embrace as though she feared he'd somehow decide to let her go. Graham held her tight, burying his face in her tangled mess of hair, grunting as she thumped her foot against his bandaged injury when she wound her legs around him.

"Your wound!" Mercy pulled back enough to cradle his face in her hands and stare at him with such panic and concern that his heart nearly burst. She yanked at his tunic, wiggling in his lap to bare his midriff and examine him for herself. If she maintained such behavior, it wouldn't be the stab wound concerning her. His man parts ached with the need for such attention and concern. She smiled and blew out a relieved sigh. "You are bandaged well." She returned her hands to either side of his face and pressed her forehead to his. "I was so afraid for you," she whispered. "I feared you lost to me. I feared my Highlander lost."

"Lore a'mighty, woman, ye feared for me when all I feared was that I'd lost ye." Graham smoothed both hands up her back and pulled her to him, his lips brushing hers as he whispered, "I feared ye dead, Mercy. My heart near broke when I saw ye lying there in the weeds. So still. So pale."

She kissed him, soft lips nibbling at his, pulling and tasting with a frantic urgency. "We are found. All that matters is we are found."

Graham tangled his fingers up into her hair, cradling her close as he responded to her kisses with all the passion, fear, and madness that had nearly drowned him over the past two days.

Ryū whinnied and snorted then, from the sounds of it, the stallion bucked and stomped in a circle.

Mercy broke the kiss and held aside the grasses, revealing her beloved horse's inquisitive nose. "Ryū...my guardian dragon. He must have found me and watched over me after I collapsed."

"Aye." Graham held out his knuckles for the horse to snuffle. "That he did. Wicked, devoted beast that he is. Thank God he loves ye as he does."

"Brother!" Duncan's concerned shout made its way to them. "Is she well? I can't get any closer for this damned horse."

"Aye, she is well," Graham called out. "And she is mine," he added as he pulled Mercy into another kiss.

CHAPTER THIRTEEN

"WHAT IS THAT?"

"A poultice of plantain and knitbone." Mercy pressed the cool, soggy mash of herbs to Graham's wound and secured them with a fresh bandage. "Drink your herbal. It will help." She cast a nervous glance around the area. Every noise, every rustling branch or fluttering leaf sent a fresh charge of panic coursing through her. The only thing giving her strength and control to get through this situation was the fact that Graham appeared to be faring well despite his injury.

"Easy, lass. Duncan and Marsden stand watch. We're a damn sight safer than we were." Graham took a sip of the meadowsweet and pine needle tea she'd prepared and made a face. He spit it out, wiped his mouth with the back of his hand, and handed the cup back to her. "I'd rather have whisky, aye? No more of that swill."

Mercy pushed the cup back into his hand. "All of it. And swallow this time. Then whisky." She rose from beside him and tossed out the remains of the pine bark brew she'd steeped to clean out his wound. The angry redness around the cut concerned her. Infection could set in and steal Graham from her. Who knew where Gobs had used that knife before burying it in Graham's side?

She walked a few feet ahead of the wagons and looked around, searching both the road and woods for any sign of Tracker and his men. They'd be back. She'd overheard them say so whilst hiding in the shallow fissure that had saved her life. Greed pushed them to find her. Mercy knew all too well how dangerous greed could be.

The touch of a hand on her arm made her jump to one side.

"Mercy," Graham said in a hushed tone with hands held aloft. Concern and heartache filled his gaze. "Come back to the wagon, lass. Ye promised me ye'd eat if I let ye tend my wound first."

"They said they'd be back." She shuddered as she spoke the words aloud, the murderers' voices echoing through her mind like the ominous tolling of a death knell. She hugged herself as she nodded toward the end of the pass. "If they don't come here to find me, they'll lay in wait for us at the mouth of the glen." She swallowed hard. "Maybe even both. There's five. They could split up to better their odds." She shook her head, panic mounting and threatening to drown her. "We are trapped, Graham, trapped for certain."

He gathered her close, tucked her head to his chest, and held her, shushing and stroking her hair as though she were a child suffering from a bad dream. She closed her eyes and fisted her hands in his tunic, clutching the material tight to her face as she hugged against him. She pulled in a deep breath. He smelled of pine, herbs, and safety. A tentative sense of calm flickered within her, strengthening with every thump of Graham's heart against her cheek. She no longer fought alone. She must not give up now.

"Come. Ye must eat." Graham shifted her into the curve of his arm and walked her back to the wagons.

Janie shuffled toward her with a lowered head, a small metal platter holding bread and a cup clutched between her hands. "Bread, m'lady," she said with a subdued curtsy, bowing again as she extended the platter. "And Cook made a cup of herb tea for yourself with what little hot water was left after you mixed Master MacCoinnich's poultices."

Graham had ordered no fires, but Mercy had insisted on heating water with the small brazier Cook had in her wagon. They couldn't risk the telltale smoke of a campfire but using the brazier inside the wagon had been safe enough. They'd covered the chimney with a wet cloth to capture what little smoke the coals generated.

Mercy stared at the platter. All she wanted right now was for Graham to hold her.

He picked up the cup and pressed it into her hands. "Drink, lass—please."

The warm liquid, strong and bitter, settled her better than she thought it would. She cupped the tea between both hands, leaning into the safety of Graham's embrace. If not for his arm around her, she'd surely shatter into a thousand pieces and scatter across the winds. She took another sip, swallowed, then pulled in a deep breath. "Forgive me for such weakness," she whispered. "Mama would scold me for having so little strength."

Graham selected the largest chunk of bread from the platter Janie held extended, then waved the girl away before pressing the crust to Mercy's mouth. "Ye're a braw, canty lass, and I'd have ye no other way. Eat now. I promise ye, your mother's smiling down from Heaven right now. Proud of the daughter she raised to be such a fighter."

Graham's words triggered a smile, strengthened her. Mama would be proud of her escape. Akio would have cheered her and shouted, *"Well done!"*. Now all that remained was to foil the snare Tracker and his men had laid.

"They said they'd watch the mouth of the pass. Tracker said it when he gave up the search for me because of nightfall." She forced herself to finish the chunk of day-old bread even though it tasted dry as dust. Washing down the final bite with what was left of her herbal tea, she pressed a hand to her chest and inhaled a calming breath, praying the basic sustenance would stay down. More of Tracker's conversation came back to her. "He knows of your clan. He fears your brother."

"Good." Graham guided her to sit on a wooden crate that had yet to be put back in the wagons. "He should fear all MacCoinnichs."

Raking her fingers through her tangled hair, Mercy picked out sticks and leaves as she spoke. "But that also means he knows where we're headed whether we go forward or turn back. He knows our destination to be *Tor Ruadh* or London. All he has to do is place men at either end of the pass."

"I can tend to your hair, m'lady," Janie said with a cautious easing out from between the wagons. She stood a few feet away with Mercy's hair combs in one hand and a brush in the other. "If you see fit to allow it."

Mercy studied the girl, debating the safety of Janie being anywhere close. She no longer trusted anyone she'd brought from Claxton House other than her horse.

"I would never hurt you, mistress," Janie whispered, her face pale and eyes filled with sorrow. "I swear it."

Mercy looked to Graham, at a loss for what to do. She wanted to trust Janie, but would such trust endanger them all again?

"Show me what ye carry, girl. Open your hands." Graham waved her closer, then picked through the combs and ran his thumb across the white bristles of the brush. He turned back to Mercy. "She appears safe enough if ye wish to allow her to help ye with your hair." He gave the girl a stern look and patted the butt of the pistol tucked in the front of his belt. "Ye will die if ye harm her. Understood?"

Janie jerked her chin downward in a quick nod as she curtsied. "Yes, sir."

Mercy felt some better but not much as she motioned Janie forward. Giving Graham a smile, she sat straighter and resettled her long, tangled locks down her back. "A simple braid, Janie. Down my back to keep the length out of the way. There'll be no more pinning it up in the latest coiffure."

"Yes, m'lady," Janie whispered as she set to the task.

"No fire means little for supper," Cook announced from the doorway of her wagon. "Two days since I cooked proper. Meat's gone but there's bread and cheese. Some vegetables. An apple or two, as well."

"'Twill be plenty," Graham said, then cupped Mercy's chin in one hand and gave her a smile that filled her heart and sent a tingling warmth through her. "I have all I need right here." He brushed a light kiss filled with promise across her parted lips.

Mercy pressed a hand to her chest. Such words. Such an intimate touch. As though no one else around them existed. And it was real—not a guise to fool the others. She smiled up at him, nestling her face deeper into his calloused palm as she pressed his hand closer to her cheek. "Yes. I as well."

Cook blew out a disgruntled huff, rolled her eyes, then closed herself up in her wagon.

Janie gave a pat to her hair, then stepped away. "All done, m'lady." With shoulders slumped and eyes downcast, she shuffled over to Cook's wagon and rapped on the door. "'Tis Janie. Let me in."

The door latch rattled. "Let yourself in," Cook barked.

Janie climbed into the wagon and closed the door. The hardware rattled as the lock settled in place.

Percy and Doughal appeared from around the wagons. "Horses and wagons are ready as they'll ever be. Leave here now or wait 'til morning?" Percy asked.

"Leave now," Graham said as he held out a hand to Mercy. "Wagons only," he added.

Mercy held tight to Graham's hand. "We're staying here?"

"Aye," Graham said, his tone vague. "For now."

Percy glanced at his son, then pointed a narrow-eyed glare at Graham before turning to Mercy. "Which way, your ladyship?"

"Graham?" Mercy wasn't quite sure what Graham had in mind, but she sensed he had a plan in the works to ensure their successful escape from the pass. He'd had her bundle a change of clothes in a blanket and strap it to the back of her saddle. It was almost as though he expected the wagons to end up at a different destination.

"Through to the glen," Graham said. "*Tor Ruadh* lies to the north-west. Once ye pass the crofts at the other side of the glen, look to Ben Nevis. Ye canna miss it."

"Through to the glen," Percy repeated. The old man swallowed hard and scrubbed his hand over his mouth as he glanced back at the wagons, then over at the road. "And what of those men? The high-waymen?"

"That's between you and them," Graham replied in a chilling tone.

A gnawing uncertainty filled Mercy as a range of unreadable expressions flashed across both Percy and Doughal's faces. Those two had never been disloyal—at least not so far as she knew. But they had been with the household for as long as she could remember. She faced Graham, turning her back toward the wagon drivers to shield her words. "Are you certain?" she whispered. The thought of sending the two into the clutches of Tracker and his men weighed heavy upon her conscience.

Graham lowered his chin in a single nod.

Duncan and Marsden rejoined the group, their looks grim as they lead their mounts by their reins, weaving in between the three wagons.

"Three wait at the entrance to the glen," Duncan reported. "Robbie and the skinny, rat-faced man were on the east side of the road. A few miles from here. Found them walking the ditches and headed this way."

Praise God that Graham had found her first. Mercy clenched a fist to her chest, pressing hard to calm the pounding of her heart. She swallowed and forced herself to remain calm. "How long until the two of them reach here?"

"They willna reach here, m'lady," Duncan said with a reassuring smile.

Marsden gave her a nod as he clapped a hand on Duncan's shoulder. "Young MacCoinnich here turned out to be quite the archer with the bows and arrows the dead men from the attack no longer needed. I assure you, m'lady, those two are returned to the dust from whence they came."

Before Mercy could comment, Graham held up his hand and turned to old man March and his son. "On now. To the glen, aye? Take Cook and the girl with ye."

"But, Janie." Mercy squeezed Graham's arm. Uncertainty filled her. Had Janie really been a part of her betrayal? What if she hadn't? What would happen to her? "Surely, not Janie. Are you—"

Graham cut her off with a curt shake of his head, his gaze intent on the senior March. "All of ye. Now."

The old man glowered at him, hands fisted, then jerked away. "Yes, sir," he shot back over his shoulder. As he passed Cook's wagon, he thumped a fist against the wooden boards.

A small square window hinged in one of the doors popped open, revealing Cook's scowling face. "What?"

"On our way," March said with a wave toward the road. "To the glen."

Cook's gaze shifted to Mercy and Graham. "The girl and me, too?"

"Aye," Graham ordered. "Now."

One by one, the wagons lined up on the road. Mercy watched them until they disappeared around the bend, the rattling of Cook's pots and pans still echoing back to her through the trees.

Guilt and frustration filled her, sending the nauseating burn of bile into the back of her throat. How could things have come to this? Tossing innocent people to those who would do them harm. Struggling to tamp down the doubt Graham's decision triggered, Mercy turned and faced him. "I assume it's safe to speak openly now? What is your plan?"

Graham nodded. "Higher ground for us. A better view of the glen that way, ye ken?"

"The wagons are bait." Mercy wound her horse's reins around one hand and started toward the far side of the road, the injustice of what they'd done choking her. What if they had judged them all wrong?

"Aye." Graham took his place beside her, pulling his mount behind him. He took hold of her arm and stopped her. "But dinna fash yourself, lass. If my instincts are right, those wagons will get through the glen unscathed. We didna feed your people to the wolves—we returned them to their own kind."

"You feel certain they all conspired against me?"

Graham gave her a sympathetic look and brushed the backs of his fingers along her cheek. "I believe so."

Lifting her chin, Mercy swallowed and stared ahead. She'd been snubbed and cast aside all her life, but the disloyalty still stung, especially from Janie. But she knew Graham, or thought she did after all these days together. He wouldn't make such a decision without reason. "How are you so certain?"

Jaw tightening as he scowled at the difficult route ahead of them, Graham paused and faced her. "Those men that took ye lashed me, Duncan, and Marsden to the wagon wheels of the flatbeds. Gagged us as well. The Marches, Cook, and Janie were put inside Cook's wagon with a bar across the outside of the rear door. The one called Gobs made out like they'd run out of rope."

"Locked in a wagon with food and water," she observed. The burden of Mercy's guilt grew lighter. It disappeared completely when revelation hit. "Janie or Doughal, either one, could have shimmied out the front door behind the driver's seat. Janie did it to escape Cook the day the woman lost her temper and threatened to boot her out the back of the wagon."

"Exactly." Graham marched onward, huffing and grimacing as he strode across the rough ground. "I dinna ken if they were instructed to wait until we were dead to seek out the horses and leave or what. All I know for certain was they were well accommodated by their captors."

Mercy stomped forward, more determined than ever to overcome her father's vile plan.

Marsden took his post on the other side of Graham, but Duncan moved to take lead of the group. "Pardon me. 'Tis my hope to get within arrow range of the enemy, m'lady," he said as he pushed past Mercy. He looked over at Graham. "Three of them. Four of us. The odds are with us, brother."

Mercy held up a hand and brought them all to a standstill before they continued the arduous climb of the rough hillside. "Please. Let me have the spare bow you found." Akio had taught her to shoot, even said her accuracy had to be a gift from the ancestors. Her brother was a critical tutor. He never would have said such if he didn't feel it was true. "I promise you, I can shoot."

Duncan glanced at Graham before answering, then rounded his horse and pulled free one of the longbows tied to the side of his saddle. With it, he handed her a *dorlach*, a quiver full of arrows. "Betwixt the two of us, m'lady, perhaps we can better our odds still."

Mercy pulled the strap of the *dorlach* over her head and slung the longbow over one shoulder. She felt better with a weapon. Empowered.

"I dinna care much for that plan," Graham said as they resumed their journey, trudging through the rugged terrain.

Mercy didn't answer, just concentrated on picking her way up the side of the mountain and leading Ryū across the dangerous ground. Once they reached the peak of the ridge, they continued leading the horses rather than riding due to the hazardous footing.

As the sun slipped below the horizon, Graham held up a hand. "We'll bed down here 'til sunrise."

Mercy glanced around, doubt filling her. Few trees grew at this elevation. Whatever shelter they hoped to find would be in the form of boulders and the land. What if Tracker and his men discovered them?

"Marsden and I will stand watch. We can sleep when we reach *Tor Ruadh*," Duncan said. He nodded to the north. "The wagons will have reached the glen by now, so the bastards might risk a search for us through the night."

"But they won't know we're here." Mercy clenched her horse's reins so tight her nails bit into her palms.

"They'll know we're close," Graham said as he walked a slow circle around the plateau and scanned their surroundings. "We canna be certain how much information the others gave them once they caught up with them."

Mercy glanced up at the darkening sky. A faint winking of stars already spattered the blue-black curtain of night falling. The dark of the moon. That would help. Mercy stumbled across the loose rocks in her path.

"Easy there, lass." Graham's comforting voice wrapped around her and held her steady. His hand slid down her arm and he took the reins. "Wait here. I'll tie the horses to that bit of scrub over there and then we'll bed ourselves down, aye?"

Bed ourselves down. The ability to speak escaped her, so she released the reins without comment. She wet her lips and clenched her hands together. She'd never lain with a man. In fact, Graham was the only man she'd ever kissed, the only man she'd ever embraced. The memory of their swim together flashed hot through her, stealing the breath from her lungs.

Pressing her legs tight together, she rubbed one against the other, remembering the slick feel of Graham's skin against hers when she'd brushed against him in the water. She looked around, squinting to make out shapes in the darkness. But here? While chased by murdering thieves? With Marsden and Duncan standing watch but a few feet away? And what should she do? Mama had given her little advice other than to say Mercy would know what to do when the time came.

"Come, lass." Graham tucked her hand into the crook of his arm and led her to a horseshoe-shaped outcropping of stones. The massive boulders, bleached white by nature's harsh kiss, seemed to give off an eerie, blue-white glow in the darkness. Graham motioned to a darker patch of ground abutted to the stones. "The moss willna cushion us much, but 'twill be softer than bedding down on hard-packed dirt or stone."

"It'll be fine, I'm sure." Mercy moved to sit. A faint, hitching gasp escaped her. A bruised stiffness had set in, a painful reminder of her brutal escape.

Graham took hold of her hands. "Lass?"

Whilst she couldn't make out his expression in the darkness, she heard the concern in his voice. "I'm quite all right," she said as she settled atop the spongy moss. "Just a little sore from where I jumped from the horse."

"Jumped from a horse," Graham repeated.

"It was my only means of escape."

Sitting down beside her, Graham scooted them both back until he sat with his back leaned against the stone, reclining but partially upright. He held out his arm and waited. "Come, lass. I ken it's no' proper for a lady to do such, but let me hold ye whilst ye sleep. I swear I'll do nothing to dishonor ye."

Mercy found his words mildly disappointing. Hadn't Graham professed his feelings for her? Hadn't he as good as asked her to be his wife? She touched the cut on her throat, then her bruised cheek and sore mouth. Her fingers found cuts, scratches, a split lip, and even a lump the size of a goose's egg just above her temple. Had she become so hideous he didn't want her anymore? Or was it because she'd brought nothing but ill-luck to him ever since stepping into her presence?

Snuggling up against him, Mercy curled into his side and rested her head upon his chest. "Have I become too much trouble to you? Do you no longer wish to have me?" She clenched his shirt in her fist and pressed it close to her mouth, holding her breath until he answered.

Graham kissed the top of her head and hugged her closer. His steady heartbeat ratcheted up a notch. "Ye're my heart, Mercy, and I want ye with a fierceness that scares me." He shifted with a deep breath, then groaned it out. "But I willna have the first time I love ye be on a patch of rock in the wilderness and rushed for fear murderers are nearly upon us."

Mercy lifted her head and looked up at him, thanking God for sending her such a man. "I haven't frightened you then? Driven you away by all the trials that follow me?"

Graham softly traced the curve of her jaw as he peered down at her for a long, breathless moment. Lacing his fingers into her hair, he cupped her face in his hand and kissed her with a tenderness that threatened to make her sob. He drew back and brushed a kiss to her forehead, then cuddled her back to his chest. "The only thing I fear in this world, m'love, is losing ye. I swear upon every breath I draw, m'heart is ever yours."

"I love you," Mercy whispered, hot tears of joy and relief wetting her face.

"And I love ye as well," Graham brushed the back of his fingers across her face, wiping her tears away. "Rest now, love. When we reach *Tor Ruadh,* I'll make ye mine good and proper. I swear it."

CHAPTER FOURTEEN

HER SOFT, REGULAR breathing shifted against Graham's chest, and he thanked God for it. He'd feared her lost. Tortured. Murdered. He'd feared never seeing her again. A weary smile overtook him. Holding her like this was a tender blessing of which he'd never tire. He yearned for an even greater closeness but not now. Not until he had her safe and true happiness shone in her eyes. He wanted the shadows of worry and fear gone. He would make this woman happy. She deserved such.

He pulled in another deep breath and let it out with just as much care. His side pained him some as he eased out from under her. He held his breath to keep from grunting against the aching twinge and waking her. Mercy gave a soft whimper and curled into a ball on her side on the moss. Graham held fast, frozen in place until she relaxed back into sleep.

Where the sky joined the earth had taken on a softer coloring, the yellow-white hue of the sun about to peer above the horizon. 'Twas time to make short work of Tracker and his men and clear the path to *Tor Ruadh*. A few steps away from where Mercy slept, Duncan and Marsden joined him. Graham put a finger to his lips, pointed toward her, then motioned for them to keep their voices low.

"Ye were right. The wagons went into the glen with no trouble.

We found Tracker and his men. They set up camp inside the tree line beside the road at the mouth of the pass, but there's no sign of the wagons anywhere. They had to have gone ahead." Duncan scrubbed a hand across the stubble covering his jaw, then stifled a yawn.

"Do you think they've already arrived at *Tor Ruadh?*" Marsden asked.

Graham snorted at having allowed the handful of traitors escape without a good horsewhipping for the lot of them. "If they go to *Tor Ruadh*, I'll be more than a little surprised. My guess is they've gone to Fort William to send a report to Edsbury."

Marsden turned and scowled at the glen below. "I find it considerably disturbing to think Lady Mercy traveled with not a single ally from her own household. Even her lady's maid turned traitor and deceived her." Marsden shook his head, his fierce feelings painting his cheeks with patches of scarlet visible even in the soft gloaming light of early morning. "Without a doubt, it is utterly reprehensible."

Graham agreed—but in much stronger terms. Now, however, was not the time to go into it. He nodded toward the exit of the pass located just below them. "By Mercy's count, there's but three of them now. God willing, we'll make short work of this and be at *Tor Ruadh* in time for the midday meal. I'll no' have those rabid curs nipping at our heels any longer."

"Aye," Duncan raised his longbow as though toasting their success. "Let's be about this then. Catriona found a new cook from the village, and the woman makes damn fine meat pies."

"I say," Marsden said with an excited bob of his head and a pat to his belly. "That does sound tempting."

Graham rolled his eyes and shook his head at the two and their distractions. They sounded like two old women. He waved them forward, creeping down the rugged terrain of the steep hillside with as little noise as possible. Boulders assisted in their descent, providing welcomed shadows. He made use of anything for cover to keep

Tracker and his men unaware.

Graham moved with raw, burning determination, rage fueling every move. There was no telling what the Marches or the two women had reported to Tracker, and it wouldn't take a stretch of the imagination for the murdering thieves to figure out that Graham and the others had taken to high ground.

He paused behind the muddy, tangled mass of an uprooted tree. Crouching low, he looked back and checked the progress of Marsden and Duncan. A fluttering of movement among some bushes higher to the right caught his eye. He squinted and blinked, staring at the spot, willing whatever had moved to make itself known, but nothing moved again. Pinching the bridge of his nose and rubbing the corners of his eyes, Graham sent up a silent prayer. *Now is no' the time for me to fail. Please clear my sight and make my aim true.* He glanced heavenward and crossed himself, then waved Marsden and Duncan forward.

Marsden and Duncan scrabbled to his side and pressed up against the trunk of the fallen tree.

"Did ye see movement above us?" Duncan asked, frowning back at the same spot that had concerned Graham.

Graham studied the spot again but still saw nothing out of the ordinary. Dawn was almost full upon them. Mayhap that was it. Shadow and light could play tricks on a man's eyes, especially when fraught with weariness and hunger for revenge. If someone lurked above them, they'd surely see them now since the higher ground had the sun full upon it. "I thought I had." He wouldn't lie to his brother, and it made him feel some better that Duncan had experienced the same. "It must ha' been the play of shadows."

"I think not, gentlemen," Marsden whispered, peering up, his attention focused on something farther down the hillside. He pointed. "Look just there."

Graham crawled to Marsden's side. Resting both hands atop the rough bark of the fallen tree, he stretched and looked over the log. A raging flood of emotions slammed into him at the sight of Mercy with an arrow nocked and ready to release, inching ever closer to the men camped below. "What the hell is she doing?"

"I think that's obvious, brother," Duncan remarked in a tone that tempted Graham to turn around and knock the man on his arse. "I thought she was still asleep," he added.

"So, did I!" Graham pulled his pistol from his belt and readied it to fire. "Damned, stubborn woman!" He sprang up and charged down the hillside. He had to get to the men before Mercy caught their attention and drew fire. Duncan and Marsden followed close behind.

As he reached the soft, loamy ground of the forest and entered the trees, shouts shattered the morning's silence. Graham ran toward the noise, ducking and dodging around the trees. Gunfire split the air. He spotted the white smoke of spent powder filtering up through the leaves and veered toward it.

The one called Gobs teetered into view, two arrows embedded deep in his chest and his side. Something hissed past Graham and another arrow, one from Duncan's bow, drove deep into Gobs's neck and took the monstrosity of a man down.

"Kill that bitch, now!" A raspy voice Graham had never heard before came from just up ahead. "Kill her, Flynn! No gold worth this!"

It had to be the one Mercy had called Tracker. She'd mentioned the man's unusual voice. Graham spotted him dressed all in black, crouching behind the trunk of an ancient oak. He leveled his pistol, took aim, then sent Tracker to the hell he deserved.

One left. Graham tucked his spent weapon back in his belt and readied his second pistol, watching his surroundings as he eased around the outcropping of limestone marking the clearing. The woods were quiet, but they'd yet to find the bald-headed man with the earrings, the one called Flynn.

Leaves crunched and twigs snapped to his left. Graham spun about, relief almost taking him to his knees as Mercy eased out from behind a tree, an arrow nocked and ready. Jaw locked and body tensed, Mercy made a single nod toward another mound of limestone boulders across the clearing. "My aim is rusty," she whispered as she joined Graham. "I aimed for between his shoulder blades but missed." She smiled as she leaned up against the rocks. "But sitting a horse will be most impossible for him until he rips out that arrow."

Graham didn't know whether to laugh because she'd shot Flynn in the arse or shake her because she had joined the fray. "What the hell are ye doing here, woman?"

Fine, dark brows arched to her hairline, she looked at him like he'd lost his mind. "Revenge," she said in a cold, hard tone. "I am not a helpless lady born to cower and wait to be saved. Society never accepted me by their standards, so I decided to create my own—in Mama and Akio's memory." Her look softened. "I hope that doesn't diminish your opinion of me. If it does, Graham, then I am sorry— because this is who I am."

With a shake of his head, Graham stared at Mercy, struggling to find the words to tell her all he felt. He reached out and touched her arm. "Ye could do nothing to lower yourself in my sight, but I must admit, ye've found many a way to scare the living hell out of me." He ground his teeth, doing his best not to sound like a scolding bastard. "I need ye safe, love. I canna have ye joining me in battle, especially no' sneaking about and mixing in when I think ye safe elsewhere."

"But—"

He held up a hand. "Ye no longer fight in this world alone, Mercy. Do ye understand me? Ye're no' alone."

Mercy stared at him, then bowed her head as she removed the arrow from her bow and returned it the quiver. She smiled, her eyes shimmering with unshed tears. She opened her mouth to speak but was cut off by a bullet ricocheting off the rocks in front in them.

"I'm not dead yet!" Flynn shouted from across the clearing.

"The hell ye're not." Graham charged from around the boulder, careened around the trees, then dropped Flynn where he stood leaning against the rocks.

Duncan, Marsden, and Mercy eased out from where they'd taken cover, moving with care as they searched the area. Captain Marsden bent and scooped up a pair of saddlebags, rummaged through the contents, and pulled out a parchment with a familiar wax seal. He unfolded the letter, his scowl darkening as he read the missive. "It appears your father gave the men a promissory note payable once they'd completed their task." Marsden shook his head as he refolded the letter. "Apparently, even he didn't trust the miscreants he'd hired to dispose of his daughter." His jowls tightened and his face reddened even more. "Deplorable man."

Mercy shook her head. "What those *miscreants* didn't realize is that my father tricked them. If his claim that Jameson Campbell owned his soul was true, then he had no gold to give them. They would never be paid and could do little to recoup the monies owed." She shrugged and gave a sad smile as she looked around the clearing. "What is the old saying? You can't get blood from a stone?"

"Then who would have paid us?" Duncan asked with an irritated look directed at Graham. "Ye said there'd be as much gold as we could carry."

"The king," Graham said. "Ye forget His Majesty is a part of this, too."

Marsden frowned, stared at the promissory note, then shook his head. "But His Majesty seemed genuinely concerned for her ladyship's welfare when he spoke of securing her a suitable match. He appeared deeply troubled over the additional information of Lady Mercy's situation provided him by the duke." He waved his stubby fingers to encompass the whole of the camp. "None of this madness fits the king's demeanor at all. I truly believe he'd be most enraged to discover such an barbarous plot regarding the lady."

"His Majesty plays a good game," Graham said as he hugged an arm around Mercy, his heart lifting when she nestled her head in the crook of his shoulder. "He controls his courtiers like a chess master moves his pawns." He pressed a kiss to Mercy's forehead and held her tighter, blowing out a heavy sigh as his gaze scanned the encampment.

"What's wrong?" Mercy asked, pulling back and studying him. She motioned toward the still form of Flynn. "He was the last."

"Nay, love." Graham shook his head. "The traitors from your own household are still free to do their evil mischief, and we've no idea what that mischief might be." It cut him to the quick to see how his words hurt her, but it couldn't be helped. Mercy was still in danger.

Who knew what the Marches, Cook, and Janie would say when they reached anyone willing to lend a sympathetic ear and report back to the king? Graham very much doubted they'd heard the last from the duke.

"Your clan," Mercy whispered, drawing a shaking hand to her brow. "What trouble might they cause your clan? How will Father misconstrue this to his own benefit?"

"We must make haste and warn them." Graham took hold of her hand and started the climb back up the hillside to where they'd left their horses tied. Determination spurred him on—that, and the knowledge that as soon as they made it to Clan MacCoinnich keep, he'd be talking to Father William about performing a wedding. It was time to make his protection of Lady Mercy Claxton official and more importantly—permanent.

CHAPTER FIFTEEN

MERCY OPENED HER eyes to the road ahead, her feeling of contentment fleeting, leaving her as quick as the wind. A smattering of dwellings filled this end of the glen. One might even call the place a village. A village protected and governed by Graham's eldest brother, Alexander, chieftain to Clan MacCoinnich. She pressed the knot along her hairline and ran her fingers down the scrapes and cuts along her cheek. What would Graham's people think of her arriving in such a state?

A meandering flock of sheep *bah'd* and barged into their path, wandering in and out between the horses, oblivious to the riders. Children laughed and played around the squat houses of mud bricks, stacked stones, and thatched roofs. Mercy could almost see the news of their arrival rippling through the village, spreading among the people. She could tell who had heard of their passing through by the way the people emerged from their houses or ceased their outside chores and waved for their children to come in close.

Women with baskets propped high on their hips climbed up from the low banks of a nearby burn, its crystal-clear waters sparkling across the riverbed stones as it snaked alongside the road and disappeared beneath a short, wooden bridge arched up ahead. The washer women shaded their eyes and studied the riders as they rode past. Mercy swallowed hard. Their scrutiny pricked across her skin like crows pecking flesh from her bones. No one smiled or waved. No one spoke. Was Graham unknown to his brother's people? Was he disliked? Or was it because of her?

Graham drew up close, riding at her side. "Dinna let them trouble ye, lass. They're still leery of folks they dinna ken, but they'll come 'round. They've been through much, and it takes time for deep wounds to heal."

"Graham!" A pretty, young woman with hair as bright and flaming as newly forged copper ran toward them, waving both hands high in the air. "Graham! Ye've a'ready returned!"

A pang of jealousy stabbed through Mercy just as surely as if the girl greeting Graham had shot her through with an arrow. Mercy sat taller in the saddle and lifted her chin. "You have one villager thrilled to see you."

Three large, white geese raced along behind the woman, trotting after her as fast as they could waddle. Following the geese, were two goats, a dog, and three laughing children.

Graham smiled and waved back at the girl. "Ahh...that's Gretna. She loves everyone and they love her."

"I see." Loved by everyone. Mercy couldn't begin to imagine how that might feel. She pulled in a deep breath and did her best to shove her insecurities aside. A pang of remorse flashed through her like a subtle scolding. Others shunned her without knowing her, and she hated it. How hypocritical was it of her to shun others on sight? She would give this girl a chance. She ground her teeth as Gretna ran along beside Graham's mount, smiling and laughing.

"Meet Lady Mercy Claxton, Gretna." Graham pulled his mount to a stop and held out a hand to Mercy.

"A pleasure, m'lady." Gretna gave a curtsy, then drew closer, shading her eyes with one hand as she peered up at her. The girl's head tilted to one side and her reddish blonde brows drew together over the startling blue of her eyes.

Mercy flitted a hand to her hair and forced a nervous smile. "Forgive my appearance. I'm afraid our trip became quite the adventure over the past few days."

Gretna's eyes widened. "Oh no, m'lady." She shook her head. "I didna mean to stare at ye like a rude bairn. I was just thinking how those bruises and scrapes of yours could use some tending." She turned and gave Graham a narrow-eyed glare. "Did ye no' take the parcel of arnica and other herbs I sent for your journey? They wouldha helped your lady here."

"Ahh…"

Mercy held her breath to keep from laughing out loud. She'd never seen Graham in such a state. The man looked like he actually feared the young slip of a girl.

"'Ahh's' arse. I'm ashamed of ye, Graham MacCoinnich! Ye know better, or at least ye should." Gretna rolled her eyes and shook her head before returning her attention to Mercy. "Once ye're settled, tell Mistress Catriona that old Elena, she's the village healer, and me will be up to tend to your aches proper since it appears ye've been ignored and treated most poorly." Gretna raised her voice, directing the scolding portion of her diatribe at Graham. "I canna believe ye werena properly tended."

Graham flushed a bright red and looked away. It was the first time Mercy had ever seen him speechless. She hurried to defend him. "You mustn't be too hard on him, Gretna. He's saved me from much evil on this trip and was also injured in the process."

Gretna took a step to the side and studied Graham. "He doesna seem injured to me."

Graham yanked up the side of his tunic. "Right here, ye sharp-tongued hen. See the bandage? Stabbed and left to die, but I overcame it and lived to tell the tale."

"Oh, here we go," Duncan warned. "Brother, can this no' wait until we're all settled in the keep with a mug of ale in our hands?"

Gretna turned away from the men, holding up a hand as though anything further they might say could just as well be tossed to the winds. She smiled up at Mercy. "Have Mistress Catriona fetch us, aye? Elena and I shall have ye feeling right as can be. I'll see to gathering the herbs and such now." She shooed the geese, goats, dog, and children back into the field from whence they'd come, tossing another smile back over her shoulder. "And welcome to *Tor Ruadh*, m'lady. We'll take good care of ye here."

Mercy now understood why everyone loved Gretna. She embodied kindness and compassion. "What a nice woman."

"Aye," Graham grumbled with a snorting huff. "If she curbed that sharp tongue of hers, she'd be a damn sight nicer. God help her husband, Colin."

Mercy laughed. She urged her mount onward, but the lighthearted feeling of the moment disappeared as she lifted her gaze to the impressive mountain known as Ben Nevis and the castle etched into its side. The rugged cliffs rose up and around, cradling the mighty fortress of stone like a mother cradling her child. *"Tor Ruadh?"*

"Aye," Graham said with a nod toward the four turreted towers. The square, main keep surrounded on three sides by an imposing curtain wall seemed to emerge from one side of the mountain, wrap around the buildings, then dive back into the mountain's side. "The ancestral Neals that built this knew a thing or two about creating a stronghold. Breaking in to save Catriona was quite the chore."

"Saving? Your brother's wife?" Mercy studied the massive stone barriers fully armed with arrow slits, crenels, and murder holes. "I understood the two clans, Neal and MacCoinnich, had joined by marriage and were now known as MacCoinnich, but I didn't realize the alliance had come about through violence."

Graham grew thoughtful as they crossed the stone bridge and approached the gatehouse. "I'll leave that telling to Catriona. 'Tis her story to tell." As they came up between the two guard towers forming the castle's barbican, Graham held up a hand and shouted. "Wake up and open the gate, Ranald!"

The iron and wood portcullis remained down.

"Who travels wi' yourself and Duncan?"

"Captain Marsden from His Majesty's guard and Lady Mercy Claxton. Now open the gate."

A thumping sound came from the tower on Mercy's right followed by a great rattling of chains and groaning of gears. The heavy barrier in front of them inched up, coming to a halt when it had risen high enough for them to pass beneath.

Mercy looked up as they road through the narrow neck of the entryway. A system of chains, pulleys, the portcullis, and then rows upon rows of lethal-looking spears hung suspended above them. The cold, gruesome sight triggered a shiver, and she urged her horse to move faster. The tunnel was a perfect defensive greeting for unwanted visitors.

Breathing came easier as the confined entrance opened up into the spacious grounds in front of the keep itself. Mercy rode close to Graham, casting nervous glances around the area and praying these people would be as welcoming as Gretna from the village.

A tall, dark-haired man resembling Graham emerged from one of the massive double doors of the keep and took a stance on the top step of the stone staircase. His initial welcoming smile crumbled into a scowl as his sharp-eyed gaze skimmed across the four of them. He strode forward, racing down the steps in great strides as Graham dismounted. His scowl grew even more fierce when he spotted the bloodstain on Graham's kilt. "Your blood or theirs?"

"Mine," Graham answered, then held up a hand to stave off his brother's reply. "But the land drinks their blood and eats their bones now. We'll have no more trouble from that lot."

The man gave a curt nod, then looked past Graham to Mercy and presented her with a wary smile, strained but polite. "Welcome to *Tor Ruadh*, m'lady. I am Alexander MacCoinnich, Graham's eldest brother and chieftain to Clan MacCoinnich."

Before Mercy could reply, a striking young woman with flaming-red hair stepped out from the doors and hurried down the steps to take her place at Chieftain MacCoinnich's side. Her gaze locked on Mercy, she paused but a moment, then rushed to Mercy's mount, waving for the men to follow. "I canna believe the lot of ye. Help her down. Can ye no' see she needs tending?"

Graham held up his hands to lift her down, but Mercy shooed him away. "No. Your wound. I don't want it to bleed again." Before he could argue, she dismounted, sliding her feet to the ground with a stiffness that triggered a squeaking gasp she hoped the others wouldn't notice. She held to the saddle a long moment to steady herself and convince her aching muscles to cooperate.

"Are ye all right, love?" Graham whispered.

"Yes." Mercy gave a quick nod, praying he wouldn't make a fuss.

Taking her hand, Graham eased her into the curve of his arm. The comfort of his nearness and silent assurance helped her strength considerably.

"Lady Mercy Claxton," he said, then pressed a kiss to her hand and stood taller, prouder. "And soon—my wife."

"Well, then. I am Catriona MacCoinnich," the red-haired woman said, a genuine welcome shining in her smile that reached clear to the brilliant green of her eyes. "And I am verra proud to meet another woman brave enough to take on a MacCoinnich brother. Welcome to *Tor Ruadh*, Lady Claxton."

"Please...my name is Mercy. I'd rather set aside the name of Lady Claxton, if you don't mind. That title no longer suits." She swallowed hard, feeling as though a weight had been lifted.

She'd never imagined it would be so easy to deny her family name. Mercy squeezed Graham's hand, thankful for the protection of his arm as a sudden shyness overtook her. Would Graham's people truly accept her so easily?

"And I am very happy to be here…to meet you all. Thank you." She glanced at Graham, concern for his well-being foremost in her mind. "We met Gretna from the village, and she spoke of a healer. Could we please summon her? Graham is injured and needs more care than I was able to give him on the trip. I fear infection might steal him from us yet."

"Dinna fash yourself," Graham argued. "I am fine."

Catriona scowled as she gave Graham a closer up and down look. "I see the blood staining your kilt now. Where are ye hurt?"

"He was stabbed in the left side," Mercy said before Graham could answer. "A deep gouge. I cleaned it as best I could with a pine needle wash and kept plantain and knitbone on it since, but I didn't have anything with which to stitch it closed."

"Enough!" Graham held up a hand. "I said I am fine."

Pressing a hand to his chest, Mercy peered up at him, willing him to cooperate. "Please, Graham. I can't bear to lose you. Let them see to you. Please."

Rolling his eyes and blowing out a deep, long-suffering sigh, Graham shook his head. "I will allow Elena to tend me as long as she tends your injuries first, agreed?"

"Agreed." Mercy felt a great deal better with that worry off her mind.

Alexander laughed as he clapped a hand of welcome on Duncan's shoulder. "Are they always like this?" He cast a side-eyed glance at Graham and Mercy.

"Aye, brother," Duncan replied with an exaggerated roll of his eyes. "Sometimes worse."

"I find it delightful," Captain Marsden said with a grin as he shook hands with Alexander. "And it is good to see you again and visit the comfort of your fine home, Chieftain MacCoinnich. The weather is much drier and more welcoming than it was this past spring when last I visited."

Catriona looped her arm through Mercy's and eased her away from Graham's side. "We shall take care of the both of ye, lass. I promise."

A stabbing pain cut Mercy's smile short and made her gasp as she started up the steps to the keep. "Forgive me. I'm still a little stiff and sore."

Catriona waved down a young lad in the process of propping open the doors leading into the main keep. "Run and fetch Elena and Gretna. Be quick about it, ye ken?"

"Aye, m'lady." The boy made a respectful hopping bob, then took off down the steps and across the courtyard at a fast lope.

"I can tell by looking at ye and by Graham saying ye're to be his wife that ye've had quite the journey." Catriona led Mercy to a cushioned chair beside one of the smaller offset hearths at the front of the great room and motioned for a maid. "Wine for the lady. Laced heavy with honey and a bit of Elena's herb mix from the larder. Buttered bread, too, aye?"

"Aye, m'lady." The maid curtseyed and hurried off across the great cavernous room filled with long trestle tables and benches.

Mercy eyed the fine, dark weave of the upholstered chair, then looked down at her filthy clothes. "I should sit on one of the benches. I don't wish to soil your furniture."

She glanced around the high-ceilinged room, not as opulent and gaudy as what she'd always been accustomed to in London, but the area had a regal air about it. Stately and refined in a strong, quiet way. The clan crest hung above both of the larger hearths, one situated on one side of the great hall, the other closer to the head of the room. Tartans and banners decorated the stone columns standing throughout the room, and gray flagstones, highly polished, made up the floor. The arches and doorways beneath the second-floor gallery circling the room were either fashioned of intricately chiseled stone or rich, reddish-hued wood carved and decorated with intertwining knots and thistles. The room shouted the courage and pride of Scotland.

"I'll be fine over there." Mercy turned toward one of the nearby benches.

Catriona snagged her arm, gave her a stern look, and pointed her back at the chair. "Please sit in the chair, m'lady. I'll no' have my future sister sitting on a hard bench when she looks ready to faint away from a journey that's left her battered and bruised." The stern set of her jaw softened into a warm smile. "I've always wanted a sister."

The young maid reappeared with a tray and slid it down upon the small table beside the chair. She poured the wine and removed the metal dome covering the plate of buttered bread, curtsied, then waited, her attention centered on Catriona.

Catriona smiled and nodded. "Thank ye, Meg. Please stay close in case Lady Mercy has need of anything else."

"Aye, m'lady." Meg gave Mercy a shy curtsy and returned to polishing the candlesticks lined up on a long table nearby.

With a firm, unrelenting nudge, Catriona steered Mercy down into the comfortable depths of the seat. She patted Mercy's hand where it rested on the arm of the chair. "There ye are now. Is that no' better?"

Mercy ran her hands along the silky weave of the furniture. "I must admit, this is a much nicer place to sit than any I've had in a while."

Handing her the wine, Catriona nodded. "I imagine so from the looks of ye. Heaven's sake, lass, ye look as though ye were dragged behind your horse rather than allowed to ride it."

"I had to dive off a horse into a ravine to escape the kidnappers. It was a rough landing but well worth it." Mercy took a tentative sip of the honeyed wine laced with herbs. Such a welcomed drink. She nearly groaned, closing her eyes to relish the sweet, reviving taste. Her stomach rumbled, growling out a loud gurgle. Mercy felt like the noise echoed through the quietness of the room. Embarrassment flooded through her. Such was not the behavior of a lady. Her eyes flew open, and she pressed a hand to her vocal middle. "Forgive me for such rudeness. It's been a while since I had anything stronger than water and bread."

"Ye dove from a horse?" Catriona waved her apology aside, pulling up a stool and lowering herself to it. "To escape kidnappers?" She leaned forward and laid a gentle hand atop Mercy's knee. "What in Heaven's name have ye been through, lass?"

Mercy almost wished that Catriona had focused on the rude gurgling of her stomach rather than her words. She wasn't ready to relive all that had transpired over the past few days. Staring down at the golden wine swirling in the bottom of her cup, she struggled to find the right words. This was Graham's family. What would they think of her when they learned the truth? "My father sent kidnappers after me." She lifted her gaze to Catriona's concerned look, begging the dear woman to understand. "He wishes me dead," she whispered, then swallowed hard. "He wishes all of us, myself and Clan MacCoinnich, dead."

Catriona studied her, compassion shining in her eyes as a quiet sigh escaped her. She squeezed Mercy's hand and gave her a sad smile. "Well, we shall just deny those wishes, won't we? My father was a monster, too, lass. And my brother, as well. We canna choose the ties of our blood, but we can choose the ties of our heart."

A tear rolled down Mercy's cheek. Such acceptance and understanding overwhelmed her. Her bruised, disheveled reflection on the surface of the wine stared back at her. Her voice broke as she clutched the cup tighter. "Graham has been so kind to me. I can't imagine how I would have survived this without him."

Catriona gave her arm a gentle pat, then squeezed. "MacCoinnich men are the best sort of heroes." She stood, took the pitcher from the table, and refilled Mercy's cup. "Drink the rest of your wine and finish this oat bread. It's Cook's finest and will build back your strength."

Returning the pitcher to the table, she stepped back and folded her arms across her middle. "After ye've eaten, we'll get ye a good long soak in a bath so ye'll be ready when Elena and Gretna arrive. I'll set the lads to moving a tub into your rooms so the maids can get to filling it. And dinna fash, I'm sure Alexander has already sent Sawny to fetch Father William from the village, too."

"Father William?" The potent wine had taken hold, giving her a warm, spinning feeling that wasn't altogether unpleasant. She took another deep sip, leaned back into the soft cushions of the chair, and gave herself to the comfortable surroundings. "To pray for our healing?" she asked with a hitching yawn, her eyelids growing heavy.

Catriona's light, bubbling laugh echoed through the chamber. "I suppose he can." Her heels clicked against the flagstones as she hurried away but the sound silenced when she paused. "After he performs your wedding, of course."

Wedding. Eyes closed and floating off into the softness of much needed sleep, Mercy fought to regain wakefulness. "We cannot marry just yet." She forced her eyes wide open and slid the pewter wine cup to the table. No more spirits until she'd explained the direness of the situation. "Graham and I must not marry until the clan is safe. I almost fear to marry him at all." There. She'd spoken the demons of her fears aloud. How could she be so selfish to endanger Graham and his people?

The murmurings of deep voices coupled with heavy boot steps cut off Mercy's confession. The footfalls drew closer, then Graham was kneeling at her side. He took her hand, gazing at her with such intensity, she could scarce breathe. "I overheard your words, lass. But tell me...do ye love me, Mercy?"

Emotions warred within her, threatening to spin her into hysteria. She swallowed hard at the threat of tears closing off her throat, praying for strength, praying for control. Panic took hold at the expectancy she saw on the faces turned upon her. Catriona. Alexander. Duncan. Marsden. They all stared at her. Silent and unreadable. Waiting to hear what she would say.

And then there was Graham, kneeling beside her, peering into the depths of her soul and looking into every shadowy corner of her heart.

"How can you ask me that?" The tears spilled over, out of her control, their hot wetness streaming down her cheeks.

"Because I would know the truth, lass," he said softly as he squeezed her hand and leaned closer. "Do ye love me?"

"I love you more than you shall ever know," she whispered, bowing her head and blinking fast to see past the tears. "I love you so much it hurts my heart to think of a world without you. But I cannot endanger you, Graham. I cannot bear to lose you or cause you the pain of losing your family."

Graham gave her a sad smile and pressed a tender kiss to her hand. "Nothing in this life is guaranteed, love. I willna tell ye we will always be safe and free from fear or pain, but know this, I will always love ye—to the end of this life and well into the next."

"Oh, dear heavens—how can I possibly do this to you?" A hiccupping gasp escaped her as she bowed her head and pressed her forehead to their clasped hands. "I am selfish to want a life at your side, even when I know it could turn into such a trial."

Graham rumbled with a low, soft laugh and pressed his cheek to the top of her head. "Ye're weary, lass, and ye've had a pitcher of Cook's strongest wine. Rest ye easy and set your worries aside, ye ken? Let Catriona and the healers tend ye so ye'll be ready for tomorrow, aye?"

Mercy sniffed and lifted her head to blink through the tears and look into Graham's eyes. She was so weary. It would be so welcome to entrust herself to Graham, Catriona, and the healers and block her mind of all else. "What happens tomorrow?"

"Why, our wedding, dear one," Graham said as he pressed his forehead to hers. "Tomorrow, I make ye mine."

CHAPTER SIXTEEN

THE STEAMING WATER provided healing heat, sending a soothing warmth through her aching body. Mercy closed her eyes, leaning back against the linen-padded incline of the metal tub. She drew in a deep breath of the herb-laced steam. Sweet notes of lavender wafted across her senses. Her knotted muscles eased. Pure relaxation. She'd needed this. Badly.

"Lie still whilst I dab this salve on those scrapes along your jawline, m'lady," Gretna said.

Mercy didn't bother opening her eyes, just agreed with a contented sigh and a turn of her head as Gretna applied a silky, cool paste to the wounds on her face. Catriona had called them badges of honor she'd earned from her daring escape.

"Arnica for the bruise, Gretna."

Mercy recognized the gruff, quivering voice of the old woman introduced to her as Elena Bickerstaff, Clan MacCoinnich's healer. The stern matron seemed wise and well-versed when it came to the healing arts, but she had no time for the pleasantry of conversation.

"Aye, Elena. I'll tend her bruises next. The ones on her arms are already looking better. We'll work in more of the salve once she's done with her bath." Gretna's gentle touch continued smoothing the cooling ointment across Mercy's face.

"Ye've the loveliest hair," Catriona said from somewhere behind the tub.

Mercy opened her eyes as she slid to an upright position and combed her fingers back through her long, wet tresses. It had taken numerous washes to rid her of all the debris she'd accumulated in the last days of the trip. "Thank you. It can be quite the chore."

"I'm sure, thick as it is." Gretna shoved the back of her hand against escaped tendrils of her own copper-colored locks sticking to her temples. "I'm fair melting in here. Are ye sure that waters no' too hot for ye?"

"Heat heals," Elena advised in a clipping tone that ended the topic.

"Aye, that it does," Gretna replied with a resigned sigh. "Lean forward and pull your hair aside. These herbs will soothe ye even more when I crush them in the heated water and rub them along your back."

Mercy complied, the scent of the herb bundle reminding her of Graham and his wound. "You're certain Graham's wound has no infection?"

"Cleaned and sewed it m'self," Elena said as she hooked a crooked finger under Mercy's chin and tilted her face upward. The ancient crone, wizened with age and crowned with frazzled hair white as snow, scowled down at her with a sharp, beady-eyed perusal. Turning Mercy's face from side to side, old Elena studied her. "The marks willna be gone by tomorrow, but they'll be a far sight better than what they were."

"There, lass," Gretna said. "Stand up now and we'll get ye dried and tucked into a chair."

Mercy rose from the water, reluctant to leave its comfort. Gretna steadied her as she stepped from the tub, then helped pat her dry. While Gretna dried Mercy's arms and legs, Catriona squeezed the water from her hair, then wrapped it in a length of cloth and coiled it to the top of her head.

"Here, lass. This should do well enough for now." Catriona held open a lightweight linen gown that looked more like a shift that had been split down the front, then sewn with laces spaced at narrow intervals to secure the unique robe-like garment in place once the sides were pulled together. "I'm afeared it'll be a mite short on ye, but it's fresh and clean."

Slipping her arms into the shift, Mercy wrapped it around her and tied the laces. What a comfortable dressing gown, but Catriona was right. It was most definitely too short. The hem hit her midway between ankle and knee. She smoothed her hands down the fine weave of the cloth. The odd garment had seen little use, if any. It appeared almost new. "Is this yours?"

"Aye. I knew how I wanted it and had the seamstress make it for me after the twins were born. Makes nursing them easier." Catriona led her to a pillowed bench beside the wall of windows overlooking the side of the mountain. "I thought ye'd find it comfortable whilst ye relax here in your room until we sort out your other clothes. Sit down and I'll brush out your hair."

"I be done here," Elena announced as she gathered up bundles and small jars and tucked them into the cloth sack slung over her bent shoulder. "Are ye coming, Gretna, or will ye be staying and telling her of that lass and the wagons?"

Mercy's fragile sense of peace and contentment shattered. "What lass? Wagons?"

Gretna gave the elderly healer a stern look. "Looks like I'll be staying now, thank ye verra much, Elena."

Elena waved away the words, hitched her way out the door, and closed it with a firm thud behind her.

"I thought we agreed to let the matter go?" Catriona said in a meaningful tone as she combed out Mercy's hair with gentle tugs. "We decided to concentrate on the joy of the wedding, aye?"

"I need to know," Mercy said, frustration building as she watched the non-spoken interplay between Catriona and Gretna. The two women were trying to shield her from something, something that had to do with the wagons. "What happened with the wagons? The people with them? I assume they're the wagons that were once mine?"

Gretna rolled her eyes and blew out a disgusted huff. "Elena stirs the shite, then leaves the smell behind for everyone else to breathe." With a glance at Catriona, the young girl perched on the edge of the bench beside Mercy. "Three wagons came through the village. Two flats and a boxy thing all painted up like some such nonsense I've never seen afore."

"Those were my wagons," Mercy said. "Were they headed to Fort William?"

"Said they were," Gretna said, her gaze shifting from Mercy to Catriona.

Catriona stepped out from behind Mercy, a dark tortoiseshell comb and silver-handled brush held in her hands. "There was a young, rough-looking girl with them. Gretna thinks she might ha' been their prisoner."

"Janie?" Mercy turned to Gretna. "Janie left with them willingly."

Gretna gave a doubtful shake of her head. "She didna appear all that willing to head to Fort William."

"What did she say?" Mercy leaned forward, intent on scrutinizing every word Gretna said.

"It wasna so much what she said, m'lady." Gretna scowled off into the distance as though sorting through her thoughts was an unpleasant chore. "'Twas more like the look about her. All haggard and angry." Gretna nodded, eyes widening as she held up a finger. "And trying to twist her wrist free of that sour-faced old woman, she was. Acted as though she'd jump down from that wagon and run, if given half a chance."

"So, she didn't speak?" Mercy fisted her hands in her lap. Janie's betrayal had hurt the worst by far.

Gretna looked to Catriona, then to Mercy, then back at Catriona.

"Tell me!" Not knowing was always worse than knowing. At least if she faced the evil head on, she knew what she battled. "What did she say?"

"Mentioned yourself, m'lady," Gretna said. "Said she'd find a way to get back to you if it was the last thing she did."

Mercy swallowed hard, staring down at her hands resting atop the clean, white linen across her lap. Remorse filled her. What would become of Janie? What would happen to the girl because Mercy had cast her aside? The soft weight of a touch to her shoulder pulled her from her tortured musing.

"I spoke to Graham about the lass. He and I agree. Ye canna be certain what the girl meant when she said what she did. 'Twas merely heard in passing and could mean she's intent on doing ye harm because of how ye acted after ye found her out." Catriona gave her shoulder a gentle squeeze. "Graham is as rough as they come. Says what he thinks and doesna care who disagrees. But he is just and fair and has good instincts. Trust Graham and rest assured he did what was best."

"And if they're headed to Fort William, as they said, there's always work to be found there," Gretna added. "Honest work, if the lass but looks and keeps her wits about her."

A knock at the door accompanied by a duet of angry wails on the other side interrupted them.

"Oh, dear." Catriona pressed a hand to her bosom. "I shouldha kent by the fullness that 'twas near time for my wee bairns to howl for their supper." She hurried to the door, pulled it open a short space, and said, "I'll be right there. Take the wee darlings to my solar." She turned back to Mercy. "I'll return once I've fed them, and we'll see about fitting ye with a dress for tomorrow, aye?"

"You can feed them here." Mercy rose from the bench and hurried to the door beside Catriona. She loved little ones, but the opportunity to enjoy them was rare. "May I...may I hold one?"

The red-cheeked maid complied before Catriona could answer. "Here's Mistress Willa. She's the liveliest of the two and will calm right down when she sees ye're someone new. Curious as a cat, she is, whilst all Master William cares about is getting his wame filled." She thrust the fussing little girl into Mercy's arms and handed the other child to Catriona. "I'll freshen their cots and blankets whilst ye feed them, m'lady. Just ring the bell when ye wish me to fetch them."

"I'll be heading back to the village now," Gretna interrupted, her face wreathed in smiles. "I'll have three at home looking for their supper, and every time I hold someone else's bairn, I end up with a new one on the way. Colin is fair worn out." She patted her middle and winked at Mercy. "After tomorrow night, ye could be the same."

Struggling to hold the plump wiggling baby in her arms, Mercy's mood lightened, a sense of contentment filling her. "Thank you, Gretna. You'll be here for the ceremony, yes?"

"Aye, m'lady. Ye couldna keep me from a MacCoinnich celebration." Gretna stroked the cheek of the angry baby in Catriona's arms. "There now, Master William. Your mam's fixing to feed ye." She made a curtsy to Catriona and slipped out the door, closing it softly behind her.

"Oh dear, m'sweet, howling son. Ye've no patience about ye at all, have ye?" Catriona hurried back to the bench in front of the window. "Let me get this beastie started and then ye can hand me dear sweet Willa, aye?"

"You nurse them both at the same time?" A sense of awe filled Mercy. How in the world did one woman manage two hungry babies at once?

"Aye." Catriona gave her a look as though she thought her addled. "If I didna feed them at the same time, I'd have a bairn suckling all the time." She pulled down the scooped neckline of her bodice and exposed both breasts. Holding William with his feet toward her back and his head cradled in her hand, she looked as though she planned to tote him under one arm like a sack of grain. The eager child kicked and nuzzled, then latched on. A gleeful grunting accompanied his ardent suckling.

Catriona looked up at Mercy and sighed. "He's a wee piglet, he is, but he's mine and I wouldna have him any other way." She held out her free hand. "And now for his darling sister."

Already working her mouth and making noisy sucking sounds, Willa squirmed and squealed as Mercy turned her and positioned her opposite her brother. Cradling a babe under each arm and holding them close as they nursed, Catriona smiled down at her offspring. "I'm truly blessed." She looked up, her smile widening. "I pray yourself and Graham will be as blessed."

"Are there many twins in the MacCoinnichs?" A sense of trepidation filled Mercy. She wanted children. Especially Graham's babies. But twins? And to do what Catriona did. Every few hours. Mercy prayed she wouldn't be charged with such a monumental task.

Catriona laughed. "I am a twin. They run in the Neal side of the family." She winked. "I'll temper my prayers with the request that ye be blessed with one bairn at a time."

Mercy lowered herself to the bench beside Catriona. "They're so precious." She placed a finger in the center of Willa's chubby little hand, her heart lurching as those tiny, tender fingers closed around hers and held on tight. "What a dear she is." Mercy looked to baby William, greedily rootling as though he couldn't empty his mother's breast fast enough. "My goodness."

"Aye," Catriona agreed. "The breast is nay enough anymore. To sate him and get a bit a peace and quiet, it takes a bowl of thinned out parritch for him as well. Gobbles it right up, he does." Catriona winked. "Eats like his father. Their nursemaid will see to a fine bowl for them both afore she puts them down for the afternoon." Her attention shifted to her daughter. "Willa's a bit more ladylike but still a fierce eater, so she'll be having some parritch, too, won't ye, dear girl?"

Watching the babies nurse, a special kinship with Catriona stirred within Mercy. The woman had opened her home, welcomed her in, and even shared such an intimate moment with her babies. Mercy caught her bottom lip between her teeth and chewed as she studied Catriona. Here sat the sister she'd always wanted. The experienced sister.

"What is it, lass?" Catriona lifted her gaze from her babies. "Ask me anything ye wish."

"The wedding night." Mercy held her breath. Had she actually said the words aloud?

Catriona nodded with a knowing look. "I ken how ye feel right now. All uncertain and mayhap a mite fearful about what ye dinna know."

Mercy shifted on the bench, pinching a fold of her shift between her fingers. She leaned closer. "I've never..." How could she say it?

"Been with a man?" Catriona finished. She smiled big and nodded her approval. "Good. I'd want nothing less than a pure-hearted lass for Graham."

"I've never even seen one," Mercy whispered.

"Truly?" Catriona shifted the babies a bit higher. "Prop a pillow under each of them, lass, the weight of them becomes too much after a while."

Mercy hurried to slide a pillow beneath each chubby baby tightly curled to Catriona's side. She reseated herself and folded her hands. "Of course, I've seen their *parts* in artwork but never the real thing. The closest I came to seeing a man unclothed was at the river when Graham was swimming."

Catriona studied her, quirked a brow, then gave her a dip of her chin. Voice low, she spoke in a conspiratorial tone. "His...ye know." She waited for Mercy's nod before she continued. "'Twill seem overlarge—if he's anything like his brother. But trust me, 'twill be a verra fine fit once your maidenhead has been dispatched proper, and ye can be about enjoying each other fully."

Mercy wasn't sure if that was good news or bad. "How over-large...exactly?"

Catriona frowned down at her children, puckering her brow as she smoothed her thumb back and forth across her son's chubby cheek as she cradled his head in her palm. "I'm afeared if I attempt to describe it to ye, 'twill make your worries worse instead of better." She leaned forward. "Dinna be afraid. I'm sure Graham will be gentle and understanding." She shrugged. "And at least your first time willna be in a cave."

"A cave?" Visions of rock slabs, bats, and spiders filled her mind. "Your first time with Alexander was in a cave?"

"Aye." Catriona laughed as she handed Willa over to Mercy, then motioned for her to pat and rub on the child's back as she did to William. A pair of loud burps popped in rapid succession. Catriona tucked her breasts back inside her gown, stood, and sauntered around the room with William held to her shoulder. She cast a glance back over at Mercy. "Trust me, lass, when the loving's right, it doesna matter where ye are. All that matters is that ye are."

"Oh, my." Mercy held Willa to her shoulder, rubbing and patting as she walked alongside Catriona. "How did you know what to do?" she whispered.

"Believe me when I say..." Catriona smiled. "Ye will know."

That's what Mama had always said. Mercy snuggled her cheek to little Willa's silky head, breathing in her sweet baby fragrance. She idly rubbed the contented baby's back as she walked. "I'll know," she repeated under her breath. *I certainly hope so.*

CHAPTER SEVENTEEN

"Y E'RE SURE 'TIS Campbell they'll be sending rather than the king's army?" Alexander asked as he held out a whisky.

Graham pulled the clean tunic over his head and yanked it down in place before accepting the wee dram. He downed the fine, golden whisky, welcoming the familiar burn in his throat. "Aye. According to Mercy, the best way that Edsbury could figure to pay his debt to Campbell was giving him free rein here with the king's blessing." Barefooted, he strode across the bedchamber and refilled his glass. "Ye ken as well as I that King William would prefer the clans kill each other so he didna have to bother with them." He held up the bottle to Alexander. "Another for ye, brother?"

"Aye." Alexander held out his glass, scowling at the bottle like a witch studying her potion. "But Marsden insists Edsbury has since fallen from favor. Said the king appeared determined to make a good match for your lady. Even went so far as to arrange one for her." Alexander gave Graham the sobering look that only an elder brother could give. "Reckon His Majesty would give ye his blessing for today?"

"I dinna give a rat's arse if he blesses us or no'." Graham pulled on his boots and reached for his waistcoat. A grunt escaped him as he shrugged it on, pulled it snug, and buttoned it. Damned old Elena Bickerstaff. She'd stirred the pain in his wound by cleaning it out and stitching it shut. He motioned for Alexander to hand him his neck-cloth. "I mean to make Mercy my wife, and we'll sort out the rest later."

Alexander nodded and strolled over to the lone window facing the inner courtyard in front of the large cave that served as Clan MacCoinnich's stables. "Sawny's bound to Fort William with a message to Crestshire. The man willna make the wedding, but I feel certain he'll arrive within a few days. After all, 'tis his duty to uphold peace and the king's justice in the Highlands." Alexander grinned and raised his glass in a toast. "He tossed Jameson's arse in the Tolbooth once before. He can do so again. A wedding present for ye and your lovely bride, aye?"

"Aye." Graham accepted the toast, emptied his glass, then plunked it on the table and reached for his best coat.

It wasn't nearly as fine as the men at court wore, but was the best he had. He arranged his plaid over one shoulder and pinned it. He raked his fingers through his damp hair, smoothed it back, and braided it, securing the end with a leather tie. He smelled a damn sight better. Felt better, too. They'd made it to the safety of *Tor Ruadh,* and he was about to claim Mercy for his bride. He turned and held his hands out to his sides. "Tell me true, brother. Will this do for her? Remember, she is a fine lady."

"Ye're missing one thing." Alexander reached into the black, leather pouch attached to his belt and withdrew something hidden inside his hand. "The MacCoinnich crest." He held out the pin with a proud smile.

A sense of awe, pride, and wistfulness filling him, Graham took the pin in both hands. "It's like Da's." Their father's crest had been lost in the upheaval of their clan during the plague that had decimated them and handed their lands to the bloody Campbells.

"Aye." Alexander took the pin out of Graham's hands, removed the one holding the plaid to Graham's shoulder, and replaced it with the MacCoinnich crest. "'Tis identical. I described it to the silversmith, and he made it so for me, but I wish ye to have it. I'll have another made for m'self."

Graham ran his fingers over the engraved lettering of the weighty silver pin, oval in shape, and the image at its center of a fist clutching a sword raised to the heavens. *"Je ressuscite.* I rise again," he whispered. Alexander couldn't have given him a more perfect gift. He clapped a hand to Alexander's shoulder and squeezed. "I thank ye, brother. For *everything.*" He'd endangered them all by coming here, but Alexander would not have had it any other way, and Graham appreciated it. Family meant everything, and he was more than a little thankful for his own.

A rapid pounding on the door startled them both. Duncan threw it open and gave them a stern look. "If ye dinna wish to sit through Father William's sermon about timeliness being next to godliness, I suggest ye move your arses. Catriona won't bring Mercy down from her rooms 'til she gets word that the rest of us are waiting in the chapel."

"We'd best make haste," Alexander said.

The three men hurried down the back stairway, the shortest route to the back of the keep and the path leading to the small chapel tucked into one corner of the skirting wall. The modest stone building with arched windows waited with its double doors propped open. Candelabras bathed the altar in a golden glow.

Father William, overly thin but resplendent in his white robes, stood in front of the altar, prayer book in one hand, and a folded length of ivory satin cloth in the other. His bushy, gray brows arched to the wispy remnants of his nonexistent hairline as Graham and his two brothers hurried into the room. "If ye wish to survive as a husband, Graham, ye'd best learn to no' keep your woman a waiting."

"Yes, Father." Graham took a stance to the priest's left, while Alexander and Duncan took their places to Graham's right.

With a nod toward the smattering of villagers sitting on the benches, Father William leaned closer and lowered his voice. "Ye ken, if ye'd waited a few days, a better feast couldha been prepared and more gathered to welcome your bride into the clan, aye?"

"We dinna have the luxury of time, Father," Graham said while keeping his gaze locked on the doors. Mercy would arrive any moment.

"Oh?" Father William gave him a judgmental scowl and pointed his holy book at him as though ready to drive out a demon. "And why not?"

"Because her father's mercenaries, the king's guard, and perhaps her betrothed, could be upon us at any moment." Graham shifted in place, growing more anxious by the moment. "Alexander will explain it to ye later. Can we leave it for now, Father?"

Father William rolled his eyes and shook his head. "Always into some such mischief, ye are. Always. Ye MacCoinnichs never learn."

Graham didn't hear the rest of the priest's diatribe because Mercy walked in the door.

Her beauty humbled him. She moved with the flawless grace of feather-white clouds skimming across the sky. She wore her long, black hair silky and flowing over her shoulders and down her back just as she knew he loved it. A simple gown of pale yellow and white had been hastily fitted for her, and it framed her dark beauty to perfection. The tawny gold of her eyes shimmered with the sheen of unshed tears, rivaling the sparkle of stars in the darkest night. Graham prayed her tears were borne of happiness. How could one such as her ever love him?

The bundle of ivy she held between her hands trembled as she made her way to him. She held herself poised, but Graham saw the way she caught her breath and wet her lips with a nervous swipe of her tongue. Lord Almighty, if she only knew what a rare blessing she was—the perfect heartmate Graham had never thought to find. He held out his hand as she neared, swallowing hard when she took it and handed her bundle of ivy to Catriona.

"Ye're a rare woman, Mercy. I swear I'll do my best by ye."

Father William cleared his throat and held up a hand. "Ahh now…I'll speak the proper vows first, if ye dinna mind."

Mercy squeezed Graham's hand but kept her gaze locked on the priest. "I have one request, Father," she said in a tremulous voice.

"What is that, my child?" Father William leaned forward with the benevolent smile.

"Would you please use the name my mother gave me rather than Claxton?" She stole a glance over at Graham, the pleading in her eyes touching his heart. "It would mean a great deal to me."

Father William pursed his lips, looked over at Graham, then nodded. "Most certainly. What was your mother's name, child?"

"Yumiko." Mercy bowed her head, pulled in a deep breath, then blew it out and lifted her chin. "And the name she gave me when I was born was Kimiko Mercy Rowena Etain."

Graham's heart ached for Mercy. His dear woman had lost so much. Heritage. Family. He strengthened himself with the knowledge that she'd bear his name now. Clan MacCoinnich would be her own.

Father William cleared his throat again, stood as tall as his small frame would allow, and peered out over the congregation. "We gather here to bear witness to the union of these two before Almighty God." He made a regal nod toward Mercy. "Kimiko Mercy Rowena Etain, as christened and blessed by your beloved mother, Yumiko, do ye hereby take this man, Graham Cauley Evan MacCoinnich, to be your beloved husband, bound together until death shall part ye?"

Tears slipped down Mercy's cheeks as she whispered, "Yes, Father, I do."

With a nod, the priest turned to Graham. "Graham Cauley Evan MacCoinnich, do ye take this woman, Kimiko Mercy Rowena Etain, to be your beloved wife until death parts ye?"

"Aye, Father, I do." A sense of peace, a feeling of things coming together as they should, swept over him. Graham exhaled a relieved sigh and extended their clasped hands for Father William to wrap with the binding cloth.

Over and under, Father William wound the length of satin around their hands, symbolically tying their lives together, joining them the old way. Pressing his hand atop theirs, he nodded to Graham. "Now say the words of your heart to the lady."

Turning to Mercy, Graham took hold of her free hand and pressed it to the center of his chest as he stared into her eyes. "My heart beats for ye alone. With every breath, I need ye. Ye are my blood. Ye are my bone. I canna live without ye. I give ye the protection of my name, my body, and my heart. Even in death, I shall find a way to ye. Never will I leave your side. I swear it upon my soul."

Lips parted, Mercy hitched in a sharp intake of breath and took a step closer. Pressing her hand harder against his chest, she smiled up at him, blinking away the tears. "Never have I known such love. Never have I known such acceptance. Always, I shall be bound to thee— today and forevermore. I accept your protection. I accept your love. And I swear to you that our children and our children's children will sing of the great eternal love we shared."

Graham leaned forward and sealed their vows with a sampling of Mercy's sweet lips. Aye, this was right and true. Thank God above for that summons from the king.

THE STRENGTH OF his hands holding hers was all that kept her standing.

A subtle trembling had overtaken her as soon as she'd donned the lovely dress Catriona had altered for this special day. A strange jitteriness shook her insides as though her heart had sprouted wings and was about to take flight.

Graham, handsome and strong, saying words she'd never dreamt anyone would say to her. Those precious vows had worsened her condition. So much love filled her. It was all she could do to keep from weeping with joy.

His eyes, the deep, dark blue of them, held her transfixed. And then the kiss to seal their vows. The enormity of what had just happened exploded within her at the touch of his warm mouth to hers. She was wife to Graham. The man she loved. The man this union so endangered.

"I fear for us." The whispered words escaped her as soon as Graham lifted his mouth from hers. The thrilling happiness of the day marred by the destruction that could overtake them at any time.

Graham shook his head, then pressed his forehead to hers. "Not today, love," he said in a gentle whisper. "Today, we celebrate each other. Tomorrow, we shall plan a way to end this madness, aye?"

"Aye," she said with a helpless sigh. How could she deny them both this day, this stolen bit of time when nothing mattered but the two of them? She bowed her head and squeezed Graham's hands.

"I hereby proclaim the two of ye man and wife," Father William said. "Let no man dare put asunder what God hath joined together." He removed the binding cloth and folded it. Looking to Graham, he arched a brow. "I would tell ye to kiss your bride, but since ye've already done it, I'll be waiting for a fine whisky to toast ye." He graced Mercy with a smile. "Dinna fear, lass. Ye've married a fine man."

"Yes, I have." Mercy never doubted that fact.

Graham offered his arm. "Might I lead ye to our banquet, wife?"

His words thrilled through her. Mercy took his arm and hugged him to her. "Yes, husband."

The few gathered in the small chapel cheered, following the couple as they made their way to the main hall of the keep. As they walked through the archway, Mercy came to a halt, staring at the view before her. The sight touched her heart and flooded her with so much emotion, she struggled to speak. "H-how?"

Catriona appeared at her side, smiling proudly. "It's amazing what can be done when we set our minds to it."

Bundles of thrift, rose, and cowslip, bound with ribbons and intertwined with braided ropes of ivy filled every nook, corner, mantle, and archway of the room. The yellows, pinks, and soft purples of the blooms made the deep green of the ivy leaves even more vibrant. The head table glowed with the finest silver candelabras, polished and lit with the glow of beeswax candles, their scent mixing with the delicate fragrance of the blossoms. Two, high-backed chairs waited at the center of the main table on the dais, draped with flowers as well.

Music filled the air. A fiddle accompanied by the jaunty drumming of a bodhran. The lively tune of a pair of flageolets, the whistles played by a pair of young men hopping in time to the song. The wail of bagpipes filled the air, coupled with the clapping of the crowd as Mercy and Graham entered the room.

Mercy pressed a hand to her throat, happiness overflowing as Graham helped her into her seat. She leaned forward, looking down the table at Alexander and Catriona. "I can't begin to tell you how much all this means to me. Your acceptance has touched my heart."

Alexander lifted his glass. "Any woman brave enough to take on Graham has our admiration! Welcome to the family!"

All in the great room lifted their tankards and cheered.

Mercy scanned the crowd, her heart swelling as they smiled back at her. These people accepted her. So few had tolerated her back in London, yet every person in this room seemed to look upon her with genuine kindness.

Graham leaned close, took her hand, and kissed it. "Ye've gone a bit pale, dear one. Are ye unwell?"

"No." Mercy squeezed his hand, cupping it between both of hers. "I'm overwhelmed by the open hearts of these people." There was no way she could explain how it felt. It was like finally finding home after searching through a blinding storm.

"Quaich!" The shout started from the back of the room, then grew in strength, rippling forward until all who were gathered, young and old, servants and clansmen, chanted the word.

Father William emerged from the shadows of the gallery, the two-handled silver bowl in one hand, and a bottle in the other. He walked to the main table and took a stance in front of Mercy and Graham. With a ceremonious bow of his head over the silver bowl, eyes closed and lips moving, the hall fell silent. In a deep, resounding voice that Mercy never would have imagined coming from the priest, he said, "Blessed Three we bid thee protect them, guide them, and bless them." He opened the bottle and poured some of the golden liquid into the quaich, then made the sign of the cross over it. "In the name of the Father, the Son, and the Holy Spirit." Lifting the quaich by the short handles on either side of the bowl, he passed it to Graham and nodded.

Graham accepted it and turned to face Mercy, holding the quaich between them. "In the name of the Father, the Son, and the Holy Spirit," he said while staring into her eyes, then took a sip and handed the bowl to her.

Mercy wet her lips and repeated, "In the name of the Father, the Son, and the Holy Spirit." She drank the golden whisky. The heat of the liquid warmed through her, bringing with it a sense of calm, a feeling of peace and well-being she hadn't felt in a very long while.

"Amen," Graham whispered.

"Amen," Mercy said with a smile, still holding the bowl aloft.

Father William took the quaich, lifted it high in the air, then turned toward the crowd. "And all God's people said?"

"Amen!" everyone responded.

Father William turned to Alexander and nodded.

"Feast!" Alexander proclaimed. Servants appeared bearing platters of meat, cheeses, vegetables, and breads. Glasses were filled with wine and plates were overloaded. The mouthwatering aroma of roasted meat, smoky and fresh from the spit, filled the air.

Sitting to Graham's left, Mercy stared down at her plate as servants filled it. Surely, they didn't expect her to eat? Not after such a day. She stole a glance at Graham. And how could she eat when soon, she and her husband would retire to what would henceforth be known as their wedding chamber where they would consummate their vows? She nearly choked from a nervous swallow of wine. Picking at a crust of bread, she popped a small bite into her mouth. She should eat, she supposed. It wouldn't do if she fainted due to lack of sustenance.

Graham leaned close, nuzzling a kiss to her cheek as he whispered. "All will be well, lass. I promise ye." He slid a finger beneath her chin and turned her to peer into her eyes. "We are one now." He glanced out across the room, then returned his attention to her. "And our clan stands united with us."

She smiled and nodded, relieved when he turned to reply to something Duncan had said. While she still worried about how they could overcome both her father and the king without endangering anyone else, that wasn't her immediate concern. She took another deep drink of her wine, smiling as a servant hurried to refill her glass as fast as she set it back to the table. Her present fear, the current worry knotting in the center of her chest, was what would happen when they got to the bedchamber? And while she felt all manner of delicious warm stirrings and aching desires, she wasn't exactly sure what to do about them. She'd never been with a man before.

Mama had never told her much other than Mercy would know what to do when the time came—especially if she was fortunate enough to love the man secured for her in marriage. Catriona had assured her of the same. Mercy took another long drink. She did love Graham. Studying him over the rim of the glass, she reasoned with herself. Not only did she love him, but his kisses, his embrace, his touch, thrilled her. Filled her with an aching need for...more.

Nibbling at a bite of cheese, her gaze lit upon Alexander and Catriona. While fitting her with her dress, Catriona had told her more of how she and Alexander had met. How they had married in a cave. How all she had feared had been resolved and then they'd been blessed with twins, Willa and William.

Children. She'd held Catriona's babies, wondering the entire time how wondrous it would be to hold a child of her own. A child fathered by Graham. She looked up at him, heart pounding as she hitched in a shallow breath. When he came to her tonight, when he taught her the ways a man and wife shared their love, would a child result? Would she soon hold her own sweet baby in her arms? Could it happen that quickly? Oh, how she wished Mama had told her more.

Graham rose from his seat and held his hand out to her. "Come, m'love."

Mercy stared at his hand, took in a deep breath, then slid her fingers into his grasp and stood beside him.

The time had come.

Chapter Eighteen

I F ANYONE HAD told him he'd be leading his Sassenach wife to their bedchamber on this fine summer evening, Graham would have called them daft. He'd never planned to marry but then again, as he'd learned years ago, life didn't always go as planned.

He held tight to Mercy's hand and kept his right arm around her as they climbed the steep, spiral staircase. She'd had a fair bit of wine and very little food. She seemed well enough but looks could be deceiving. When she'd risen from her chair at the main table, she'd weaved a bit from side to side and stumbled more than once.

The lass remained silent as they made their way up the steps and that worried him. Did she fear him? Did she fear what was about to happen? He'd heard tell of some wedding nights that had gone very wrong, and the women hated their husbands forever after that.

Graham halted. He wouldn't allow that to happen. Mercy must realize how much he cherished her and would never do her harm. The torchlight from the iron sconces embedded in the walls set a glow to Mercy's fair skin, mesmerizing him as he gazed down at her and struggled to find the right words. He swallowed hard. Lord, how he wanted her, but he had to put her at ease first. He had to be gentle. Patient.

"Are ye afraid, lass?" he asked in a halting whisper. "If ye're no' prepared to take me to your bed, I shall abide by your wishes until ye're ready. I swear it."

Mercy stared up at him, her brow slowly drawing into a scowl as she muddled over his words. "Do you not wish to share our marriage bed?" She pressed a hand to the bruise along her high cheekbone. "Am I so repulsive because of my bruises?"

"Lord no, woman!" Graham slipped his arms around her and gathered her close. Tilting her face up to his, he pressed tender kisses along the lines of scrapes and bruises marring her face. "I want ye more than ye could ever imagine, love, but I want ye to treasure tonight as much as I do."

Mercy gave him a tremulous smile as she cast a glance up the staircase. "Then let us be on with it, shall we?"

Graham scooped her up into his arms and cradled her close.

"You must not!" she said with a light swat of her hand atop his shoulder. "You risk tearing your stitches!"

Welcoming the return of the righteous fire in her eyes, Graham ignored her scolding and held her tighter as he made his way up the stairs, strode down the hallway, and shouldered open the door to their chambers. Once inside, he lowered her to the floor.

"If you've set your wound to bleeding again, I've half a mind to thrash you!" She glared at him, arms crossed in a tight fold across her middle and skirts shifting with the frustrated tapping of her foot.

"I swear to ye, I'm fine, love." Graham held his hands aloft and turned as he looked about the room, the opulence of the chamber catching his eye. "And just look at all they've done for us." He didn't add that judging by the looks of the room, they could survive in here for days without wanting for a thing.

A large table had been set in the corner beside the wide window taking up one end of the room. Candles flickered in twin candelabras, and replacement candles were piled in a narrow wooden box on the windowsill above the padded and pillowed window seat. Plates of cheese, bread, and dried fruits filled the table. Decanters of whisky. Bottles of wine. Jugs of water. Cups and tankards stood at the ready. In the opposite corner, placed on a long dressing table, were two ceramic washing bowls, four pitchers that probably held more water, and a pile of drying linens. He'd have to remember to thank his dear sister-in-law. Catriona had forgotten nothing when it came to the comforts of his new bride.

Mercy moved to the hearth, a welcoming fire already burning. Bundles of lavender cascaded across the wooden mantel, the sweetness of their scent filling the room. She peeped inside the jars and crocks on the dressing table, sniffing the contents and smiling. "Roses. Lavender. Scented soaps and lotions." She looked inside the narrow drawers, patting her fingers across more linens, oils, and balms. She hugged herself. "I feel like a queen," she said with a shy glance back at Graham.

"Ye are a queen to me." Graham poured from one of the bottles, pausing to sniff the contents. Fruity. Potent. "Port. Do ye fancy a glass? 'Tis stronger than the wine of our feast." 'Twas only fair to warn her. He'd not approach her until he was certain she wished him to do so, and neither would he attempt to ply her with alcohol to lower her defenses. He needed her to want him as much as he wanted her.

"Perhaps one." Mercy accepted a glass and hurried to take a sip. She hitched in a nervous breath, wet her lips, and took a step toward the window. She stopped and looked back at him. "Might we open the window?"

"Of course." Graham set his glass on the table, then moved past Mercy to unlatch the multiple casings of the wide windows and push them open. He turned and smiled, holding out a hand. "'Tis a lovely night. Come and see. We're in the tower that looks out across the mountainside."

To his profound relief, Mercy took his hand and stood close beside him. The cool night breeze greeted them, wafting in and riffling through Mercy's dark tresses. Entranced by the silkiness dancing in the wind, he slid his hand close to her neck and allowed her hair to pour across his fingers. "I love your hair loose," he whispered.

Mercy glanced down at her hands for less than a moment, set her glass upon the windowsill, and lifted her gaze to his. "Might I have a kiss, husband?"

Graham's heart thrilled, and the fiery ache burning within him raged all the stronger. Without a word, he slid his arms around her, pulled her close, and ever so tenderly covered her mouth with his. Mercy's hands smoothed up his back as she opened and took him in, matching the flicks and touches of his tongue. She tasted of wine, and to his relief, a growing urgency that matched his own. Graham drew back from the softness of her lips, nuzzled along her jawline, then paused and looked into her eyes. "Ye're a rare gem, Mercy, and I'm thankful to have found ye."

Peering up at him, worry shadowed her eyes as she trailed her fingertips along his cheek as though memorizing every detail of his features. "I almost fear loving you," she whispered, then shook her head before he could speak. "Not just because of the dangers." A sad smile curved her lovely mouth as her focus dropped to his chest where she'd taken to tucking and twisting the ends of his neckcloth. "I fear if I allow myself to love you—then fail you..." She shrugged a shoulder and knotted her fists against him. "If I'm a disappointing wife, you shall be forced to set me aside, and I'll be alone again." Lifting her gaze to his, she stared at him, turmoil churning in her eyes. "And this time, alone will be much worse, because I shall be without you."

Cupping her face between his hands, Graham silenced her with a long, deep kiss, then drew back and pressed a lighter kiss to her forehead before gathering her to his chest and holding her tight. "Ye willna be a disappointing wife. How could ye disappoint me? I'm the one who should be worried, lass, but I'm so smitten with ye, I'm too selfish to let ye go."

"What should you be worried about?" Mercy sniffed and nuzzled closer, the heat of her breath warming the center of his chest where she'd buried her face. "You've been nothing but kind and understanding."

"Maybe so," Graham countered with unabashed pride as he gently swayed back and forth with her in his arms. He so relished the feel of her against him. At least, she thought well of him. "I don't have home or land to offer ye. We're dependent on the generosity of my brother and thankfully, Alexander wants family around him. We dinna have a home of our own. I dinna ken where we might settle and claim our own place."

"That doesn't matter to me," Mercy whispered. "But I have a confession."

Graham braced himself, after all Mercy and her family had endured, whatever else she was about to confess had to be horrid. He swallowed hard, then kissed the top of her head. It didn't matter what it was—he'd love her all the same. "What is your confession, lass? Tell me. I swear ye've nothing to fear."

She shifted against him, burying her face into his chest. Her gentle mumbling into his shirt alerted him she'd said *something*. Although, for the life of him, he hadn't heard what.

He eased her back and looked her in the eyes. "Again. Tell me so I can hear ye."

For a short, uneasy pause, Mercy caught her lip between her teeth and chewed it. "I have never seen a man." She paused and cleared her throat. "Without clothing," she whispered. "Except for your shoulders and chest that day at the river," she hurried to add.

Graham clenched his teeth to keep from laughing aloud. This was his dear love's confession? It was a boon to know his bride to be so pure and untouched. If possible, it made him love her even more. She would truly and utterly be his.

"I can remedy that easy enough." He slid his hands to his jacket to strip it off, but Mercy stopped him.

"Wait!" She snatched up her glass of port, emptied it, and held it out. "Don't think me a coward, but could I please have another drink first. I am certain these feelings I'm having right now are most unseemly."

Not trusting himself to speak, Graham gave his beloved wife a polite bow. He took her glass, refilled it, then handed it back to her. What unseemly feelings was she having? Such words sounded most promising. Hopefully, the brazenness he'd witnessed at the river with her was about to return.

Mercy held the glass between her hands as she circled him, her gaze skimming up and down, flitting across his clothing, and having the same effect as if she touched him in the intimate ways a woman could touch a man. If he didn't get relief soon, his ballocks would surely explode. The sobering thought made him pull in a deep breath. It had been a long while since he'd had a woman, he'd best get control, or tonight would end before it even started.

"Should I..." Mercy started as she stared down at her dress. "Should I don my nightrail first?"

Graham wished to tell her not to bother, because if he had his way about it, both of them would soon be naked as the day they were born and remain that way for what he hoped would be a very long while. But judging by Mercy's expression, he thought better of it before the words slipped out.

He nodded toward the intricately embroidered privacy screen, framed in wood, and consisting of three panels. Thank God for Catriona. His sister-in-law had seen fit to place the thing in the corner of the room beside the wardrobe, knowing Mercy might need a bit of privacy over the course of their first nights together as man and wife. "It appears the maids hung your night dress there. Shall I help ye with your ties before ye slip behind the screen?"

Mercy's hand went to the back of her neck, recollection alighting her features. She turned and gave her back to him, sweeping her hair to the side in the process. "That would be most kind," she said in a tremulous whisper.

Graham's fingers shook as he took hold of the ribbons and set to their undoing. With every pull of the tie through the loop, the dress opened wider, exposing Mercy's silky back. Graham swallowed hard and shifted in place, widening his stance. At last, the loving of Mercy had begun.

THANK HEAVENS FOR the cool breeze from the open window brushing her nape. Mercy closed her eyes as she held her hair out of Graham's way while he undid the ties of her gown. The gentle tugging started at the top of her shoulders, traveled down her back, then finished at her waist, the snug bodice of the gown relaxing away from her body as Graham moved downward. Before the gown fell completely away, Mercy caught it up to her bosom and held it in place, pressing both hands against the hammering of her heart in the process.

Graham brushed a kiss across the top of her bared shoulder, triggering a tingling shiver through her. She ached for him. Oh, so badly. But did not understand what to do to sate this heated anxiousness that made her feel as though she was about to burst into flames. He kissed the top of her other shoulder and nuzzled his way up the back of her neck, pressing against her as he did so. Even through the layers of clothing between them, there was no doubt that Graham wanted her, too. And soon, *all* would be revealed.

She hurried behind the screen and removed the dress. Hands at the tied waist of her petticoat, she paused, reliving the sensation of Graham's ardor so long and hard against her backside. She'd seen sculptures and portraits of men's *parts*. But none of them had seemed as large as Graham's had felt pressed against her. She fanned herself for a moment before removing her petticoat and stays, then bent and smoothed her stockings off her legs. Much better.

Discovering a washstand with a small basin and a pitcher of water beside the cabinet holding the chamber pot, Mercy splashed water on her face and patted it dry with a linen. Excitement, desire, and worry churned inside her. Her head was swimming. She'd had entirely too much to drink.

Breathing in slow, deep breaths, she slipped the lightweight night rail over her head and shook it down around her hips and to her ankles. She smoothed her hands over the cloth, mildly alarmed that the darkness of her nipples and the triangle of hair between her thighs was easily discernible through the thin weave. *Oh, dear.* Well...it wasn't as though Graham hadn't seen her before. After all, he'd quite clearly watched her disrobe and walk into the river for her swim. Oh, what she wouldn't give for the bravado and daring she'd possessed that day. But that day had been safe. Nothing could happen with the possibility of Janie or one of the others discovering them. Tonight was different.

"Are ye well, love?"

She could hear Graham moving about the room, no doubt impatient for her to find her courage and join him. "Yes. Quite well." She stepped out from behind the screen, crossing her arms in front of her body. Her breath caught at the passion she saw in Graham's eyes. It was now or never.

She gave a shy nod toward his jacket. "You may remove your jacket now."

His smoldering gaze locked with hers. Graham's large, calloused hands moved slow and steady, peeling back the jacket, slipping it from his wide shoulders, and tossing it to a chair. With slow, teasing pulls, he untied his neckcloth and unwound it. His hands went to the buttons of his waistcoat, fluttering them open in rapid succession, shedding the garment, tossing it over to join his jacket. Then his hands dropped away, and he stood staring at her in his tunic, kilt, and boots. "Come closer," he whispered.

Mercy complied, powered more by his mesmerizing hold on her than her own free will. She came to a halt within two strides from him.

"Closer, lass," he urged her softly. "I need another sample of your sweet lips." His gaze raked across her. The look in his eyes professing that Graham wanted a great deal more than just a kiss.

Stepping close enough that his heat embraced her, Mercy rested her hands on his chest. The rock-hard heat of his muscles through the linen never ceased to thrill her. She slid her hands higher, reveling in the cut contours of his body. This must be how a sculptor felt upon caressing a wondrous creation.

Graham responded with a groan before taking her mouth with his, smoothing his hands down her back, then cupping her bottom and pulling her harder into him.

The kiss left her breathless, aching, needing. She gathered the hem of his tunic in both hands and lifted it upward. "I would see you. *All* of you." She grazed a kiss against the span of chest, touching the tip of her tongue to his salty, sweet flesh. "Please."

"Aye." Graham pulled away the tunic, unbelted his kilt, and allowed it drop into a puddle around his boots. Heel to toe, he worked off the footwear and kicked them aside. "I hope ye dinna mind." He grinned. "I unlaced them whilst ye donned your night rail."

Mercy pressed trembling fingers to her mouth as she took a step back, taking in the glory that was Graham. A broad chest, perfectly sculpted with a dusting of black hair that accentuated his muscular build. Trim waist and oh... How in Heaven's name? No sculpture, tapestry, nor any form of art had ever depicted a man such a way. So...formidable. Mercy swallowed hard. How could it possibly not rend her in two?

Awareness flashed across Graham's countenance. He stepped forward, taking gentle hold of her shoulders as he bent and peered into her face. "Trust me, lass. There will be some pain, but I swear to ye,

I'll be as easy as I can. And once we're past your maidenhead, the pain will be no more." He brushed a soft kiss across her parted lips. "Trust me."

She allowed her hands to fall away and closed her eyes as he removed her night dress and it puddled to the floor.

"Such beauty." Graham's whispered words tickled across the bareness of her flesh as he kissed along her shoulder, then moved lower. "Ye may touch me, if ye like, m'love. I ken ye're curious."

He had no idea how curious. But overwhelmed and slightly afraid, too. She pressed a kiss to his shoulder, then lowered her hand and touched him. So hard yet so velvety smooth.

"May I carry ye to our bed, love?" Graham eased back a pace but trailed his fingers from her jaw, to her throat, then down between her breasts and settled both hands to her waist. "Let me love ye, Mercy."

Not trusting herself to speak, Mercy nodded, holding tight to Graham as he scooped her up into his arms. He walked over to the four-poster bed and gently placed her on it. Sliding back into the pillows, Mercy smoothed her hands along the sheets. "I see you turned back the bed as well as unlaced your boots while I undressed. Was I really behind the screen all that long?"

Graham gave her an intense look and grinned. "Long enough, lass." He slid into the bed beside her, pushing one arm beneath her shoulders and pulling her close. Kissing her with a need that chased all other thoughts and worries from her mind, Mercy shuddered and held Graham tighter. The more he touched, the more she needed. The more he tasted, the more the breathless, frenzied feeling grew. Skin against skin. Sensations stronger than she ever thought possible. Fire burned within her, overtaking her. His fingers teased and taunted ever higher along her inner thighs, then slipped deep inside her. A sudden stinging caught her unawares.

Mercy tensed, digging her nails into his shoulders, biting her lip to keep from crying out.

Holding her close, Graham tenderly cradled her, brushing light kisses across her face as he shushed her. "I'm sorry, lass. 'Twill be better now, though, when I actually join with ye."

They lay like that for a little while, Graham doing nothing more than holding her and trailing his fingers up and down her spine as they lay on their sides facing one another. Heart to heart. Two halves needing to become a whole. Mercy nuzzled her face deeper into the crook of his neck, breathing in the scent of him as his chest pressed against her breasts, his body molded into hers. The need returned. Her fire was ready to be stoked, then quenched. Mercy hugged a leg over Graham's hips and rolled to her back, pulling him with her.

"Show me," she breathed. "Show me what it is to be your wife."

"Gladly, love," Graham groaned as he settled between her legs. Gently. Slowly. He pushed into her, then waited, kissing her as he trembled above her. "Relax love. Relax and let me in. It willna hurt again as it did earlier."

She feared him wrong. After all, his manhood was so much larger than his fingers. Mercy forced herself to relax, breathing deeper and giving herself to the promise of ecstasy. The wondrous fullness convinced her Graham was right. This wasn't pain. This was a powerful, maddening pleasure. She matched her thrusts with his, their rhythm quickening. Whirling pleasure exploded and spun her away. Rapturous sensations thrummed across her body in unrelenting waves of bliss. She cried out in delight.

Graham roared, plunging hard and deep, then held fast and spasmed within her embrace. He sagged atop her with a satisfied groan, rolled to his side, then pulled her into the curve of his arm. They both gasped to catch their breath.

"I love ye, my wife," Graham said between kisses to her forehead, "More than ye shall ever ken."

"And I love you, my husband," Mercy murmured as she melted into him and hugged a leg tight around him. "With all my heart."

CHAPTER NINETEEN

H E AWAKENED TO her breath tickling across his chest. With every deep inhale and gentle exhale she made, her breasts brushed against him. She shifted in her sleep, hugging a leg around him and pressing closer. Graham hardened, aching and ready to return to the pleasure of his wife's sweet warmth. It didn't matter that they'd loved and learned of each other 'til the rosy glow of the rising sun had filled the room. Morning birdsong had bid them good rest when they'd at last succumbed to an exhausted sleep. He'd never tire of her. Not after an eternity of sunrises and sunsets.

The room was dim again, filled with the ever-darkening shadows of early evening. Cooler night air wafted in through the windows. A smile overtook him. After a long night of loving, they had slept through the entirety of their first day as husband and wife. A promising start to their marriage.

Mercy shifted again and hummed out a low, soft moan followed by a light breathy snore. Graham eased his way out from under her, his stomach choosing that opportune moment to growl its displeasure at being empty for so long. He held his breath as Mercy emitted a sleepy sound resembling the mewling of a kitten, then rolled over to her other side, her fine, firm bottom giving a tempting wiggle as she nestled deeper into the covers. As much as he ached to awaken her in a most enjoyable manner, a trip behind the privy screen was sorely needed. A tankard of ale and a bit of bread for his empty stomach would not be amiss either.

After a visit to the chamber pot and a splash of cool water to his face, Graham padded over to the table filled with food. He selected a few dried plums, a chunk of cheese, and a bannock in one hand, whilst filling a tankard with ale. Lounging down into the corner of the window seat, Graham propped his back against the wall after settling down. He breathed in the night air and peered up at the rising moon, thanking God for blessing him with such bounty. A beautiful wife. A generous brother who had told them to stay as long as they liked. The opportunity to start anew after the decimation of all he'd known and loved when his clan had died away.

Rustling from the direction of the bed pulled his attention away. The sight of her caused his breathing to hitch, and he nearly choked on the bite of bread he hurried to swallow. Her beauty never ceased to amaze him.

Mercy stood beside the bed, stretching her arms to the ceiling, oblivious of her breathtaking nudity. Her pale skin took on a pearlescent glow in the half light of the room. The dark river of her hair rippled across her form like a silk curtain. At the end of her stretch, her sleepy-eyed gaze found Graham. She hurried to gather up her nightrail and slip it on.

Graham found her modesty both endearing and amusing.

"Food. What a good idea." She flashed a shy smile at him. A smile that made him consider setting his food aside whilst he bent her over the arm of the chair and reawakened the temptress who had shared his bed last night. "Stay there," she said in the low, soft voice that stoked his need to an urgency. "I'll join you."

Graham drained his tankard, stretched to hook the pitcher from the nearby table, and poured himself another. He patted a spot on the cushion. "I've a place for ye right here, love."

After pouring herself some wine and selecting a whisky-soaked slice of sweetmeat, Mercy sauntered toward him with such a slow, seductive swing of her hips, he thought he'd surely die. *Ah...but what a fine way to go.*

She bit into the juicy cake, then tortured him even more by licking away the excess juice of the delicacy as it trickled down the side of her hand and dripped off her wrist. Setting her wine glass on the ledge, she set her knee between his legs, then leaned in and held the treat close to his mouth. "Would you like a bite?" she asked with smiling innocence.

"Only of yourself, m'love." Graham couldn't bear it any longer. He'd never get enough of her. He set his hands about her waist, lifted her up over his lap, then thrust her down atop him, returning to the wondrous pleasure that consumed him.

"Oh my," Mercy gasped in breathless abandon, her dressing gown bunched up around her hips.

"Oh my, indeed." Graham nuzzled his way down her neck, pushed aside the neckline of her gown, and kissed the satin of her collarbone as he cupped her breasts.

The cake fell out of her hand as Mercy shuddered. "Oh my...yes."

Graham lifted her up and lay her back across the window seat. "Aye, love. Yes, indeed." He settled down between her thighs and buried himself to the hilt, rocking into her with an age-old rhythm.

Mercy arched beneath him, meeting him thrust for thrust. She raked her nails down his back and cried out, her wet heat clutching around him and pulling him deeper. Heart pounding, Graham hammered forward and roared out his release.

Arms propped on either side of her to keep from crushing her, Graham collapsed. He pressed a kiss to her damp temple. "Lore a'mighty, love. I'll never get my fill of ye."

Stroking her fingertips up and down his sides, Mercy breathed out a happy sigh. "Nor I you, my love. Nor I you." Her stomach whined out a delicate growl between them. "Oh dear."

Graham chuckled, raised up a bit, and kissed her forehead. "Perhaps, I shouldha waited until ye finished your cake."

The prettiest shade of red stained her cheeks. Mercy tucked her face into the curve of his throat. "Perhaps we should eat. Do you wonder if anyone has ever grown weak and died in this manner?"

"If I had to choose a way to die, this would be it." Graham wrapped an arm around her, and resituated them to a seated position on the bench with Mercy cradled in his lap.

A look of sadness flashed across her face. She pressed a hand to his chest and leaned closer. "Promise me you won't die first. I could never bear to be alone again. Not after being with you."

"Shh…'tis all right lass." Graham laced his fingers through her hair. "Ye mustn't dwell on what we canna control, ye ken? 'Twould be a damned shame to let one unknown moment in the future steal away the happiness of all your days. Leave tomorrow's worries to tomorrow, aye?"

Mercy smiled and covered his hand with hers. "How are you so wise?"

"I'm a Scot."

Mercy laughed, but soon stopped as she shifted on his lap and discovered he was hard again. Her eyes widened. "Again? So soon? Is that normal?"

"Like I said, lass, I'm a Scot."

She took hold of his shoulders and gave him a stern look. "Before we start again, sir, I would like to make it clear, I want a daughter first."

Graham clamped hold of her fine, round behind and rubbed her back and forth against his rigid member. "Nay, love. A son first. Then a daughter if ye like. That way she'll be protected by her brother."

"Just two children?" Mercy asked as she stretched out across the bench and reached for him.

"Oh no, lass," Graham argued as he dove into her embrace and returned to the pleasure only Mercy could give. "At least six or more." He pounded harder, nearing the point of no return. His poor man parts had never had so much enjoyment in such a short span of time. "Mayhap a dozen wee bairns, aye?"

"Yes!" Mercy cried out. "Yes!" she shrieked, arching and bucking beneath him.

Her release was all it took to finish him. Graham held her fast and plunged faster, emptying into her with a throat-burning roar.

"A dozen it is," Mercy rasped out between gasps.

Wrapping his arms tight around her, Graham pressed a kiss to her damp forehead. "And dinna forget—a son first."

"Hmm," Mercy responded, nuzzling her cheek to his.

A loud horn shattered their peacefulness.

Mercy pushed him away, scrambling to get them both up from the bench. "What is that?"

A chilling, ominous sense of doom filled Graham. "An alert to the clan."

"What kind of alert?" The look she gave him struck him in the heart. Mercy was terrified. Damn it all to hell. Their brief, carefree happiness was at an end.

"It could be nothing," he said as he yanked his tunic on over his head and hurried to wrap and belt his kilt around his body.

"But it could be something very dire." Mercy rose from the bench, hands knotted. "It could be Campbell and his troops, couldn't it?"

Graham hated to fill her with even more fear, but he'd never lie to her. Planting false hope was far crueler than the truth. He nodded as he shoved his feet into his boots. "Aye. It could be." He pondered for a moment. There had been but one blast of the guard tower horn. That did bode well, indeed. If something dire was about, the horn would still be sounding. "But I dinna think it is. The horn sounded the alarm but once."

Rushing over to the wardrobe beside the bed, Mercy threw open the doors. "Thank goodness Catriona had my clothes mended and put them in here." The few garments Mercy had rolled up inside blankets and lashed behind her saddle before they'd sent the wagons away hung in a neat row inside the cabinet. She snatched one of her odd pantalette skirt creations with its adapted petticoat, a strangely short chemise, and the jacket that matched. With her clothing clutched to her chest, she hurried across the room and slipped behind the privy screen to the pitcher and bowl of water.

Between the sounds of splashing, Graham heard Mercy muttering under her breath but couldn't make out a word. Finished with his own dressing, Graham strode toward the door, knowing in his heart he was about to start a battle he'd never win. He stared at Mercy's silhouette showing through the screen, willing her to cooperate with what he was about to say. "I wish ye to remain here until I send for ye, ye ken? I want to make sure 'tis safe before ye come down and join me."

The splashing of the water stopped. "What did you say?"

"Ye heard me, lass." Graham braced himself for the worst. He felt the storm of Mercy's stubborn determination coming.

"I will be coming downstairs to face whatever is about to happen. Now you can either wait and escort me down, or I shall find the way myself. The choice is yours."

Graham scrubbed a hand across his face, clenching his teeth and forcing himself to wait a moment before responding so he wouldn't raise his voice. Leave it to him to marry a woman with a will as strong as his own. "I would have my wife safe," he stated carefully. "And I would have her do as I ask."

"Then you have the wrong wife," Mercy said as she emerged from behind the screen, fully clothed, with shoes and stockings in hand. "Our marriage will not be one where I cower behind my husband." She perched on the arm of the chair by the hearth, pulled on her stockings, and secured them in place with a ribbon tied snug above each knee. Pinning him with a determined look as she slipped on her shoes, she added, "I shall fight at your side until I no longer draw breath."

The thought of endangering her, of losing her, threatened to make him roar at her until she understood and bent to his will. "Ye begged me to no' die first because ye feared being alone. Think ye I wish to be abandoned because of your stubborn unwillingness to allow yourself to be protected?"

The guard tower horn sounded again, longer and louder this time. Graham pointed a finger at the window. "Do ye hear the horn? 'Tis an alarm to the clan. Wait here until I send for ye. Do this for me, Mercy, I beg ye. I swear I'll send one of the maids to let ye know what's about and if it's safe to come down." He strode across the room and took hold of her, staring into her eyes for the span of a heartbeat before kissing her long and hard. Tearing himself away, he lifted his head and set her away but still held tight to her shoulders. "Swear ye will wait here, aye?"

Mercy reached up and touched his face, her emotions clearly at war with his. The coolness of her palm pressed against his cheek threatened to weaken him. Brow furrowed and mouth clamped into a tight frown, her delicate nostrils flared as she huffed out a hard, ladylike snort. "I shall wait here for a time." She pointed to the half-spent candle burning on the table. "'Til the flame reaches the bottom of the candle. I can bear no longer." She turned away and moved to stand by the window. With frustrated jerking motions, she replaced the spent candles in the candelabra and lit the new ones. "This danger is because of me, Graham. You must allow my help in diffusing it." She looked back at him, the glow of the freshly lit candles revealing a sudden weariness in her expression. "This is my battle. It's been going on far longer than you have known me."

Her pain and frustration reached out to him, took hold of his heart, and twisted. Woman or no', Mercy was a warrior, and Graham knew well enough the raw, choking rage it was to be set aside and not allowed to wade into the thick of things, especially when the battle was your own. He reached down and pulled his *sgian dhu* from his boot, strode across the room to her, and before she could react, he slid the knife down between her breasts, tucking it snug behind the rigid stomacher at the front of her corset. "If ye get yourself killed, I swear to God Almighty that I'll cross over right behind ye and tan your arse. Do ye understand me, wife?"

Mercy lowered her gaze, but Graham could tell damned good and well that she only did it to hide her joy at wearing him down and getting her own way. "I understand, husband."

He took her hand and led her to the doorway, pausing as he took hold of the latch. What in Hell's name was he doing endangering her so? He was a damned fool not to hold fast and make her stay where he knew her safe at least for a little while.

"It will be all right, Graham," she said quietly, with a squeeze of his shoulder. "I can face anything as long I'm at your side."

"Ye shouldna have to face anything, love." Graham brushed a tender kiss to her hand and hugged it to his chest. "Not while I live and breathe. 'Tis my duty to face it for ye."

Mercy's eyes shimmered with unshed tears. Her head tilted to one side and her lower lip quivered as she studied him. With a sudden hard dip of her chin, she released his hand, took a step back, then withdrew his dagger from its concealed spot between her breasts. She held it out. "I shall wait until you call for me. I shouldn't have treated your wishes so lightly."

Graham stared at the *sgian dhu,* warring with his emotions. She understood. He shook his head and pressed it back to her. "Put it back where I placed it, lass. In case ye need it."

With an obedient nod, Mercy tucked the knife back in place. As Graham pulled the door open and moved to step out into the hall, she caught hold of his arm. "If you get yourself killed, I swear to God Almighty that I shall cross over after you and tan your *arse.* And my brother and mother will be there to help me. Understood?"

An even deeper appreciation for this rare woman flooded through him, nearly taking him to his knees. Graham chuckled. "Aye, m'love. Understood."

CHAPTER TWENTY

M ERCY BOLTED THE door behind Graham, then hurried to the bench in front of the window. Hiking her skirted pantalettes up to her knees, she crawled up onto the window ledge and perched in one of the casings. With a tight hold to the iron supports surrounding the panes of glass, she leaned out as far as she could. If only their chamber was at the front of the keep rather than located in the rear wing of the stronghold overlooking the mountains. And it was full on nighttime by now. Granted, the sliver of moon shone bright, and not a cloud hid the stars, but she still couldn't see a blasted thing. She strained to pick up on any noise that might give her more information.

No shouting. No metal on metal. No gunfire. That gave her some comfort. She slid back down to the window seat and fisted her hands in her lap. She had half a mind to sneak down and spy from the staircase, but she couldn't. Not in good conscience. She had told Graham she would wait for him here. So, wait for him she would.

"I am a fool for saying such," she said to the room in general.

She jumped up from the seat, poured herself a glass of honeyed wine, and downed it. Smacking her lips, she eyed the bottle of port. *Better not.* It took very little port to make her head reel.

Depending on what developed downstairs, she most certainly needed to keep her wits about her. She poured another glass of wine and took to pacing. As she walked back and forth across the room, she smiled at the awareness of a subtle soreness with every step. She was a true wife now. A moment of happiness thrilled through her. Perhaps they'd even seeded a child already. Her cheeks heated. Their love had peaked many times. She'd never imagined such sensations, such feelings.

The door rattled, startling her out of her musings. She froze in place, holding her breath, hand pressed to her chest to draw the dagger.

"'Tis me, lass. Open the door."

A noisy exhale escaped her. Graham. Thank God. She rushed to undo the latch and open the door. "You've returned so soon! Good news, I pray?"

Graham's dark look dashed her excitement.

"Tell me," she said, taking hold of both his hands. "Are we under attack?"

"Not yet." He motioned her toward the hall and extended his arm for her to take. "But we soon will be if we dinna piss out this wee flame threatening to blow into a bonfire."

They rushed down the hallway. Energy surged through her, making it difficult to breathe. As they hurried down the staircase, Mercy steadied herself by sliding her hand along the rough surface of the stone wall. Her heart pounded into her throat. She swallowed hard to keep it from strangling her. What threatened them now? Had father sent more men? Had he unleashed the Campbells? "What flame, Graham? Are the Campbells about to attack?"

"They have reported ye as kidnapped." They reached the first level of the keep and Graham picked up the pace, turning them toward the great hall. "His Majesty's guard as well as Campbell's regiment have been dispatched to recover ye and they've been informed to give no quarter."

Mercy stopped in her tracks. "Kill any and all in their path?" She closed her eyes, pulled in deep breaths, and struggled not to sob out her fury. "How could they?"

Graham steadied her, holding her close. "Dinna give up hope, lass. Soldiers from Fort William are here to investigate. 'Tis the Earl of Crestshire's regiment. He is friend to us. Fostered with the MacCoinnichs for several years before my clan fell ill. He and Alexander are like brothers."

The faintest hope flickered within her, easing the panic. "So, His Majesty suspects the report of kidnapping to be a ruse?"

"It is our hope." Graham halted as they reached the last stone archway, the entrance to the great hall. "We will get through this, love," he reassured with a kiss to her temple.

She buried her face in the crook of his neck, wrapping her arms around him and squeezing with all her might. His warmth, his strength, the steady beating of his heart against her lips, steadied her. "I love you," she whispered.

His arms tightened around her even more. "I love ye, too, m'dear sweet lass. Love ye more than ye'll ever ken."

Mercy eased out of Graham's embrace, smoothed her clothes, and lifted her chin. "I am ready."

Mercy assumed the pleasant demeanor Mama had taught her. *One must never appear vulnerable. If the enemy senses it, your weakness will grow, and you will be conquered.* Mama had survived so much. Mercy would honor her memory by surviving. They entered the great hall and alarm pulsed through her.

"Janie," she said from between clenched teeth in a voice for Graham alone.

Janie, wide-eyed, and red-cheeked, stood slightly behind the tall, broad-shouldered commander. Janie's hands twisted into trembling fists in front of her waist. With her red hair mussed and clothing smudged and torn, the maid looked worse for her alliance with those who would see Mercy fall.

The commander, immaculate not only in his uniform but with perfect blonde hair and sharp blue eyes, stepped forward and bowed. "Lord Crestshire at your service, Lady Claxton. It is my upmost pleasure to meet you."

"Actually, Lord Crestshire, my name is now MacCoinnich, but you may address me as Lady Mercy." She gave a slight curtsy along with a reserved smile. Graham had named the man as friend, but she'd decide for herself whether he warranted that designation.

Crestshire gave a curt nod, and his military stance appeared to relax. He gave Graham a genuine smile and then shared it with her. "Congratulations to you both, Lady Mercy. May God bless you with a long, happy life together."

"My husband tells me I have been reported kidnapped." She riveted her stern glare on Janie. "Who filed such a report?"

Janie jerked, then lowered her gaze to the floor. "Not me, mistress. I've done nothing but try to prove to you I would never wrong you. I swear it." The girl's voice trembled. "I'm here to help you any way I can."

Graham squeezed Mercy's arm. "The lass speaks the truth. We judged her poorly. Hear what Crestshire has to say."

Crestshire motioned toward Janie. "Miss Hughson came to the garrison and refused to leave until I granted her a meeting." He stepped back, took hold of Janie's arm, and walked her forward until she stood in front of Mercy. "She reported all that had happened during your trip through the Highlands, including the attack by the miscreants hired by Lord Edsbury. Your husband confirmed everything she said." He looked first at Graham, then at Duncan who had taken a stance to Mercy's right. "She also attested to the protection given by these two MacCoinnichs." Amusement softened his stern demeanor. "But she failed to tell me you had married one of them."

"I didn't know she married him. I only knew she loved Master MacCoinnich." Janie gave a dismissive shrug. "I knew she wasn't pretending like her father told her to."

Mercy had treated her so badly. Misjudging poor Janie.

Mercy held out both hands. "Can you ever forgive me?"

Janie slid her hands into hers. "I understand why you acted as you did. Especially after everyone turned on you." She squeezed Mercy's hands. "I hope you know I'd never betray you, m'lady. Never."

Mercy pulled Janie into a tight hug. "I am very sorry, Janie." She blinked hard against the threat of tears as she took hold of Janie's shoulders and squeezed. "But you're here now, and here you will stay—if you wish it."

"Oh yes, m'lady." The frazzled weariness fell away from Janie, replaced by a vibrant, joyous glow. "I was hoping you'd ask me to stay. I've nowhere else to go."

Catriona stepped forward. After a nod and smile toward Mercy, she waved one of the kitchen maids forward to stand beside Janie. "Jenny, this is Janie Hughson. Help her get cleaned up and settled in, so she can serve her mistress properly."

"Yes, m'lady." Jenny bobbed in place, then took Janie by the arm and led her away.

"I feel so badly about the way I treated her." Mercy watched her maid hurry away at Jenny's side, both girls already chatting as though they were fast friends.

"Ye had no way of knowing," Catriona said. "Not after the way the rest of them betrayed ye." She turned aside. "A curse on every one of them."

"They're doomed for certain now." Alexander took hold of his wife's arm and hugged her to his side. He grinned at Mercy and the rest of those gathered.

Catriona smiled. "Cook said supper's ready. Sit and eat whilst ye plan your battle."

Battle. The word sent a chill clear to the marrow of Mercy's bones.

"Easy, lass," Graham said, his deep, calming tone soothing her.

"We have the beginnings of a plan." He led her to her seat, then took the chair beside her.

"That we do," Lord Crestshire agreed. "This very evening, I shall send an urgent missive notifying His Majesty of your happiness, your willingness, and your obvious consent to be Graham's wife." Crestshire folded his hands above his plate, casually observing as a servant reached in between him and Duncan to fill his wine glass. "But I have concerns. I fear it will not be enough for the king to call off his guards or the Campbells." He shifted with a deep inhale. "King William does not like to be made to look the fool, even when he is wrong."

Mercy agreed. Memories of her family's dealings with the king, both personal and public, validated Lord Crestshire's observations. "Lord Crestshire is right. King William never admits when he's wrong."

"Ye could go to France," Catriona suggested. "Surely, he'd leave ye be there. He's too busy warring with the French and doesna have money to spare. He'd no' have the time to send Campbell chasing after ye."

"But he could send Campbell here," Mercy replied, looking to Alexander at the head of the table as she did so. She could tell by his expression that he'd thought the same thing but just hadn't said it aloud. "I have to find a way to convince King William to accept my marriage *and* call Campbell off."

"You shall be hard pressed to do that, m'lady," Captain Marsden said from farther down the table. "There is the matter of the betrothal His Highness arranged for you. He is sure to be most displeased when he discovers his plans will not come to fruition and will have to notify all concerned that the betrothal is off."

Mercy bowed her head and massaged her temples, willing it all to go away and leave her to the happiness of her new life. A dismal, sickening realization came to her. "I have to go back," she whispered without lifting her head.

"What?" Graham leaned in close, took her hand, and squeezed. "Go back where?"

"To court." Mercy took a deep breath and stared at the center of the table. It was the only way. "I shall seek a private audience with the king." She turned to Graham, wishing she could stay here forever. "He's never denied me any requests in the past."

Graham raked a hand through his hair, still loose about his shoulders. He looked a wild, untamable warrior, and she loved him for it. "I dinna like that at all. What about your father?"

"If King William listens to me and calls off Campbell, that should silence my father as well." She gave Graham a sad smile and brushed a finger along the day's growth of stubble along his jaw. He'd been clean shaven when he'd taken her to their marriage bed. "Few will listen to a penniless duke banned from court and His Majesty's presence." She almost added that her father might finally understand all that she, her mother, and her brother had endured, but she knew better.

"Would ye accompany us, Edward?" Alexander asked, his calm focus sliding over to Lord Crestshire.

"What?" Mercy interrupted before Lord Crestshire could answer. "This is not your concern, Chieftain MacCoinnich. In fact, if I could find a way to do so, Graham would stay here and I would go alone."

"Ye no longer bear the burden of being *one* in this world, m'love. We are *one* together, ye ken?" Graham said.

"Well said, brother. And let us make something else clear whilst we're about it." Alexander leaned forward, his scrutiny pinned on Mercy. "I'm no' Chieftain MacCoinnich to ye, good sister. I'm your brother, Alexander, ye ken?" He waited for Mercy to acknowledge his words. "And I'll also add that a MacCoinnich never fights alone. Your battle is our battle as well."

"If I could come along, I would," Catriona said. "But I willna take my babies into such dangers, nor will I leave them to the nursemaid as yet." Catriona smiled. "But dinna doubt for a moment if Willa and

William were older, I'd no' hesitate to travel at your side."

"Will ye come with us then, Edward?" Graham asked. "I dinna care overmuch for the pomp and foolery of court. An Englishman at my side might help."

"I doubt that," Lord Crestshire said with a snort. "But I will go and do my best to keep you from getting into trouble."

Graham scratched his chin, squinting as he stared off into nothingness. "Even with the best horses, 'twill take us at least a sennight or more to get to London. And that's at a hard, steady ride with but a few hours of rest each day—just enough for the horses' needs." He kissed Mercy's hand, released it, and reached for his tankard. "Do ye ken the whereabouts of Campbell and the king's guard? And how many? I dinna care overmuch about leaving *Tor Ruadh* to the wolves."

"We can defend ourselves just fine, brother," Catriona said. She glared at Graham as she reached over and rested her hand atop Alexander's arm. "MacCoinnich warriors will guard us well and keep us safe. I grant ye that."

Mercy made to sip at her wine but didn't attempt to eat. Emotions threatened to overcome her. Her new family overwhelmed her with their caring. They'd been complete strangers only days ago, but now they were willing to risk everything to protect her. They'd taken her in and embraced her. Treated her with an accepting love she hadn't experienced since Mama and Akio.

A tear escaped and raced a hot trail down her cheek. She swiped it away, sniffing to prevent anymore from falling.

Catriona jumped up from her seat and raced around the table to hug her. "Dinna cry, lass. We'll get through this, and soon our wee bairns will be tumbling and playing across the heather together."

The men shifted in their seats, giving each other uncomfortable glances, and taking deep draughts of their ale. They could plan battles and killing all day long, but not one of them had the courage to face a woman in tears.

"I'm fine." Mercy sniffed as she patted Catriona's hand still on her shoulder. "Thank you so much, dear sister."

"Think nothing of it, lass. Ye're our own now." Catriona hugged her one last time, then returned to her seat.

"So, Lord Crestshire." Mercy sat taller and fixed the commander with a polite smile. "As my husband asked, how many men are we dealing with?"

"I'd say about a hundred men. Campbell's regiment is only about fifty or so now. They broke off from Argyll's six hundred after Glencoe. The king's guard is massive but are dedicated to other causes." He took a healthy swallow from his tankard, then supported his assessment with a slow nod. "They have already made their way into Scotland, but I received a report they've been instructed to report to Fort William before coming here. That will work to our advantage. They can be delayed there while we seek an audience with His Majesty."

"Can we be ready by morning?" Mercy looked to Graham, then turned to Alexander. "We must make haste."

"Aye, lass," Alexander said.

"Then tomorrow it is," Graham said. "The sooner we end this, the better."

CHAPTER TWENTY-ONE

"**B**UT HOW CAN we refuse her?"

"We tell her she is to wait here. Simple as that." Graham turned and glared at the *her* in question—Janie, perched on the back of a sturdy mare.

Fidgeting with the reins, the maid looked as though she feared the horse would unseat her at first opportunity. He didna like that girl. Nor did he trust her no matter what she or Mercy said. His gut told him loud and clear, the lass was trouble.

Graham jabbed a thumb in her direction. "Look at her. Scared to death. Does she even ken how to ride?"

"She can ride." Mercy glanced at Janie, and a faint cringe betrayed her lie. "She'll be fine. What better way to hone her skills?"

May God have mercy on his soul; he'd married an impossibly stubborn woman. Graham widened his stance and folded his arms across his chest. They didn't have the luxury of time to argue over something as inconsequential as that maid. Mercy needed to leave go of this ill-conceived idea. "Six riders is plenty. We dinna need to slow our pace by adding a seventh. Especially one that canna ride."

Mercy glared back at him. "I will not set her aside again. She wishes to resume her position. A position she's earned with loyalty, even though she wasn't believed."

"Ye dinna need a lady's maid on a hard ride across Scotland and England. There'll be no tents. No dressing gowns. And no time for extended ablutions." He motioned for Alexander, but his coward-of-a-brother shook his head, held up a hand to fend off any words, and walked faster in the opposite direction.

Mercy stepped forward, smoothed her hands up Graham's chest, and pressed so close her sweet scent surrounded him. "Please?" she said soft and low. "I yielded to your wishes once before to set her aside and look what came of it. I cannot refuse her, and I swear she won't slow us down."

Graham ground his teeth. Something about Janie wasn't right, but he couldn't place what it was. Graham scrubbed a hand across his face, doing his best to ignore the tempting warmth of Mercy pressed against him. The woman wasn't fighting fair, and she was wearing him down. "The girl understands we shall ride long and hard?"

"I will make certain she understands." Mercy stretched on tiptoe for a quick kiss. "Thank you." She gave his chest a victorious pat and hurried away to her horse.

The horse looked at Graham, flicked an ear, then bared his teeth and tossed his head as if laughing at his inability to control his wife.

Graham stomped over to his own mount, saddled up, and wound the reins around one hand. An ominous weight settled deep in his gut as he nodded to the other riders. Alexander. Duncan. Crestshire. Marsden. May God watch over them all and bless this journey with success.

Alexander waved him forward. "Lead us, brother."

"Stay close to me, aye?" He waited for Mercy's subtle nod. She fell in beside him without a word. Janie followed her, then the other four took up the rear.

Graham urged his mount to the fast pace they'd keep as long as the horses' energy allowed. Thankfully, the fierce warhorses bred by the Neal clan were known not only for their strength and size but their stamina.

A deep pull of the fresh morning air reassured him that no threat of rain rode upon the wind even though a bank of fluffy white clouds shadowed with gray bellies marred the sharp blue of the sky. The rising sun warmed his flesh, urging him onward. They'd make good time in this fair weather, and good timing was sorely needed.

"If Crestshire's missive doesn't reach the king before we arrive, what shall we do?" Mercy asked as she rode beside her husband. "What if the king has left Kensington? He travels during this time of year."

Graham had wondered the same thing but dared not say it. What was the use of worrying over something he couldn't control? He kept his gaze focused straight ahead. "If His Majesty is there and he's no' received the message, we shall surprise him with our visit. If he's not there, we will find where he's gone and follow."

Mercy didn't respond and that concerned him. He wished he could shield her from this. Leave her back at *Tor Ruadh* and handle it himself. But good sense bade him bring her. King William would be hard pressed to accept the word of a Scot without Lady Mercy present to corroborate his story.

As they entered the pass, Mercy spurred her mount to a full gallop and took the lead. Graham understood completely. She needed to get through the pass, especially this section of it, as quickly as possible. Her wounds, both internal and external, were still too raw for her to stomach this area for very long.

He tried to catch up with her, but her horse had superior speed. She was getting too far away. He couldn't protect her with so much distance between them. "Mercy!"

Her glance back assured him she'd heard him, but she still didn't slow down. "Dammit, woman!" Graham pulled free his pistol and fired a shot into the sky. This was not the proper beginning to this accursed journey.

Reining in her steed, Mercy came to a halt. She cast a wild-eyed look at the woods and the rising cliffs around them. "Who did you see? Where are they?"

Graham rode up close enough to take hold of her arm and give her a gentle but stern shake. "Did I no' tell ye to stay close? No matter what?"

Mercy wet her lips and looked away. "Forgive me. I had to get through here as fast as I could."

Graham's protective rage faded to a frustrated irritation. He slid his hand down her arm, took hold of her fingers, and kissed her knuckles before pressing them to his cheek. "I understand that, but ye must keep your head about ye and stay close." He gave her hand a squeeze. "The enemy triumphs if we give them our wits on a platter."

Alexander, Duncan, Crestshire, and Marsden thundered to a stop around them.

"I say," Marsden huffed with a red-cheeked grin. "That was quite the jaunt."

Graham leaned to the side and looked past them, down the road from whence they'd just came. "Where's the girl?"

All the men shifted in their saddles and turned to stare back down the trail.

"She was right behind us," Duncan said. "We rode past her."

"I'm sure she's just beyond that bend. We'll see her shortly," Alexander added with a wave of his hand at the curve in the road. "The lass wasna sure at all about riding. She's most likely struggling to catch up with us as we speak."

Mercy turned her mount around. "We should go back for her."

Graham snatched hold of her reins, yanking them out of her hands. "Duncan will go back." He turned to Marsden. "Ye go with him, aye?" This part of the woods gave him the chills as well. They'd gone well past the point where the first ambush had occurred, but they'd not cleared the pass yet. There was still another good mile of narrow, winding road prime for attack.

Duncan and Marsden turned their horses and rode until they were well out of sight.

"I dinna like this." Graham shifted in the saddle, staring at the point of the road where they'd disappeared until his eyes burned with the need to blink.

"She should no' have fallen that far behind," Alexander said, fidgeting in his own saddle.

Duncan and Marsden reappeared with Janie's horse trailing behind them.

"She must have fallen." Mercy yanked her reins back from Graham and urged her horse forward.

Graham, Alexander, and Crestshire followed close behind until Graham spurred his mount forward ahead of them. He was damned tired of this feeling of losing control. He'd had his fill of it. "Ye found the horse. Any sign of the girl? Where she might ha' fell?"

Duncan and Marsden shared a glance, then Duncan focused his troubled look on Graham. "I dinna think she fell. We found the horse beside the road. Thought she might ha' stopped to relieve herself or wretch from the rough ride, but we searched and found nary a sign. No broken branches, no crushed leaves, nothing."

"She appears to have disappeared," Marsden added. "No footprints. Almost as though someone lifted her from the back of her horse and spirited her away."

Graham turned his mount. "We need to leave this place. Ride hard and dinna stop 'til we reach the bridge. We'll stop and water the horses there." He pointed at Mercy. "Ride hard but stay at my side, ye ken?"

"But Janie…We must search for her. How can we leave her?" Mercy made to retrace their trail, but Graham blocked her way.

"Nay." He shook his head. "We canna risk it. She didn't fall or leave any sign of dismounting from her horse. There was no sign of struggle, Mercy. Do ye ken what that means?"

Mercy stared at him, then looked back at the road, her mouth tightening into a hard, fierce line.

"Do ye understand, Mercy?" Graham repeated. They had been tricked again. Janie was a traitor planted among them to gather information.

Sparing a last nervous glance at their surroundings, Mercy nodded and turned her mount. "Lead on, husband."

She understood now. He could shield her from it no longer. And she sensed it just as he did. Someone watched them. Ready to pick them off one by one at the most opportune time. He knew in his heart that no ill had befallen the maid. This had to be Edsbury's doing. The man planned to use the maid as a witness even if he had to torture her to make her say what he wished. Graham grit his teeth as his horse pounded along.

They finally reached the bridge, and Graham dismounted before his horse sloshed into the water. He helped Mercy dismount, hugging her to his side. The feel of her centered him. "We'll rest here for a bit. Give the horses a chance to catch their wind."

Mercy stared back in the direction from whence they'd come. "What do you think happened to her? I want the truth, Graham."

"'Twas too clean for highwaymen." Graham strode forward, scanning the horizon as the rest of the men dismounted and led their horses to the stream. "More of Edsbury's mercenaries and the Campbells. Sassenach troops dinna possess such stealth."

"As much as I hate to admit it," Lord Crestshire said as he joined them. "The man is right. This was not the doings of His Majesty's guard." He turned to Graham. "It was my understanding that Campbell and his men had been ordered to report to Fort William."

"A Campbell obeys the orders that suit them." Graham pointed toward a thickly wooded area right below a plateau overlooking the pass. "There." He'd nearly missed them. Two horses, very possibly three or more. But two for certain. One with a single rider. The other with two riders—one of them short and dressed in drab clothes with a light-colored covering in the front—Janie's apron. The white cap fringed with the fuzzy curls of red hair confirmed the girl's identity. They disappeared into the protection of the copse, but not before Graham spotted them. At this distance, he couldn't discern the pattern of the rider's plaid. But he'd bet his pistols the man was a Campbell. The other rider looked to be wearing trews.

"Will they hurt her?"

Graham could tell by the hitch in Mercy's voice that his dear wife still wrestled with her conscience. "They'll use her as a witness against us. They'll only hurt her if she refuses."

Mercy's mouth tightened into a hard line and she nodded. Moving to her devoted horse's side, she rubbed his withers and pressed her forehead against his sturdy neck.

Graham envied the horse's ability to give his wife the comfort he couldn't provide. He blew out a long, disgusted sigh. He was a large part of Mercy's dilemma. Had been from the start. Thank God the woman still loved him in spite of it.

Glancing up at the sky, Graham gathered his horse's reins and looked to the others. "Time to move. We'll go slower since we rode hard for such a stretch, but they've some travel left in them yet this day."

"Aye," Alexander agreed, mounting, then scanning the landscape. "And open land ahead of us for a good while. We need that for now."

Duncan, Marsden, and Crestshire followed suit, waiting with their attention focused on Graham as he walked over to Mercy where she stood beside her horse, staring off into the distance. The woman had known mostly tragedy. Her strength filled him with awe. But how long could such strength last? She looked spent, ready to give up.

"Come, dear one," he said. "We best be on our way."

Mercy blinked as though waking from a dream, turning to him

with such sorrow reflected in her expression that Graham gathered her up into his arms and held her. He didn't speak. Didn't know what to say.

"I'm sorry," she whispered against his chest. She hugged him tight, then pushed away, lifting her chin and giving him a tremulous smile. "We will get through this and return to *Tor Ruadh* to have our babies. Will we not?"

"Aye, m'love." Graham nodded, forcing himself not to reach out and touch her. Her fragile strength forbade it, and he'd do nothing to risk the composure Mercy struggled to maintain. "We'll fill the place with our braw, bonnie bairns. Lassies as beautiful as yourself, and sons as stubborn as me."

"Yes." Mercy's smile grew as she took her seat in the saddle. "Let's be on with this so we can put it behind us, yes?"

"Aye." Graham mounted and waved them all forward. "Onward."

Chapter Twenty-Two

T HE GNARLED ROOTS at the broad base of the ancient oak cradled her perfectly as Graham pounded into her. Mercy tightened her legs around his hips and dug her nails into his shoulders. She needed this. Graham gave her strength, gave her hope, gave her the excruciating ecstasy of escaping the madness of the world for a moment lifted out of time. A soft shriek tore from her throat as sensation after wondrous sensation exploded through her, spinning her into welcomed oblivion.

Graham growled out a huffing groan, shuddering as he held her pinned against the tree. Gasping for breath, he kissed her upturned face and smoothed her hair away from her damp temples. He pressed his forehead to hers. "I thought this would help us sleep better and no' disturb the others in the camp. But I no longer think that's true. I willna be able to lie beside ye without wanting ye again. I canna get enough of ye, m'love."

Mercy squeezed her legs tighter around him. "And I, you. But we do need to try to sleep when it's our turn. You said we are to leave before dawn." She didn't add that currently, they were supposed to be keeping watch while the others slept. Thankfully, Marsden patrolled the other side of camp. If her husband felt safe enough to fill their time with loving rather than watching the woods for the enemy, she'd not say anything.

Graham slid his hands under her bottom and lifted her, stepping back from the tree. His resigned sigh as she unwrapped her legs from around his hips and slid to the ground made her smile. She always hated the parting of their bodies too. Recovering her unique pantalettes from the ground, she shook them out before donning them. A pat to her hair smoothed the errant tendrils back in place, but it was still quite tousled. She fanned her heated flesh. They'd ridden hard, and the day had been quite warm. Surely, Graham wouldn't mind her bathing in the pool near camp. They still had time left on their watch.

"While you check with Marsden, I'm going down to the water to freshen up." She waited as he mulled her proposal over, his scowl deepening at the prospect.

Her heart fluttered at the way the blue-white light of the moon washed across his powerful features, making him appear mythological. Graham wasn't the only one stricken with unquenchable lust. Cool water splashed across her flesh would be most welcome. "I promise I'll stay at the pool. I won't be long."

Graham nodded. "Ye tucked your blade back in place, aye?"

Mercy patted the space between her breasts, the weight of the dagger and its carved haft giving her a sense of security. "It is. And I promise when I'm washing, I'll keep it close at hand on the bank."

"Dinna be gone overlong." Graham stepped over the roots of the tree and took to higher ground. While scanning the woods, he motioned in the general direction of the water. "When ye've finished, go to camp and seek your rest." He looked back at her and grinned. "I'll try to control m'self and no' wake ye when I join ye on our pallet."

Longing washed across her all over again, forcing her to pull her dress away from the sweaty stickiness of her flesh. She lifted her pantalettes to her knees and cast a teasing glance back at Graham as she made her way down the slope. "I'm a very light sleeper. You are most welcome to join me in my dreams."

Graham rewarded her with a quiet chuckle as he moved off deeper into the woods, climbing the low ridge surrounding the area.

Mercy glanced around. Good. Alexander, Duncan, and Crestshire were so quiet they had to be sleeping. She hiked her skirts even higher, reveling in the air kissing across her thighs as she made her way down the embankment to the water.

A wall of limestone rose at one end of the pool. Bubbling water reflected the moonlight, tumbled down the layers of rocks, and emptied into the small, circular pool that narrowed on the other end and wandered off into the woods. A perfect place for bathing.

Mercy shucked off her clothes. No wonder she'd grown so warm. She should have had her seamstress fashion a set of pantalettes without so many layers of petticoats attached. Modesty and the possibility of nearby danger bade her keep on her chemise that only reached her mid-thigh.

Mercy eased into the cold water. Goosebumps rippled across her skin, and her nipples tightened as she moved forward until waist deep. She splashed the water across her arms and shoulders, then submerged to her chin. She dove downward, swimming across the pool, reveling in the peaceful silence under the water. The serenity of the moment filled her, strengthened her for whatever lay ahead.

Kicking her way to the deepest part, she dipped her head back, and worked her fingernails across her scalp. A bit of the rose-scented soap Catriona had shared would have been nice, but Mercy was still grateful for the cooling embrace of the spring. She swam back to the spot where she'd disrobed and climbed out onto the moss-covered bank. As she reclined, she indulged herself with a brief moment of staring up at the stars and the bright waxing moon.

A long yawn beset her. Time to move before weariness overpowered her. Forcing herself up, she shook out her clothes and donned them, wishing there had been time at least to rinse out her pantalettes and for them to dry. But she couldn't risk it.

As she tucked the dagger back in place, a rustling sound from the far side of the pool caught her attention. She froze. She barely breathed as she scanned the area, praying the noise had simply been some foraging creature or even Graham patrolling the area.

The rustling grew louder. Mercy took shelter behind a boulder, crouching low and peering around it, afraid to call out for Graham or anyone from the camp. What if it were just an animal? It didn't sound too loud. Whatever it was had to be small. And it was on the other side of the waterfall. She shouldn't disturb the others from their much-needed rest.

Her breath caught in her throat as Janie stumbled out from behind the bushes, bathed in the blue-white light of the moon. The girl crawled to the pool's edge and scooped up handfuls of water, first to drink, then to splash across her face. One arm clutched tight to her side. Every move she made caused a twisted grimace. Mercy could tell that Janie's lip was swollen, even split. It looked to have once been bloody. She'd been beaten.

Mercy held fast, fighting against the urge to rush from her hiding place and help. What if the kidnappers were still about? What if they waited in the woods while Janie tended to her wounds? There was little danger of the girl running. Janie moved as though the slightest twitch pained her. Guilt filled Mercy. They had misjudged Janie again. Abandoned her. Left her to be treated with cruelty.

Janie wilted to one side, almost rolling into the water, one hand submerged in the edge of the pool.

She had to go to her. Mercy scanned the area one last time. There had been no other movement. Mercy ran to the narrow end of the spring and leapt across it. Hurrying to the maid, she knelt at the girl's side and hovered over her.

"Janie?" She held a hand in front of Janie's parted lips and nose, praying to feel the girl's breath across her fingers.

A strong, calloused hand slammed across her mouth. Raging panic shot through her as an arm snaked around her waist and yanked her upward. Mercy flailed against her captor, ripped the dagger from between her breasts, and stabbed upward. The blade made hard contact but glanced away. She had to have hit bone.

A horrific yowl confirmed she'd done some damage but apparently not enough. The man's hold on her tightened as another figure appeared, grabbed her wrist, and twisted the knife away. Janie came into view, pressing her face close to Mercy's and gifting her with a chilling smile right before she spit on her. "Whore," she said in a growling tone filled with hatred. "Just like your mother."

Janie pranced around in front of her as the two men wrangled her toward a group of waiting horses—one of them with a rider. Janie shook a club-like object in Mercy's face. "You're goin' to get yours now, *m'lady*. I been waiting a long time for this." She struck the side of Mercy's head with such force, sounds grew distorted. Just as her sight cleared, Janie struck her again.

"Enough!" One of the men cuffed Janie away. "Ye can torment her in a bit. His lordship is waiting with the horses."

His lordship? Her father? Mercy screamed loud and long, praying her muffled shrieks would be heard. The hand across her mouth tightened and the arm around her middle clamped upward, cutting off her air. "Ye keep it up, and we'll gut your husband like a felled deer. We're all over these woods. Ye just didna ken it because we didna wish it." The knife pricked her skin again. "Remain silent, and we willna kill him 'til we lay siege on *Tor Ruadh*. That can be your last gift to him. The peace of dying with his brothers."

An enraged roar shook the trees.

"Mercy!"

Graham. Her beloved husband. Mercy flailed and fought her attacker as he dragged her closer to the horses. She could not allow him to get her on a horse. With one well-placed, backward kick, she managed to trip him. They both went down, the heavy brute landing hard on top of her. She didn't care. Elbows flying, she fought and clawed, the chance of escaping charging her with the will to fight.

"Graham! Here!" she screamed.

The man caught hold of her ankle, yanked her back down, then rose above her. Burying one hand in her tangled mass of wet hair, he jerked her along on the ground beside him, stumbling across the rugged terrain.

Mercy caught hold of his leg and bit hard. She clamped down until she tasted blood. The man howled, then knocked her away. Mercy twisted around and bit him again.

The man clubbed her in the face, then whipped her around by her hair whilst trying to kick her forward. He backhanded her again just as Graham, Alexander, and Duncan burst through the trees. She prayed they had truly burst through the trees. The strikes to her head had scattered her senses. Her vision blurred in and out of focus, grew dark, then lightened again. All sounds were muffled, and she couldn't make out words. She lost her hold of the man's leg and landed hard at the base of a tree.

Gunshots. More shouts. Horses screaming. All she knew was the safety of the tree. She held on to it for dear life. The rough bark scraped against her cheek as she clamped her arms around it and hugged hard.

Someone pulled her hair hard enough to make her cry out. Cursing in a high-pitched voice sliced through the fog of her miserable confusion. It had to be Janie. A hand took hold of the back of her head, yanked her head back, then slammed her face into the tree. Janie attacked her as though possessed by demons.

Gunfire split the air again. Close. Then a body fell across her and didn't move. It wasn't as heavy as the man's had been. A warm wetness seeped into her clothing and trickled down her sides and back. The weight on her didn't move. Whoever it was, was dead.

Mercy prayed it wasn't someone she loved. She couldn't look. It wouldn't do any good to open her eyes, anyway. Every time she did, all she saw were nauseating swirls of darkness and light.

Then, gentle hands touched and tugged at her. She pulled in a deep breath. Someone had taken the body off her. Now she could breathe so much easier, but she had to keep a tight hold on the tree. Just in case...

Fingers pried at her hands, at her arms. "No!" She held on tighter, dragging herself closer to the tree.

Someone spoke close to her face. She couldn't make out what they said. She couldn't even tell if it was a voice she knew. But it sounded calm. She recognized the *feel* of the voice. The intent behind the tone.

Suddenly, shouting surrounded her again.

Someone pulled her upward.

A new voice hit her like a punch in her stomach. Her father's voice. She'd recognize that dreaded voice no matter her condition. A horrendous sense of loss hit her. If her father stood above her, then Graham had to be gone.

Gunfire exploded close by. Acrid smoke filled her nostrils. She hit the ground, but the pain in her heart far outweighed the thudding in her head.

Sobbing overcame her. Graham must be dead. Her greatest fear had come to fruition.

"Please, God, take me, too," she cried out, going limp as she gave herself to the darkness.

CHAPTER TWENTY-THREE

GRAHAM HELD MERCY close and brushed a kiss to her bruised, bleeding forehead, then lowered her to the pallet. Her head rolled to one side, and her arms splayed across the blankets. Graham eased an arm under her shoulders and lifted as Marsden slid an additional folded blanket beneath her head. Tucking her arms in close to her sides, Graham knelt beside her.

Shame and gut-wrenching guilt twisted so hard within him, he yearned to roar out his remorse. How could he have been so careless? How could he have been such a fool? How could he have let this happen to her? He bowed his head and closed his eyes.

"Forgive me," he whispered. Hot tears stung his eyes as he rocked in place beside her.

If Mercy died, it would be no one's fault but his own.

"With your permission?" Marsden paused, speaking in the hushed tones used by those in the presence of the dying.

Graham forced open his eyes and lifted his head. Marsden stood beside him with a pot of water in one hand and a cloth in the other.

"We should clean her wounds and apply cool cloths to reduce the swelling above her eyes." Marsden held up the items. "I shall tend your lady whilst your brother wraps your shoulder. Yes?"

"Nay." Graham took the items from Marsden, set them beside the pallet, and dipped the cloth in the cool water. With the gentlest of touches, he dabbed the linen across the angry scrapes across Mercy's forehead, temple, and jawline. That damned Janie had done a great deal of damage. He felt no remorse at all for killing the bitch for all the pain she'd caused his beloved.

"Well then," Marsden said with a nod. "I shall leave you to it. But when you are done, you must let Alexander or Duncan bind your shoulder. The bleeding must be staunched until a healer can remove the bullet."

Graham still had use of his left arm, so the bullet hadn't damaged any bone. Nor had it exited his body. The shot had burrowed into his chest, close to his shoulder. Painful but nowhere near bad enough to put him down. The pair of Campbells and Edsbury had soon discovered the error of their aim and the consequences such a mistake incurred. All were dead, Edsbury by Graham's own hands.

"I willna leave my wife's side." 'Twas as simple as that. The rest of the group could do whatever they damned well pleased.

"Brother." Alexander paused until Graham looked up. "I ride to *Tor Ruadh* to increase the guard and prepare for attack. I'll send back a wagon with additional men to guard ye on your journey and Gretna with supplies for Mercy. I doubt old Elena can make the trip—especially not all the way to London."

Graham pulled in a deep breath and looked back down at Mercy. "She liked Gretna. Mentioned her more than once."

Crouching beside him, Alexander took hold of Graham's uninjured shoulder and squeezed. "Dinna speak as though she's already gone. As long as she breathes, there is hope." He clenched Graham's shoulder tighter. "Ye must hie yourself to His Majesty, Graham. For the sake of your wife, yourself, and our clan. 'Tis most urgent that ye seek the king's mercy or else ye'll hang for killing the duke."

"I willna leave her side, brother." Graham wet the cloth again and wiped down Mercy's scraped and scratched arms, her bruised knuckles, her torn and bloody fingernails. "Besides—think ye truly that King William will listen to a Scot?"

"We shall stand at your side and testify to what happened here this night," Crestshire said.

"You have two of the king's finest willing to testify on your behalf," Marsden added. "We will not stand idle whilst you and your lady are in need."

Duncan moved to Graham's injured side, strips of cloth clutched in one hand. With a grim look, he motioned toward Mercy. "If we get both of ye well enough to travel, I believe your wife will be the key in settling this. From all she said, her father was the bastard behind this plot. Ye and Marsden both said the king seemed truly fond of her. Do ye think he'd approve of the way her father treated her?"

Graham pushed him away as Duncan moved to cut away his bloody tunic and tend to his shoulder. "Leave me. All of ye. I canna reason about anything other than her right now." His foolish choices had cost his wife dearly.

"Hold him, Alexander," Duncan said.

Alexander sprang into action and twisted Graham's good arm behind his back, holding him in a firm but brotherly headlock. "We willna listen to mumblings of misplaced guilt. Tonight was no' your fault, ye stubborn arse."

Graham arched against Alexander's hold, renewed rage pounding through him. "I'll whip your arse! Let me go! Give my wife the respect she deserves."

Shifting Graham around, Alexander faced him toward Mercy's still form. "She's no' dead! Stop mourning her and concentrate on saving what ye have left. Ye rid her of her bastard-of-a-father, now all that's left to do is convince the king to leave us in peace."

Duncan ripped away the sleeve of Graham's tunic and poured a splash of whisky into his wound.

Searing pain burned through his shoulder. "Damn ye, Duncan!"

Alexander released him and stepped back. "I'll leave ye to bandage him." He paused, stared down at Mercy's still form, then crossed himself, his lips moving in silent prayer. Lifting his head, he gave a curt nod to Crestshire, then to Marsden. "Help Duncan guard him, aye? I willna contemplate a world without my brother in it."

"Take this wee squirrel wi' ye afore he strangles me with these damn bandages!" Graham shoved Duncan back and attempted to return to ministering to Mercy's wounds.

Duncan laughed and yanked him back. "Now, there's my brother full of piss." He snugged a length of torn linen even tighter around Graham's shoulder and chest. "Use that anger to fight for your lady, brother."

A faint moan interrupted them, and Mercy stirred, scowling as she lifted shaking hands to her head.

All else ceased to exist for Graham. "Oh, dear love, thank God for bringing ye back." He wet the cloth again and pressed it to her face.

She batted his hands away as she rolled to her side and clutched her head in her hands. A sobbing moan rose from her. Cradling her head, she rolled back and forth, wrestling with her pain.

"Can ye hear me, love? Mercy, can ye hear me?" Graham leaned close, keeping his voice low, forcing himself not to touch her. "Ye're safe, lass."

Mercy didn't respond, just continued the pitiful moaning and thrashing that tore at Graham's heart.

Stab wounds, he understood. Broken bones. Gunshot wounds. He'd had them all and knew well enough about their stages of healing. But Mercy had taken more than one severe blow to the head and had been unresponsive until now. And this responsiveness was more like that of a blinded, wounded animal fighting its last before it died. A sense of helplessness overtook him. He stared up at his brothers and friends. "What can we do to help her?"

Captain Marsden gave a sad shake of his head. "Keep her as comfortable as possible and pray."

"Mayhap, Gretna will ken a better way to help her. I'll prepare her with a description of Mercy's injuries," Alexander said. "I'll get her here, and more protection, as fast as possible."

Graham reached up and clasped Alexander's forearm. "God be with ye, brother. Race the wind, I beg ye."

Alexander squeezed his arm in return, then strode to his horse, mounted, and galloped away.

"Marsden, stand guard. I shall circle about and search the woods to see if any others remain." Crestshire nodded to Marsden, then looked to Duncan. "Between the three of us, we can rotate until reinforcements arrive."

Duncan nodded, picked up one of the larger water skins, and held it aloft. "I'll fill it with the spring water straight off the falls. It should be coldest. She can rest her head on it, aye? Cooler and softer than the blanket."

"Ye always were the most cunning of our brood." Graham wrung out the cloth and eased it across Mercy's hands still clutching at her temples. As soon as the coolness of the cloth touched the backs of her fingers, she snatched hold of it and clamped it tight across her eyes.

"She needs easing in the worst way. Hurry, Duncan." Graham had never felt more useless in his life. He prayed Gretna would know of some way to ease Mercy's suffering.

Scuffling through the underbrush yanked Graham away from his musings and forced him to his feet. He drew his pistol and pulled back the hammer. "Who goes there?"

"Stand down, man," Marsden called out as he breached the line of trees. "All appears quiet. It is my hope Lord Crestshire shall bring news of the same farther out."

Graham lowered his pistol and returned it to his belt just as Duncan reappeared with the swollen skin of water.

"I didna fill it tight, but it should support her head well enough.

Can ye lift her without throwing her into more distress?" Duncan held the skin aloft, staring at Mercy, fear and worry creasing his brow.

"I dinna ken." Graham shook his head. He leaned down beside her and whispered, "Duncan made ye a wee pillow, m'love. It should help with your pain." He watched for any reaction, any sign she had understood him.

Mercy ignored him, just kept fingering the damp cloth against her eyes and crying out.

Graham looked to Duncan. "Get ready. When I lift her, she's certain to set to thrashing, but it is my hope that once she feels the cool of the skin, she'll calm down."

As soon as he slid his arms beneath her shoulders, she fisted her hands and fought him, wild and flailing as the cloth fell away from her swollen eyes. Graham's heart ached with every pitiful strike, not even closing his eyes as she slapped and clawed at him.

Duncan yanked away the folded blanket and slid the water skin in place, nodding to Graham to lower her.

Graham eased her down, then hurried to soak the cloth for her eyes and draped it across her face.

The cooling worked as planned. Mercy calmed almost immediately, nuzzling her head against the water bag and clutching the wet cloth back against her face. Even her crying ceased, and she grew still. Whether sleeping or unconscious again, Graham didn't know, but at least she seemed at peace and breathed.

"Praise God," Duncan whispered.

"Aye," Graham replied. "I'm also thankful He gave me such a wise brother."

The rest of the night and through the following day, Graham stayed by Mercy's side.

Head propped in his hands as he sat beside her pallet, the sound of approaching horses jerked Graham awake. Duncan was already on his feet with pistol drawn, and Crestshire stood beside him.

"Marsden's on watch. He'll see them and report," Crestshire said.

Graham rose from the ground, drew his pistol with one hand, and his dagger with the other. "Help him. I dinna wish them close to Mercy. I'll stand guard over her."

Both men took off toward what sounded like a large group, the thundering hooves growing louder by the minute.

"'Tis safe!" Duncan's shout echoed back through the misty gray of the woods still shrouded with the gloaming before sunrise.

"Put away your guns, Graham MacCoinnich! I'm a coming to ye!"

Graham exhaled and bowed his head. Gretna had arrived. If anyone could help Mercy, she could. He holstered both pistol and dagger. "Over here!"

A glance down at Mercy told him it was time to switch out the water skins again. Whenever the water bags warmed too much, Mercy grew restless. He feared she'd gone feverish. Her flushed coloring didn't bode well, but it disturbed her when someone touched her so, he didn't ken for certain. But Gretna would know. Some said her talents even surpassed Elena Bickerstaff's when it came to the healing arts.

An unholy crashing through the woods soon revealed Gretna stepping high and fighting through the underbrush, cloth sacks over both shoulders and clutched in both hands. "Where is she?" she asked, still gasping from her struggles.

"Here." Graham motioned toward Mercy who was growing more agitated. "We've been keeping skins of spring water beneath her head. Seems to help with the pain." He knelt down, lifted Mercy's shoulder, and slid a fresh, cool water skin in place of the warm one.

She didn't fight him as much now. It seemed as though she finally understood he meant her no harm. He moistened the cloth and pressed it to her face. Looking up at Gretna, his voice cracked, weariness and worry threatening to break him. "Help her, Gretna. I beg ye."

Gretna piled her supplies to one side, then crouched over Mercy, making soft cooing sounds as she flitted the lightest of touches across Mercy's face and head. Her gaze swept down her curled form and across Mercy's bruised arms and hands. She turned a concerned scowl on Graham. "I'm glad ye killed the bastards for what they did to your fine lady."

"Tell me ye can help her." Graham fisted his hands and sent up the thousandth prayer that Gretna would ken what to do.

"They battered her so," Gretna said softly, her grim look striking fear into Graham's soul. "Alexander said the sooner we get the two of ye to the king, the better. But she canna travel yet. 'Twould kill her to do so." Gretna's mouth tightened as she rose, went to her bags, and started rummaging through them. She paused in her digging, frowning down into the bag. "And her dying would no' be an easy one, Graham. She would suffer badly."

"We will no' travel until ye deem it safe for her." Graham paced back and forth at the foot of Mercy's pallet. "I dinna care if I spend the rest of my life in these godforsaken woods as long as Mercy lives."

Gretna nodded. "Verra well then." She pointed at the small pot of water at the head of Mercy's bed. "I need a fire and a great deal more water. Then I'll need your help to give her the deep healing rest she needs." She stole a glance around the woods, then took a step toward Graham. "But ye mustn't be alarmed by anything I do, and I beg ye— keep what I do to yourself for my own safety, ye ken?"

A leeriness swept across him. He'd heard the rumors about Gretna but assumed they were just lies spun by vicious women jealous of Gretna's status in the clan. Everyone loved her. Well...most loved her. A select few hated and feared her, fueling their envious wickedness with accusations of witchery. Alexander had put his fist down on the rumors, but the ugly lies persisted.

"Graham—d'ye hear what I'm asking of ye?"

"Aye, and I dinna care what it takes. Save her." Graham scooped up a spare water skin as well as the discarded one that had grown too warm for Mercy's head. "I'll fetch the water and build ye a fire. What else d'ye have need of?"

"I'll need ye to help hold her once I've made the tonic, then I want ye to sleep. Ye look like hell." She nodded toward his shoulder. "Once ye've rested a bit, I'll be ridding ye of that bullet and cauterizing the wound. Have ye even washed it? Those bandages look filthy."

Graham glanced down at the bandages. He'd been so caught up with Mercy, he'd forgotten about the wound. "Duncan cleaned it with whisky. Burned."

"I promise it didna burn nearly as bad as it will when I get hold of ye."

"Take care of Mercy. Dinna worry after me."

Gretna waved him away. "Then fetch that water so we can get this healing started."

The area seemed more peaceful now with Gretna's arrival, more ordered. Controlled. Graham hurried to the spring, knelt at the water's edge, and splashed his face before tending to the water skins. The sound of footsteps across the pool drew his attention and made him reach for his gun. "Who goes there? Speak now or be shot."

"'Tis me, brother," Duncan said as he shoved aside the bushes and scooped up a handful of water to drink. Swiping the back of his hand across his mouth, he grinned at Graham. "Alexander not only sent fifteen clansmen but twenty of Crestshire's guard from Fort William, too."

Thirty-five men to guard them. The knotted muscles across Graham's shoulders eased up. He gave Duncan a smile. "I hope they brought supplies. Gretna says it could be days 'til it's safe to move Mercy."

"Three wagons," Duncan replied. "One filled with Gretna's supplies, the other two for the men. I'll set them to hunting for extra meat." He glanced up into the woods toward camp. "I ken it might take a fair spell or so for her to get Mercy strong enough to travel, but she needs to make haste. Crestshire's captain said the Campbells and the king's guard have already arrived at Fort William and merely wait for the king's order to carry on with the attack."

Graham submerged the leather water skin at the base of the trickling waterfall, watching the bag as it slowly filled with water. "Do ye no' find it odd that the king sent the men first to Fort William and ordered them wait until he signals to attack? It doesna make sense. If the royal went to the trouble of sending the mix of Campbells and king's guard, why did he no' unleash them immediately?"

Duncan splashed water on his face and rubbed it across the back of his neck. "I'm telling ye, brother. The man's giving his goddaughter a chance to tell her side. Marsden said her father had been banned from court, remember? What king will ban a man, then take that same man's word for gospel—especially when it comes to a clan war whose cost could be avoided when resources are needed in the colonies against the French? King William willna risk England's battlefront on this side of the sea. He doesna want this fight."

What Duncan said made sense, but that didn't change the fact that Mercy was too weak to travel. Graham finished filling the bags and stood. "We'll leave here when Mercy's able. Not before." He gave Duncan a grateful nod. "Thank ye, Duncan. Please see to everything for me, aye? I ken I can trust ye whilst I'm busy tending Mercy."

"Done without asking, brother."

As Duncan disappeared into the woods, Graham hurried back to Mercy. The area had changed dramatically in the short time he'd been gone. Gretna had set the place straight, cleared it free of soiled linens, tossed aside cups, and extra water skins. She held out both hands for the water. Nodding toward Mercy curled on her side on a clean, straightened pallet, she scowled as she hefted the sacks of water over to a large boulder she'd turned into a makeshift table. "She didna take to cleaning her up well at all. Poor lamb. She doesna ken what she's doing." Gretna heaved out a heavy sigh. "But the strength she had fighting me is a good sign. She'll need that strength for healing."

"Aye." It pained Graham to admit it. "There hasna been a glimmer of her escaping that hell she's trapped in since it all happened."

Graham propped his hands against the boulder and stared at all the items Gretna had strewn across it. Bundles of dried herbs. Knobby looking chunks of roots. A particularly pungent pile of something impossible to identify. Several small knives. Twine. A stone mortar and pestle waited in the center of all the mysterious items.

"What is that?" Graham pointed to the hairy chunk of something Gretna snapped off into the tiniest of pieces and placed into the mortar. "Almost looks like a body. Arms. Legs. Even a knob for a head." He must be delirious from weariness.

"Mandrake." Gretna spared him a sharp glance, then set to grinding the root into a pulp.

"Witch's root?" The words escaped him before he realized it. So, the rumors had been true. Graham decided then and there he didn't give a damn if Gretna was a witch or not. Her helping Mercy was all that mattered. "Forgive me. I misspoke."

Gretna's jaw tightened, and she didn't look up from her work. "Aye. Witch's root it is. But 'twill help your lady along with the henbane, makings for laudanum, and a few other ingredients I managed to acquire." She stopped pounding the pestle into the mortar and looked up at him. "Dinna judge me, Graham. 'Tis merely herbs that aid in healing. 'Twill make her sleep deep enough that her mind can heal and no' feel its terrible pain. 'Tis no' the work of the devil. I swear it."

Graham reached out and laid a hand on Gretna's arm. "I trust ye, Gretna. Ye're a good, kind lass that would never hurt another. Dinna fash herself over those red-arsed hens and their clacking tongues."

Gretna smiled and motioned toward a patch of ground she'd rid of leaves and brush. "I thank ye for your words. Now build me a fire so we can steep this and get it down her." She shifted with another heavy sigh as she pounded the mixture even harder. "Me thinks we'll be keeping her buried in the deep rest for a few days, and then we'll see."

"We'll see what?" Graham dreaded hearing the answer aloud.

"We'll see if we can raise Mercy up out of her hell and get her to speak to us. That's the only way we'll ken for certain if she'll ever be right again."

CHAPTER TWENTY-FOUR

IT HAD BEEN nearly a sennight. Graham lowered himself to the ground beside Mercy's pallet and leaned back against the tree shading her. Almost seven days of the vile tonic's healing. He set his feet apart, propped his arms atop his bent knees, and didn't give a rat's arse if anyone looked up his kilt.

Whenever the noxious herbal had run its course, they would force another dose down her throat and send her back to her peaceful darkness. Mercy always fought them. He'd begun to doubt she'd ever escape the prison of her pain.

Eyes burning with weariness, he scrubbed his hands across his face. Such doubts brought madness. He refused to allow them. Maybe today would be the day she returned to him. Thank God above Duncan had thought of the cool water. Gretna had said they could have done nothing better to bring Mercy comfort and help with the swelling than by keeping her supplied with the waterskins.

"I swear, Graham, would your ma want ye showing your uglies to all and sundry? Cover yourself." Gretna gave him a stern look as she walked by, hands filled with fresh linen and a steaming kettle of water. She plunked the articles down atop her crude work table fashioned from a rock, then wiped her hands on the apron tied around her middle. Turning to Mercy, she smiled down at her. "She's doing better

242

today, Graham. Fever's gone and look at her color."

Graham stretched out his legs and crossed them at the ankles, covering his man parts as requested. "I pray she'll do as well when time comes to let her awaken completely." The men were restless, eager to head to London. But Graham dared anyone to rush his dear Mercy. They wouldn't attempt moving his wife's little finger if it wasn't blessed by Gretna.

Gretna squatted down and examined Mercy's face closer. She raked her fingers through Mercy's hair, combed and finally free of blood, sweeping it back out of the way. Frowning, she felt her way all along Mercy's hairline, starting at her forehead and working her way back. "The swellings are all but gone, but I'm worried about the inside of her poor head. 'Tis my hope the swelling on the inside has lessened as well."

"The rise on either side of her nose looks better," Graham said. The swelling across Mercy's eyes and down the ridge of her nose was gone, but the poor lass was black and blue as though masked. They'd managed to clean the blood from each of her nostrils, then packed them with linen to keep the bones aligned. Mercy breathed through her mouth. Her poor lips were dry and cracked even though Gretna kept them coated with an oily-looking salve.

"A pity ye shot Janie. I would no' have minded watching her receive the same treatment she'd meted out." She looked up from Mercy, fixing Graham with a glare. "Eye for an eye, ye ken?"

"There was no' time to consider such." Graham rose and paced around the small area that the men had dubbed the healing camp. He was restless, too, but he'd never dream of rushing Gretna.

"This afternoon, when the next time of the dosing comes, we shall hold off and see if she wakes from her sleep without pain."

"Are ye certain?" He'd take no risks. "I willna have her suffer needlessly."

Gretna took hold of his arm and squeezed, her consoling demeanor striking fear deep in his heart. "We need to see if she's able to come back to us. I would warn ye—hurt as she was, she could be blind, deaf, or completely lost to us." Gretna shrugged. "She could be nothing more than a shell. A soul unable to cross over until her body dies."

Graham jerked out of her hold. "Ye will stop such talk! I shall no' consider it. Mercy will be fine, ye ken? No more of your dire predictions!" They'd kept Mercy alive this far. She would be fine. It would take a while, months maybe, but she would be well. "Ye must have faith, Gretna. Faith in yourself. Faith in God. Faith in Mercy. My wife is a fighter. How else could she ha' survived thus far?"

Gretna stepped back, hands in the air, but Graham could tell by her expression she pitied him. She feared him ill-prepared. "We shall see this afternoon." She clasped her hands in front of her. "Might I suggest ye tell the men so they can pray?"

Before he could answer, a horn sounded to the north of the camp. The warning. Someone approached. Graham drew his weapons and handed both pistols to Gretna. "Guard her and keep yourself safe as well, aye?"

"Aye." She hefted the weapons in both her hands. "No one will get to your lady. I swear it."

The horn sounded again, but 'twas two short blasts this time. The signal to stand down.

Gretna started to hand the pistols back as Graham drew his sword. He shook his head. "Nay. Keep them until I find out what the hell those horn blasts mean."

He crashed through the woods and made his way to the road where several men had gathered, including Duncan and Crestshire. "What is this about?"

Duncan looked disturbed, and Crestshire looked amused. The tension pounding through him eased somewhat but was quickly replaced by a simmering rage. His nerves were raw. He wouldn't bear stupidity well. They'd best take care.

"Father William," Crestshire said. "On his mare. The sentry sounded the horn when he spotted movement, then sounded the stand down when he realized it was the priest." He gave Graham a serious look. "Better for the man to be quick to alert us than not."

Grudgingly, Graham agreed although his current state of mind didn't need the additional excitement over nothing more than Clan MacCoinnich's priest. "Why did the man no' come with Gretna and the others? 'Twould ha' been safer for him."

"I suggest you ask him," Crestshire said as he waved Graham forward. "Father William's reasoning is known only to himself."

"My son!" The priest waved at Graham, then dismounted from the mare that most of the clan had decided was more Father's William's wee pet than his mount. He kissed the wooden cross hanging from his neck and lifted it to the sky. "Thanks be to God for my safe and successful journey." He patted the cross back in place on his chest and crossed himself. "How fares your poor wife?"

"We mean to see if she'll be able to awaken in a few hours, Father." Perhaps it wasn't so bad to have him here after all. He could lead them all in prayer. "Why did ye no' come with the others? It wouldha been safer."

"I was safe with God." Father William gave him a haughty look, then hooked his thumbs in the pockets of his brown robe. "And I bear a message since Chieftain MacCoinnich could spare no more men until this issue is ended."

"What message?" Duncan asked as he joined them.

Father William gave the man a withering glance. The two had never gotten along. The priest's attention shifted back to Graham, completely ignoring Duncan. "A message from the king himself."

A chill washed across Graham, making him swallow hard. "Tell me."

Father William gave a knowing nod. "His Majesty wishes to see Lady Mercy immediately."

Graham scrubbed a hand across his face. They all wanted Mercy in front of the king. But thanks to the mongrels the king had unleashed, it seemed impossible. He turned about and motioned for the priest to follow. "Come with me, Father."

Stomping through the woods, Graham led Father William to Mercy's side.

As soon as the priest set eyes on her, he pulled out his rosary beads, closed his eyes, and started praying, "Heavenly Father, all healing comes at Thy bidding and all diseases and infirmities heed Your commands. Redeem this woman's life from this terrible destruction. Crown her with Thine loving kindness and mercy..." The prayer tapered off into fervent whispered words as he walked circles around Mercy, holding the crucifix over her as he moved.

"At the chapel, his prayers are always in Latin," Gretna whispered from behind Graham, poking him in the center of his bare back.

"Perhaps, he wishes to give us more comfort by making the words easier to understand." He turned and gave Gretna a sad smile. "Some of us struggle with Latin." How many times had Mam sent him to Da's solar to study his lessons with Alexander, only to find them play-fighting with their wooden swords instead? How he wished he'd paid more attention to the tutor who had bored them beyond measure. Then he could have prayed for Mercy himself.

Gretna gave him another not quite so gentle prod. "Strip your kilt off here and go to the pool and bathe. I've washed and mended your tunic, and I'll brush out your kilt whilst ye're scrubbing."

"Are ye mad?" They were about to awaken Mercy. Had Gretna lost her mind?

"Do ye wish your wife awakened by your words or your stench? Ye smell like shite, Graham MacCoinnich. Go wash while Father finishes his prayers. Then we'll see to opening your lady's eyes." Gretna poked him in the middle of his bare chest. "Do it. Now."

Graham bit his tongue and fisted his hands to keep from cursing in front of Father William. "Ye're no' my mother. Dinna behave as though ye are."

Gretna's challenging stance told him all he needed to know. She didn't speak, just glared at him.

"Damn your stubbornness!" Graham handed his pistols and dagger to Gretna, then stripped off his kilt and tossed it over beside his boots. With the warm weather and his torn tunic, he'd taken to walking around camp barefoot, wearing nothing but his bandages, kilt, and weapons.

Gretna didn't spare him a glance, just rolled her eyes before returning to her worktable and setting his weapons aside. She waved him onward as she selected a brush from her pile of tools and headed toward his kilt. "A clean bandage awaits ye as well. On wi' ye now."

"And ten Hail Mary's for your swearing, my son," Father William shouted from behind him as he stomped away toward the pool.

"Ten Hail Mary's, my arse," Graham muttered, sweeping branches and bushes aside.

"Twenty!" Father William shouted.

Damned priest. Had the hearing of a bat.

SHE WAS FLOATING upward again. Mercy pointed her toes and pushed her hands harder down through the darkness, shoving against the rise. She had to dive deeper. The dark waters swirled around her and kept her pain at bay. Soothing relief. No sound. No light. The place suited her.

But whenever she floated upward, whenever the liquid around her grew lighter, the incredible pain and suffering returned. Agony returned. Fear. Sorrow.

"Mercy. Come back to me, lass."

A voice? Here? Mercy shied away from it even though she knew it.

Somehow, it sounded kind. Loving. It stirred a strange aching warmth in her heart. But how? How could she know a voice here? This was her world alone.

The surrounding light increased. Sensations swirled about her, grew stronger. An aching swept across her body. A foul taste. A hollow roaring in her ears. She couldn't breathe unless she gasped in and out through her mouth. A popping when she swallowed—or tried to swallow. Where was the peace of the dark waters? Why had it spurned her and forced her into the light?

"Mercy. Can ye hear me?"

A woman's voice. Panic flooded her. A woman. A muddled fog of jagged memories filled her mind. Flashes of suffering. Betrayal. Pain. Hatred. She shielded her face with her hands and veered away from the madness the woman's voice stirred.

"Talk to her, Graham," she said. "She fears me. That wretch's voice may ha' been the last sound she heard before we lost her to the darkness."

Graham. The name centered her, made her heart beat harder, made it more difficult to breathe. She held her head in her hands. Graham. The name made her feel safe.

"Mercy, love. Try to open your eyes. Come back to me, dear one. I beg ye. 'Tis me. Graham. Your husband."

A dull pounding battered inside her skull, right above her eyes. She curled to her side, burying her face in the crook of her arm. Her beloved darkness was gone. Hard ground beneath the rough blankets tormented every soreness across her shoulders, hips, and knees. She laced her fingers through her hair, wincing as she discovered tender spots all across her scalp.

"Mercy, 'tis me, love."

The kind voice. Graham. Husband. The memories surged. Her heart and soul leapt with joy. Graham. Yes. She loved Graham. He was alive!

"Graham." Her dry mouth made it so hard to speak. "G-graham," she repeated louder, wincing as the sound of her own voice rasped through her skull.

"Aye, love, 'tis me." Tender laughter or was he sobbing? Why?

She risked lifting one hand from her aching head and reached toward the sound of his voice. A trembling kiss pressed into her palm and then the familiar curves of her beloved husband's face, the scratchiness of his stubble, the hard cut of his jaw. Yes. Graham. But tears? Graham's cheeks were wet.

"D-don't cry." Such a struggle to speak. To choose all the right words and sort through them. To say them properly.

"Aye, love. Now that ye're back with me, all will be well." His mouth moved against her hand as he spoke. "Can ye try opening your eyes, Mercy? Open your eyes, love, so Gretna can look into them? 'Twill help her heal ye."

"Gret...na?" Memories of her newfound friend emerged, dashing away the dark scenes of Janie. Gretna was the woman's voice. The knot in her chest eased. Gretna and Graham were here. She was safe.

"Aye, m'lady," Gretna said. "I ken the brightness of the day will be a struggle to bear, but if ye can manage it…"

Fighting against the dull pain, Mercy cracked an eyelid open, flinching against the light. "So, bright." She shielded her eyes and closed them again. "Too much." She shaded her eyes and tried opening them again. Blurriness greeted her.

Gretna gently pulled her hands aside. "Let me look into your eyes, m'lady."

The longer she kept her eyes open, the more the pain from the light eased. She sensed movement, made out cloudy shapes and faint colors in the shifting fog in front of her, but nothing else. She blinked hard, trying to clear the fog away. "B-blind," she finally blurted. Panic rising, her eyes stung with tears and the pounding in her head increased. "I am blind," she repeated.

"Tell me what ye see," Gretna said. "Exactly what ye see."

"Light. Dark." She struggled to pick out the words to describe the confusing world to which she'd opened her eyes. "Shapes," she finally said, sobbing as she covered her face with both hands. "Some color."

A strong arm slid beneath her shoulders and cradled her, holding her close with the gentleness of handling a newborn babe. A kiss brushed across her forehead. Shushing sounds reached her ears. "'Tis early, lass. Give your sight time. As ye heal and grow stronger, it may improve, aye Gretna?"

"Aye," Gretna said. "I am relieved that ye can see and hear. Even speak at all. And ye remember us. 'Tis a good sign, m'lady."

In her weakened state, Mercy could tell Graham and Gretna were doing their best to comfort her. She might not be able to see their faces, but she picked it out in their tones.

"N-no lies," was all she could force out. The more upset she got, the more difficult it became to string words together.

Graham held her tighter, the moment between them suspended time. Ever so slowly, he lowered her back to the pallet. "Ye're alive, and ye've returned to me, love. That's all that matters." He lifted her shoulders again and propped more blankets behind her, lifting her to a slightly inclined position. A cup pressed against her mouth. "Water, dear one. Just a wee sip or two for now."

Mercy struggled to swallow, then pushed the cup away. Too painful. She pressed her fingers alongside her sore nose and felt the tender ridge of her brow.

"Broken nose, love. 'Twill heal, but I ken it makes swallowing hard." The cup pressed to her mouth again as Graham said, "A few more drops and then I'll leave ye be. If ye take to the water well, Gretna will fix ye a fine broth later."

All she wanted Gretna to fix was her sight. Mercy forced down another sip to make Graham leave her alone. The longer she remained upright and awake, the more her mind cleared and flooded her thoughts with all that had happened. She knotted her hands in her lap and bowed her head. Janie had hated her.

A shifting in the blurry fog beside her startled her. She shied to the side, one hand clasped to her chest.

"Forgive me," Graham said. "I didna mean to give ye a fright. I rose to get ye a damp cloth for your face. It seemed to bring ye comfort before."

Mercy pressed a hand to her face, struggling not to cry. Tears hurt worse, filled her head with such pain she'd surely vomit. How could she live like this? How could she be a wife? A mother? Graham should have let her go. He should have allowed her to die.

"Gretna," she forced out, her tongue more manageable since she'd forced down the water.

"She's gone to the fire to start your broth and steep ye another tisane." Graham took her hand, his blurred shape hovered beside her, blocking out the light. "Shall I fetch her? Are ye in more pain?"

Panic filled his voice. And more. Worry. Fear. Poor Graham. Saddled with such a useless wife.

"No more pain," Mercy forced out. No more pain for either of them if she had her way about it. "Talk to Gretna. Alone."

Mercy marveled at the fact she heard his every breath, felt the heat of him, and if she concentrated hard enough, swore she heard the beat of his heart. Graham didn't wish to leave her side.

He scooped up her hand and pressed a kiss across her knuckles. "I shall fetch her for ye, but know this, Mercy, I willna allow ye to harm yourself in any way, ye ken? Ye may be blind, but I am not. I see what ye're thinking."

Mercy pulled her hand away. She didn't argue. She would save her energy to speak with Gretna. The healer would understand. She was a woman already widowed once before finding Colin and starting life again. Gretna would help her. And if the woman refused, Mercy swore by every trace of agony flickering through her mind, body, and soul—she would find a way to free both Graham and herself from this nightmare life had become.

CHAPTER TWENTY-FIVE

IT HAD BEEN another sennight, and Mercy's sight fared no better.

"She rarely speaks." Graham watched Mercy propped upright in the shade of the same ancient oak that had cradled them while they'd made love on that fateful night. Her eyes were clear and alert, her bruises fading, but her gaze registered nothing. She stared out into the woods, seeing nothing of the world.

"Words still dinna come easy to her yet." Gretna paused in her tying of the bundled herbs she'd gathered that morning. "Your lady fears appearing weak and helpless more than anything else. Stumbling to speak angers her. Anger makes her struggle to grasp the words all the harder."

She tucked the bundles into a small sack, cinched it tight, then packed that sack into a much larger tote hanging from the knob of a nearby tree. Returning to the table, Gretna cast a wistful glance Mercy's way. "And since I refused her the belladonna, she willna speak at all unless I nettle at her like a herd dog until she snaps." Gretna shook her head. "Just because she canna speak, dinna think her mind has not returned to her. She's a wily one. Tried to convince me the nightshade would help her eyes." She turned and pinned him with a fierce look. "Ye must convince her to live, that she's worth everything to you. The two of ye can still live a full life, if she'll only try."

"Do ye no' think I've been doing my best to make her believe such?"

Graham skinned the bark from the staff he'd fashioned from a sturdy rowan sapling. He'd chosen the tree as protection for Mercy, praying she'd accept the walking stick for the loving gift it was. His heart ached for her. "'Tis my hope when we reach London and she speaks with the king, she'll see she's got a future worth living." He prayed such. Constantly. He refused to consider the other possibilities.

"Has she agreed to speak to the king? I canna imagine she'd do so from the way she struggles with words right now." Gretna hooked another tote on the tree limb and set to packing it. "She nay understands that the more she speaks, the easier the task should come to her. I can work with her whilst we ride."

"Have ye told her that?" Graham scraped the blade of his dagger across the knob of the staff, ensuring the area Mercy would grip was smooth to the touch.

"I can hear both," Mercy said without turning her head in their direction. "Blind. Not deaf."

"Shite," Graham whispered under his breath.

Gretna shrugged, then pointed first at Graham, then at Mercy. "Convince her," she mouthed.

Aye. He would. Slipping his dagger back into its sheath, he ran his hand over the knob of the staff and down the length of cane. Good. 'Twas slick as waterweed and had a good weight to it. It should fit her well. With a deep fortifying breath, he approached Mercy.

She didn't look up, but he could tell she felt his presence. She might be blind, but the woman's other senses were keen as a huntress.

"I've a gift for ye, m'love." Graham did his best to sound lighthearted. He laid the staff across her lap and stepped back. "'Twill help ye when ye walk about. Find your way better."

Mercy's dark brows drew together as her fingers flitted up and down the stick. She gripped the end with the knob, then brought it close to her face, scowling at it. "Cane?"

"Aye, love. A cane to help ye feel your way about. Ye seem to hate asking anyone to walk with ye." Her strength had increased since she'd stopped taking the herbal mixture. She could even breathe through her nose some, and her sense of smell was returning. He prayed the trip to London wouldn't set her back. "We leave at dawn for London. When we stop to rest, ye'll be able to walk along the roadside all by yourself. I ken how ye are about your independence."

Using the cane for balance, Mercy pushed up from her seat on the log. She turned to him. "I'm a burden on you. Leave me there. Return to your home. I will beg king to pay you. Marriage annulled. Because of this." She motioned across her eyes.

Those were the most words she'd spoken since she'd awakened, and they rent his heart and soul in two. Graham closed the distance between them, knocked away the cane, and gathered her into his arms. "Ye are my wife 'til death parts us and even then, our souls are bound beyond the grave. Ye're no' a burden, and as far as I am concerned, ye never spoke the words ye just uttered." He gave her a tender kiss and cradled her close. "Come back to me, Mercy. Find yourself. Return to the courageous woman I married. The woman willing to fight for those she loves. Dinna let them win by stealing your courage. Dinna let them steal your joy. Your light. Your soul. Those bastards took everything away from ye but me. I beg ye, Mercy, I pray ye, tell me I am enough for ye. Enough to pull ye back into the light. Please. I beg ye."

Mercy shuddered and bowed her head, burying her face into his chest. A low howl rumbled against him as she fisted his tunic and kilt in both her hands and pounded her fists against him. "So... hard," she cried.

Men came running from all directions. Gretna held them at bay, motioning for them to remain silent with such a threatening look none of them dared cross her. Father William drew out his rosary, cast a glance skyward, then folded his hands around the beads and bent his head in prayer.

"I ken it's hard for ye, dear one, but ye can do it. I know ye can." Graham wrapped his arms tighter about her and gently rocked as though she were a fretting babe. "Cry all ye like, love. Let it out. Scream, if ye wish. I ken ye've been robbed and left raw and hurting, but dinna give the bastards another moment of your life. We can move on from this. Together."

"B-babies," she wailed against his chest, shaking with angry sobs. "No babies."

Every man at the edge of the clearing cringed, then shied away, disappearing into the woods.

Graham looked to Gretna, willing her to help him find the right words. Gretna widened her eyes and fixed him with a pointed scowl.

"We can still have bairns," he whispered into Mercy's hair, rocking back and forth. "We've a clan to help us. No woman raises a child alone at *Tor Ruadh*. Not even the sighted ones."

Gretna smiled and nodded at him. Praise God. If only Mercy would accept his words.

"I'd never see them," she choked out.

God in Heaven, please give me the words. "Nay, love, but ye will. Maybe ye willna see them with your eyes, but ye'll ken them well and good in other ways—just like any mother." Graham set her back a step, took her hand, and pressed it to his face. "Ye see different now but ye still see. Ye'll know them by their cries, their laughter, their tears. Ye'll know them by their scent, their touch when ye nurse them at your breast. Ye'll know them by the way they hug ye when they clamber into your arms for your kisses."

Mercy settled down some. Graham prayed that meant he'd achieved some small success at calming her down.

Mercy gradually lowered herself to the ground, patting along the dirt until she located her fallen staff.

It took every ounce of strength Graham possessed not to lunge forward and put the stick in her hand. She needed to do this herself.

She picked up the staff, patted along the length of it, and discovered which end was which. Plunking it upright, she grabbed hold with both hands, supported herself, and rose. She lifted her chin and hitched in a shaking breath. She wet her lips and swallowed hard as she rested both hands atop the staff. "I…"

The waiting stretched on for what felt like an interminable span of time, but Graham bit his tongue to keep from speaking. She struggled worse when agitated. All she needed was a bit of peace to put her thoughts into words and speak.

"I will try," she finally said.

Graham rushed to her, and she threw herself into his arms, clutching him tight.

"Love you," she whispered.

"And I love ye, my rare, fearless woman."

≫≫≪≪

SUCH A RIDE. Exhilarating. So much better than the endless hours of riding in the wagon.

She'd known in her heart she was strong enough and could trust Ryū to know where she wanted to go without her having to guide him. A pleased sadness filled her. What a struggle it must have been for Graham to watch her ride. But he had understood her need and finally allowed it. God had blessed her with a fine husband. A man she couldn't imagine ever deserving.

Her dear horse nuzzled his warm, velvety nose against her cheek, then rumbled in her ear, his whiskers tickling along her neck. *Ryū speak,* she'd always called it. The beast understood and loved her.

"Love you, too." She hugged him and snugged her forehead against his powerful neck. Even though she didn't say all the words she wished, Ryū understood. "I walk. You drink."

The horse shifted beneath her hands, moving forward a pace. Water sloshed to her left, then he snorted. She could just make out his shadow as he stood beside what sounded to be fast-running water trickling and gurgling across rocks. A shallow burn most likely. With the sun on his other side, Ryū's silhouette focused for her better than normal.

Maybe that was the key. Keep her face to the brightness of the sun to make out more shapes and colors. She squatted down, patting along the rocks and hard-packed ground for her staff. She'd convinced Graham to let her take her horse for water and let her walk for a while alone. That was one of the worst things about this accursed sightlessness, she had no privacy whatsoever. Graham had promised her time to herself, but she sensed whoever it was hovering just outside her shadowy vision. Someone watched her. Probably Graham, Gretna, or Duncan.

She set her jaw and swallowed hard. No matter. This was life now. Time to move on and make the best of the situation. Mama would have done so. As would Akio. She sent up a prayer for an ounce of their immense strength and fortitude.

Mercy lifted her face to the warmth of the sun, closed her eyes, and pulled in a long breath. They might've crossed over into England, but the fresh greening floating through the air reminded her of Scotland. Thank goodness her sense of smell had returned fully. Graham assured her she looked the same although she didn't know for certain if she trusted his word on that or not. Graham was not above lying to protect her feelings.

Gretna had told her she'd packed Mercy's nostrils with linen and straightened it as best she could while Mercy was in deep sleep. Mercy wiggled her nose as she walked, remembering the day Gretna had removed the cloth. She would ask Gretna if she looked the same when they returned to their tiresome speaking lessons.

Her toe bumped into something hard. Mercy tapped it with her staff, tracing the large perimeters of the boulder. Leaning forward, she touched the stone, patting along its jagged surface. This would be a pleasant place to sit.

"Mercy."

So, it was Graham shepherding her this time. Surprising. She'd thought for certain he'd be busy setting up camp. With all the men they'd gained and the wagons, their traveling time had slowed to a snail's pace. It had taken them well over a week to reach Hadrian's Wall. She turned toward his voice. "Yes?"

Graham looped an arm through hers. "We're in England now but still nearly a solid fortnight or so from Kensington."

"I...know." Mercy's staff thumped against the smooth river rocks as they strolled along beside the water. "Gretna and I work hard on speaking."

Graham patted her arm, leaned in close, and pecked her cheek. "Ye're doing a braw job, lass. I ken ye'll overcome this in short order."

Mercy huffed out an angry snort. Graham had no idea of what he spoke. "Do not humor me." That was another irritating facet of this new existence. Everyone treated her like a child.

"Forgive me, lass." Graham slowed down, took hold of both her arms, and led her to a seat on what felt to be a felled tree. "Sit down, m'lady. Let us enjoy the peace of this place for a while."

"R-ryū." She'd left him by the stream.

"I can see him from here. Duncan just brought the lad a carrot, and your beast is verra pleased with him. I'm sure he'll lead him back to the other horses."

That knowledge settled her somewhat. She brushed a hand across her forehead, pushing back tendrils of tickling hair. She must look a mess. Gretna had said she'd done a good job with tying up her hair, but she had to have failed in securing it somehow because she hadn't ridden hard enough to loosen it this bad. "Messy."

Graham smoothed her hair away from her face. "Ye're lovely as ever. No' a mess at all." She could tell by the shifting of the tree and the movement of Graham's shadow he'd risen from his seat and moved to stand behind her. "I've done well by a braid or two in my time. Shall I have a go at it?"

Her husband braiding her hair. Mercy couldn't decide if it was laughable or an embarrassment. What would the others think? Were they watching? Did they pity her? Or worse yet, did they pity Graham? They had to. The only time Graham touched her anymore was to guide her or give her a loving peck on the cheek like a cherished pet. Every night, he kept his pallet settled an arm's length away from hers, stating he feared jostling her or causing her discomfort whilst they slept. She'd been a fool to worry about children. At this rate, there was no danger of them ever having any.

Enough. Such mindset was poisonous. She flitted an impatient wave in his direction. "Fix it."

A few gentle tugs of her hair and Graham's fingers fluffed her tresses out across her shoulders. "I ken it's too warm to leave it down, but I do love it like this."

Mercy closed her eyes, pulled in a deep breath, and gave herself to the sensation of Graham raking his fingers through her hair, over and over. Combing it out. Tender and gentle, taking care to work around the parts of her scalp that were still sensitive. She'd healed well but certain spots along her hairline still had a strange tingling numbness that turned to a burning when touched abruptly. At least he was touching her.

"Describe where we are."

"We're off to ourselves here. Sheltered from the camp by this great oak that must ha' uprooted during the spring rains." Graham's fingers worked through her hair and massaged her scalp. Gentle, rhythmic tugs told her he'd set to braiding. His ministrations paired with his low, deep voice entranced her, eased the tension of the day out of her aching shoulders. "The burn runs to our right, and there's a thick green patch of sedge off to our left, snuggled up into the curving of the tree."

A patch of sedge. Off to ourselves. A rush of warmth flushed through her. She slid to her feet, one hand balanced against the log and one holding her staff.

"Wait, love. I've no' bound the end of the braid yet." Scrambling sounds and Graham's blurred shadow seeming to float over the tree as he climbed across it to reach her.

Mercy paused, the certainty of what she was about to do strengthening with every breath. It was time she and Graham returned to behaving as husband and wife.

A final tug and Graham patted her shoulders. "There, love. Feel better?"

"Yes." Her fingers trailing across the rough bark of the fallen tree, Mercy extended her staff and skimmed it across the ground in front of her as she walked. The rocky, hard-packed earth beneath her feet changed to the tangled softness of the grassy area Graham had described. "How large…a patch?"

"Good sized." Graham's tone sounded thoughtful. Strained.

Mercy suppressed a smile. Good. He needed relief as much as she but feared to take that first step. All she needed to do was put his mind at ease. She turned and faced him, holding out a hand. "Large enough…private enough for two?"

Graham took her hand, his strong grip sending a thrill through her. He moved closer, close enough that his warmth embraced her, welcomed her, and took her in. "Are ye certain, m'love?"

"It has been too long, husband." She lifted her face to him. "I need you."

Her staff clattered against the trunk of the tree as Graham swept her up into his arms, cradling her against his chest as he moved forward, then lowered her to the ground. Hovering above her, he whispered, "Ye're certain?"

The sun at his back, Mercy swore she could almost see the contours of her beloved's face. The sight brought tears to her eyes. She reached out to him, opening her embrace. "Never more certain in my life."

Graham closed in, covering her mouth with his, kissing her the way a husband should kiss a wife. A hungry husband filled with need. She tangled her fingers in his hair and kissed him back in such a way as to leave no doubt as to what she wanted. She arched against him, thrilling at the rock-hard neediness that greeted her.

It was still daylight, and they were close to camp. With all her strength, she pushed against Graham's chest, hanging on tight as he rolled to his back. Running his hands up her skirts, he squeezed her buttocks, groaning as she yanked his kilt up and out of the way and slid down on him.

"Yes," she said in a whispering groan, grinding atop him to seat herself to the hilt. She'd so needed *this*. The union. The wondrous joining. *This* made her whole again. The sensations spun her into oblivion, ripped a joyous cry from her throat.

With a growling groan, Graham bucked beneath her, joining her ecstasy as he spasmed inside her, spilling his seed. "God Almighty!" he shouted. He jerked a few more times, then pulled her down atop his heaving chest, locking his arms around her. "I needed ye something fierce, Mercy."

A glowing peacefulness filled her, the first real happiness she'd felt in a long while. Mercy pushed aside the opened neckline of Graham's tunic and kissed his sweat-drenched chest. "I needed this, too. You will return to my bed for good now?"

"Aye, lass. Most definitely."

CHAPTER TWENTY-SIX

"SHALL MARSDEN RETURN or meet us at the edge of the city?"

Graham pondered his brother's question and wished like hell Duncan had asked it before they'd sent the captain on his way to secure a meeting with the king. "I dinna ken. My primary concern was ensuring we didna get shot as we approached Kensington."

"Is King William even there? Rumor amongst the troops has the man in Ireland."

"Why do ye ask me such a thing? How would I know?" Duncan had always had a talent for riding his last raw nerve. He'd done it since he was a wee bairn learning to talk. Graham shifted in the saddle and glared at him. "If ye've nothing useful to say, shut your maw and stop your yammering, ye ken?"

"Your husband has a case of the red arse today, m'lady. I'd advise ye tread lightly," Duncan warned with a snide laugh as he edged his mount to one side and ahead to permit Ryū and Mercy to take their place beside Graham.

"Stop chiding the bear, Duncan," Mercy said with a smile, aiming it in Duncan's direction. "He has much on his mind."

With every passing day, Mercy's speech improved measurably thanks to Gretna's tireless tactic of forcing her to chatter on about absolutely nothing. Graham made a mental note to mention to Alexander just how much the MacCoinnichs owed Gretna. He would never live long enough to repay the woman for all she'd done.

He cast a glance over at Mercy, sitting tall in the saddle, proud and in complete control even though she couldn't see. This was the fearless woman he'd married. The rare woman he loved more than life itself. "If Marsden is successful, this could all be ended within days, m'love."

Mercy nodded but her forehead creased with a frown. She smoothed a hand down her braid draped to the front of her shoulder. "We must be presentable before we see the king." She brushed her hand along the layers of her skirts, ragged and dusty from the trials of the trip. "His Majesty will be so distressed by the filth, he will not see the truth."

Mercy made a fair point. Court ran on pomp and circumstance. If they showed up at the palace looking like beggars, they'd be treated poorly.

"I'm sure he expects little from a Scot but..." Graham's observation trailed off.

"He will expect much from me."

Graham held up a hand and brought the caravan to a halt. They had to resolve this now. With her father dead by her husband's hand, Mercy could not show up on the doorstep of her former residence in London and expect to be welcomed. They would have to find an inn and secure appropriate attire before meeting with the king. He motioned for Duncan to fall back and rejoin them. "Ride on and secure reputable lodging. Two rooms. A good place providing baths and meals. Close to the shops, ye ken?"

"Two rooms?" Duncan leaned forward in the saddle, obviously relishing the chance to ride alone.

"Aye." Graham looked back at the first wagon. Reins clenched in her hands, Gretna stretched forward to hear their words. "One for

Mercy and m'self and another for Gretna. I'll need ye to camp with the men at Gray's Inn Fields. Keep them in line." He turned to Crestshire. "I assume Marsden and yourself will make use of military lodging, aye?"

Crestshire nodded. "Yes. We shall accompany you to meet with the king, but it would be best if all those wearing His Majesty's colors abided by military protocol whilst in the city." He gave a judicious shrug. "Such behavior would lend more substance to our words when we speak on your behalf."

"Fifteen for ye to control," Graham said, directing his words at Duncan. "Once ye've made the arrangements for us, meet us at the west edge of Gray's Inn Field to take lead of the men, aye?"

"'Twill be done, brother." With a curt nod, Duncan thundered away.

Drawing closer to Mercy's mount, Graham reached over and touched her arm. "Can ye and Gretna manage the shops?"

Mercy's eyes narrowed as though struggling to suppress a flinch. Her chin lifted and her jaw hardened. "I will send a message to my seamstress, Madame Zhou. She was the only shop keeper in London who treated me with respect."

"I will see to it that ye're always treated proper, love. I swear it."

"Their acceptance doesn't matter anymore." Mercy smiled. "The shallow people of London will never be as happy as I am." She turned toward Graham, her gaze fixed upon him. "I have you. My heart is full now."

Graham scooped up her hand and kissed it. "As I said before, ye're a rare woman, Mercy. I thank God for bringing ye to me."

He motioned to Crestshire as he spurred his mount forward. "Ride ahead of us, aye?"

Mercy trusted her devoted beast, but Graham feared the horse would decide to bolt. With one of them beside her and one to her front, they could correct that if it happened. The dark stallion was made for racing. It was true the steed loved his mistress, but Graham didn't know if the horse loved Mercy more than he loved speed.

"Can you see the city yet?" Mercy asked.

Graham studied the surrounding land. Rolling hills tamed into farmland dotted with sheep and the occasional cow. Thatch-roofed houses with walls of stone, surrounded by stone fences. Gardens were littered with chickens, geese, and children. Graham felt it in his bones. They no longer road through open country. "I canna see the main city yet, lass, but we're close. Listen. Do ye hear the sounds of farming around ye?"

Mercy tilted her head and smiled. "I hear the laughter of children."

"We'll reach the city by sunset." Graham studied her, pondering whether he should speak his thoughts aloud. Aye. He'd risk it. "Ye're speaking is almost back to normal. Ye've worked hard, and I'll have ye know I admire your strength and dedication."

Her cheeks turned a lovely shade of red. "I...thank you."

Crestshire halted in front of them, holding up a hand as he cast a warning look back at Graham. "Riders approaching."

Graham reached across and squeezed Mercy's arm. "Stay here, ye ken?"

Thankfully, Mercy nodded, clenching the reins in her lap.

Graham squinted to bring the riders into focus. "Is that Marsden?" The portly captain had an odd way of sitting a horse that made his identity easy to discern.

"Yes." Crestshire scrubbed a hand across his mouth. "And those men with him are wearing the uniform of the palace guards."

Graham's gut knotted, causing him to rest a hand on his pistol.

"Take care, Graham," Crestshire warned. "To win this game, do not engage the palace guard."

The group of three thundered toward them with alarming momentum.

Graham rushed back to Mercy, dismounted, and hurried to her

side. Taking hold of her arm, he pulled. "Come, lass. I'd rather ye sit with Gretna. I'll tie Ryū to the wagon."

"Who approaches?" Mercy complied, patting the side of her saddle in search of her staff holstered at its side. She slid it free and thumped the tip of it hard against the road.

"Marsden and two palace guards. Hurry. We've no' much time." Grasping her by the elbow, he rushed her to Gretna's wagon and lifted her up to the seat. He pulled both his pistols from his belt and held them out to Gretna. "Just in case."

Gretna nodded and took them without a word. Her grim expression said it all.

Hurrying back to her mount, Graham tied off the horse to Mercy's side of the wagon. "He's right here beside ye, love."

Mercy held out a trembling hand, waiting for him to take it. "Heed Marsden and Crestshire. They will protect us."

Graham squeezed her hand, then kissed it. "Bossy woman. I'll do me best."

Her quivering smile spurred him onward.

Graham saddled up and rode to Crestshire's side just as Marsden and the two palace guards reached them.

Wary. That was the first word that came to mind when Graham saw Marsden's face. The man looked ill at ease. Graham half expected him to fall from the saddle in an attack of apoplexy. "Marsden."

The captain gave him a slow nod, spared a glance at the two stoic-faced palace guards, then swiped a hand across his forehead. "His Majesty—in all his generous wisdom—has not only granted a *private* audience with yourself and Lady Mercy, but has also ordered that you be accommodated to the palace and given a private suite at Kensington until such time as your business with court is concluded."

Crestshire reacted with a sudden clearing of his throat, increasing Graham's alarm all the more.

"Stay at the palace?" Graham glanced around the area, searching for soldiers hiding to ambush them whilst they were in shock at such an announcement.

Marsden held up a hand at the two palace guards, giving them each a stern look. He urged his mount forward until they stood nose to nose with Graham and Crestshire's horses. After stealing a glance back at the king's men, he tucked his chin and lowered his voice. "I apprised His Majesty of every detail." He paused and darted a look at Lady Mercy. *"Every* detail."

An odd combination of irritation and relief swept across Graham. "That's why we wished to meet with the man. To tell him our story ourselves."

"The king does not appreciate surprises," Marsden warned. "Trust me. It was far better that he learned all the details from me before he meets with you."

Graham wished they could return to Scotland "How did he react?"

"His Majesty does not *react*." Marsden shook his head. "His thoughts are known only to him until he so wishes to share them."

Graham clenched his reins so tight his knuckles popped. Never in a thousand years had he dreamed he'd ever face such a situation. He turned and looked back at Mercy, locking his gaze on her. Emotions churned within him. Love. Protectiveness. Sorrow. Guilt.

He turned back to Marsden and nodded. "Lead on."

"I DON'T LIKE you leaving the palace grounds without Marsden." With a light exploring patting of the table in front of her, Mercy located the small, handle-free cup of the heated drink beside her breakfast plate of toasted bread. She lifted it to her mouth, and sipped, closing her eyes and savoring the milky, sweet flavor. Tea. Imported from the east. Very good. This should help settle her nerves nicely.

Graham's shadowy form, sitting opposite her at the small table on the garden balcony, shifted from side to side in the way Mercy had come to recognize as a signal that he was frustrated. He didn't possess a talent for being idle. She'd lost the benefit of seeing his expressions but gained a sensitivity to his mannerisms that aided her just the same. "I must see to Duncan and the men. Tell them of our meeting with the king the day after next."

They'd already spent three days at the palace. Mercy feared the time on what Graham considered enemy ground would surely be his end. The unknown outcome of their meeting with the king plagued him like a festering wound. With care not to spill anything, Mercy returned her tea to the table, located her spoon, then tapped her fingers along the rim of her bowl of chopped apples and berries.

"I...understand." She pointed her spoon at him before dipping into the fruit. "Just t-take care. Please?"

Graham reached across the table and tickled his fingertips across the back of her hand. "Aye, love. And when I return, perhaps we can enjoy another bath?"

Heat rushed through her at the memory of last night's bath they'd shared in the opulent tub of steaming hot, rose-scented water. The scandalous tub had been fashioned for two, and she and Graham had made good use of it, staying in the water until it had grown cold and been sloshed to the floor with their sensual thrashing. "I am sure it can be arranged." Choosing words had become easier. The delightful distraction of another bath would do them both good.

"Did ye get a message sent to ye're seamstress?"

"Yes." Resting her fingers around the rim of her bowl, Mercy spooned up some fruit and popped it into her mouth. She scooped up the cloth napkin from her lap, pressing it in front of her mouth as she chewed. Goodness. She had not meant to take such a large mouthful.

"Let me slice those into smaller bites for ye." Graham's shadow leaned toward her, clinked in her bowl for a few seconds, then retreated back to his seat. "There now. I'll speak to the servants and ask them to pass along to the cook that your meals should be better attended."

Mercy patted the napkin to the corners of her mouth and returned it to her lap. "Please don't." A sigh escaped her as she shook her head. "I must do as much as I can for myself. I should have taken more care with the fruit before I put it in my mouth."

"Ye didna hesitate to speak!" Graham rushed around the table, knelt at her side, and hugged her to him. "I'm so verra proud of ye."

Relief and joy filled her. He was right. She hadn't failed at a single word. Wrapping her arms around Graham's neck, she kissed him soundly.

"Mmm," Graham rumbled as he nuzzled her mouth. "Apples and cream."

A sharp rap on the door tossed the enticing possibilities of an after-breakfast pleasuring to the winds. Graham rose and pecked a quick kiss to her forehead. "Finish your breakfast, love."

Mercy folded her hands in her lap and angled an ear toward the opened doors leading into their suite from the balcony. The sunny, open-aired breakfast had been quite nice, but she needed to hear who was at the door and learn what they wanted.

"I am Madame Zhou. These are my assistants. Your presence here is unnecessary while we tend to Lady Mercy. I suggest you leave."

Mercy rose from her seat, retrieved her staff from where she'd propped it against the stone banister of the balcony, and scooted her chair back under the table. The brightness of the day helped so much with her sight. She could almost make out all the shapes around her and their colors. "Madame Zhou. Thank you for responding so quickly."

Mercy made out the blurred forms of Madame Zhou and two of her assistants hovering close to the suite's outer door. It was moments such as these that reminded her of just how much she'd lost by losing her sight. She couldn't see their expressions.

Graham hurried to her side and took her arm. "This is your seam-stress?"

The short shadow of Madame Zhou marched forward until she stood so close Mercy picked up the nose-tingling scent of the exotic herbal sachets the eccentric woman kept tucked in her clothing to ward off evil spirits. Angry wormwood. Mercy remembered her telling her the name of the pleasant-smelling plant. It was her herb of choice for protection, far surpassing the famed protective properties of dill or lavender.

"Your presence is dismissed," Madame Zhou announced to Graham. She stepped closer to Mercy and firmly pulled her a few paces away. "Your staff should be made of kingwood. More protection. And covered with the proper symbols to guide your steps. I know an artisan. I shall see to it."

"Mercy!" By the sound of Graham's tone, a possible explosion was very close.

Graham took hold of her arm and gathered her up. "If ye dinna mind, I shall kiss my wife good and proper before I'm dismissed."

He kissed her with such fervor her knees weakened. Graham lifted his head, and Mercy actually felt the smug look on his face. "I look forward to our bath this evening, love. Enjoy your day of picking out your fine dresses." Then he strode from the room and slammed the door behind him.

"Strong, that one," Madame Zhou observed. "But ill-informed. I am under His Majesty's service to complete your entire wardrobe. It has already been paid for." She snapped her fingers, and one of her attendants jumped to her side. "Master Lang shall fashion Lady Mercy's proper staff, by tomorrow."

The blurred form of the attendant darted out the door, clicking it softly closed.

"His Majesty?" Mercy repeated. Madame Zhou's announcement set her stomach to churning worse than it had when she'd smelled

Graham's breakfast. Mercy swallowed hard, pulled in a deep breath, then blew it out. "My husband and I requested your services, Madame Zhou—not His Royal Highness. We are only guests for a short time here at the p-palace."

Madame Zhou stepped closer. "Acupuncture and herbs will help with your speech and sight." She circled around Mercy. Her adept fingers patted and prodded Mercy's shoulders, elbows, and the curve of her waist as she moved. "The needles and herbs will not endanger the child. We shall administer the treatments during your stay here at the palace." She snapped her fingers, and her other attendant popped to her side. "Inform His Majesty's servants of our additional needs, then fetch the red box and the black one." The attendant disappeared.

"I need to sit." Mercy felt her way across the room to a pillowed bench beside the open doors leading out to the balcony. She sagged down into the cushions, concentrating on taking deep breaths and not losing her breakfast. His Majesty paying for an entire set of clothes? A complete wardrobe? She pressed a hand to her stomach. And a child? How could Madame Zhou say such a thing? "Please explain to me about His Majesty's generosity, but more importantly, tell me why you believe I am with child."

Madame Zhou idly paced back and forth across the path of sunlight shining across the floor. "His Majesty's servant included a missive from the king himself when he delivered your message. By His Royal Highness's order, a complete wardrobe shall accompany you when you leave the palace. I know not why." The clicking of her heels across the marble floor slowed. "However, he did mention you had been under great duress for several weeks. I have made your clothes for years, Lady Mercy, as I did your mother. I am no stranger to abuse." Her voice grew quieter. "Your body already prepares for the child you carry. Softer in some places. Fuller in others."

Mercy covered her face with shaking hands, overwhelmed by the joyous yet terrifying news. A child. She nearly wept.

"You do not want the child?"

"Of course. More than anything." Mercy dropped her hands to her lap, then hugged herself, shaking uncontrollably. "But there is so much danger right now. And I have no idea what His Majesty intends."

"There is always danger in this world," the woman announced. "Teach your child to be strong. Like you. Like your husband."

The curt woman perched on the edge of the bench beside Mercy. "We shall always be at the mercy of the court. Enjoy when you find favor with the king." She shifted, doing something Mercy couldn't make out.

She took Mercy's right hand, opened it, and pressed a small cloth bundle into her palm. Closing Mercy's fingers around the packet, she squeezed it tight. "Angry wormwood for the child. Wear it wherever you go. That along with your new staff will keep you safe." She released Mercy's hand, stood, and marched across the room. "I shall request hot water for steeping herbs. You shall drink it and feel better. When my assistants return, we shall make preparations for later. Perhaps I shall try my hand at a christening gown for the babe."

CHAPTER TWENTY-SEVEN

"I FEEL LIKE a trussed goose headed toward the oven." Graham tugged at the snug waistcoat, then ran a finger around the inside of the overly tight neck cloth. "I think that man wouldha rather hanged me as dress me."

"Probably," Duncan agreed, rolling his shoulders and stretching his neck to resettle his own new garments. "Gretna said she felt the same when that rude woman measured her for a gown. All poking and prodding and such."

"Aye, rudeness itself that woman is." Graham shook away the chill rippling across his flesh. At first meeting, he'd wanted to wring Madame Zhou's neck, especially since Mercy had been in such a state after the seamstress's first visit. But the woman had promised a cure for Mercy's ailments and perhaps even help with her blindness before their meeting with the king. He'd bargain with old Scratch himself if it meant helping Mercy.

A blessing in some ways, a curse in others, their meeting with King William had been postponed a fortnight. Some sort of emergency gathering of the European coalition against France that His Majesty could not ignore. So, they had waited, biding their time.

Two weeks in the palace had rubbed Graham's nerves raw, but it was worth it all to see Mercy gifted with such fine clothes. He had yet to be told the cost, but it didn't matter. He had gold set aside. Madame Zhou could have all of it.

And he had to give the woman respect; she had done exactly what she had claimed. Mercy said her vision was much clearer. For that alone, Madame Zhou deserved the world.

"I'll fetch Gretna," Duncan said, interrupting Graham's thoughts. "Me thinks making the king wait would be ill-advised."

"Aye," Graham agreed as they entered the marble hallway lined with elaborate paintings and statues. Duncan hurried onward toward a gilded door on the right as Graham stopped in front of the next door on the left. Another of Madame Zhou's eccentricities. The woman had insisted she dress Mercy in a chamber, keeping them separated as though it was their wedding day.

Graham rapped a knuckle on the door. "Mercy, love. 'Tis time."

The latch clicked, and the door slowly swung open.

Graham caught his breath. Such loveliness. How could his beloved wife grow more beautiful with each passing day?

"Say something. You know I can't make out your expression."

Mercy stood framed in the sunlight flooding through the arched window behind her. Bathed in its golden rays, she looked like an angel. The ivory shade of her dress and the golden trim of satin and silk along the full, flowing skirts and paneled sleeves were beautiful. Her glorious hair had been swept up and piled high, tendrils allowed to trail down on either side of her face.

"Your husband appears to have been struck mute by your beauty," Madame Zhou observed from behind the door.

"She's right," Graham said in a low, rasping whisper.

Mercy laughed. Her cheeks bloomed with color.

Graham hurried to her side and eased her hand into his. He was almost afraid to touch her. "I am humbled by your beauty. Ye're a glorious woman, m'love."

"We should go," she said as she slid her hand through his arm.

Pausing she turned to Madame Zhou. "Will you be here when I return?"

"No. My work is complete here." She studied Mercy, then slid her piercing gaze over to Graham. Her scowl deepened, then she shoved a hand deep into the hidden pocket of her skirts. She withdrew a small, bundled bit of linen filled with something Graham couldn't identify and tied with a purple ribbon.

She jerked Graham's arm out of the way, opened his coat, then stuffed it into the small pocket of his waistcoat. Jerking his clothing back in place, she glared up at him. "Protection. Keep it with you always."

Mercy squeezed his arm and bowed her head. "Thank you, Madame Zhou, for everything."

She gave a curt nod, clasped her hands in front of her, and marched down the hallway, her assistants scurrying to gather her things and follow.

"What an odd woman," Graham said under his breath.

"She risked her reputation by taking on Mama and myself as clients," Mercy said with a rueful smile. "She makes clothes for many royals."

Marsden came careening out of a side hallway, the sturdy heels of his perfectly polished boots striking hard against the floor. "Are you still here? We must take our places in the library now. His Royal Highness will arrive at any moment."

The knot in the center of Graham's chest tightened. He patted Mercy's arm.

Mercy nodded, hurrying along with her husband. "Just remember," she said. "His Majesty always speaks first."

Graham slowed his pace. "I promise to behave, love." Or at least attempt to. He cleared his throat and gave her arm a reassuring squeeze. "We must think only good shall come of this meeting, and then we can get on with our lives."

Mercy gave him a sharp look he didn't quite understand, but they'd reached the entrance to the library, so there was no time to ask.

Crestshire stepped forward to greet them. "Thank goodness. I feared the king would arrive first." He leaned to one side to look behind them. "Well done, Marsden."

Marsden patted the perspiration away from his brow as he bobbed his head and waved away Crestshire's praise.

Duncan and Gretna stood near the front of the room, close to the dais holding the king's chair.

Straightening his clothes, Graham looked to Mercy. "Ready, love?"

Graham sent up a silent prayer as they joined Duncan and Gretna at the head of the room and just in time. The door known as His Majesty's private entrance opened, revealing the king.

He entered the room, and the door closed behind him as though tended by a spirit. His long face was set in a dark scowl, and he marched to his chair.

Graham's instincts made him wish he'd tucked his faithful dagger into its hidden sheath at his back. But the king was alone. No servants. No lordlings. A private meeting was a bad sign.

Releasing his arm, Mercy lowered herself into a deep curtsy.

Giving Duncan and Gretna a sharp nod to do the same, Graham bowed, glancing to the side to ensure they had understood.

"Rise," King William snapped, his glare fixed on Graham. His Majesty stared at him overly long. His scowl shifted to Mercy, and everything about the king changed. There was sadness in his expression, genuine concern. "Are you able to come to us, child? Can you see anything at all?"

Mercy lifted her chin and smiled. With the aid of her staff, she moved with the grace of a sure-footed deer walking through the heather. "I shall always see my way to you, Your Highness." She paused when she reached him, frowned for a moment as she stared back and forth at the space in front of her, then held out her hand as she lowered herself into another curtsy. "Forgive me, Your Highness. I am unable to find your hand."

King William moved forward and took hold of Mercy's hand, tears in his eyes. "Rise, child. Sit with us as you once did so long ago, when your troubles were farther away."

Graham widened his stance and clasped his hands at his back, unsure what to do or say. Best stay silent. He stole a glance at Duncan who rewarded him with a wide-eyed look.

Holding tight to Mercy's hand, King William slouched back in his chair, closed his eyes, and pressed shaking fingers to his temple. He pulled in several deep breaths and released them with loud sighs.

Graham wished the man would get on with it and spare them the drawn-out dramatics. He understood the king had always been fond of Mercy, but apparently, he'd underestimated the depth of the king's feelings for his only goddaughter.

As though he'd heard Graham's thoughts, King William opened his eyes, sat straighter in the chair, and glared at him. "We bade you to guide and protect our goddaughter through the Highlands. Did we not?"

"Aye, Your Majesty, but—"

King William held up a hand. "We are aware of the duke's abominable actions. While we condoned testing your loyalty and that of Clan MacCoinnich's, we did not approve of anything else. Is that clearly understood?"

"Yes, Your Majesty." Graham tried to relax. He had to say more. He couldn't resist. "Have ye truly been apprised of all Lady Mercy endured?"

King William's look hardened as he settled Mercy's hand upon his knee and covered it with his own. "We are aware our goddaughter has endured unimaginable abuse. We are also aware she married you."

"Aye." Graham took a step forward. "She is my wife."

King William shook his head. He turned to Mercy. "Did this man force himself upon you? Did you marry him to protect your honor?"

Mercy rested her other hand on top of the king's. "I love him, Your Majesty. He has cared for me in more ways than I can ever describe. He is a good man ..." she paused, stole a glance in Graham's direction, then turned an even brighter smile back on the king. "...even though he is a Scot."

King William nodded down at her. For the first time since he'd entered the room, he looked more at ease. Turning back to Graham, he pulled in a deep breath and slowly blew it out. Coldness settled across him. "You realize she has nothing."

"Beg ye're pardon?" Confusion filled Graham. What did the man mean?

"You murdered her father." King William shrugged. "The man deserved it, but there are no assets. No inheritance. Lady Mercy is penniless thanks to her father's debts. You can also forget whatever gold was promised as payment for her tour through the Highlands. We consider that a failed task, and we are not in the habit of compensating failure."

Graham grit his teeth, rage simmering hot and fierce at the insult. "I killed her father because he was a cruel bastard. I dinna give a damn about any inheritance or payment for my services." Graham strode forward another step. "I married the woman because I love her. Nothing else. Ye can take yer insinuations and yer gold and rot in hell with them."

"Graham!" Mercy gripped the king's hand. "Please forgive him, Your Majesty. I am afraid my husband is a very passionate man and speaks before he thinks."

King William smiled, a genuine smile that lit up his face. The man was pleased. He nodded, then motioned for Crestshire and Marsden to come forward. "Please escort these two..." He motioned at Duncan and Gretna. "To our personal solar. We shall all enjoy some refreshments after we finish our *private* business with Lady Mercy and her husband.

Crestshire and Marsden both sprang into action and led Duncan and Gretna from the room, closing the door quietly behind them.

King William turned to Mercy. He kissed her fingers, then gently patted her hand. "I loved your mother very much," he said softly, his voice filled with pain.

Mercy's lips parted, but she remained silent.

Graham tensed. This sort of conversation made him more than a little uncomfortable. Such intimate knowledge about the king could end badly.

King William released a deep sigh and smiled. "She was so much more to me than a mere mistress. In another world, another time, she would have been my cherished wife. She was my heart, dearest Mercy, and always will be." King William scooted forward to the edge of his seat, slid a finger under Mercy's chin, and tilted her face upward. "You are so like her."

He turned and looked at Graham. A weariness settled back in place, pulling a deep sigh from his lungs. "When Yumiko placed this precious child in my arms for the first time, our very own baby, I was filled with such indescribable joy." He shook his head. "And sadness. You see...I held my daughter, the beloved child I could never claim as my own."

He lifted Mercy's hand to his mouth, pressed another kiss to her fingers, then bowed his head. "It is I who must ask forgiveness, my daughter, for allowing all this misfortune to befall you. I promised your mother you would always be under my protection. I failed both her and you."

His Majesty lifted his head and leveled his gaze on Graham. "You and your clan are safe as long as you care for Lady Mercy and treat her as the cherished woman she is. But know this, if any more harm befalls her, I shall see that Clan MacCoinnich are wiped from the face of this earth. Is that understood?"

"Aye." Graham stepped forward and rested a hand on Mercy's shoulder. She'd grown pale, and he feared she was about to swoon. "Are ye all right, love?"

Mercy clutched her hands to her chest, took in a deep breath, and eased it out with a nod. "I had heard rumors," she said as she turned back to the king. "And Mama always spoke so fondly of you."

King William leaned forward, his lowered voice weak and filled with pain. "I still miss her terribly."

"So do I," Mercy whispered.

Graham suddenly felt very much the outsider. He shouldn't be here right now. Mercy needed this chance to come to terms with her truths. She needed to speak with the father who had always loved her. "By your leave, Your Majesty, shall I wait in the solar for yourself and Lady Mercy to join us? I feel ye have much to talk about. Alone."

"You see? A good man." Mercy smiled up at the king.

"A good man," the king repeated. "A rare thing these days." He nodded. "We would be most grateful if you would do so, Master MacCoinnich, but we must bid you keep the particulars of this conversation secret for reasons we are certain you understand."

"Aye, Your Majesty." Graham gave the man the polite bow he'd earned. "I shall take this secret to my grave. I swear it."

THE CURVED BANISTER surrounding the balcony held Mercy steady. She upturned her face to the sun, closed her eyes, and sent a silent prayer. *I will be all right now, Mama. Rest in peace.*

And she truly believed it. Life had not gone the direction she'd thought it would, but she would take it, relish it, and be thankful.

Illegitimate daughter to the king. Blind wife to an unruly Scot. Mercy pressed a hand to her stomach, still smooth and flat, but according to Madame Zhou, not for long. She had earned many titles in what seemed like the blink of an eye and also rid herself of many burdens. Life was now filled with promise.

"Mercy?"

She smiled at the loving concern she always heard in Graham's voice. "Here. On the balcony."

"Sunning again, are ye?" Graham's arms slipped around her from behind, and he hugged her back against him. Resting his chin on her shoulder, he nuzzled a kiss to her ear. "Ye're warm as a bannock straight from the oven. Are ye feeling better after your wee nap?"

"Much better." The meeting with the king had drained her. She had begged to be excused after their talk, feeling too sick to speak to anyone. The many revelations had left her emotionally drained. The quiet rest had done her good. "When do we return to *Tor Ruadh*?"

"Tomorrow." Graham chuckled as he hugged her tight, kissed her ear again, then shifted to stand beside her at the banister, his arm still curled about her waist. "Gretna and Duncan are seeing to the packing of the wagons. 'Tis my understanding that ye've four trunks of clothing? Is that no' a bit excessive?" He leaned in close and whispered, his breath tickling her ear, "Even for a king's daughter?"

Mercy smiled. Wait until he understood why. Perhaps clothing trunks were the best way to introduce Graham to the subject. "Madame Zhou prepared a complete wardrobe for me now, one for later when I am much larger, and a christening gown, as well as the first few months of swaddling and wraps for the baby."

Graham's arm dropped from around her waist. He took hold of her and turned her toward him. His hands trembled. Oh, how she wished she could see his face. Unable to resist, she reached up and felt his features. Satisfaction filled her. He had taken the news well.

"A b-bairn?"

"Yes." She took his hand and pressed it to her stomach. "According to Madame Zhou, we await our first child."

Graham roared, gathered her hard against his chest, then jerked a step back, still holding her by the shoulders. "Lord. I'm sorry. Please forgive me. Did I hurt ye?"

Laughter spilled from her. What a fine father Graham would be. "No. You most certainly did not hurt me." She wrapped her arms around his neck and kissed him. "I am not a fragile flower."

He tucked his face into the curve of her neck and rumbled against her in a growling whisper, "Nay. Ye're no' a fragile flower. Ye're a rare, fearless woman, and ye're all mine."

EPILOGUE

Tor Ruadh
Summer 1694

T HE SIGHT OF Mercy cradling their son in her arms nearly brought him to his knees in gratitude each and every time. Her laughter paired with their son's contented cooing was the sweetest song he'd ever heard. Aye, life was good, and he'd been blessed a damn sight more than he deserved.

Graham leaned back against the low, stone wall of the inner court-yard, contentment filling his heart. He nodded toward the women, Mercy, Catriona, and Gretna, enjoying the warm spring sunshine of the garden with all the bairns. "This happiness could be yours, brother."

Duncan shifted in place, then elbowed Sutherland leaning against the wall as well. "He's talking to ye."

"I think not," Sutherland said with a pointed look at Gretna. "She's widowed six months now, has three young ones to feed, and the two of ye have always been close." Sutherland graced Duncan with a knowing smirk and poked him in the chest. "He's speaking to yourself."

Graham caught Mercy's head barely turning in their direction.

She'd bade him speak to Duncan about Gretna, and he'd agreed to do it to keep the peace, knowing full well it would more than likely not go as she wished.

"Besides, I leave for Skye tomorrow," Duncan said. "The Mac-Donald pays a fair price for a good smuggler able to slip past the excise man, and I need some coin." He pushed away from the wall and rolled his shoulders, his eagerness apparent. His tone faltered as his gaze followed the women moving about the garden. "Gretna's a fine woman. Deserves better than me. I'm no' the sort to sit about and bounce bairns on my knee. I could never keep her happy."

"Alexander and I felt the same way before our wives changed us," Graham said with the wisdom of time and experience forcing a smile he couldn't wipe off his face if he tried. "Fate had other plans for me."

Duncan clapped a hand to his shoulder. "My fate is to be the favorite uncle of all my brothers' bairns, ye ken? I'll regale them with stories of my exciting adventures. Just ye wait and see."

Graham laughed, and Sutherland rolled his eyes.

"Godspeed to ye, brother," Graham said as Duncan sauntered away. "May God and fate, both, have mercy on your soul," he added under his breath.

"I'm off before the lovely Lady Mercy decides I'm next to be fitted with a wife." Sutherland strode from the garden at the quickened pace of a man running for his life.

Graham shook his head and huffed out a silent laugh. Fools, his brothers. The both of them. Someday, they'd long for the contentment he'd found. He joined the trio of women herding the children. Coming up behind Mercy, he wrapped his arms around her waist and propped his chin atop her shoulder. "We shall have to look elsewhere for a match for Gretna, dear one," he whispered as he nuzzled a kiss to her neck, then smiled down at his son. "Duncan and Sutherland are fools."

"I heard." Mercy lifted the babe to her shoulder and kissed his chubby cheek. The child let out a gurgling laugh, hands grabbing for Graham's nose. Mercy laughed. "Little Ramsay loves the garden. It always puts him in the best of moods."

Graham took Ramsay out of Mercy's arms and lifted him high until the child squealed with delight. "That's because he's an adventurous wee lad who love his Highlands." He cradled the child in the crook of one arm, took hold of Mercy, and led her a few steps away from the others. "I have news I think will please ye."

"What?" Mercy leaned closer, hugging his arm to her side.

"Alexander has asked we stay here. Permanently." Graham watched Mercy closely. She feared herself a burden on those at *Tor Ruadh,* especially since Ramsay's birth. But she worried about managing a home should they build a keep of their own. "Alexander needs my help with the running of the clan. The Neal-MacCoinnich union has been prosperous and grown."

Mercy rested her cheek against his shoulder, caught hold of the baby's hand. "You are certain it's not charity? Pity?"

"Nay," Graham reassured. He glanced back at the others at the far edge of the garden. "He and Catriona both said they need us here, and since Gretna lost her husband, she needs ye as well. Helping ye gives her comfort." He pressed a kiss to her furrowed brow, praying the news would ease her worries. "They both said the entire third level of the keep is ours to fill with our bairns."

Ramsay squealed and kicked his tiny feet back and forth, rubbing his heels together as though dancing.

Mercy brightened. "Your son appears pleased with the news that he'll live here and grow up with his cousins."

"And what of his mother?"

Mercy's peace and happiness meant more to him than anything. Graham watched the emotions play across her face.

Mercy's brow smoothed and she smiled. "Yes. I am pleased too." She tickled her fingers across the babe's tummy and leaned close enough so he could pat her face. She laughed and cocked her head as though listening. "What's that, my son? What's that you say?"

Ramsay gurgled and cooed and kicked his feet even faster.

Mercy straightened and gave Graham a pointed look. "Ramsay says he wishes he had a sister."

Graham laughed and pulled Mercy into a hug as he looked down at the wee lad. "I shall do my best to grant that wish, my son—as soon as ye take a nap."

If you enjoyed THE GUARDIAN, please consider helping to spread the word about it by leaving a review on the site where you purchased your copy, or a reader site such as Goodreads or BookBub! Reviews help an author more than you know and they are SO appreciated. You could help another reader decide if they'd like to give THE GUARDIAN a try!

I love to hear from readers too so drop me a line at maevegreyson@gmail.com

OR visit me on Facebook:
facebook.com/AuthorMaeveGreyson

I'm also on Instagram:
maevegreyson

Twitter:
@maevegreyson

Visit my website:
maevegreyson.com

If you'd like to receive my occasional newsletter, please sign up at:
maevegreyson.com/contact.html#newsletter

Follow me on these sites to get notifications about new releases, sales, and special deals:
Amazon: amazon.com/Maeve-Greyson/e/B004PE9T9U
BookBub: bookbub.com/authors/maeve-greyson

Many thanks and may your life always be filled with good books!
Maeve

About the Author

"No one has the power to shatter your dreams unless you give it to them." That's Maeve Greyson's mantra. She and her husband of almost forty years traveled around the world while in the U.S. Air Force. Now, they're settled in rural Kentucky where Maeve writes about her beloved Highlanders and the fearless women who tame them. When she's not plotting her next romantic Scottish tale, she can be found herding cats, grandchildren, and her husband—not necessarily in that order.

SOCIAL MEDIA LINKS:
Website: maevegreyson.com
Facebook Page: AuthorMaeveGreyson
Facebook Group: Maeve's Corner
facebook.com/groups/MaevesCorner
Twitter: @maevegreyson
Instagram: @maevegreyson
Amazon Author Page: amazon.com/Maeve-Greyson/e/B004PE9T9U
BookBub: bookbub.com/authors/maeve-greyson

Manufactured by Amazon.ca
Acheson, AB

14052886R00162